THE DEVILS THEY ARE

BOYS OF WILLOWBROOK #1

STEPH MACCA

Contents

Dedication   XI

1. Chapter 1   1

2. Chapter 2   15

3. Chapter 3   24

4. Chapter 4   33

5. Chapter 5   41

6. Chapter 6   50

7. Chapter 7   60

8. Chapter 8   69

9. Chapter 9   80

10. Chapter 10   89

11. Chapter 11   98

12. Chapter 12   107

13. Chapter 13   118

14. Chapter 14   128

15. Chapter 15   138

16.	Chapter 16	149
17.	Chapter 17	159
18.	Chapter 18	169
19.	Chapter 19	181
20.	Chapter 20	194
21.	Chapter 21	206
22.	Chapter 22	216
23.	Chapter 23	227
24.	Chapter 24	237
25.	Chapter 25	245
26.	Chapter 26	255
27.	Chapter 27	264
28.	Chapter 28	273
29.	Chapter 29	282
30.	Chapter 30	290
31.	Chapter 31	299
32.	Chapter 32	308
33.	Chapter 33	316
34.	Chapter 34	327
35.	Chapter 35	336
36.	Chapter 36	345
37.	Chapter 37	355

38.	Chapter 38	364
39.	Chapter 39	373
40.	Chapter 40	382
41.	Chapter 41	391
42.	Chapter 42	400
43.	Chapter 43	410
44.	Chapter 44	420

Playlist

Listen on Spotify here
(https://shorturl.at/2tCnw)

1. Castle – Halsey

2. Strut – Emeline

3. Don't Blame Me – Taylor Swift

4. Control – Halsey

5. Mad Hatter – Melanie Martinez

6. Holy – King Princess

7. My Demons – Starset

8. Blood // Water – grandson

9. I Like You Best – Ella Red

10. War of Change – Thousand Foot Krutch

11. Southbound – Artemas

12. Dynasty – MIIA

13. Throne – Bring Me The Horizon

14. Like A Villain – Bad Omens

15. Demons – Imagine Dragons

FOREWORD AND TRIGGER WARNINGS

Dear Reader,

I'm so excited for you to read The Devils They Are! The Boys of Willowbrook are ready to meet you.

If you have read some of my previous books, you'll know that I often write dark romance – anywhere from morally gray to pitch black. When writing this book, particularly after the Dance With My Demons series, I thought it seemed tame compared to some of my other works. But mental health is important, and although this book isn't super dark, there's still some topics and scenes that may be confronting and upsetting.

Your mental health and wellbeing is my priority, followed by having a good time on this journey. So, if you have any potential triggers or would like a sneak peek at the menu before diving in, please find a list of the full triggers here:

HTTPS://STEPHMACCA.MYSHOPIFY.COM/PAGES/TRIGGERWARNINGS

The series will darken as it progresses. More triggers will be added to the above page as the Ridgeview Valley characters complete their story. Please feel free to check back before diving into the next book in the series. I'll do my best to avoid spoilers but please take care of you! You're precious and beautiful.

Anyway, time to dive in!

Yours in love and smut,

Steph

*To everyone who knows that a spit roast isn't something you eat
and the Eiffel Tower isn't just a place to visit...*

CHAPTER ONE

BEXLEY

If you'd ask me how I ended up with a glowstick shoved into my nether region like some kind of flesh lantern, I should probably lie and say... *I don't know.*

But the truth is I'm too stubborn to turn down a dare. Showing signs of weakness or fear leads to nothing but trouble, and I didn't spend the past few years fighting my way to the top, just to be dethroned by a pink neon light in *my pink bits.*

Some people might ask why I let such a ridiculous dare even be considered. Where are my morals? My dignity?

It's just a vagina, for fuck's sake. People waste too much time panicking over their genitalia—it's not like they have razor-sharp teeth and a thirst for blood. And the quicker people accept their sexuality and needs, the better it is. If you're in control, there's less chance that someone will take advantage of it. Let's face it... there are plenty of people out there who would take your hesitation and fear and use it for their own victory and repulsive needs. But at the end of the day, sex is just sex. It's as normal as it comes... *No pun intended.*

We shouldn't feel ashamed to want to be touched, to feel wanted—*to feel beautiful.* And we should always get a say in our own autonomy and choices.

I'm not ignorant though. I know what people say about strong-willed women who know what they want—the slurs painted on us while our male counterparts receive all the glory. That's just bullshit if you ask me. If a guy has sex, he's a legend. But if a woman does it...

But back to the point and my current dilemma.

Unfortunately, the sole photo capturing the dare had made its way into the wrong hands and now there must be consequences. But when I say *unfortunately*, I don't mean for me.

"Find Joshua and bring him to me," I say, handing the cell phone back to Archie.

Arch pockets the black device, giving a stern nod as his hazel eyes scan my unbothered face. "I'll go find him now."

"Good," I reply, slipping one of the black hair ties off my wrist and pulling my dark purple hair back into a high-arched ponytail. If memory serves me, the name on the dye box was called *Midnight Royal.* Like any woman who loves to accessorize, I matched my fingernails to it tonight. The violet painted tips are curved into a classic almond shape, perfect for gorging out eyes if need be—especially *here.*

The abandoned warehouse off seventeenth and south is lit up with strobe lights, a smoky mist hanging above everyone's heads. The haze is a mixture of cigarettes, vapes, and if my senses are correct... cigars?

I'm not sure what fancy fucks thought they would be able to show off with Lonsdales and Panatelas, but in here during fight night, money means nothing.

Maybe in central Ridgeview Valley or on the Willowbrook side it can be used as a weapon, but in the dusty, dark confines of the warehouse, there's something else we value a lot more.

Tenacity. Strength. Power.

We call this the lawless land. On the outskirts of the city, along the border just before the cavernous mountains that travel for miles, the warehouse is pretty much smack-bang in the center of Ridgeview Valley.

It's also just a mile away from the damn miniature crater that our town celebrates. Or is it commemorates? Either way, I suppose Ridgeview Valley doesn't have much more to offer once you've visited the caves and deep canyon if your cardio is up to the challenge.

I did it once–freshman year. Before needing three business days to recover.

But the canyon and *au naturel* views aren't the town's pride and joy. Once a year, the mayor likes to throw an event to remember the day a random piece of space junk smashed into Ridgeview Valley.

It didn't kill anyone, but it did leave a lasting mark in the form of a small dent in the CBD. No doubt the town *could* have fixed it–but why waste the opportunity to attract tourists for extra cash?

Come see our three by three hole in the ground! Suitable for all ages!

If you searched up Ridgeview Valley on Google Earth, you could almost draw a straight line from the hole to the warehouse. And to appease the symmetrical Gods, the lawless land sits perfectly centered between the Cedar Heights and Willowbrook Academies.

Therefore, we have shared custody of this renovator's dream.

But it's the perfect place to do what we want and what we do best—fight. The abandoned warehouse was repurposed back in 1984 to give the rival crews a safe space to burn off steam and test our power against our rivals. Let's face it... no one wants brawls in the streets where innocent people might get caught up in it.

It sounds barbaric—criminal even. But we're not bad people. We just follow the long standing feud and our elders wanted a place to safely fight it out if we needed—under control and with rules of course. And we all abide by them.

Outside of this building, we keep to our own spaces, turning a blind eye on the street if we see our sworn enemies, aside from snarky remarks and the occasional middle finger.

In the center of the room, where the haze of the smoke lingers around the top, the makeshift cage stands. The rusty circular fencing has long lost all its paint, but if you look closely, dried blood clings to the metal giving it a splash of color. It's been here for at least a decade, with various monetary and material donations from both sides keeping it in somewhat decent condition. I mean, how many times can a body be slammed against wire before it starts to buckle and weaken? But I guess it beats the alternative of fighting old school, where everyone just stood around in a circle. I've heard past stories of one-on-one scraps that turned into all-out group brawls before they finally put a cage in the warehouse.

Among the sea of blue and white, I spot an argument forming between a few people, but it's quickly dissolved by the cops standing by. Only, it's hard to tell they are cops, dressed in all-black casual wear.

Former members of Cedar Heights Academy and Willowbrook Academy, they kindly dedicate their time to their old stomping grounds. Some might say they are corrupt for engaging in what a normal person would describe as illegal activities, but I would argue it's a community service. Outside of here, we're all model citizens.

I'm surrounded by the crowd of blue jerseys—my fellow classmates from Cedar Heights Academy. Across the room, it's a different color scheme–stark white attire with black writing. It's laughable, utterly fucking ridiculous even—a color used to depict purity and innocence... two words you would never associate with the assholes of Willowbrook.

Somewhere in the middle of the room around the cage, that's where things start to get a little *mixed up*. People from the rival schools pass each other as they head to the restrooms or drinks line, no clear barrier between the two groups. We co-exist *mostly in peace* while we wait for the scheduled fights to start. But even through the large crowd, I can spot *them* easily.

The so-called Kings of Willowbrook.

Rylan Astor, Hunter Lannister, and Tai Beckett.

On their side of the room, they've set up makeshift thrones—if you can even call it that. Made from chunks of metal, barbed wire, and oak, the three of them sit a foot and a half above their people—staring down at them like self-proclaimed Gods among men.

They aren't Gods though. They are Devils—evil in poor disguise.

As if sensing my heated hatred coming his way, a pair of baby blue eyes snap in my direction. His lips curl into a smirk, fingers dressed in silver rings strumming along his jaw.

Rylan Astor is the bane of my existence. Wait, that's far too polite.

He's an abomination, an odium to my very being.

A dash of moving light reflects little hints of caramel in his dark brown hair as he turns to his left, responding to something Hunter has said.

If there was ever a walking contradiction, it would be Hunter Lannister. His sharp forest green eyes never miss a single thing, but he loves to pretend to be naive. An apex predator, he will lure you in with false pretenses, waiting for the perfect moment to strike when your back is turned.

I can only assume that's why he's dyed the tips of his jet-black hair red—to warn people that he's not afraid to spill blood.

Well, neither am I.

Hunter's father might be the dean of Willowbrook Academy, but while that doesn't give him an exact automatic pass to do whatever he likes, he does grab the nepotism perks by the balls. Which is why he's a conniving snake.

You'd be stupid to fall for his charms and good looks. Designed to be the perfect predator, he will draw you in until you slowly suffocate to death.

But despite all their questionable doings, they are well protected. People often make the mistake of thinking Hunter is the number one threat in their group, but I'd argue they are all equally fucked up.

Rylan definitely snapped that title up with ease a few years ago. His father, Max Astor, is the mayor of Ridgeview Valley. At least until the next election in a few months.

It was a close count in numbers, but I have no doubt it will swing back to us again. It's never a popularity contest—just merely a battle of numbers. And a whole bunch of us from Cedar Heights just turned eighteen and we're ready to flip the numbers as soon as we get the chance.

It's easy to tell I'm the current topic of their conversation, the two of them watching me closely. They don't even bother to hide it. And of course, their attention and heated whispers grab the awareness of the third member of their little kingdom.

Tai Beckett looks over, finding me easily in the sea of blue, a wide smile flashing my way. Some days, I would love nothing more than to wipe that smug look off his face.

Pushing his ashy silver hair back, I can't help but notice his fingertips as his eyes scan over me. His black nails match his soul—I guess he can accessorize too.

His hazel eyes are more on the green side, but close up, there's specks of orange and blue around the irises.

When he doesn't shift his gaze from me, I lift my hand, slowly raising my middle finger shamelessly at him.

After I fell down the Wikipedia rabbit hole and learned that purple was the color of royalty, I decided to adopt it for the foreseeable future. Unlike them, I don't need a dick to rule—let alone three. I'm strong enough to hold that title on my own.

Rylan raises an eyebrow, amused at the exchange between Tai and I. But I stop wasting my energy on them when a body is shoved toward me.

Joshua falls down onto the concrete floor with a heavy smack, groaning for a brief second before pushing quickly to his feet. Archie remains behind him, blocking the escape with his arms folded.

"Joshua," I start firmly, folding my arms. "Have you been sharing pictures that don't belong to you?"

His eyes snap to mine, trying to keep his expressionless, but panic quickly flashes back at me. "I didn't realize it was *your* cunt," he answers defensively. "I just found it... amusing."

Liar liar. I bet this asshole jerked off to my photo at least five times.

"Right," I mock-agree. "And how *did* you even obtain the photo in the first place?"

Creases form around his eyes, a telling sign of rising fear as he tries to pull a lie from his puckered funnel of doom. After this, I would recommend he visit the doctor because it can't be healthy to have shit coming out of your mouth.

"It was sent to me anonymously," he says quickly—*too quickly.*

When I smile slyly, a few people step back.

Archie rolls his eyes as Joshua takes in my expression, unsure how to react. He has every reason to be nervous, especially since I know that only one person had that photo. The person who dared me and took it.

Steele is a long-time friend—and my current *stress reliever.* I know without a doubt he'd never share anything intimate. He's a good guy, but gets easily distracted and has no password on his cell. What kind of person doesn't password protect their cell these days? I'm surprised he hasn't been taken advantage of before now.

The only time that Steele is away from his cell in public is in the locker room. And who is his locker neighbor at the academy? Ahh, that's right. Dear Joshua here.

I raise my hand, looking over my shoulder. I tap the back facing me, watching as Steele turns around, grinning.

"What's up, Bex babe?"

His light brown eyes sparkle but when he takes in my expression, they harden, looking behind me. He pauses on Joshua, a frown appearing as he steps closer to me.

"What did he do?" Steele asks curiously, instinctively tightening the chocolate-colored man-bun on his head like he's getting ready for a fight.

"Joshua here says that he received a picture of my pussy anonymously," I tell him. "With a glowstick in it."

As the seconds tick by, I'm grossly aware of the circle of people watching our interaction. Some seem perplexed about the glowstick comment, while others appear amused. But Steele's expression darkens, connecting the dots. "You fucker! You went through my phone!"

"I didn't mean to!" Joshua argues, throwing his hands up defensively. "I thought it was mine. It was on the bench."

"Bullshit!" Steele snaps back. "I have an Android, and you have an iPhone. They don't even look the same, you wet, flaccid noodle-fucker."

I place a hand on Steele's chest, holding him back as he takes a step toward his teammate. "I don't like liars, Joshua. And I hate people who share intimate things without consent even more."

"I'm sorry," he mumbles apologetically, colliding with Archie's chest as he steps back. "I won't do it again, I promise."

My eyes flicker to Archie, giving him a nod. "I know you won't. That's why I've taken the liberty of arranging your apology."

Archie smiles, holding in a snort as he braces for what's coming. Just because I rule alone, it doesn't mean I don't have a right-hand man or see value in having someone watch my back. We're a family at Cedar, and Arch and I have been friends since elementary school. But in chaos, there still needs to be order. Which is why I have to do this.

"Oh." Joshua sighs with relief. "What can I do for you?"

I nod my head toward the cage. "Since you're such a big, tough man, you're going to fight on behalf of Cedar Heights tonight. I know you won't let me down. It's an honor, after all."

For a linebacker who spends his days shouting aggressive taunts at people, he sure looks like he might piss himself right now. Where's that brute mentality from the field gone? Well, you know what they say... fuck around and you shall find out.

"Wait!" Joshua squeals as Archie starts to push him toward the cage. "Bexley! Please!"

I ignore him, holding in a sigh as I scan the cage to check out his opponent. He won't do this again—let this be a lesson on behalf of not just me, but all women. And certainly a lesson not to shit where you eat. I do everything I can to protect my people, and he crossed the line when he violated my trust.

Willowbrook's first fighter dances around in circles, trying to boost crowd morale as he waits. If I had to guess, I'd place money on this guy being a jock too—except he's bigger than Joshua.

As much as I hate losing a fight to these assholes, sometimes the lesson you learn and price you pay is more valuable. We can always win the next fight.

Archie pushes Joshua into the cage with a slap of encouragement on the back, closing the door behind him. Instantly, my ears ring as the crowd screams loudly in excitement.

On the other side of the room, Rylan leans forward with interest, locking his eyes on Joshua. His lips twitch into a smile, quickly assessing that our fighter is no match for his.

His gaze moves away from the cage, finding me again, probably to gloat.

I give him a sweet smile back, letting him know with a silent message that this was deliberate. Even though I can't hear it, Rylan laughs, slumping back casually in his seat as he turns his attention back to the cage as the bell rings for the fight to start.

I didn't deliberately give Joshua a losing match—I don't even know who this other guy is or what his abilities are. But the message is still the same. Don't fuck over your family.

Fight for them.

As I hoped, Joshua perks up after receiving a solid punch to the cheek. His ego takes over, arms wildly swinging in retaliation as the two guys exchange blows.

Out of the corner of my eye, I see Archie pull out his cell, glancing down. The crowd roars as Joshua hits the side of the cage, but I still hear the little *"Shit!"* that comes from Archie.

Before I can ask what's wrong, he hands me the cell with an open text message from his dad. William Roberts is the fire chief, so instantly I know it's bad.

> **Dad: There's a fire at Cedar. We're on scene but it's not looking good. Arson suspected.**

The noise of the room fades as I read and re-read the text message. Our school is on *fucking fire*? Why would someone do that?

A loud bellow rips me back to the present. Joshua is on his back in the cage, clearly unconscious, while the Willowbrook fighter runs around in victorious circles.

"Send someone to check on Joshua then call your dad," I direct Arch, handing him back the cell. "We need to find out what happened."

He nods, pushing his way through the crowd while I turn my attention back to the other side of the room.

Not many people would benefit or get a kick out of burning our school into ashes. *Except...*

I glance at the three of them suspiciously. Hunter is on his feet, alternating between clapping and pumping his fist into the air while Rylan holds out his hand as someone slaps a wad of notes into it.

But when I look at Tai, I find him staring right back at me. He throws me a wink, my insides burning with rage.

If I find out they are responsible for this, we're going to war.

Rules be fucking damned.

CHAPTER TWO

BEXLEY

I can't hide the look of disgust from my face as I glare up at the chestnut shaded building, squinting as the morning sun whacks me in the face.

Beside me, Arch lets out a sigh, rubbing the side of his face with exasperation.

"This is the worst idea in the history of ideas."

I snort. "It's certainly not my first preference. Or my second. Hell, is there a position after last?"

White jerseys float around us, taunts and cat calls bouncing off me without making a dent.

One guy—Perkins, according to his football jersey—decides to be brave, getting right up into my face as he jeers at me, bristles of spit flying out of his mouth.

"Welcome to Willowbrook, bitc—"

My hand snaps out, cutting him off as I wrap my fingers around his neck in a tight grip. My nails are blood-red today—a warning.

It's the only one they will get.

Perkins splutters for a moment, in shock, trying to take a breath. Caught off-guard by my reaction, he quickly slaps my arm out of the way with ease, stepping back. "What the fuck?" he gasps, clutching at his neck.

Giving him a polite smile, I take pride in the angry-red crescent moon marks that now blemish his skin. "Touch me again and next time I'll gouge your fucking eyes out. Okay, sweet pea?"

I sense a plethora of bodies behind me, a blue wall appearing into my peripheral vision as other Cedar students step up protectively behind and beside me.

Even though we're being forced to attend Willowbrook until our school is repaired, it was a unanimous decision to continue wearing our own blue jerseys. Like Willowbrook, we have a few different jerseys among the cohort—such as the football players having their own unique ones with their names and position numbers.

Most of us just wear the plain version without the extra detail. They all have Cedar's emblem on them—a tarnished coat of arms engulfing a wildcat. It's not much different from Willowbrook's attire, and it's an unpleasant reminder that we're in wolf territory now.

Perkins takes a few steps back, stumbling into his friends as his eyes scan the Cedar crowd with unease. "Whatever," he spits out vehemently, before turning and disappearing through the entrance doors.

I start to turn toward Archie, tugging down my new–well, secondhand that I sourced off Facebook Marketplace–Willowbrook black and white tartan skirt, when the sound of slow clapping reaches my ears. Snapping my neck toward the obnoxious sound, I find none other than Rylan *fucking* Astor standing at the top of the steps in front of the entrance, a smirk on his face.

"Quite a performance, Spencer. Shame it ended prematurely."

My eyes narrow glaringly. "Are you volunteering to switch places, Rylan? I'd be happy to give you an up-close and personal view of my nails if you want to continue where Perkins left off."

Rylan casually moves down two steps without breaking eye contact. "Thoughtful—but I prefer them running down my back."

I resist the urge to scoff and gag at his suggestion. You couldn't pay me to sleep with the monster. Even if I was dead, my corpse would still roll around with repulsion to get away.

"Unfortunately, you already turned me off by saying *ended prematurely*. But don't worry, Freudian slips happen, even to the best of us."

I start making my way toward the stairs, feeling the others follow close behind. Rylan steps to his right, blocking my incoming path. Without missing a beat, I follow suit, barging him with my shoulder as I skate past toward the doors. He laughs loudly, amused, and when I glance over my shoulder to make sure he doesn't touch any of my people, he's still watching me.

Surprisingly, he seems to have an ounce of self-preservation, moving to the side as the others walk past. They all glare at him heatedly, and Millie—my little five-foot nothing firecracker freshman—mimics my actions and jabs his shoulder with her backpack.

Her blonde hair is tied in a ponytail, and she swishes it deliberately as she walks, whacking him in the face with the ends.

When we lock eyes, she grins back at me, electric blue irises dancing wildly with a silent plea to let her loose.

It's always the fun-sized ones you need to watch out for. On many occasions, it's crossed my mind that in a few years, she'll probably be in my position. I'm not sure who will take over next year when I'm gone, but whoever it is, they better watch out for her once she's a senior if they are still around. Or worse, considering other replacement options.

Rylan holds up his hands in a seemingly act of retreat, but I know better than to believe it's coming from a genuine place. This is his way of warning me too.

There's no doubt in my mind that he was here deliberately, waiting to greet me—to remind me that I'm on his turf now.

But like the warehouse, it doesn't matter where we are. I won't bow down to anyone. These people behind me, they rely on me, and I have their back just as much as they have mine.

We're a family—a band of misfits from similar walks of life. Unlike the richer snobs of Willowbrook, we're known as the *other option*. If you can't afford Willowbrook or meet their selection criteria, then the only other option you have in Ridgeview Valley is to attend Cedar Heights–and we don't turn anyone away.

That's what makes us a threat though. We lean into our pasts, not run away from it. Rejection and heartache make us stronger, and we don't bat an eyelash at the prospect of new enemies. We survive—that's what we do.

Which is why when Mayor Astor told our principal that we would need to merge for a few months, we didn't rile up or shy away from the challenge. And yes, these obnoxious pricks like to rub it in every chance they get that they are privately funded while we rely on the State.

But it doesn't matter though. You can take the kid out of Cedar Heights, but you can't take the Cedar Heights out of the kid.

Bring it on, Rylan Astor. I hope they bring their A-game. I would never want to just dethrone them without a fight. I want to earn it, so that when I do, everyone will know that I deserve it.

It's a long morning.

The administration staff scramble to confirm everyone's details and pass out schedules and maps. But eventually, we all head in our separate directions with some slight understanding of what's to come and where to go.

Unfortunately, there's not enough lockers for all of us, so the staff tried to suggest that we leave our belongings in the auditorium for now. Fat chance of that. Textbooks are expensive and we had no choice but to bring whatever they could recover from our lockers back at school.

Thankfully, the fire didn't cause too much damage to the halls where the lockers are, but many classrooms, the administration building, and our sports facilities were painted in charcoal ash or obliterated completely.

Even our beloved library, full of worn old books and computers that run slower than windows 97, is gone.

Archie and I compare schedules and I'm happy to see that we have a few classes together during the week—but none today. First period, I have history while he has biology. Following that, I have a free period where I plan to use that time to explore the grounds to figure out what the hell I'm doing.

I never intended to step foot inside this academy, so the idea never popped into my mind that I should learn the blueprints.

At least for the most part, the Willowbrook students have kept their distance. I told my guys to let me know if anyone gives them shit, but so far, it's been relatively smooth sailing. But I'm not being complacent. It's still early days and I know that somewhere around here, Rylan is stalking around with Hunter and Tai. It's only a matter of time before they show their faces again, and it's best we keep our heads down and stay out of trouble.

Staring at the map, I follow the wide hallways, turning left, then right, before confirming I've gone past the nurse's station as needed. Then, I find myself face to face with room 228 for history.

I push the door open, letting my hand drop down with the paper as I glance up. All eyes fall on me, the teacher pausing his spiel as his lips purse with disapproval at my tardiness.

Wow—talk about not getting a break. It's only day one and he expects me to magically know everything. To be fair, I would have been here sooner, but I hung back, waiting until all of the Cedar Heights students had been processed and paired up with a buddy to find their first classes.

Judging by numbers, I'm the last to arrive. There's a handful of blue jerseys in the class with me, and they beam at me happily.

As I scan over the students, my face deadpans at Tai's grinning expression. He's in the back row, last in line. Leaning against the wall lazily, he shoots me a wink before turning his head to the free seat next to him.

The last available seat.

Fucking great.

Forced proximity is one issue, but close proximity? Dammit.

"And you are?" the teacher asks when I make no effort to move from the doorway.

Turning my focus back to him, I try to ignore the obvious hairpiece staring right at me. His dusty-brown toupee is crooked, brushing over the tops of his wide-rimmed spectacles.

"Bexley Spencer," I answer, glancing at the paperwork again. "I assume you are Mr. Hardwood."

Fuck me. What an unfortunate name. I do my best to keep my face expressionless, biting my tongue as he nods.

"You're late, Ms. Spencer. I don't tolerate tardiness in my classroom. However," he pauses, clicking his tongue as his eyes skim over my jersey. "Given it's your first day, I'll let this one slide. You can take a seat next to Mr. Beckett up the back."

"Thank you," I say politely, walking past him as I head to the back row while swallowing a curse.

Apparently, politeness toward our elders is not a trait that Tai and I share—his legs lifting up and perching themselves on the edge of my new history desk, ankles crossed.

I drop my bag on the desk and without hesitating, I shove his feet, letting them fall to the floor with a bang. Sliding into my seat, I give Mr. Hardwood an innocent smile while Tai readjusts himself.

"As I was saying," Mr. Hardwood grumbles, finally looking away and continuing on.

Reaching into my bag, I take out my textbook and pens, getting set up. I feel burning eyes on me, daring me to look his way but I ignore him. That's how nuisances like Tai work—they feed on attention. But if you ignore them, *eventually* they burn themselves out.

I listen closely to the teacher, trying hard to pay attention as his toupee shifts with his movements. Focus... Focus and figure out what page I need to turn to.

My fingers are pressed into the spine of the textbook when Tai leans toward me, lowering his voice.

"Hey, Sexy Bexie. I can help you."

Cringe.

Not the first time I've heard someone use the terrible nickname, but it sounds far worse coming from his lips.

"I've got it under control," I mutter back, still glancing straight ahead. "But call me that again and I'll staple your balls to Hardwood's desk."

Tai doesn't react, his face stoic, but I do notice his hand casually disappearing under the desk. "We can do this the easy way or the hard way, Spencer."

"And let me guess," I whisper, turning to finally face him. "The easy way is to let you boss me around? I'll pass, thanks. Just because we've been forced here for the time being, doesn't mean you get control over us."

He finally cracks with a smug smile. "I have no problem going down the hard route, babe. I was just trying to do you a one-time favor."

"Don't bother," I shoot back, looking away. "The day any of us bow down to you is the day that hell freezes over."

"Fine," he replies, playful demeanor vanishing. "Don't say we didn't warn you. We're going to make your life unbearable. And when the lowlives from Cedar start to crack, I'll make sure they know why—or rather, who is to blame."

My jaw clenches at his words, but I don't bother dignifying his threat with a response. If hard is what they want, then hard is what they are going to get.

Chapter Three

"Mom, I'm home," I call out, closing the front door behind me.

It's quiet, which can mean only one thing.

Dropping my bag at the doorway with a sigh, I make my way to the other end of the house, finding her bedroom door open. As I thought, she's passed out on top of the duvet, an empty bottle of cheap-ass wine on the bedside table.

She doesn't move a single muscle as I approach, soft snores coming from her petite frame.

I hate that she's withering away in front of me. It wasn't always like this. Once upon a time, I had a sickeningly happy family. But four years ago, my dad lost his job and went into a spiral. Eventually, it tore their marriage apart, and he walked out one night and never came back.

I stood at my bedroom window that night, watching him pack our only car. I silently begged him to look over at my window, to see me. My heart knew he was leaving, but if that wasn't enough solid evidence, their screaming had been.

I heard the whole fight. He had cheated with a neighbor while Mom was at work and I was at school. But despite knowing they had marital issues, a part of me thought—*hoped*—maybe I could change his mind. Maybe I would be enough for him to stay—or at the very least, not stray too far.

But sometimes wishes don't come true. Life isn't a fairytale.

All I remember is him kissing me goodnight, tucking me into bed before the screaming had started. I stayed awake listening to it, doors slamming, before eventually all I could hear was sobs and the sound of the trunk being opened outside my bedroom window.

We never did find out where he went. All I know is nothing could save his mental spiral, not even me. And eventually, Mom went into a spiral too.

After she removed all traces of him from the house, she found solace in the bottom of a bottle. And from that day forward, I became the parent of the house. I was forced to grow up and take charge, making sure we kept on top of things whenever she was in one of her depressive moods–which slowly became more frequent until it was the norm.

Sadly, it's because of my forced hardness that I ended up ruling Cedar Heights. People loved that protective, fierce nature. They looked up to it. I guess in a way it was a comfort for them too—many having their own challenges in life and needing someone to step up that was willing to help them. Or probably just the fact that someone *wanted* to take care of them.

No one takes care of me. But I've long learned to accept that. There's no use breaking down, crying for my parents to change–I already tried. I'm here now, and that's what I need to focus on. I can't change the past, but I control my future.

Grabbing a spare blanket from her dresser, I drape it over her, grabbing the empty bottle of wine and discarding it into the trash. I replace it with a glass of water and two Tylenol for when she wakes, before heading to my bedroom.

Sitting down at my desk by the window, I open my bag and place my schedule in front of me. Memorizing tomorrow's classes, I switch out my textbooks for what I need before grabbing out my cell.

I had asked Archie to organize a bonfire night down at the beach. By beach, I mean it's more like a small lake with rocks and sand, on the opposite side of Ridgeview Valley away from the caves. It's only about half a mile long, but it's on Cedar's side of town, so we hang there when we need to unwind.

I think after the day everyone has had they deserve a night to vent and decompress. Moody Mondays are already sad enough without throwing Willowbrook bastards into the mix.

Opening my cell, I read Arch's newest text message, confirming that everything is sorted. There's still a few hours before I need to head down, so I go raid the fridge and make some cheap pasta with cheese before putting on some music and stare at the ceiling.

There's already a crowd of people on Cedar Beach when I pull up in my old blue Ford pickup.

Climbing out of the cab, I spot Archie immediately on the sand, red solo cup in his hand as he laughs and chats with a few people.

Sneaking up behind him, I surprise him when I pinch the cup from his hand, taking a sip as his eyes light up. "There you are! Was beginning to think you had gotten lost."

Swallowing the warm beer, I hand the cup back to him. "Got distracted doom scrolling for a bit. Thanks for getting this all sorted."

He nods. "Took us a while to get the fire going. Damn wind kept putting it out."

Out of the corner of my eye, I see a figure bouncing toward me, and when I turn, Millie is there with two cups in her hands. "Bex!" she greets, holding out a cup. "I got you a drink."

"Thanks, Mills," I say warmly, taking it from her. "How was your first day?"

She visibly cringes, rolling her eyes with a sigh. "It was *fine*. How long did Principal Samson say we need to be there for again?"

"Hopefully not too long," I tell her softly. "Just keep your head high and be on your guard."

Something flashes in her eyes, but she doesn't voice it. There's no need. I know she's itching to give back whatever bullshit someone throws at her. But I've made everyone promise to keep out of trouble...

However, if someone else starts it, they have my permission to *end it*.

This girl has been begging me to let her fight in the cage for months. But while I have no concerns that she could hold her own, her older brother, Parker, has forbidden her from stepping inside the rusty cage.

Parker is a junior, and just as *passionate* as his sister. If anyone can take her on or hold her back, it's probably him. God, I can only imagine what their sibling rivalry was like growing up.

Someone steps up behind me, snaking their arms around my torso. Leaning back, I recognize Steele's scent immediately, the smell of beer and crisp citrus cologne.

"Hey," he murmurs quietly into my ear.

Turning around to face him, I rest my arms on his shoulders, careful not to spill my drink. "Hey, Steele. How's your *friend* doing?"

His nose upturns at the mention but he just nonchalantly shrugs under my arms. "A few bruises but fine. His ego is more bruised than anything."

I nod. "And did *you* learn anything?"

Steele grins at me. "I've put a passcode on my cell. But I also deleted the photo."

Pushing up onto my toes, I kiss him softly. "Good."

"I'll leave you to mingle," Archie says from behind me. "I see Abby over there so I'm gonna say hi."

I look over my shoulder, giving him a nod of acknowledgement. "Have fun."

As he walks off, I watch as he makes his way over to the blonde senior by the edge of the water, surrounded by other cheerleaders.

Archie has been lusting after her for years, ever since they became neighbors in our freshman year. She was in a relationship with one of the football players until a few months back, and now that she's single, the two of them have been nearly inseparable. Though, he swears black and blue nothing has eventuated between them yet—*yet* being the key word. I give it a few more weeks at max. They've been looking pretty cozy lately, hugging and whispering in corners.

"Want to come over to my truck?" I ask quietly, gazing back at Steele. He nods eagerly, letting go of my waist to grab my hand.

He leads us over the sand and rocks to the gravelly parking lot, making a beeline for my Ford. I fish my keys out of my black ripped denim mini skirt, unlocking the driver's door before climbing in and reaching over to lift the lock on the passenger side.

Steele climbs in and when he shuts the door, the sounds of the beachgoers fade. Instantly, he charges across the seat, kissing me. I laugh, kissing him back while blindly trying to put my drink on the dash.

When it's securely and safely out of reach from tangled limbs, his hand lands on my thigh, sliding up my legs as I part them for him. Steele groans into my mouth when he reaches my hipster briefs, rubbing me through the thin material before carefully peeling it to the side with his fingers.

That's what I like about Steele and our arrangement—there's no expectations, no awkwardness. We both know what we want, and we go for it. And after the day I've had, an orgasm is high on my priority list of needs.

The tip of his finger slides up and down my slit, teasing me, and I buck my hips toward him. He smirks wickedly against my mouth, deliberately pulling back as his hand firmly presses into my inner thigh, squeezing the soft skin.

"Dammit, Steele," I grumble. "If you don't touch me, I'll—"

"You'll what, Bex?" he replies, kissing my neck. "Tease me back? Beg?"

"I don't beg," I mutter playfully. "I'll take matters into my own hands and make you watch. You won't be allowed to touch me. You'll have to sit there and watch my pussy get wet, listen to my moans while I come."

I hold back a laugh, biting my lip as his body tenses against me. I know he hates not being able to touch me, but we're both headstrong, constantly fighting for power and control. Secretly, I think he gets off on the fact that he gets to bring me to my knees. But I don't think he realizes that even when we're on our knees, we're still in control.

Before he can make a move toward me, I slide back, pushing his chest firmly with my hands. He falls backwards, lips parted as his eyes sparkle with defiance and challenge.

"Look at me," I say, bringing my leg up between us. I place one foot on his thigh while the other rests on the dash, giving him the perfect view of my cunt.

Slowly, I mimic his earlier actions, pulling the material aside as he watches. Swallowing, a rush of panic falls over his face when he realizes just how serious I am. His hand tries to come out to touch me and I smack it playfully away, waving my finger at him. "Uh, no. You had your chance, babe. Now, you get to be a spectator."

"Oh, come on," he groans, dropping his hand into his lap. He kneads his groin with his fist, eyes locked on the spot between my inner thighs.

My other hand trails down my pelvis, finding its way to my aching center. I start by rubbing lazy circles around my clit, before dipping lower, pressing a finger inside myself.

Steele's eyes blow wide, barely blinking. When I add another finger, pumping them in and out, he groans again, reaching for the waistband of his shorts.

"No," I tell him, shifting my foot from his thigh to his hardened cock. "If you can't touch me, you can't touch yourself either."

A string of curses fall from his lips as his head falls back onto the passenger window.

Grinning, I free a finger from the bunched-up material, using it to stroke my clit while my other hand continues to press into my core. I press my foot into his cock harder, earning myself a scattered groan as his hips jerk into me.

"Bex," he begs, and I can't help the tiny laugh that spills out of my lips.

"I don't beg," I reiterate. "But you do, don't you, Steele?"

Steele nods, just once. "You're being mean."

"Am I?" I tease, removing my fingers and leaning forward as I hold them out in front of his face.

He hungrily pulls them into his mouth, sucking my fingers clean with a shit-eating grin.

My throbbing body reminds me that I've forgotten it, and as I start to drag my hand back down, I've barely touched myself when a knock on the window behind me stops me in my tracks.

Whipping my head over my shoulder with a look of frustration, I relax when I see Archie. He looks uncomfortable and annoyed at having to interrupt, but I know he wouldn't do it unless it was something urgent.

Bringing my legs together, I sit upright in my seat, winding the window down. "Arch?"

"I'm sorry," he starts, apology evident in his tone as he looks between us. "I didn't want to interrupt but we have a bit of a situation."

"What is it?" I ask urgently, brows dipping.

Archie's face hardens, glancing over his shoulder at something.

"We have company, Bex. Those bastards from Willowbrook are here."

Chapter Four

Rylan

I grin at the wide berth the Cedar crowd gives, forming a semi-circle around us. I can't tell if they want to fight us or if they are terrified of our presence. Either way, it's downright amusing.

Hunter, Tai and I stare back at them, not the least bit bothered.

My eyes scan the lineup of Cedar flops as they block our access to the beach, but it's the tiny blonde girl that gets my attention for a moment. She's front and center, tapping her foot as she leans forward, locking eyes with me and silently muttering. Judging by the way her lips form the unspoken words, it appears to be something like *'Come on'*.

"How cute are they?" Hunter mutters, not bothering to lower his voice or hide the menacing tone. *"Adorable."*

Shaking my head, I smile smugly. "Very cute. It's like an army of fluffy blue bunny rabbits."

To my right, Tai snorts. "Incoming."

I don't bother looking, my face still on the group in front of me. One by one, they turn their heads toward the parking lot, faces relaxing slightly. I don't need to check who's approaching—I already know.

"What the fuck are you doing here?"

When her footsteps stop a few feet away, I finally turn my attention to her, lazily pivoting my frame. "There she is," I proclaim, digging my hands into my pockets. "Hope we weren't interrupting something."

My gaze flickers behind her to the tall, dark-haired man who's mirroring her angry expression. Judging by her flushed cheeks and burning eyes, I can only assume—and hope—that we just successfully ruined her evening.

"This isn't your neck of the woods," Bexley answers heatedly. "And you sure as shit aren't wanted here."

"Ouch," Tai murmurs, feigning disappointment as he cradles a hand to his chest. "I'm hurt."

Bexley's eyes swing between the three of us, her arms folding over her chest. "It's bad enough we have to deal with you on a daily basis now. You won't be ruining our time outside of school hours. Now, leave before I make you leave."

Hunter laughs, glancing over at me. "I think we should stay—make sure they are keeping out of trouble. You know, since Dad is worried about their behavior. After all, they are representatives of Willowbrook now."

There's a protest of angry voices, some louder than others. In my peripheral vision, that girl is trying to lunge forward, but a guy next to her grabs her arm, whispering something in her ear. Bexley's eyes fall on her too, a look of admiration and fondness washing over her face. Ahh—ten bucks says this is her little protégé. But it's obvious that where Bexley has experience and control, that little psycho has yet to learn how this world works.

"Regardless of your father's position," Bexley says with a scoff. "We don't answer to him or anyone from Willowbrook. You're merely a means to an end."

"While you're on our turf, you'd do best to follow our rules," I answer first. "That goes for all of you," I add, glancing at the group.

Bexley laughs, dropping her arms as she steps closer to us. I watch her carefully, interested to see how far she's willing to push back. My eyebrows raise when she finally stops, inches from my chest as she glares up at me. "You can take your threats and shove them into your rectal cavity, Rylan. They are as empty and vapid as you are."

I lower my head, bringing our faces closer. There are more murmured whispers from the crowd, gawking at our close proximity. But to Bexley's credit, she doesn't flinch or pull back. We're locked in a game of chicken with neither one of us backing down.

"This is your only warning," I tell her loudly, addressing her peers as well. "We came here to give you the opportunity to fall into line before we *make you*."

She smiles sweetly at me, no doubt ready to defy my words. Most people shy away from us, fearful, but I wouldn't expect the same from Bexley Savanna Spencer. In fact, I'd be disappointed if she did.

"*He*," she pauses, pointing toward Tai without breaking eye contact. "Already tried to warn me. And barely managed to leave with his balls intact. For the sake of your lack of comprehension, I'll repeat what I said to him; We're not bowing down to you. We're not *falling into line*. You can save your breath because nothing you say or do will change that."

I grin at her, flashing my teeth as I run my tongue along the back of them. "I hope you realize that we're going to enjoy breaking you, Bex. You're at a disadvantage here. A good leader tries to save their people, not send them into the wolf's den. I guess I mistook you."

"You did," she agrees. "But don't you for a second make the repeat mistake of assuming you know us. We might be at a *disadvantage*, but don't underestimate us. That will be the last mistake you ever make."

A few people yell '*Yeah*' and '*That's right!*' but I pay them no mind. My attention is locked on the woman in front of me. Even with my 6'2" frame, she's not that far off me, maybe four inches, if that. It's tempting to close the gap and leave a bite mark on her pale skin to show who's in charge here. That guy behind her is still watching us with wild eyes, obviously hating how close I am to what's his.

But if this is the game she wants to play, I'm more than happy to participate. Because by the end of it, she'll be nothing but a product of my destruction—a broken, soulless mess. But I like it better when they fight back. It's the sweetest victory, breaking someone who acts like an untamable mare.

Everyone is tameable though. She has weaknesses and I'm going to find it, exploiting them one by one until she cries for the mercy that will never come.

"Best of luck tomorrow," I murmur with a tight smile. "You're going to need it."

I step back, turning and pushing my way through the crowd of people with Hunter and Tai close behind. As I reach the parking lot, I dare a glance over my shoulder, giving her a wink before we climb into my black Chevy Silverado and peel out of the beach entrance.

"Any more comments in that Facebook group?" I ask Tai, stepping out of the truck as I shield the sun from my eyes.

He's parked next to me in our reserved spots, Hunter lingering on the pathway in front of the cars as he waits patiently.

It's still about fifteen minutes before other students start to arrive, but we agreed to meet early to go over our plan for today.

"Just a bunch of nonsense about our visit last night," he answers, swinging his bag over his back. "Idiots still haven't figured out we're in their little secret group."

Amused, I laugh, giving Hunter our usual handshake and fist bump as I approach. "Typical. Keep it on the down low though."

As soon as we heard from Hunter's dad that they were heading to Willowbrook, Tai did some digging around on social media. After all, that's how everyone communicates these days, so I figured that Cedar students would do the same. And wouldn't you know it, I was correct.

They run a closed group on socials, but after doing some investigation work, Tai set up a fake profile of a student who is listed in the Cedar Heights system but doesn't appear to have social media. As long as he doesn't draw attention, they won't know that the profile is fake unless they investigate or ask questions.

Tai's a bit of a tech genius. While I like to run, he spends his free time coding and ripping apart computers to put them back together.

Hunter, on the other hand, loves his music. The guy can play Beethoven's 5th Symphony and not hit a single wrong key. To be fair, he only mastered it because I made a bet that he couldn't. The competitive shit just had to prove me wrong. I'll never admit it, but I was probably never going to win that bet. Hunter's been playing piano since he was seven. I don't know how he can read all that gibberish sheet music, but props to him.

"Dad said they're trying to incorporate some of the Cedar staff to assist with teaching pressures," Hunter says. "Most have been making a fuss about not being able to work so the State suggested that Willowbrook cooperate to ease the burden on both sides."

I snort. "Ease what burden? The curriculum is nearly identical. A few extra kids here and there won't kill our teachers. As for the Cedar staff and their money woes, it sounds like their problem. We don't need any more of them hanging around here. Even one brainless Cedar student or teacher is overkill."

"Did your Dad say much on the matter?" Tai asks me. "I bet he's *really* pleased."

I can't help but laugh at his sarcastic tone because as usual Tai's right. My father was pissed when he found out it was his responsibility to handle the Cedar mess. As mayor, he's been ordered by the State to help.

"His office is helping with organizing repairs, contacting builders... that kind of thing. He's not thrilled."

Hunter nods. "Our dads are meeting tonight for drinks to try to work out a solution–get them out of here as fast as they can."

"Good," I say shortly as we walk through the entrance. "The sooner they are out of our hair, the better. Though, it is fun toying with them."

"Can't say we didn't warn them," Tai remarks.

"Yeah, about that," Hunter cuts in. "What was the go with that comment last night?"

Tai shrugs casually. "I have the utmost pleasure of sharing History with Bexley–we're even desk neighbors."

"Sucks to suck," I grin. "You'll be able to keep an eye on her at least. She's a fucking snake. They all are."

We pull up to the lockers, dumping our belongings and collecting what we need for first period.

"I give it until the end of the week," Hunter says. "She's not as tough as she makes out to be."

My lips pull up into a lopsided smile. "Wanna bet?"

"Fuck off with your bets. It's too early for that shit."

"I'm just saying; The bitch has balls. She didn't even flinch when I got up in her face."

Tai leans back against his locker, resting one foot against it. "She's certainly got a mouth on her."

"Muzzle her then," Hunter suggests, rolling his eyes with clear annoyance. "We just need to do whatever is necessary, as quickly as possible."

"The repairs are going to take weeks easily, maybe even months according to Dad," I say. "So, leaves us little choice other than making them fall into line. What a pity."

They nod, the sound of the first students starting to arrive as people move through the hallway to their lockers.

"Wolf Pack," Tai grins, holding up his knuckles. Hunter taps them with his own before I do the same with theirs.

"Wolf Pack," I repeat. "Let's rip them to pieces."

Chapter Five

Those assholes ruined my orgasm, and now they have ruined my Tuesday.

I was ready to be all peppy and optimistic, but as soon as I turned the corner to the hallway, I spotted their backs as they walked off in the other direction. Thankfully, they didn't see me, but I did have half a mind to fling something at their heads.

After they left the beach, the vibe kind of died so we called it a night. Yesterday was exhausting—mentally and physically—and we decided it was better to get some rest for school today.

Gym for first period should be illegal and punishable by law. It's way too early to be running around and the weather is already heating up for the day. The Ford doesn't have a working A/C, so I had both windows down on the way here, but the stale, warm breeze just made me want to go back to bed.

Following the hallway to the other side of the building, I vaguely remember my bearings from yesterday. Thankfully, the track isn't hard to miss when I emerge through wide double doors and I make my way down to the female locker rooms by the edge of the field.

It appears empty as I pull into a stall, changing into the slightly too-small black shorts, and an extra-large white shirt. It's not ideal, but at least the shirt partially covers my ass since it's threatening to break loose. Though, I'm not confident that it will help once I start to run. I hope the stitching is premium on these shorts and they don't rip and flash my ass to everyone.

There's still no one in sight when I walk out of the stall, but a sudden "*Fuck sticks!*" has me jumping and looking around wildly.

"Uh, hi?" I ask, determining that the voice came from one of the toilets and not God himself.

"Oh, thank goodness," a soft voice mutters in relief. "This is embarrassing but do you have a spare tampon? Hell, I'll even accept a pad. Anything except for this one-ply sandpaper."

Laughing at the toilet paper comment, I open my bag and start to dig around. "No offence but you'd think with Willowbrook's money they would at least provide some decent toilet paper."

"You're telling me," she groans, letting out a tiny squeak when I reach under the door and hold out a Tampax. "You're the fucking best."

For some reason, I feel compelled to wait. It seems rude of me to run out now, so I stand by the basins, until the toilet flushes and a blonde girl with vibrant pink ends walks out.

Her green eyes look at me warmly and I take in our matching outfits, surmising she must be a senior about to start gym as well.

"Oh, I see," she laughs, nodding at the blue sleeve poking out of my bag. "A Cedar Heights comrade."

"Comrade is a stretch," I joke back. "But yes, I'm still getting used to the toilet paper situation too since it's only my second day."

She grins, washing her hands under the tap. "I hate to break it to you, but you never get used to it. There's a constant fear you're going to accidentally finger your own asshole. But hey, that's probably the least of your concerns. I bet it feels like you're trying to swim in a pool of lava right now."

"Something like that," I admit. "I can handle it though."

Her eyes meet mine through the mirror. "I bet you can. You're Bexley, right?" she asks confidently.

"I am," I confirm.

There's something about her presence that seems friendly. Even saying my name, there's no animosity like I'd expect.

She doesn't seem so bad. Easily the nicest person I've come across the past two days. I actually think I might grow to like her. I'm not completely against the idea of an ally in this school, even if most of them are entitled dickwads. But she doesn't give that kind of vibe. If anything, she seems *normal*.

I still have to be on my guard though. I've learned never to trust people until they prove themselves. But hey, if anything was going to bring mortal enemies together, it was always going to be our disdain for periods. That's why women should be in positions of power. Dick fights? Unproductive. Sharing tampons? World peace.

She flicks her hands over the basin, wiping the residual water on the sides of her shirt. But before she can respond, another voice cuts in.

"Argh, look what the trash dragged in."

I turn my attention to the doorway, eyes landing on three cheerleaders. Ahh, yes—this was the drama I was expecting.

"Fuck off, Liv. Don't you need to get your nails done or something?" the blonde girl mutters, walking away from the basin to stand next to me.

The girl in the center with auburn hair holds up a hand lazily, turning it over. "No need—got a fresh set yesterday since I can actually afford it."

I know that's a dig toward me, but I couldn't care less. Despite the fact these shorts are strangling my ass cheeks, I make do.

Crossing my arms, I face my bright-red nails toward her. "You're blocking the entrance," I tell the cheerleaders, noting the small crowd that's gathered behind trying to get in. They are watching on, some with interest, while others glare at me. There's not a single familiar Cedar face among them but that's fine. If they don't move, I'm not above shoving my way through if need be.

"Don't pay her any attention. That's just Liv," the blonde girl murmurs dryly.

"Just Liv?" she laughs. "Try head cheerleader."

Oh, goody. I love a walking cliché first thing in the morning.

"Amazing," I reply sarcastically. "Well done, you."

Liv turns to the girl on her left. "Sierra, aren't they your old shorts from freshman year?" she laughs.

The tall, tanned cheerleader with a fresh caramel balayage snickers. "You know what Mommy is like—loves donating to charity."

"God, she can't even get the right size," Liv mocks. "They are so small on her."

And here come the fat jokes. Not an original thought or brain cell between the three of them.

I'm not overweight by any means, but I expected the bitchiness. When people have no more ammo, they target your physical appearance. I don't care though, but the girl on Liv's right shifts awkwardly. Her friends don't notice, but when her light brown eyes meet mine, she quickly looks away.

I take a few steps forward. "You're still blocking the entrance," I point out.

Liv smiles, glossy pink lips upturning smugly. "They can wait."

Rolling my eyes, I take a step to my left, but Liv follows, blocking my path.

"Move," I order with a warning to my tone.

"I'm not done speaking to you."

"That's hilarious because I have nothing to say to you. Just keep out of my way and I'll keep out of yours."

Liv laughs, stepping forward and closing the distance between us. She lifts one of her perfectly manicured nails, shoving it into my chest. "You listen to me—"

My hand snaps up, coiling around her finger and painfully squeezing it. Her words cut off as she tries to jerk her hand back, but I grip tighter, pulling her finger backwards. Not enough to break it, but enough to warn that I'll dislocate the damn thing if she touches me again.

"I don't think so," I start, pressing my thumb against the back of the tip of her nail. "I don't waste my energy on vapid, shallow bitches. Whatever you are going to say, forget it. Yes, I'm from Cedar. No, I'm not going to fuck your boyfriend. But yes—I will absolutely break your fucking finger if you touch me again."

I release her finger, the force sending her stumbling back into the black-haired girl.

"Peyton!" Liv hisses, apparently deciding it was her friend's fault.

Making use of the distraction, I stroll past them, stopping in the middle of the gawking crowd. "You coming?" I say to the blonde girl, not keen to leave her behind to deal with the fallout of my actions.

"Absolutely," she laughs, following.

When we're on the track, she turns to me, grinning from ear to ear. "That was epic. I love seeing bitches get eaten for breakfast."

"Not friends of yours, then?"

"Hell, no. Me and cardio don't get along at the best of times—much less with a group of girls that will gouge your eyes out if you so much as disagree with them. I'm more of the reading type."

I laugh softly. "I hate cardio too."

A group of blue jerseys start heading toward the locker rooms, their faces lighting up when they see me. I wave them over, warning them to give the cheerleaders a wide berth before I turn back to the girl.

"I suppose we should do proper introductions. You know my name and I'd hate to just refer to you as Tampax girl," I say, holding my hand out.

She takes it, giving it a firm shake. "Sophia. But please don't call me Sophie. I'm one more incorrect name away from having a menty b."

"Noted."

"What the hell are you wearing, Spencer?" a deep voice asks from behind with a laugh.

I don't even need to turn around to know who it belongs to. His voice is embedded in my head, like nails down a blackboard.

"Fuck off, Rylan," I reply sharply.

He steps up next to me, giving me a full body scan before looking at Sophia. "Wow, this is early for you, Soph. I can't believe you're out of bed already."

"Oh, bite me, Rylan," Sophia retorts, but it's surprisingly playful. "Not everyone likes to get up at sparrow's fart like you."

Both Rylan and I turn to look at her, completely baffled. She chooses to face me, giving a sheepish smile. "Heard it on TikTok. Apparently, Australians say it when referring to early mornings."

A part of me wonders if I read her wrong. Maybe she's not as innocent as she seems if she's friendly with this jerk. But still, I laugh at her weird comment, wondering how the hell bird farts have anything to do with early mornings.

I'm still perplexed by the exchange though. While I have made the effort to be an approachable leader for the Cedar Heights students, most of Willowbrook seem to fear their masters—tending to every command like they aren't worthy or equals. But this girl doesn't flinch at all with Rylan's remarks. And he doesn't seem upset at her snark reply. If anything, he seems amused.

I hope they aren't dating or fucking. That would be awkward.

"I'm happy to bite you anytime, Sophia. You just have to ask."

"You can leave now," I shoot at him. "It's too early to be dealing with you, and to be honest, I've already used up my quota of patience for you this week."

Rylan gives me his usual smug smile. "Is it because of last night? Did I ruin your dicking?"

Sophia gawks at us in confusion. I turn to face him, propping a hand on my hip. "You ruin everything. Your presence alone in a five mile radius has that effect."

He scans me again, raising a quirky eyebrow at my itsy bitsy teenie weenie shorts that are barely visible. Returning the favor in an attempt to make him uncomfortable, I notice he's dressed in gym clothes too—dammit, apparently he's in this class as well. I have the worst luck.

Wearing black shorts and a white shirt with the Willowbrook crest on his pec, part of me wonders if it was custom made for him since it fits him so well. His muscles cut through the white material, and I take a moment to breathe a sigh of relief that they opted for black as the bottom half of their uniform. I can only imagine the chaos that would ensue with white shorts if it rained. No one wants to see wet sausage flinging around.

"Well then, prepare to have every day ruined, Spencer," he grins, unfazed by my intruding eyes.

Before I can respond, the coach summons everyone over. I whip around, giving Rylan a view of my back.

He laughs quietly behind me. "You seem to be missing your shorts."

I bite my tongue, ignoring the comment.

"Alright, folks. Let's begin," the coach says. "Cedar Heights students, you can place your bags by the seats next to the track. Then come back here and we'll start splitting you into groups to start warmup laps."

CHAPTER SIX

BEXLEY

Warmup laps, my ass.

Coach Carter is almost as brutal as our coach from Cedar. For a second, I was taken aback by his appearance. Easily in his prime, he's tall and buff, with light hazel eyes and a bald head. But unlike some men, he pulls it off *very well*. He reminds me of Arnold Vosloo in *The Mummy*—the first movie I ever watched that made me question my sanity when I fell in love with a villain.

Except, just like a villain, he made me run. I feel sick. Send help.

Next to me, Sophia is hunched over, groaning. "Someone kill me. Put me out of my misery."

"Hang in there," I laugh while panting, patting her back. "The endorphins will hit soon. And we will feel *so good*."

"Not likely," she grumbles. "I'm glad I didn't eat much for breakfast, otherwise I'd be painting the grass and reenacting the vomit scene from *The Exorcism*."

When the two of us finally catch our breath, we start making our way toward the locker room, detouring to the pile of bags by the seats.

The cheerleaders finished just before us, a few making snide remarks and comments as we ran past, but thankfully, they all disappeared from the locker room before laps were complete.

Standing over the pile of bags, I do a double take. I remember exactly where I left my backpack—so why isn't it here?

"What's wrong?" Sophia asks when I stay frozen.

"My bag is gone," I hiss quietly.

"What?" She looks around. "Are you sure?"

"Positive."

A wolf whistle catches my attention, the two of us spotting Rylan as he walks past with a group of guys, grinning at me. You can't even tell he just ran several laps of the track, his slicked-back sweaty hair the only indication. I hate him for that. Fuck him and his damn cardio stamina.

"Might want to invest in some new shorts, Spencer," he calls out. "We could see your ass starting to hang out." His friends all make crude remarks and cat calls but I just flip him the bird and turn around.

"Fucking cheerleaders."

Sophia doesn't even try to offer a possible alternative explanation, doing a check of the field to see if they are gone. "Want me to help you look? Mrs. Camerons usually doesn't care if I'm a little late to American Lit."

"Nah, you're fine," I say, waving her off. "I'll see you later no doubt."

Despite just running and near dying, I find my second wind and take off in a jog toward the main building. That bag has all my stuff in it—clothes, cell, textbooks. I swear if they have touched anything, I'm going to lose it.

People are casually strolling through the halls when I enter, my eyes scanning the crowd of people for either wolves in cheerleader costumes or familiar blue faces.

A tall body walks out of a classroom, and I sag in relief, pushing past people to head over.

"Arch!"

He stops in his tracks, looking around until he spots me. "Hey!" he greets. "What are you wearing?" he laughs, but it's not the same tone as Rylan. It's amusement, sure, but more like he understands the ridiculousness of this situation and the sacrifices we are making just to receive an education.

"Former cheerleader shorts that are burning my groin and a shirt that has a stain I'm trying to ignore," I reply, stopping in front of him. "Someone stole my bag."

"What?" he yells, startling a few students passing by. "When?"

I jerk my finger back toward the door I just came through. "Gym. Help me look for a bunch of vapid bitches? You can't miss them–cheerleaders," I finish, giving my poor attempt at spirit fingers.

He nods, digging into his shorts for his cell. "I'll ask Abby as well. A few of our girls were going to try to meet up with them this week to ask about potential open spots, just to train and keep up their routines."

"Doubt this bunch will be welcoming to the idea," I reply as he clicks away on the screen.

"Agreed," he mutters. "But it doesn't hurt to ask, I guess."

I smile, knowing he's only saying that because of Abby. Deep down, he knows just as well as I do that the attempts will be futile, but it's cute that he wants to remain hopeful for his girl.

When his cell dings, we both glance down at the screen to find a message from Abby.

> **Abbs:** *I think they are in the courtyard. I heard there's a cheer performance to-day.*

"Well, there's your answer," Arch murmurs, quickly typing back a reply before shoving the cell into his pocket. "I'll come with you."

The two of us head through the white maze of Willowbrook, navigating the crowd of students and long hallways until we reach a set of open doors. Through them, the courtyard is bustling with students, and when Archie and I step out, I take my first good look around since I didn't get to this section yesterday.

It's a perfect square in the middle of the main building, high glass windows lining the four sides. Students walk past on the other side of the glass, occasionally stealing glances to those outside as they head to their destinations.

Toward the other end of the large courtyard, there's a fountain—an actual working water fountain. Its tarnished bronze metal is shaped into a wolf, water spurting out of its mouth like sound waves as it stands frozen mid-growl.

Strategically placed benches are spaced out along the sides, people sitting and chatting casually, while others lounge on picnic blankets on the grass.

My eyes continue to scan until I find what I'm looking for. Under a large shady tree, the cheerleaders are laughing to themselves.

Arch follows me as I take off across the courtyard, but my gaze is locked and loaded on the laughing brunette as she flicks her hair dramatically, talking to her friends.

As I approach, I finally take a good look at their uniforms. The two-piece outfit perfectly matches the academy col-ors—a black dual-layered skirt with thick pleated white strips while their tops are white with a black waistband, the word *Wolves* written across the chest. Well, let's see if wolves are afraid of wildcats.

The group falls quiet as we approach, drawing Liv's atten-tion. Her laughing face turns into a look of disgust when she spots me.

"What do you want?"

"Where's my bag?"

"How would I know?" she shoots back, but the smug smile on her face tells me that she knows *exactly* where it is.

I step forward, keeping my eyes trained on her. "I'm only going to ask you *one... more... time*," I warn. "Where is my backpack?"

Liv laughs, the shrill sound taking place with Rylan's voice on my list of most annoying noises. "Oh, yeah? What are you going to do?"

"Do you like your acrylics?" I ask sternly.

Her face darkens at the threat, hands dropping to her sides. "Fuck off."

"Right," I mutter, lurching forward and placing her straight into a choke hold. Dragging her body back, I check Arch from the corner of my eye. He does exactly what I hope—placing himself between us and the group of cheerleaders. This isn't their fight.

"Get off me!" Liv shrieks, clawing at my skin.

Pain shoots through my arm but I tighten my grip, pushing my forearm harder into her throat. She starts coughing, and a sharp pain in my arm means that there's blood dripping down from scratch marks, but that just spurs me on.

People are watching us grapple now, the cheerleaders screaming while a few brave ones try to get past Arch who blocks them with his body. Well, shit—I hope this doesn't ruin Abby's chances of fraternizing with the enemy. Not that they deserve her. They would be lucky to have any of our girls on their team—even temporarily.

"Tell me or else you're going to take a nap," I warn, focusing on placing pressure on her carotid arteries to show how serious I am.

I have to hand it to her—she's stubborn. Even as spots start to assumingly appear in her eyes, and her nails retract, she refuses to tell me.

"Tai Beckett has it!" one of the other cheerleaders blabs out.

Looking up, I spot Peyton, watching with wide, frightened eyes. She meets my gaze with a desperate plea.

"I gave it to him," she admits quietly, sounding embarrassed. It's obvious she was acting under instruction.

"Thank you, Peyton," I reply, releasing Liv and letting her drop to the ground with a thud.

Arch and I step aside, the cheerleaders flocking over to check on their captain who pants and coughs.

Liv glares daggers at me from the ground, clutching her neck. "You'll pay for that."

"And you'll need to pay for nail repairs," I point out, nodding toward her two broken acrylic nails. "But it's okay because *you can afford it*, right?"

I tap Archie's arm and gesture for him to follow me before she can reply. "Come on, Arch. Time to go find Tai Beckett."

Turns out finding Tai was easier than playing Hide and Seek with the cheerleaders... because all I had to do was follow the paper trail.

The paper trail of my textbooks.

Word must have spread fast about our encounter in the courtyard because the hallways were eerily deserted when we stepped back into the building. But that asshole had left me a trail of torn-up pages guiding us to the computer science lab. How nice of him.

Stepping through the door, I'm met with the sound of ripping pages.

Across the room, Tai sits atop the teacher's desk, legs parted with the contents of my bag all over the floor and around him.

"Took you long enough," he grins, holding eye contact with me as he shreds another page from my biology book.

Arch slams his hand on the doorjamb, glaring at Tai as we both scan the pile of destroyed textbooks. But despite how much this hurts, because there's no way I'm going to be able to afford to replace them, I won't give him the satisfaction of seeing me angry. Not yet anyway.

"I didn't take you for a toddler, Beckett," I merely say.

He pauses. "Why do you say that, Sexy Bexie?"

Ooft. Double whammy. He's really going for gold in the Olympic sport of being punched in the jugular.

"Toddlers love to tear up paper to entertain themselves. But, I mean, if that's what you like..." I trail off with a shrug.

Tai slams the biology book down, jumping off the desk. "Aw, you're not upset, are you?" he asks with a patronizing tone.

I shake my head. "Not at all. In fact, you've just given me the perfect excuse to leave this shithole for the day. Since I don't have any material for class, I'll have to head home. What a shame."

He laughs. "Nice try. Maybe try the library—we actually have a decent one here. Most of the books were purchased brand new. Hell, even our second-hand ones are probably in better condition than what you are used to. Consider it a treat for yourself, sweetheart. And you can thank me later."

Archie steps in front of me, fists curled. "Pick her shit up," he demands.

Instantly, Tai's playful face vanishes, replaced by a flare of anger as he glances at Arch. "You going to make me, lap-boy? Must suck knowing she has your balls in a vise. I bet your manhood hates having a *woman* in charge."

I place a hand on Arch's shoulder, moving in beside him. "Weird flex, but props to you for admitting there's room for improvement among the students here."

Sexist comments mean nothing to me. I've been dealing with them long before schoolyard taunts got thrown into the mix.

"That's funny," Tai shoots back. "Because we outperform you in every measure." He straightens up proudly, tapping the Willowbrook crest on his shirt.

"Except for the dick measuring contest," I quickly reply. "Mine is several inches bigger than yours, even on the flop."

Arch snorts next to me, not bothering to cover his mouth like he usually does. Tai, on the other hand, picks up the biology book and stalks forward.

Without saying a word, he stops in front of me, flicking open the book. Slowly, he rips another page while maintaining eye contact with me, scrunching up the torn paper and dropping it on top of my head.

"Oops," he says as the paper bops me on the nose.

Okay–now my patience is wearing fucking thin. He *did not* just bop me on the nose with a piece of my destroyed book.

"Arch," I start through clenched teeth. "Can you check my bag to make sure everything is there?"

I block the doorway while he shoves past Tai, barging him with his shoulder. Tai laughs in response, raising an eyebrow at me as if to say, *"You really think you can stop me from leaving?"*

Placing my hands on either side of the doorjamb, I smile, daring the fucker to try. But surprisingly, he doesn't budge, his eyes scanning over my face, then down my chest, before stopping on my bare thighs that show too much skin because of these shorts. Fuck–I forgot about my stupid shorts.

He grins to himself, and I resist the urge to knee him in the dick. Though it's tempting... So damn tempting.

Fucking creep.

"Cell phone, jersey, skirt," Archie says from the desk. "Anything in particular you want me to check?"

"Nope, that's all good," I reply, dropping my hands from the frame. "Off you fuck now, Beckett."

Tai's amused eyes flick back to my face. "Enjoy the rest of your day, Peach Queen."

Chapter Seven

"Man, I'm good. I got it," I say with a laugh, throwing my backpack onto the ground.

Rylan and Hunter look up at me, following me all the way down until I'm at their level.

"No shit?" Rylan asks, impressed.

I grin, stealing a quick glance to the familiar wolf statue beside us. I love the damn thing. It actually reminds me a little of Calvin.

Dad paid the donation for the construction of it two years ago. I lean over and give the little plaque on the sandstone a rub, proudly reading the words *Donated by the Beckett Family* like I've done hundreds of times.

When the sun is nice, like today, we sit outside in the courtyard. We had already planned to meet up since the three of us have a free period next, but I'm the last to arrive since I took a brief detour after English. Rylan had texted and asked me to go find the girls, saying they had a present for me.

And what a present it was.

Apparently, he ordered the cheerleaders to steal Bexley's bag while she was out running on the track.

Since he has gym too, it gave him the perfect view to make sure Bexley was distracted while they quickly grabbed it at the end of cheer practice and took off. After I got the bag from Peyton, I ducked into the restrooms to take a sneak peek, unable to help myself.

It was just the usual shit, and even though I didn't have time to jailbreak into her cell, I was able to open the camera and snap a pic of my ass. I can't wait for her reaction when she finds it in her gallery. Hell, maybe she'll even flick the bean over it.

I was also able to see her list of ICE contacts. Even though it doesn't display their numbers, she stupidly saves them with first and last names like she's trying to be a corporate professional. So now, it's just a matter of me doing some easy work on my PC later to find them. That idiot lapdog she was with is one of them, of course. But also a few other people I'm interested in learning more about. You know what they say—keep your friends close and your enemies closer.

Best of all, I dialed my burner cell from inside the emergency settings, giving me her phone number. If she tries to call my burner back, she's in for a special treat. I hope she enjoys my little creation. I'd give just about anything to be a fly on the wall for *that* too.

By the time I had finished fucking around with her cell, Hunter texted me to say that Bexley had Liv in a sleeper choke hold in the courtyard and to be ready because she would be hunting down my ass any second. The guys were lucky enough to watch the whole thing from inside the building through the floor-to-ceiling glass windows, and I can't wait to hear the play-by-play. Liv might be stubborn as fuck, but even I'll admit she's out of her depth trying to take on Bexley without our help. It's a rookie move, but no doubt Liv's just even more motivated now to go for the kill. Oh, well—her mistake. At least it will be entertaining.

Don't get me wrong, Liv is hot as fuck. But damn that girl drives me insane. I don't know how Rylan can stand her. Apparently, she gives decent slop-top and puts out whenever he wants, so he puts up with her presence from time to time.

"I'll text it through to you both," I say, grabbing my cell from my pocket and sending them Bexley's phone number. "Your little girlfriend doing okay?"

Rylan wrinkles his nose. "Not my girlfriend, T. But Liv is fine. Whined more about her nails than anything. I had to kiss her just to get her to shut up."

"Of course," Hunter sighs. "First world problems."

I share a look with Hunter, thinking the same thing: *Play stupid games, win stupid prizes.*

"I'd stay on guard for some Cedar backlash," I murmur, leaning back on my hands as I bask in the warm sunlight. "Spencer is pissed."

"When isn't she?" Hunter snorts. "That's been her whole personality this week."

Rylan finishes saving her number and puts his cell down. "I assume you did more than steal her number."

"Let's just say I need to make a quick trip to the library after this."

Hunter snorts. "Well, I took a visit to Dad's office and *accidentally* obtained a copy of her schedule. And I may have switched a few of our classes starting next week."

That thought makes me excited but Rylan groans.

"Small sacrifices to make," he grumbles. "But you better not have touched my business management class. I need that for college."

Hunter shakes his head. "You're all good, brother. I switched you to advanced English—where you should have already been."

Rylan narrows his eyes. "Smythson makes me want to claw my eyes out with Liv's acrylics. That's why I refused to take her class."

"You'll survive," Hunter laughs. "Smythson is actually considering a small break so that one of the Cedar Heights staff can fill in."

"That's even worse!"

I shush him playfully. "What about me?"

"You've switched from Statistics to Algebra."

This time, it's Rylan who cackles while I scowl. They know how much I detest that stupid bullshit class. It makes no sense. Why did they have to add letters into the mix? I've tried to avoid it for as long as possible, even if I knew it was inevitable since it's a core part of the college course I want to take. Letters and numbers in coding are easy. In math equations? Blasphemy.

"I might actually hate you now."

Hunter holds up his hands defensively. "I tried. All the other math classes were full. The Cedar twits have made it just a bit more difficult moving things around. Apparently, we can't pull them from their enrolled subjects. We have to be the *perfect hosts*."

"Fuck that," Rylan mutters to himself.

"Or fuck Liv," I offer.

He raises an eyebrow at me. "Go for it."

"I'll pass, thanks."

"Anyway," Hunter says, cutting us both off. "One of us will be in most of her classes. But as a special treat, I did put us all together in graphic design."

My ears prick as I perk up. "Another computer class?"

He grins. "See—Don't say I don't do anything nice for you."

I tap my jaw, thoughtfully. "I won't even need to destroy textbooks for that one. I'll just be able to hack into the server to access her saved work."

Ahh, yes. If you think I'm finished with you, Spencer... You're in for a rude awakening.

When I get home that afternoon, I head straight to my bedroom to start the fun stuff.

I've been counting down the minutes until I could get here, excited to see what I can find.

Is it wrong of me to stalk Bexley Spencer? Probably. Do I care? Absolutely not.

Turning on the PC, I swing around in my chair, lazily checking the room while it fires up. The four curved screens flash as the multi-tonal keyboard lights up. The light reflects off the dark gray walls as my eyes fall onto my bed at the other end of the room. Pushed against the wall in the center, it appears Mary made my bed this morning. Dammit. I've told her countless times not to worry about it, which forced me into the habit of doing it myself. But the early start to the day had me rushing out the door and I figured she wouldn't check since she hasn't had to make it in months.

I should have known. She never misses anything.

Mary's been looking out for me since I was four. With Dad traveling a lot for work, it's just me here. So, he decided we needed a housekeeper. And eventually, Mary wormed her way into our hearts—well, mine anyway. Dad is pretty indifferent to *the help* as he calls them, but to me, she filled the void after Mom passed.

She even dotes on Rylan and Hunter, constantly fussing over us.

I'm making sure I don't forget my bed tomorrow.

The welcome screen appears, and I type in my password, opening Facebook first. I head straight for the Cedar Facebook group, reading through the new messages. My lips curl into a grin when I spot a post from Bexley herself, warning people to keep an eye on their bags at all times.

But still refusing to ask for help. She probably thinks she's seen the last of me.

There's no mention of my little paper art display, though I have no doubt they all know. It wasn't exactly like I was subtle.

Next, I start typing in the names of her ICE contacts. Archer is first, and while we already know about him, I still take a few minutes to stalk through his details. The smart cookie has his profile locked, but a search shows a few different groups, and when I switch to Google, I also find an article about his father. Interestingly enough, it happens to be one about the Cedar Heights Academy fire.

Ahh, good memories.

When I punch in the next name, I recognize her boy-toy in the pictures straight away. And this idiot has *nothing* hidden. His whole entire profile is on public mode.

Steele Turner.

Plays football, likes to drink, ripped his groin muscle two seasons ago—typical stuff. But there's a few photos of him and Bexley together, posing with big smiles and 'peace signs'. I save a copy and move onto the third and final name.

Surprisingly, nothing comes up.

At all.

Zilch.

I try a few different methods such as LinkedIn, Google, other socials, even government related sites and still find nothing concrete.

Annoyed that I can't find anything, I'm too focused on the screen that I don't sense the person creeping in behind me. It's not until two soft hands rest on my shoulders that I jump six feet in the air, spinning around.

"Mary! Jesus. I'll have to start calling you Scary Mary. When did you get so stealthy?"

She smiles down at me, wrinkles crinkling around her cheeks and eyes. Her chestnut hair is fading with silver streaks, but she's still as beautiful as ever.

It's not fair that she's wasting her life here when she should be out living it. But even when I turned eighteen and begged Dad to let her go, it wasn't just him that refused.

"Oh, Tai. Maybe I'm just learning from the best," she jokes. "Or you're too busy to hear little old me."

I grin. "The first one, definitely. I like to think I have some good influence in your life."

"You're the best influence in my life, Bear."

That sense of maternal warmth floats through me as I watch her chocolate irises dance. Even after all these years, I never forget the day she saved me.

Mary had only been with us about a month when Mom passed. The final week before she died, we were able to move her back home from palliative care so she could be comfortable with family. Even though I sometimes wish Dad had stopped me, I stayed by Mom's bed, holding her hand while she slept longer and longer. Mary stood by my side the entire time, and when Mom left this Earth, I was gifted with a white teddy bear by my new friend. It even had one of Mom's old dresses repurposed into a miniature version, with our names embroidered across the bear's chest. Apparently, her and Mom worked together to surprise me, so that I'd always have something to remember.

Poppins is still in my room to this day. But he's in his special box, just in case Calvin gets any funny ideas.

"You didn't have to make my bed," I playfully scold, crossing my arms.

"Oh, enough of that," she smiles softly. "You barely let me do anything these days. Which reminds me; dinner will be ready in about fifteen minutes."

"Okay," I beam back. I may not want her to make my bed, but dammit Mary makes a mean dinner. I can't cook to save my life, so it's our little tradition that Mary cooks, we eat together most nights, and I wash up.

Well, she tries to fight me on that too, but I'm incredibly quick with my food.

I watch as Mary leaves, and when the door closes, I turn back to the enigma on my screen.

Who are you, Lark Kory?

CHAPTER EIGHT

BEXLEY

"The males barge and jostle one another to reach her, and several mates succeed, one after the other. Male right whales have gigantic testes, the largest in the world. They weigh a ton and produce gallons of sperm."

Why the hell am I listening to a documentary on sperm whales by Sir. David Attenborough?!

I stupidly wait until the end, checking to see if there's any indication of whose phone number this is. There's nothing, just the loud *beep!* signaling for me to leave a message.

"What the fuck?!" I curse, ending the call a few seconds too late.

Well, I guess I left a message.

It has to be Tai. He's the only person who could have gotten ahold of my cell and dialed a random number since he stole my bag. Speaking of which...

I survey the ripped remains of my books in front of me. Despite my earlier threat, I did end up staying at school. The rest of the day was tricky without the required material, and one teacher even threatened to write me up for not being able to use my textbook. It took all my effort to bite my tongue and just say sorry. Talk about victim blaming.

I'm finally able to get a closer look at the damage and as I suspected, he made sure to damage every single one beyond repair. At least I'm only carrying around what I need for each day. However, that's three I'll need to replace immediately if I don't want to fall behind.

Even though I hated taking his advice, I did try the Willowbrook library. But even after being messed around and scolded by the librarian because I didn't have a library card, it turned out to be useless anyway. *Apparently*, someone had just checked out all the books I needed during second period. I only need one guess as to who.

"Bex?"

A soft voice travels in from the doorway, and I glance up from the bed, offering Mom a smile.

"Hey, you," I say, swinging my legs over the side and climbing off the mattress. "How are you feeling?"

"I'm fine, baby," she answers, rubbing her temple. "How long was I asleep?"

The honest answer would be that I don't know. She was passed out again when I got home. Judging by her glassy, red eyes and softly spoken slurred voice, it was a bad day for her. But she's coming out of the intoxication fog, and I try to spare her from the usual guilt she harbors in these moments.

"Not long," I answer with a warm smile. "About forty minutes."

"Oh, good," she murmurs. "Want me to make us some dinner?"

She asks this almost every day, as if it's her way of reminding me that she's a mom that cares about her daughter. Even though she struggles to do much, she always asks to do things for me, despite her demons. I love that about her. As usual, I decline with my usual excuse about not being hungry, suggesting she go for a shower to freshen up instead.

I don't know the last time she actually ventured to the fridge, but we haven't had any food for days except raw pasta and cans of beans. Luckily, she gets paid this week, so I'll do the grocery shop.

On paydays, I wait for the funds to hit and immediately transfer a small amount from her account to my own to buy us food with whatever the food stamps don't cover and put away some extra for gas and utilities. It's always the same amount, and for whatever reason, she never questions it. Part of me wonders if she just checks the balance and assumes that's her normal SSI payment and rolls with it. But I think deep down, she knows what I'm doing, but she's too ashamed to bring it up. Which in turn, makes her just buy more alcohol to numb her feelings until the funds are gone until the next pay cycle. Rinse and repeat.

I'm just thankful that Dad paid out the mortgage during the divorce proceedings so that we had a roof over our heads. It was the least he could do since he abandoned us. I often wonder if he thinks about us—about me. If he ever thought about coming back... or if he even knows the damage he did walking out.

Does he know what we live like now?

Probably not. The guilt would eat at him, so I bet he avoids ever checking to spare himself the self-condemnation.

It's just a shame that we got nothing else from him. Sure, he paid a scrap of child support monthly once he landed another job, but the second I turned eighteen, they stopped.

We had to fight tooth and nail to get Mom on disability payments after he left. For months, we struggled hard, and more than a few times, I actually thought we were going to die. I'll never forget the summer where I would have needed a belt to hold Sierra's stupid skimpy shorts up.

Sitting back on the bed, I grab my cell and start to shoot off a quick message to Steele. I really need to cash in on that dicking those douchebags ruined. But before I can hit send, a text notification appears.

Unknown: *Open your photo gallery.*

What the fudge?

I have a suspicion I know who this is, so I quickly cross-check with my call log. Yep—*that* number.

Ignoring the message, I hit dial instead, listening as it goes straight to voicemail. There's no way he turned off his cell that quickly. It has to be DND mode.

Curiosity gets the better of me and I open up the gallery to see what I have to deal with. A squeak rips out of me as I drop my cell in disgust.

WHY IS THERE A PICTURE OF AN ASS ON MY SCREEN?!

That son of a bitch. It was already bad enough that he tore up my stuff and stole my number, but to taint my camera with pearly white globes? Hell. No.

Huffing, I go back to my inbox and punch out a reply.

Bexley: *You're disgusting.*

I really shouldn't waste energy responding, but I'm so mad at his sheer audacity.

It only takes a few seconds before his reply comes back.

Unknown: *Come say it to my face, Bexley. I'll even meet you on your turf.*

The nerve of him. Do these guys have a sensor on them that every time I want to get off, they have to interrupt?

Bexley: *Hard pass.*

While I wait for him to respond—because I know he will—I save his number to my contacts. When his next message comes through, I have a little giggle to myself.

Ball-less Paper Fucker: *Suit yourself.*

I take a screen shot, sending it through to show off his new title. Within seconds, there's a reply—a retaliation screenshot, with the words *Peach Queen* followed by the associated fruity emoji plastered as my contact name.

Peach Queen: *Come say it to MY face tomorrow, Tai. I owe you a date with the stapler.*

Ball-less Paper Fucker: *So, you wanna touch my balls, Peachie?*

Peach Queen: *Go fuck yourself.*

Ball-less Paper Fucker: *Already did, actually. You should try it. Might loosen up that attitude of yours. Feel free to use my peach as inspiration.*

Peach Queen: *Trust me. No one is using THAT as inspiration.*

Ball-less Paper Fucker: *If you say so.*

Peach Queen: *I'm blocking you now.*

Grumbling and cursing, I block the number and close my cell screen, slapping the device onto the blanket. To be fair, it's not the worst ass I have seen. Tai is all muscle and dammit it's reflected in his glutes.

And there goes my libido, fighting for its life. Muscles are a weakness for me, but thankfully, my brain comes to its senses, fighting off the need to orgasm.

Lady boner deflating... and gone.

Sorry Steele. No snu-snu for you either now.

Mom walks past my bedroom on her way back from the shower, calling out an early goodnight, and I decide to follow suit. Shower, music, doom scrolling then sleep... that's all I need.

Not an orgasm.

Nope.

Definitely not one of those.

The rest of the week goes smoothly oddly enough. I barely cross paths with any of the Three Musketeers, except for classes like gym, and as I later found out, chemistry with Hunter. Even worse, apparently, we all share graphic design. But despite the odd glares here and there, they didn't actually try anything.

Friday night rolls around and even though Arch asked me to reconsider, I put my name down for a fight.

It's not my first time in the cage, but usually I let other people volunteer so everyone gets a fair turn.

Unsurprisingly, this week we had a record-breaking number of requests from people wanting to fight. Apparently, I'm not the only one that needs to blow off some steam.

"Are you sure you want to do this?" Arch asks, the two of us standing outside the cage door.

"Absolutely."

I'm listening to him, but my eyes are locked on the opponent in the ring. The girl waiting for me looks like she could be the younger version of Miss Trunchbull in a spring production of Matilda. She's not quite as tall as me but damn she's fit and muscular. I bet she slings around athletic weights as part of her chosen sport.

"Alright," Arch concedes with a sigh. "Go get her, Tiger."

Giving him a wicked smile, I step into the cage, looking around.

It's been months since I last fought, but the feeling still gets me every time.

The first time I ever circled these metal walls, I wondered how people could concentrate with the surrounding crowd and noise. But then it all faded. The faces vanished, my ears fell quiet, and all I could focus on was my opponent.

It was a thrilling rush. Addictive, almost.

Miniature Trunchbull sizes me up with a smirk, already thinking she's got this one in the bag. But she's mistaken. What I lack in muscle size is compensated by speed, height, and best of all, the ability to read my opponents.

Sparring isn't about who can throw the hardest punch. It's a strategic dance and battle of wits. And if you walk into the cage underestimating your opponent, you've already lost.

I know she's going to make me work for it. And hell, I bet I'll be sporting some nice bruises tomorrow. But the pain is worth it. The escape is everything.

The crowd of blue cheer loudly and I can't help but smile. They love seeing me fight as much as I love fighting for them.

This is what a good leader does—she faces the enemy straight on. No hiding or sitting on makeshift thrones like you're scared to get hurt.

Unable to resist, my eyes dart over to them, wanting to see their reaction. They've seen me fight plenty, but this time, it's personal.

This time, I'm out for blood to make a statement.

Hunter's mouth twitches as he mutters something to Rylan. He nods, Tai leaning in to join the conversation. Their eyes stay on me while they speak, and I give a little satirical wave, lifting an eyebrow.

"I'm going to kick your ass, Spencer," the girl snarls.

Glancing back over to her, I shrug. "We'll see. What's your name so I can add it to my list?"

"Fuck you."

"Odd name, but okay."

She curses at me just as the bell rings, and immediately, goes straight for my face. It's clear she wants to make a statement too. Fists swing at me, and I jump into action, darting and blocking all of them. But I don't throw a punch back yet. I wait.

Calculate.

Fuck You tries again, switching tactics and faking a punch before slamming her knee into my ribs. The crowd groans as if they feel the pain of her blow too, but I keep moving. This was all premeditated. You can't get a read on an opponent if you don't take a few hits.

Right. So, that's her plan. She's going to go for lower extremities since she knows I'll block the face. It means she's going to toss uppercuts, side hooks and knees into the grapple. Easy peasy, lemon squeezy.

When she comes for me again, I eye her stance carefully. When her knee tenses up, I count to a quick two before pivoting to my side, letting her knee brush past my stomach as she tries to launch it into me.

The move throws her off balance, so I swing to test the waters. As I suspected, she's not strong with reflexes. There's no time for her to block, still stumbling to recover when my fist connects with her cheek bone.

Oof. That's going to leave a mark.

Hissing, she takes a few seconds to shake it off, eyes flaring as she throws a side hook at my head. I speedily lift my arm into a L shape, deflecting the move away but her other fist comes out straight away, this time smashing into my jaw.

I rotate my neck to clear the little head spin. "Is that all you've got?"

The fighter, formerly known as *Fuck You*, soon to be known as *Toast*, smirks, the two of us dancing around in circles. "Not even by a long shot."

"Good," I breathe out, darting forward to drive my knee hard into her lower stomach.

She hunches over with a groan, struggling to pull up from the pain as she clutches her torso. I decide enough is enough and to put her out of her misery early. I'm not a monster.

Tackling her to the ground, I maneuver her onto her stomach while I push my weight into her back and place her into a choke hold.

One... Two... Three.

Tap. Tap. Tap.

And just like that, it's all over.

Chapter Nine

Monday morning rolls around, just like the random clouds that have appeared overhead today.

Maybe it's a sign or an omen.

A new week, a fresh start.

"Ms. Spencer," a voice calls out to me as Arch and I step through the main entrance.

I glance over at the tall, stern looking woman in her dark brown dress suit. Her arms are folded, looking like she's never smiled a day in her life. Being here, I can't blame her.

Arch shoots me a confused look and follows me over.

"Yes, that's me."

"Dean Lannister needs to see you in his office," she informs me, completely ignoring Archie's presence.

My brows furrow. "No worries. Lead the way."

As Arch steps to follow, she finally acknowledges him with a sharp glance.

"Head to class. Your attendance isn't required for this."

He looks like he wants to protest, but I put my hand on his shoulder.

"It's okay," I tell him with a soft smile. "I will catch up with you afterwards."

"Alright," Arch says suspiciously, heading to join the crowd of students flocking to their classes.

I follow Miss. Power Suit up a staircase to an open office setup. Besides the initial landing, there seems to be only one other room up here, with two large polished wooden doors blocking my entrance. There's a desk outside the room on the landing, and my personal escort sits down, gesturing her hand toward the door. "Straight in."

"Okay," I nod, as she turns to her computer without so much as a backward glance at me.

Pushing open the large doors, I'm immediately whacked in the face with sunlight, resisting the urge to hiss like a vampire. Apparently, the sun has chosen to break out from behind the clouds at this very moment. When I finally manage to claw back my irises from fiery destruction, I see why I was temporarily blinded.

The spacious room only has three walls. Across from the door, the entire back panel is made entirely of glass, overlooking the sports field. Dean Lannister looks up from his paperwork, face expressionless.

"Sit down, Ms. Spencer," he motions to a chair in front of him.

I take a seat, dropping my bag next to me as I try to figure out what all this is about.

For such a large room, there's not much in here. Besides his desk, there's a bookshelf lining the wall on one side, and a cabinet on the other, filled with trophies and medallions.

"Do you know why I've summoned you, Ms. Spencer?" the dean asks, grabbing my attention.

I shake my head. "No, sir."

His lips purse, apparently either suspecting that I'm lying or that I'm stupid for not immediately knowing. Unfortunately, I'm yet to master the art of mind reading. He lays his hands atop the desk, holding my gaze.

"You were involved in an altercation last week."

Altercation? Wait—Does he mean Tuesday?

"I'm sorry," I say. "Could you please elaborate?"

An eyebrow twitches back at me. "I'm told you assaulted one of our students. I'll have you know that despite what happens at *Cedar Heights Academy*," his vibrato increases with the words. "Here at Willowbrook, that kind of behavior will not be tolerated."

"Once again, sorry—but I'm still not following," I play coy. "Are you referring to Liv the cheerleader?"

Head cheerleader. Her voice is a shrill memory in my mind.

"Precisely," he confirms, annoyance clear on his face. "Now, we're doing our best to accommodate your cohort, however, I will not have our students placed in danger."

I hold back a laugh because I know it will just make the situation worse. But we're not a goddamn danger and he knows it. This is just a power struggle, but still, it doesn't add up. While I have no doubt she would love to see my downfall, it's been nearly a week. I'm missing a piece of the puzzle. Why is this only being brought up now?

"Sir, are you aware that her and her friends stole my belongings?" I ask, testing the waters.

"I don't see how that is relevant," he tuts back. "According to multiple sources, the physical altercation was one-sided."

You bet your ass it was.

My eyes deliberately drift down to the long red scratch on my arm that's nearly healed, the only time she managed to maim me. "That was nearly a week ago," I point out. "And even though it appears my side of the story won't be taken into account, I have to ask: why is this only being brought up now?"

The dean glowers at me from across the table. "Ms. Winston only came forward over the weekend. Apparently, she was so frightened by the attack that she needed encouragement from some of our academy leaders to speak up about the incident."

I bite the inside of my bottom lip. That makes sense. So much for a fresh, new week.

"I can only assume that these academy leaders are the ones who not only instigated the theft of my belongings but the irreparable damage to them."

He pauses for a moment and there's not a doubt in my mind that he knows about these details. He's just choosing to overlook them.

After all, one of these so-called leaders is his precious son.

"Unfortunately, the witness reports do not corroborate your story, Ms. Spencer. Now, as this is your first violation, I'm willing to apply a lighter disciplinary action. However, next time, there will be more severe consequences."

My eyes narrow suspiciously. "And this disciplinary action includes?"

"You'll have detention after hours each day this week. Thankfully for you, Ms. Winston isn't seeking restitution."

"Restitution for what, exactly?" I snap back, unable to hold it in any longer.

This whole situation is ridiculous. She snapped two nails and they think I should pay, while I'm the one who ends up with no textbooks?

"Tone, Ms. Spencer," he growls. "Now, as I have said, this is your final and only warning. You will behave while at Willowbrook or else we will have no choice but to pull your temporary enrollment. At this point in the year, that would likely mean not graduating."

I stand up, dropping my arms to my sides. "I'm not afraid of a shakedown, Dean Lannister. We came into Willowbrook agreeing to peace, but if your students try to force our hand, we will retaliate."

His sharp green eyes remind me so much of Hunter's. It's easy to tell they are related. Especially with the glare he's giving me right now—like father, like son.

"One more word, Ms. Spencer and the disciplinary action will increase to two weeks. You're excused."

There's a threat in his tone, one that as our current educational supervision he can't voice. But I can read between the lines well enough.

Scooping up my bag, I don't bother to close the door behind me. Ms. Stuck Up Power Suit can do it.

She grunts in annoyance as I skip down the stairs to the now empty hallway, and I do everything to control the rage threatening to break loose.

I was going to play nice. This didn't have to be difficult. But the time for pleasantries is over.

W

"The arson report came back," Arch announces, dropping a piece of paper on the desk in front of me.

Intrigued, I pick it up, quickly scanning the words.

Fire is estimated to have affected at least forty percent of Cedar Height Academy's structure. Extensive damage was found in the administration office, with traces of accelerant. There appears to have been multiple sources of initial ignition spots. One in the administration building, one in the library, and one in the main Ridge wing where majority of classrooms are situated.

Investigators obtained a copy of footage from the night of the attack. However, footage appears to have encountered technical difficulties. Recording ceased approximately thirty minutes before the fire initiated.

"Well, that just confirms what we already suspected," I sigh.

Archie slumps into the seat across from me. The library is oddly quiet for the middle of the day. Besides us, there's a few other Cedar students lurking around, but not a single Willowbrook face.

"Yep," he answers. "Cops have put out a statement requesting people come forward with information—"

"But they won't," I finish. "Willowbrook twits protect each other."

He nods. "What did they have to gain from it though? That's what baffles me. They didn't want us here."

"Maybe they didn't expect we'd be shoved here. Probably just trying to stop us all from graduating."

Arch leans back in his chair. "So, what was this morning about?"

I give him a look somewhere between a smile and a sneer. "Detention for a week for snapping acrylic nails."

"What?" he asks, perplexed. "From last week?"

"Yep," I grumble. "I suspect it's to do with ignoring Beckett's request and the fight at the warehouse. They are punishing me."

"Did you tell them about your bag?"

Laughing, I raise an eyebrow at him.

He sighs in defeat. "Good point. Wait," he pauses. "Circle back. What message from Beckett?"

"It doesn't matter," I finish. "It just means we're going to start hitting back. I'll put a post in the Facebook group later."

"Bex," Arch warns.

I lean forward, lowering my voice. "Arch," I mimic his tone. "If we don't do something now, then they are going to think they got away with it. They won't just be coming for me. Everyone will be a target."

"We need to play it safe though. If you're on the dean's radar, it's just going to make things worse for you."

His worried expression is wholesome. It's nice to know he's worried about me—I'm not though.

"Don't worry about me," I tell him, packing up my stuff. "I can handle it. Come walk with me to next period."

The two of us exit the library, a body nearly slamming into me at full speed.

"Whoa," I breathe out, spotting familiar blonde and pink hair. "You don't need another tampon that badly, do you?"

Sophia blinks, before breaking out in a huge smile. "Bex! I was wondering when I'd see you again."

"Is that why you stalked me to the library? Did you know I had a thing for academic literature?"

"I was hoping," she says playfully, lifting a book. "Just have to quickly make a return before next period. I'm one more late slip away from Mr. Hardwood blowing his toupee off."

I laugh, glancing down at the textbook in her hands before frowning. "Is that... a biology book?"

Sophia holds it up. "Yeah. I don't need it anymore. Or the others in my bag. Just don't want to get slapped with a late return fine."

Biting my tongue, I nod. "Well, I'll let you head inside. I'll see you tomorrow for gym?"

"It's a date." She rushes past, squeaking as the warning bell rings throughout the speakers.

Arch watches her through the doors, finally glancing over at me. "New friend?"

"I don't know," I answer honestly. "Maybe. But also... that's the textbook I needed the other day. The one that was mysteriously checked out before I could get to the library."

"How can you be sure?"

"The librarian said they only had one copy."

Once again, I'm faced with the reality that I need to be on-guard. It could be one hell of a coincidence, but I've also learned that sometimes, *it's not*. Especially when it comes to situations like this.

It's also strange that being this far into the school year, someone would need to borrow a mandatory textbook when they would have already had it. But still, I'm not making assumptions yet. That little tidbit of information is being filed away for later use. Maybe I'll bring it up tomorrow, see what she says.

I just have to get through detention first.

Chapter Ten

Bexley

In Cedar world, detention means sitting at the desk doing extra study work.

But apparently, at the Willowbrook Academy, it means free labor.

No wonder the fuckers are rich.

As soon as I stepped into the assigned classroom, the teacher had shoved a bucket of supplies at me. My job for the next hour is to repair some desks and tables. Which, if you ask me, makes no sense.

I'm all for repairing things to extend its life, but these folks don't care about that. They will happily buy new equipment, just not until I've attempted to fix someone else's mess and destroy it even further.

I notice that I haven't been given any actual power tools to fix them—literally just superglue, sandpaper, and coating. But judging by the state of this current desk, no amount of glue in the world is going to fix it.

About halfway through the detention, the teacher, Mrs. Smythson, announces she's going to use the restroom and threatens a punishment worse than death if I even consider taking off in her absence.

Rolling my eyes, I don't address the threat, continuing on with my ridiculous task. When footsteps walk into the room a few minutes later, I jump when the voice doesn't match.

"On the dirty ground where you belong, Duchess."

I peek over my shoulder, finding an amused Hunter in the doorway. "Duchess?" I snort.

He smirks. "Just to remind you of your place here. They are below Kings in the hierarchy, just in case you weren't aware."

"Well done on having basic knowledge, Hunter. I'm thrilled for your achievements."

Turning back to the desk, I try to ignore the footsteps as they get closer, until the asshole places his foot on my lower back.

Hell. No.

Spinning around, I launch to my feet, glaring at him. "Don't fucking touch me, Lannister, or I'll break your foot."

"I'd like to see you try, *Duchess*."

A moment of frustration overpowers me, and I shove my hands into his chest, sending him backwards. Immediately, his eyes darken. Two large steps toward me and I find myself torso to torso with Hunter Lannister.

"What's wrong?" I goad. "Don't like being touched?"

His jaw hardens as he stares daggers at me, but I just straighten up further, refusing to look away.

I slip my hand behind my back, squeezing the tube in my palm as I count to five in my head and calm the wave of emotions. He doesn't get to come in here and torment me—he and his father can go to Hell. This whole situation is their fault, and I'm not about to bend over backwards and let him intimidate me.

"You're worthless, Spencer. You'd be lucky to touch me."

Walking over to Smythson's desk, I drop the tube and sandpaper on it, dusting my hands. Hunter watches me carefully as I approach him again, narrowing his eyes.

"Is that a fact?" I ask casually.

He nods. "I would *never* allow someone like *you* the honor of touching me. You're not worth my time."

"And yet, here you are."

Hunter shoots me a wicked smile. "Just doing my civic duty to make sure you don't fuck up anything while unsupervised."

"Ahh," I say thoughtfully, nodding. "Does this count?"

My hands shove him again, but we've switched positions. Hunter stumbles back, this time catching himself on my little renovation project. He grips the side of the desk with one hand as he steadies himself, hovering over the top. I step forward, slamming my hands down on his upper thighs. The movement startles him for a moment, forcing him to put his weight on the desk to regain his balance. There's a small sense of satisfaction at my handiwork and repairs as the desk somehow doesn't buckle and collapse under his weight, before his hands quickly whip out and snap around my wrists painfully.

"I'll fucking end you," he hisses, squeezing so hard that my bones start screaming in pain.

But my face remains expressionless, unwilling to let him see that he's hurting me. That's what he wants, after all.

"You can try." I repeat his words back to him. "But I don't think you'll get very *far*."

Hunter goes to stand, to tower over me, except...

I can't help but laugh like an insane person at the sudden panic on his face.

Walking over to the corner of the room, I scoop up my bag from the floor, stopping at the teacher's desk. Picking up the tube of superglue again, I hold it up. "You know, I might just keep this. Seems to work really well."

"You fucking vicious bitch!" Hunter yells, the whole desk now an ass attachment. It's completely off the ground, the adhesive stuck to his black pants which has him stumbling to find a new center of gravity.

"That's right," I agree, swinging my bag over my shoulder. "And don't forget it. Good luck getting the desk off your pants. I'm sure Mrs. Smythson will give you a hand when she returns."

My laughter drowns out his curses as I head out the door. Because judging by the look on Hunter's face, Mrs. Smythson is now long gone for the day.

Now that we'd all but declared war, I decided it was time to bring in the cavalry.

Tuesday morning, I hunted down someone from Cedar to escort me to the field. Given it was before first period, I was surprised to find someone so easily—Millie.

She jumped at the chance to come on a *mission*—her words, not mine.

We made sure to arrive early to the locker rooms, so I could change into my gym clothes and give my backpack to Mills to guard during first period.

While standing around waiting for the rest of the class, the usual taunts and catcalls started. But my focus was elsewhere, waiting for it.

"Nice ass, Spencer," Rylan calls out with a laugh.

Next to me, Sophia shakes her head. "Ignore him."

"I am," I reply.

When Coach Carter splits us into groups, I'm happy to be placed with Sophia. The two of us jog at a glacial pace, glaring at the cheerleaders as we pass their practice spot.

The comments don't get any better—from the men or the women—which just solidifies my motivation.

At the end of class, I pause on the track, watching as the men head into the locker room. Rylan shoots me a wink before disappearing out of sight, and this time, I'm ready to go for the kill.

"Soph, could you do me a favor?"

"Sure!" she answers happily somehow, breathing heavily through dry-retching sounds.

I cross my arms as my voice drops low. "Don't let anyone in, okay?"

Sophia gives me a look of pure confusion, but I don't elaborate, merely smiling before I stalk straight into the male locker room.

The layout is nearly identical to ours, and it takes about three seconds for the men to react when they spot me.

"Girl!" one yells, apparently forgetting he co-exists with them every day.

"Out!" I shout back, glaring at all of them.

They share a look between them as if to ask if I'm being deadly serious. I pick up an abandoned towel—because men are messy as fuck—and whip one of them in the ass. "Now!"

I like to think it's the look on my face that persuades them to listen. One by one, they grab their stuff, exiting to the field.

When they are all gone, my eyes fall on the closed door of the shower stall, stepping forward. The water is running, the sound of someone moving around inside the cubicle.

I walk over to his locker, which, of course, has his own name personalized on it, and start going through his things.

Completing phase one of my plan, I decide against stealing his cell. I have no desire for his number, but something else grabs my attention. Slipping the little black card into my bra, I walk over and slam my hand on the cubicle door.

"Yo, what?" Rylan snaps back. "I'm showering."

"You need it," I say back, holding in a laugh. I can picture him tensing up in surprise, the shower quickly turning off.

"What the hell are you doing in here, Spencer?" he growls.

Snorting, I turn away and start heading back to the entrance without a word.

When I emerge through the doors, I'm not surprised to find the group of guys still waiting, some only in towels and staring daggers at me—likely pissed at themselves for listening to my demand.

Sophia gives me a bewildered look, before bursting out into a fit of laughter. "Fuck. Fuck! I'm dying."

"Do you have your cell?" I ask her. She nods, handing it to me and I flick up the camera app.

There's a string of loud, booming curses from inside the locker room, and less than two minutes later, a steaming Rylan storms out.

In my booty shorts.

"Nice ass, Astor!" I mock, snapping a picture.

He glares at me, the tiny material stretching to unimaginable lengths, looking more like swim briefs than shorts. His eyes rake down my body, landing on *his* shorts that I'm currently wearing.

I guess he didn't check the trash bin for his uniform slacks.

"Give my fucking shorts back," he angrily orders.

"Nah," I say, amused as a few of his buddies take their own pictures while whistling. "They are quite comfortable. Thanks!"

Grabbing Sophia's arm, I'm barely able to pull her behind me as she hunches over, still cackling wildly. I glance over my shoulder, watching as Rylan tries to give chase, but the shorts wedge into his ass cheeks, causing a huge wedgie.

I wave, grinning as the two of us start running toward the main building. Rylan yells out for us to come back, but our laughter blocks him out, before eventually, we dive through the double doors inside the building.

"That was the best thing I've ever seen," Sophia pants, wiping a stray tear away. "Oh, shit. He's so pissed."

"Good," I mutter, leaning against a locker. "Asshole deserved it. Here's your cell back."

Sophia takes a deep breath, trying to regain a normal level of oxygen intake. "Those guys are going to share the fuck out of those photos. If I were you, I'd call *Witness Protection* immediately."

My lips twitch into a smile. "I'm not scared of him, Soph. And it's about time someone took them down a few notches."

"Early morning gym was worth *that*," she grins, looking at the photo in her camera gallery before hyperventilating with laughter again.

I mull over whether or not to bring up the books but decide to leave it for now. I'm riding a high, and soon, there will be definite retaliation. So, for now, I live in the moment, permanently burning a place in my brain of Rylan Astor in teenie-tiny booty shorts.

There's still one more thing I plan to do. Well, two—but the first needs to happen straight away while I have the chance.

Saying goodbye to Sophia, I retrieve my belongings from Millie and duck into the restroom. After changing, I whip out my cell and google a few key words before I find what I am searching for.

As I tap out the information, I bite my lip to stay quiet, not the least bit surprised when the idea works.

Ha! This is gold.

The little blue checkmark notification appears on the screen, and I snort, covering my mouth as my body shakes.

I warned them.

And I always follow through on my promises.

CHAPTER ELEVEN

HUNTER

Tai and I are deep in conversation when the doors to the courtyard fling open so fast and hard that the sound of them bouncing off the glass wall echoes through the entire quad, silencing everyone.

To my surprise, Rylan is storming through the crowd, steam practically billowing from his ears. He makes a beeline for us by the fountain, bowling his bag to the ground with a sickening thud.

"Fuck her!" he yells loudly.

My eyebrows shoot up, watching as he finally takes a seat, pressing his curled fists into his forehead.

"Hello to you too," I say, exchanging a quick look with Tai as we both wordlessly ask, *"What the fuck?"*

Rylan breathes heavily, shaking slightly with unbridled anger. Finally, he opens his eyes, a forced look of calm replacing his earlier rage.

"We need to take down Spencer," he exclaims. "Now. No more half-assed pranks. She goes down this fucking second."

I'm double surprised by his words because I'm yet to tell either of them about my own encounter with her yesterday. Just thinking of it threatens to send me into the same spiral of fury as Rylan. But given all the eyes on us currently, I ignore the impending explosion, lowering my voice.

"What happened?"

Rylan snaps his head up. "She stole my goddamn shorts and pants. I had to wear those stupid fucking gym shorts she's been parading around in."

My mouth pops open as I process his confession. Tai quickly covers a snort when Rylan glares at him.

Sighing, I look between them. "She superglued my ass to a desk yesterday."

This time, Tai can't hold it in, bursting out in a fit while Rylan splutters. "She, *what*?"

I quickly fill them in about detention—how I organized to clear Smythson out of the room so I could have some fun tormenting her. But embarrassingly, she got the upper hand on me.

I'm so angry at myself for letting her do that. I should have seen it coming, but I got complacent—mistook the moment for a bout of weakness.

Since everyone had left for the day, I had no choice but to call Peyton for assistance. My dear cousin was just finishing a late cheer session and helped grab a pair of spare shorts from the admin office. The only way I was getting that thing off my ass was by shimmying out of my pants. But there was no way I was walking around in my boxer trunks with Dad lingering around.

It was on my to-do list to fill Rylan and Tai in about it this morning, but I never expected that Duchess would get to him first.

I think we may have underestimated her willingness to start shit on our turf. We're going to have to hit back hard, make her regret the day she stepped foot inside Willow-brook.

Rylan is still muttering curses when we all pull out our cells to check whether the little stunt has made its way onto social media. We need to do damage control as soon as pos-sible.

But before any of us can check, both Tai and Rylan yell at the same time.

My eyes widen, switching between the two of them, won-dering what I've suddenly missed.

"Why am I missing two-thousand dollars from my ac-count?!"

"Why am I being sent *dick pics*?!"

The two of them pause, staring at each other in complete silence. Sighing, I pluck Rylan's cell from his hand—because I don't want to see wrinkly balls—and check his screen.

"Tarven INC?" I read the newest transaction on his bank-ing app. "Tai, search it up."

He nods in reply, quickly tapping his screen before his eye-brows disappear into his hairline, eyes snapping up to Rylan. "Oh, man..."

"What is it?" Rylan growls, ripping the device from his palm. He scans the screen, fingers clenching the sides tightly. "The fucking *Conservation Mission for... Wildcats.*"

Oh, Spencer. You're fucking dead.

Dead and then I'll resuscitate her just so I can end her a second time.

There's a small yell of disgust from Rylan as he flings the cell back to Tai. "You're getting dick pics one after the other. What the fuck?"

"She's obviously leaked my goddamn number," he grimaces, shoving his burner back into his bag. "That has to be it. There's been seventeen so far and they just only started at the end of first period."

That sneaky bitch.

Whispers behind me have us all whipping around, Rylan yelling at the gossiping girls to fuck off.

This is bad. Really bad.

"And there's pictures of you in the shorts," Tai mutters low. "It's popping up on social media. But it looks like it's coming from Willowbrook students."

Rylan massages his temples. "Right. We need a plan. Tai, can you get the picture wiped? If my dad sees it, I'll never hear the end of it."

Giggles ring out around the courtyard. "I think we might be a little late for that," I murmur darkly, watching as people gasp at their cells and send amused looks in our direction.

"I need to find the source of these text messages. But I can't do it until I'm off school grounds," Tai grunts.

"I need to get my damn credit card back," Rylan interjects. "Who knows what else she'll do with it. What's her schedule?"

I glance over at the courtyard doors, popping an eyebrow. "No need. She's right *there*."

The other two look up, easily spotting what I'm already staring at.

Across the courtyard, Bexley is standing, eyes locked on us with a crowd of blue-wearing jerseys behind her. A dozen easily, they all stare at us with cunning smiles, and it makes my blood fucking boil.

Bexley's gaze falls onto me first, her pink lips twitching. She then does the same to Tai, before landing on Rylan, who powers up to his feet and takes off toward her.

Tai and I quickly follow, jogging to catch up as his heavy footsteps approach her.

I nearly expect some of them to retreat with how murderous he looks, but none of them flinch. Bexley actually takes a few steps forward, meeting Rylan face to face.

"You changed your shorts," she says softly to Rylan, body scanning him.

His fingers spasm by his sides, itching to reach out and strangle her. "My card, Spencer," he spits out with a threatening tone.

She smiles, not answering immediately as we flank his sides. "And here we have three little Musketeers," she tells the group behind her. "Pretending to be wolves."

Rylan finally snaps, hand shooting forward. But Bexley catches his wrist in her grasp, holding it tight. "Don't bother, Astor. All it will do is make me smile. And you know what they say about a woman if she smiles when your hands are around her neck..."

My eyes flick to the glass windows lining the courtyard, hissing quietly as I find people pressed up against it, watching our encounter and power struggle. Around the courtyard, everyone has stopped what they are doing, a silence lingering in the crisp air.

We're in trouble. We need to defuse the situation and take back control as quickly as possible. With all the eyes and ears on us, and things spreading fast on socials, damage control needs to happen *now*.

Sensing that it's still too raw for Rylan to chill, I step forward, taking over their exchange.

"Listen here, Duchess. You've made a grave mistake fucking with us. We were going easy on you out of pity, but if you want a fucking war, then that's what you'll get."

Her emerald irises flick to me with interest. "Is that right, Hunter? Out of curiosity, did you know that the classrooms have cameras?"

Of course, I did. It's not as if they are hidden from sight. But my bewilderment at her question diminishes instantly with realization, body shaking with growing fury. "Don't. You. Dare," I whisper darkly. "You'll regret it, Spencer."

Bexley turns to her side, to that little errand boy of hers. "Arch?"

He taps his cell, grinning with a nod. "Done."

As his hand drops, I catch a glimpse of the screen, and as expected, there it is... *A video of me in Smythson's room with the desk affixed to my ass.*

She turns back to me, offering a sickly-sweet smile. "I know how much you hate being kept out of the know. So, we posted it on Youtube for you and shared the link to the public Willowbrook forum. Hopefully, you can find it. Your father is a member of that group, right? Since it's full of alumni?"

Tai actually appears offended by the idea that someone has hacked into the cameras—like he's taking this one personally. But I don't have time to dwell on his feelings. Not when I need to get rid of that evidence.

I realize that Bexley is still holding Rylan's wrist, so I slap her hand down, forcing her to release him. I shoot a dirty glare at Rylan, wondering why he didn't bother to escape already when he could have easily done so.

People are still gawking in disbelief, and my stomach sinks when I spot a few people with their cells up, recording our standoff.

"Enough of this!" I snap, turning to the nearest Willowbrook student I can find. "Grab our bags and follow us."

I walk around the Cedar Heights group, silently demanding that Rylan and Tai follow.

Tai follows but Rylan stays put, again asking, "Card, Bexley."

"I don't have it," she shrugs lazily. "Maybe it fell out of your bag in the locker room."

The longer we stay and argue, the worse it makes us look. So, I snap at Rylan again to follow, which thankfully, he does this time.

Once we're back inside the main building, I head straight for Dad's office. Elizabeth will at least be able to delete the post from the Facebook group since she's an administrator. Then, we can use the staff credentials to delete that footage of me from the servers—not that it will do any good now that they have a copy. But it will make me feel a little more at ease.

After that, I'm going to beat the shit out of everyone who shared the picture of Rylan, even if they've already taken it down.

Tai might even be able to locate the source of his anonymous number spree and block it, so he doesn't have to wait until the end of day.

But even with all those plans, I try not to focus on the fact that the boulder is already rolling down the hill. We can't stop it. By now, screenshots and recordings have already been saved and exchanged hands. All we can do is stop it from getting worse, but deleting all the footage is near impossible—even with Tai's skills.

The only thing we can do is strike back immediately.

Hard. Fast.

Painfully.

Break her so that she remembers who she is dealing with. Make her regret what she's done.

End her miserable existence and send her packing.

Perhaps, Dad can suspend her. She's already on a warning from her altercation with Liv. But still, not having Bexley here is not the solution either.

The best thing we can do is force her to remain on Willowbrook turf, so she can't hide from us.

At the very least, she has detention this afternoon. I'll get her then.

Just hopefully I'll have Rylan and Tai there as well to make sure I don't actually murder her. Because that's a real possibility right now.

CHAPTER TWELVE

BEXLEY

Midway through second period, I feign the stomach flu, ducking through the quiet hallways to the nurse.

I was pleasantly surprised to find she's a delightful, middle-aged woman, who seems to actually care about the well-being of her students.

Therefore, she was more than happy to excuse me from classes for the rest of the day, including an exemption from detention.

Running away has never been my thing, but I'd be stupid to allow myself the opportunity to be left alone with the three wolves. I know they will try to jump me in detention. I would do the same.

Alone, after hours. It would be the perfect time and place for them to seek revenge for today.

So, I took that away from them.

All the Cedar students were advised to be on their best behavior for the rest of the day, as to avoid the same fate. Arch graciously stayed back with Abby after school, to make sure everyone left without troubles, before sending me the *all-clear* text message.

Tomorrow, we'll work out a plan to maybe get a few more Cedar students into detention with me or to stand guard outside, just so we can't be ambushed.

But for now, I start making dinner, relieved to see the fridge full of food again.

Mom is awake and moving around, and I'm happy to see that today is a better day for her. Small glimpses of her old self are shining through, her petite frame swaying to music as she helps chop up some vegetables.

"Do you remember when we used to cook together when you were a child?" she asks, slicing an onion.

I nod. "After I set microwave popcorn on fire, you made it your personal mission to ensure I knew how to cook."

She laughs softly. "And you still burned it again. But after that, you demanded to cook for us every Wednesday night."

The indirect reference of Dad makes us both still, but neither of us voice our thoughts. At least we're in sync with that. I guess I share that trait with Mom—compartmentalize your trauma. If we don't talk about it, it never existed.

"And every second Friday, we used to go to Olive Garden. You loved those damn bread sticks," I reminisce.

Mom sighs happily. "They are delicious." She pauses, placing the knife down on the chopping board. "Let's go tomorrow."

I glance over my shoulder at her, stirring the mashed potatoes. "To Olive Garden?" I ask, surprise obvious in my voice. "Like a Mother-Daughter date?"

"Absolutely," she gushes. "It's been so long since the two of us went out and enjoyed ourselves."

My foot taps thoughtfully. "I came home sick today," I admit quietly. "I told them I had the stomach flu."

Mom frowns in concern. "Are you actually sick?"

"No," I laugh, feeling a touch nervous at admitting my little white lie. "Just pissed some of the Willowbrook boys off and wanted to make sure I made it home for dinner. But anyway, how about I skip school tomorrow and we have a whole day together? Think about it—manis, pedis, bread sticks."

I half expect her to say no, that I have to attend school. But she beams at me. "Let's do it! I just have to go to the doctor's office in the morning for my follow up SSI physical, but you can come with me."

Spinning around, I forget about the potatoes. "Really?" I ask, heart pounding in excitement. "You wanna do it?"

It's been so long since I've seen her like this—happy, aware... *alive.*

I don't want to waste an opportunity. The good days are scarce, and right now, I have the chance to spend time with her before her demons pull her back into the abyss.

"I do, Bexie," she murmurs with a smile. "Tomorrow—it's just us."

"Just us," I repeat, skipping across the kitchen to pull her into a hug. "It's a date."

Just us. Plus, Doctor Lavings.

The aging man in his fifties looks just as pleasantly sur-prised to see Mom in her current state as I was. He gave us both a warm smile as he ushered us into his clinical room the next morning.

I wait in front of the curtain as Mom changes into a dress-ing gown, making small talk with the man. We joke about the weather, the release of new music that we both like, and finally, about Mom's improvement today when she emerges in the grayish gown with red socks.

"Alright, Savanna. You know the drill—I'll check your blood pressure, heart rate, breathing rate. Then, we'll have a discussion about your current overall health and touch on how you feel. You'll also need to fulfill a pathology request so we can check your bloodwork. But I have to say, I'm loving this improvement today."

Mom looks at me, beaming with pride, and I can't help but share it back at her.

After the last two weeks with Willowbrook, putting those assholes in their place and seeing Mom like this, really made it all worth it.

Last night, it was all over social media—and I don't just mean the Cedar Heights pages.

The Youtube video had skyrocketed in views before it had finally been shut down. But copies of the video appeared all over Facebook and Instagram, with students front and center at the table—the *tea table*, that is.

Steamy, hot tea in the form of three Willowbrook legends, who were meeting their downfall.

How do I know it's a downfall in progress?

Comments.

Behind screens, people aren't afraid to say what they feel. Keyboard warriors were out in full force, suddenly questioning their so-called leaders. Many were disappointed that '*a lowlife from Cedar Heights*' had managed to get the upper hand on all three of them.

Others were amused, talking about how they had it coming. Many were also angry, siding with their friends and swearing vengeance on me—but whatever. Bring it on.

But the more news got around, sharing not only our encounter in the courtyard, but Hunter's ass-accessory, Rylan's new booty strut, and Tai's alleged love of dick, people were concerned. They were scared. And suddenly, there was a feeling of trepidation looming in the air at Willowbrook.

Not that I know anything about it. I'm here, enjoying my day off.

Arch's updates have been entertaining, and I fully intend to dive more into them later. But for now, I'm focused on this moment with my mom.

"Uh-huh," the doctor mutters to himself, shining a pen light in her face. "I just want to check your liver enzymes which will be included in the blood panel. You have a little bit of jaundice, but I assume you've still been consuming alcohol. It's probably nothing, but I'd just like to be sure."

Mom hangs her head down, shame written across her face. "I want to give it up," she whispers. "I haven't touched a drink since Monday."

"That's fantastic," the doctor rejoices. "Well, let's see what the bloodwork returns, and we can discuss next steps. I know you've mentioned previously you'd like to return to work at some stage."

"I do miss my design work," she nods.

Before Mom became a victim of Dad's spiral, she designed wedding dressings—well, the sketches, anyway. She was such a sucker for love that she fell hard into the wedding in- dustry, determined to make brides feel as beautiful on their wedding day as she had done. But when he left, love was nothing more than a wasteful emotion that she disregard- ed. Except, that's the problem with love. You can't stop it, and you certainly can't just turn off the feelings of heart- break—unless you numb them.

Mom looks at me, a ghost of a smile appearing. "Who knows? In a few years, maybe my beautiful daughter will be walking down the aisle."

I snort, not wanting to burst her bubble, but truthfully, I'm not sure I'll ever get married.

Men are great for orgasms. But life commitment? The jury is still out on that one.

"We'll see," I tell her, not keen to fully destroy her mental image of me dressed like a white, fluffy cupcake.

"Head down the hall to the laboratory and get your blood-work drawn," Doctor Lavings directs, sitting down and typing on his computer. "Our in-house team will be able to fast track the results to me. Given it's for SSI reporting, I expect we should have them back within twenty-four hours. I'll have my receptionist schedule an appointment for tomorrow, that way we can decide straight away what you would like to do. In the meantime, I'll collate some information regarding rehabilitation for you."

She throws him a panic-stricken look. Noticing, he smiles gently.

"You wouldn't need to attend a facility if you didn't want to. There are many support options available, and I'll support whichever route you choose. But we'll need to decide and set up a management plan, as if you intend to return to the workforce in the near future, we'll have to notify Social Society. The last thing you want is to be in debt for an overpayment."

I nod, squeezing Mom's hand. "That's right. We'll work it out together. This is a good thing, Mom."

"I know," she breathes out, giving me a shaky smile. "I'm just..."

The words remain unspoken, but I know. I'm scared too—but life is meant to be scary. How would we build character if we weren't challenged?

Doctor Lavings beams at me. "Little Miss Bex is correct. We'll support you, Savanna. And Bexley," he pauses. "You're due for your annual check-up too."

After our trip to Olive Garden, I waddle back to my bedroom when we arrive home, feeling more stuffed than I have in years.

There was a fraction of guilt at how much we had spent today—the two of us also taking a quick trip to the spa, but I always say that memories are more important than money.

Money will always come back again, but memories? You can't replace them.

Mom and I said goodnight as she went for a shower before an early sleep. She's doing fantastic this week, but I know fighting those mental demons is exhausting. The best thing she can do is sleep, to silence them when they creep out of the shadows at night.

But as for me, I'm completely wired. Part of me is scared to go to sleep, worried I'll wake up and it will have all been a dream, or that she'll be gone again.

Packing my bag for tomorrow, I snuggle into bed, scrolling on my cell when an unknown text comes through. It's a new number, since I blocked Tai's, but I can guess with accurate certainty who it belongs to.

> **Unknown:** *Spencer. Give me my damn credit card back. You weren't at school today. I swear to God if you put any more charges on it, I'll wipe you from the face of the Earth.*

Snorting, I start writing back a reply to Rylan. I'm in such a good mood from today that not even he can ruin it.

> **Bexley:** *Maybe I underestimated you, Rylan. I thought you didn't have a heart. But that generous donation to the conservation of wildcats was selfless. Don't worry, I'm sure you can deduct charitable contributions on your tax return.*

I see the little bubble pop up immediately as he writes back, grinning to myself. It was perfect, donating to something he associates with hate.

> **Rylan:** *I'm serious, Spencer. Just give me the card back and we'll call it even.*

> *Bexley: We're not even close to being even, Astor. You started this war. I was more than happy to be amicable, but you all crossed the line. I'm just giving back what you deserve. If you want it to stop, then you know what to do.*

The idea of Rylan Astor giving in and admitting defeat is slim-to-none, but I mean what I said.

It doesn't have to be like this. Our feud can stay in the warehouse, just like it was intended to be. But if they continue to push me, I'll fight back. I'm not afraid to get my hands dirty and they have a lot more to lose than I do.

I expect some snarky reply, but his next message manages to shock me.

> *Rylan: Meet me tomorrow after detention. Just us two.*

This is a trap, for sure. But I'm interested in hearing what he has to say.

It will require some logistical planning with Arch, to make sure they don't ambush me. But alright—let's see what the great Rylan Astor has to say for himself when his castle is crumbling.

Bexley: *Fine. 4 o'clock sharp. Text me the location. But if you even so much as think of pulling a fast one, just know that yesterday was a warm-up.*

CHAPTER THIRTEEN

RYLAN

"How could you be so careless, Rylan? I taught you better than this!"

My jaw ticks as I force myself to stay still, eyes glued to my father while he rants from behind his desk.

As hard as we tried to contain the social media outbreak, we weren't quick enough. And if the fact that Bexley fucking Spencer managed to embarrass us wasn't bad enough, my father is making sure to remind me of my failure.

We've spent the past thirty hours trying to mitigate the damage. Tai was able to wipe the videos off the platforms, but every time we pulled one off, another three appeared in its place.

People were saving and sharing the content, and although most listened once we started making personal *visits* to posters, the truth was... we couldn't stop it.

When I received a message earlier that my father wished to speak to me, I knew he had seen—or heard.

Max Astor is a proud, esteemed alumnus of Willowbrook, and as mayor of Ridgeview Valley, very little slips past him.

He makes it his mission to know everything about everyone, and while he pushed me to this position, to be in power at the academy, he's taking great pleasure in reminding me that I've fucked up.

"I know," I manage to grunt out. "We thought we had control of the situation."

I thought I had control of her.

Truthfully, I agree with him.

We should have pushed harder. Instead of wasting our time pushing her limits, we should have just taken her down from the beginning.

Initially, we relied on the home ground advantage, knowing that Bexley wouldn't be able to do much in the way of retaliation. Setting up that meeting with Hunter's father, we had hoped that she would realize that any attempts of revenge would be useless—that she'd be thrown out of Willowbrook so fucking fast that her head would spin. Dean Lannister took no issue with involving himself, threatening her enrollment. I assumed that she would concede, since I know she wouldn't leave the Cedar Heights cohort on their own to manage.

But this—the ridiculous videos—was not something I was expecting.

Because the damn reality is... Bexley didn't take them.

She found a loophole in our schemes, setting us up for failure, knowing that no matter who someone was, people would always take pleasure in someone's weaker moments.

Sure, she stole from me, but how would I even explain that to the dean? There are no cameras in the locker room, no indisputable proof. And she didn't force my so-called friends to take videos and pictures. They did that all on their own.

Trust me, they are paying for it. But it's an uncontained virus now.

We can't even get her into trouble for what she did for Hunter. He was never meant to be near the room in the first place. The most we could do is have her punished for leaving detention early—but given we ordered Smythson to leave before the end of detention, all Bexley has to say is she left at the same time.

Regardless of the video evidence, Hunter provoked her. And Dean Lannister knows that if we spin it to blame her, the reputation of Willowbrook would be at stake. A poor, defenseless female, cornered in detention by a male after a teacher abandons her post. The media would have a field day with it. Willowbrook wouldn't survive such allegations—neither would Hunter or Dean Lannister. Their reputations are stellar, both prominent members of society.

And in turn, as Willowbrook community members, we would all be branded and tied to the actions.

Therefore... *my father*.

"You stupid boy," he hisses, infuriated. "Marcus is doing damage control as we speak, to ensure that these reports stay out of the hands of journalists. But do you understand what this would do to my campaign if word got out? It's an election year, Rylan. You know what's at stake."

I nod. "I understand. It won't happen again."

Dad stands from behind his desk, palms flat on the polished wood. "See to it that it doesn't. We've contacted George to see what else can be done but he's currently in Europe dealing with a criminal investigation."

When isn't George traveling? For the past few years, I can single-handedly count the number of times I've seen him in the Beckett residence. I envy Tai in that regard, whereas Hunter and I have the utmost pleasure of having our fathers breathe down our necks constantly. It's why I can't just cancel my credit card and get a new one. He would be notified and the situation would get worse.

"I'll speak to Dean Lannister tomorrow," I promise. "To see what we can do."

I watch as his knuckles crack, forming fists. "Marcus doesn't need your assistance. You need to keep your head down and remain out of trouble. I cannot even fathom how you let someone from *Cedar Heights*," he pauses, spitting out the words as if they contained poison. "Get the better of you. I'm disappointed. Do better, Rylan."

Sitting back down, he turns his chair, facing away from me. His dismissal is clear, and without another word, I leave his home office.

The urge to punch something is consuming me so I head down the stairs, taking a sharp right until I end up in the gym. Bypassing the weights, I go straight for the punching bag, not even bothering to glove up before I swing and punch it square in the middle.

My fists rain down on the hard bag, one after another, until I'm panting with bright pink knuckles. My skin screams to stop, but it's nothing compared to the feeling of euphoria that creeps through my body, relishing in the pain.

I keep hitting, until eventually, my knuckles split, and little droplets of blood drip down my hands. Only then do I finally stop, dropping to the ground with my head in my hands.

I hate that I'm in this position. And like Dad, I blame myself too.

When news broke about the fire at Cedar, I didn't stop and consider for a single second that it would mean sharing our school. But even when Dad and Marcus were forced to accommodate the Cedar students, I felt nothing but joy.

Joy in the prospect of tormenting them. Taking our rivalry to another level, to truly show the kind of power we had at our school.

But fucking Bexley Spencer decided to be difficult.

I never expected her to just give in, to accept the situation, but I also never expected to be betrayed by my own.

Recovering from that embarrassing situation with the shorts, that was easy. We all do dumb shit. It's partly my own fault for not packing trunks. But it was the fact that Bexley went after all of us and succeeded.

Hunter's should have stayed under wraps, but Tai has already in the past expressed concerns that the security system at Willowbrook could be tighter. Yet, when Cedar invaded our space, we didn't stop and consider that we should circle back to that issue.

They are pathetic, worthless. How could any of them have any experience in hacking or breaking into systems? I guess we should have known better. After all, they are more likely to be criminals than we are.

Even Tai's attack, that should have been easy to conceal. But prying ears and our lack of awareness got the better of us. We were pissed, distracted, and of course, people heard—not hard when T was yelling about dick pics to the entire quad.

That showdown in the courtyard should have ended differently. But there's no way we'd be able to explain an all-out brawl. The rules are simple—keep it to the warehouse.

My breathing finally starts to regulate when I hear footsteps come into the room. I glance up, face deadpanning at the figure by the door.

"What the hell are you doing here, Liv?" I ask, exasperated.

She twirls her hair, leaning against the doorjamb. "I missed you after school today. I thought we could hang."

I regret that one drunken night a few weeks ago where I accidentally blurted the access code out loud when bringing her here. Now, she tends to turn up at the worst possible times.

Normally, I'd be all for a bit of stress relief, but my mind is stuck on another woman, and I'm too angry to deal with this.

"Now's not a good time," I grunt back, pushing to my feet and turning away from her. God, I'd kill for my AirPods right now. Because I know she's going to fight tooth and nail on this.

"But babe," she whines, walking toward me. "I came all this way. Come on, you don't even need to do anything."

Her hands run up my back, and she takes my tensing muscles to mean something else. I don't want to be touched right now, but Liv doesn't understand personal boundaries. To her, she thinks my body is reacting to her touch in a lustful way, shivering in anticipation. Wrong. I'm recoiling, desperate for her to read the damn fucking room.

Spinning around, I grab her wrist when she claws my shoulder, jerking her arm away. Liv blinks, confused, and I lean down toward her.

Little breaths catch in her throat as her eyes blow wide in excitement. And for a moment, I almost feel bad for the incoming rejection. But she needs to learn the word *no*.

Ever since we were toddlers and our families met, Liv has struggled to be anything except the center of attention. Don't get me wrong, I love a confident woman, but there's a time and a place... and that doesn't include stalking and breaking into houses.

"No," I say sternly, letting her see just how serious I am.

"Why not?" she pouts, unbothered by my grip on her arm. "I don't care about the video—"

I rip my arm back, taking a step back as her mouth gapes open. "Shut up about the video, Olivia."

Liv lets out a little annoyed huff. "Honestly, Rylan, you're being ridiculous. Don't let that Cedar trash get to you."

"I'm not," I bite back. "But I still don't want to fuck right now."

"We don't have to," she offers, jutting out her hip. "I'll blow you."

Sighing, I squeeze the bridge of my nose. "For the last time—no. I need to take care of a few things. And for the record, you cannot just turn up whenever you feel like it. Just because you know the code, doesn't mean you can come and go as you please."

"But as your girlfriend—"

"For fuck sake, Liv!" I shout, scaring her. "We're not dating. We're *fucking*. That's not going to change anytime soon, so drop the point."

The rejection finally registers, a cold chill crossing her face before she stomps her foot—like a damn toddler—and glares at me angrily.

"Do you know what people are saying about you, right now?" Liv spits back. "About all of you? I'm throwing you a bone here, Rylan. We can put these issues to bed. Your bed."

"Fucking you is not going to fix this," I hiss. "And I don't have time to waste. Get out of my house."

Liv growls, tossing her hair over her shoulder. "Right now, I'm the only solidarity you have. If you don't take advantage of this, people will continue to talk."

"People are talking no matter what," I point out. "Now, stay here if you must. But I'm leaving. Be warned though, my father is upstairs and in a foul mood."

As I stalk past her, Liv quickly follows, jogging in her cheer uniform to catch up. "Don't let her win, Rylan. That's what that bitch wants. She wants us to be apart—"

Stopping, I almost laugh when she crashes into my sturdy back. Any other time, I'd find it amusing, but not right now. Turning, I glare down at her. "Bexley couldn't give two shits about our relationship, Liv. I guarantee that's the last thing on her mind. Stop making this situation about *you*."

I know I've hit the nail on the head when she falls silent, expression tugging into annoyance.

Olivia doesn't care about the destruction of my reputation. She just wants to make sure hers doesn't suffer the same fate. I have no idea why she wants to attach herself to me when I'm in the midst of a crisis. Most people are running far away, not willing to be associated with any of us until we take back control—fucking cowards.

But the head cheerleader is so far up her own ass, that all she sees is appearance. For months now, it's been *The Dance* this and *Cheer Comp* that. In her mind, having a legacy on her arm will seal and secure her fate—make her seem untouchable. But doesn't she realize how wrong she is? Not heeding Bexley's warning was a mistake on her part. We encouraged her to go to the dean, to report the altercation. But if she continues to poke the bear, eventually she's going to get hurt. And we won't be able to defend it.

The key to this is playing checkers while everyone else is playing chess—to fly under the radar, to grab control from the inside. The only way to do that is...

"I'm not making this about me," she argues, placing her hand on my chest. "I care about you."

Even the admission falls flat, the words empty as she pleads with me to reconsider. But like before, I pry her hand off me, letting it drop before walking away.

"See yourself out, Olivia," I demand, heading up the stairs to my bedroom.

Thankfully, she finally takes the hint, leaving with a curse and mimicking a huffing train. I don't want her around for this, it's already threatening to send me into a blackout rage.

I pick up my cell, scrolling through the contact until I sneer at her name.

I hate myself for this.

But I'll hate myself more if I don't take back control.

That's why I need to play it smart, lead everyone into a sense of security. Punching out the text message, I swallow down bile as I hit send.

I can't tell Hunter and Tai about this yet. They won't agree. But it's the only way to get on top of this. If getting into bed with the enemy is the only way to win, then it's a sacrifice I need to make.

Chapter Fourteen

The school day drags on, causing me to question the concept of time.

I swear, all the clocks are at half-speed, taking forever to reach the end of day.

My mind has been a blurry mess all day—stuck on the thoughts of Mom at her follow-up appointment today, and my agreed meeting with Rylan this afternoon.

When I arrived at Willowbrook this morning, I gave Arch the brief update after he filled me in on yesterday's antics. It brought me great joy to hear how people taunted the three guys, the academy in shambles as staff rushed to control the students.

The videos are still being shared at an alarming rate, and despite putting on a brave face, it was apparently easy to tell they were frustrated.

Even today, I was stuck in a classroom with the three of them, and they barely glanced my way. A few heated looks here and there, but for the most part, they kept away.

I organized for a small group of Cedar students to hang around after school, standing guard in the hallway to make sure no one tried to sneak into the detention room. Mrs. Smythson barely glanced at me when I arrived, and surprisingly, I was instructed to study rather than fix desks.

Huh—I wonder why that is.

Four o'clock rolls around and I meet Archie, Millie, Steele, and Parker outside the room. Millie, of course, volunteered to assist, which meant Parker was hot on her heels, guarding his baby sister. According to our sources, Hunter and Tai left academy grounds when classes finished, but they hadn't seen Rylan. That was surprising to me because I thought for sure I'd be facing the three of them, even if Rylan did say it would be just us.

Pulling out my cell, I double check the time, and reread Rylan's message with the meeting location. "If you stay outside the main building, you'll probably be able to hear if I need you. I'll shout down."

"Are you sure being on the rooftop with him is a smart idea?" Arch asks as the others nod in agreement with him.

"I can handle him," I say, offering a small smile. "Steele will catch me if I get pushed off the roof."

Not one of them laughs at my little joke. Rude.

Steele steps forward at the mention of his name, placing a hand on my waist. "I can come with you. I don't mind."

I pinch his cheek. "You're so cute when you're protective, Steely."

He grimaces at the nickname, rolling his eyes but yields his argument.

I gesture for them to follow to their station at the back of the main administration building. According to my research, if I go past the staircase to the dean's office, I'll find an emergency door further down the hallway. Behind it, there should be a stairwell leading to the roof.

It doesn't exactly scream *safety procedure* but alas, we should be able to keep our meeting private. Personally, I don't mind if people see or hear, but something tells me that Rylan doesn't feel the same.

Waving goodbye, I push inside the quiet building, daring a glance up the staircase to check the coast is clear. Most of the staff have appeared to have left for the day, and no one interrupts me when I duck through the emergency doors.

The stairwell weaves and curls upwards, and I grumble to myself about the extra cardio workout. Trust that asshole to make me do extra exercise when I barely survive gym at the best of times.

Finally coming to a door, I push it open, relishing in the feeling of fresh breeze as it whacks me in the face. My hair whips around my face, the orange hues of the sun casting shadows on the rooftop.

Rylan is standing on the other side, back facing me as he looks over the field with his hands in his pockets. The door slams closed behind me, and I mutter, "Shit", watching as he turns around at the sound of my arrival.

"You actually listened," he scoffs. "I half expected to be cornered by your little posse."

"I'm not afraid to be alone with you." I roll my eyes, the two of us meeting in the middle of the rooftop.

His eyes rake over me, a small, amused smile appearing as he watches my hands hold down my skirt.

"Keep your comments to yourself," I direct when I take notice. "If your academy wasn't so sexist, I'd actually be able to wear a pair of shorts outside of gym."

My comment lands exactly where I take aim, his expression dropping at the unpleasant reminder.

"Chill, Spencer," he grunts. "I'm in no mood for your attitude today."

"And yet, you're the one who summoned me here," I quip back. "What is this all about? Another warning? A threat?"

"A truce."

My body stills at the suggestion. I never pictured Rylan Astor saying those words in a million years. I almost had to strain my ears to hear them, and even now, I'm still not entirely convinced I heard him correctly.

"Sorry, what was that?" I ask, entertained.

Sharp blue irises narrow on my face. "Don't push your luck, Spencer. You heard what I said."

Snorting, I let go of my skirt as the breeze eases off, folding my arms. "You're not capable of a truce, Astor. Save the fake attempts of power and admit I've got you by the balls."

Rylan's jaw tenses, his eyes darting back to the field. "You do," he admits quietly. "Which is why no one can know about this meeting."

Well, I'm getting more and more surprised as this progresses. The great Rylan Astor wants to pretend he didn't come crawling to me? That's exactly where he should be though—on his knees.

"Still not buying it," I laugh softly. "Let me guess... election season?"

The way his eyes spring back, clashing with mine, gives me all the answers I need. It's no mystery that word spread like wildfire, and with enough video proof filling social media, I can just imagine Mayor Astor is not happy with the latest development. They need all the numbers they can get when we hit the poll booths again in a few months.

"Don't waste my time, Spencer. Are you willing to negotiate or not?"

I shrug, walking over to the stairwell entrance and lean against the wall. "Possibly. But things need to change around here. We don't want to be here anymore than you do, but there's no reason to be constantly at each other's throats."

"Fine," he snaps. "Name your terms."

"Wow," I muse. "It took me less than two weeks, Rylan. Two weeks to follow through on that promise that I'd push back."

He runs a hand through his hair, slumping down to the ground. My brows furrow, unsure what to make of his behavior.

The simple gesture, letting his guard down, sitting at a lower height—either he's playing me, or he's genuinely stuck between a rock and a hard place.

I push off from the wall, walking back over and sit down in front of him. For the first time, I'm looking at an equal, a product of this feud we've been forced into.

What happened this week, it wasn't even that bad. Sure, the videos were embarrassing, but he's strong enough to recover from something like that. The man in front of me is full of pure exhaustion, feeling the weight of this forced proximity.

I can relate.

It's hard trying to be *on* all the time. To put your own personal demons aside for the sake of saving face. And this could be a game, a tactic to blindside me, but if it's not... then Rylan Astor is really breaking to be asking for help.

I've only met Mayor Astor once, during the last election campaign. As part of the rounds, all the candidates had to visit the schools and local community venues. Even with trying to hide his displeasure at being present in Cedar territory, he was easily one of the worst humans I've ever come across.

Cruel, brutal, a real piece of work.

The apple doesn't fall far from the tree, but we're still young, and I bet that's a lot of pressure for someone like Rylan.

I wish I didn't feel pity for him. He doesn't deserve it. They spared no pity for me when they harassed me, set the cheerleaders on to me, destroyed my belongings knowing I'd be shit out of luck trying to replace them. Yet, I still feel a little *sad* for him.

My home life may not be perfect, but I have a mom who loves me, even when the demons swallow her whole. The pressure I feel at home is my own doing, a reaction to wanting to save her. I couldn't imagine having a parent like Max Astor, what that must be like.

"Do you want to talk about it?" I ask when Rylan continues to stay silent.

His eyes dart over to me, hardened, the mental wall blocking me from seeing what's on the other side. But his body language has already said more than words can express.

"I don't know what the hell you are talking about," he snaps back angrily.

Ahh—deflection. Classic move.

"Suit yourself," I shrug. "I'm not the one who has something to lose, Rylan."

He straightens up his back. "Don't worry that pretty little head of yours with things above you, Spencer. This is purely business."

"Exactly, business," I repeat. "So, if you want my help, you'll speak to me properly. I'm not the one who started this. I'm not the one who set fire to Cedar Heights Academy."

Rylan glowers at me. "What exactly are you implying?"

"Oh, spare me the theatrics. We all know someone from Willowbrook started that fire. You may have been at the warehouse at the time, but I'm not stupid—I know you knew about it."

His expression falters. "I knew *nothing*," he scoffs. "Why the hell would I waste my time setting fire to your school? I didn't want you here. I still don't want you here."

"Do you honestly expect me to believe that?" I challenge. "One of you lit that fuse. And I won't rest until I know who."

Rylan stands suddenly, glaring down at me. "This was a waste of time. If you've already decided in your head that we're the perpetrators, then there's no way you're going to agree to a truce."

My hand stretches out, grabbing his as I tug him back down. Surprisingly, he lets me, eyes blown wide with frustration. He could have easily walked away—we both know that. But something tells me he's fighting a battle right now. So, I keep pushing.

"My terms are these," I start, locking eyes with him. "No more pranks, no more taunts. We co-exist until the repairs at Cedar are done. Any animosity we have is reserved for the warehouse. You leave my people alone, and we'll keep a clear path."

His face remains stoic as he listens. "And the videos?"

I shrug. "I can't speak for your people, but I'll have anyone from Cedar remove the indiscriminating videos. We can display an alliance, if you wish. You rule over your people, and leave me to do my job."

"Your job," he murmurs, bewildered. "That's what it is to you?"

"Of course."

It feels like we're both lost in translation now. In all honesty, it does feel like a job to me. It's a requirement, a leadership role that I'm now bound to. The idea that it could be anything more or less is perplexing.

Rylan's face softens. "Did you even want it?"

Now it's my turn to shove those walls up. A few years ago, all I wanted was to live my life peacefully. I wanted to be a normal teenager, making mistakes and learning from it. I wanted to go to school dances, be taken out on dates, and focus on my future.

But when everything fell to shit, I forced myself to be strong, to hide my broken heart. People grasped onto me, desperate for strength to guide them. And over time, it became easier to focus on being that person for them, to separate my life. It gave me a purpose, a reason to always be strong. But the reality of always needing to be on guard, unable to make mistakes, and having people rely on me, it's exhausting.

"I love looking after everyone," I finally say, running my fingers over the rough texture of the ground. "Don't you?"

When he doesn't answer immediately, I gaze up, heart missing a beat when I find his relaxed baby blues watching me closely.

"It was just... *expected*," he mutters quietly. "I didn't have a choice."

I nod, for once understanding what he means. "It's not all bad," I tell him with a small smile. "It's just hard at times juggling both worlds."

Rylan hums, leaning back onto his palms. "Sometimes, I just want to run," he says, trailing off. I'm confused by his words, letting a silence fall betof us as I wait for him to fill in the blanks.

His eyes scan my face—boyish, carefree features revealing themselves as he smiles. It's the first time I've ever been on the receiving end of a genuine one from him, and it makes my stomach flip. Here, right now, we're just two normal people, trying to figure out where the hell we go from here.

"Running makes me happy," he confesses. "It's so freeing. Nothing but me, my body, and the elements. It's the only time my mind can switch off and focus on something other than the surmounting pressures from all of this."

"Music," I reply. "Mine is music. My neighbors are probably sick of hearing my playlist, but it zones me out."

The two of us smile, tension disappearing as more shadows cast over the rooftop.

Remembering that I have people waiting for me, I dust off my hands on my skirt, holding one out to him.

"Alright, Astor. I'm not saying it's a truce, but we'll call it a *trial run*. If you can keep out of our way and be amicable toward us, maybe we'll get out of this thing alive."

Rylan reaches out, not shaking my hand but grasping it in his palm. My eyes fall to our connected hands, trying to ignore the strange feeling brewing in my chest as his eyes linger on my face.

"To friendliness," he proclaims, my skin itching as his thumb runs a singular stroke over my hand.

Clearing my throat, I pull back first, clenching my fist by my side as I stand. He watches for a few seconds, before pushing to his own feet.

"Here," I say awkwardly, reaching into my bra and extracting his credit card. "Consider this the first step toward an armistice. The wildcat foundation thanks you for your support."

Chapter Fifteen

"And local meteorologists are advising that members of the Ridgeview Valley community should stay inside this weekend unless absolutely essential. Now, back to Julian in the weather room with more updates on this storm of the year and the predicted rain for the next week."

I'm almost thankful for the thunder outside. Between that and my music, I'm successfully able to drown out my thoughts.

True to his word, Rylan and the Willowbrook cohort behaved themselves today. While some jeers and slurs were inevitable from others, the three of them barely looked at me today. Which turned out to be a blessing.

After returning home from the rooftop meeting with Rylan last night, I found Mom sitting on the couch, a somber look on her face.

Immediately, I knew something was wrong, and after pushing her for answers, she finally caved and admitted that her bloodwork had shown some issues.

To be on the safe side, Doctor Lavings had requested that she present to Ridgeview Hospital for monitoring. When I tried to press for what it all meant, all she said was, "It's just my actions catching up to me. It will be okay."

I had fully intended to stay by her side, expecting that maybe it was just a quick visit to do further tests. But unfortunately, she was admitted under Doctor Lavings' request.

Now, we have the storm of the year hitting us, two months' worth of rain forecast over the next week. Because of the storm surge, the hospital had told me I was unable to stay past visiting hours but could return tomorrow. Mom promised me all was fine, but being stuck at home was torture. To be on the safe side, we also agreed to cancel the warehouse fights tonight, just to make sure no one was caught out in this weather.

At least she's getting help—that's what I keep reminding myself. After she left, I realized that there was not a single drop of alcohol in the house. The trash bin was piled high with empty bottles and the sink suspiciously smelled of liquor. I'm hopeful that this is a step in the direction of her recovery. I know it's not going to be that easy—demons never are. But she's already faced the biggest hurdle which I'm so immensely proud of.

I'm doom scrolling TikTok to distract myself when a text notification comes up. Flicking open the inbox, I can't help but smile at the words.

Rylan: *I thought you'd be interested to know that I received an email about my wildcat donation. Turns out they were so grateful for my generosity, that they named a baby wildcat after me.*

Rylan: [Picture Attached]

My grin is wide as I open the attachment, spotting the tortoiseshell creature. Even more amusing is the fact that it has striking blue eyes that remind me of Rylan.

Bexley: *There's finally an adorable Rylan in the world. Do you feel fulfilled?*

Rylan: *I feel like my credit company does. What are you up to?*

I wonder if he feels as lost as I do right now. It's been forever since we had to cancel a fight night. And because of the weather, we can't even venture to the beach.

Okay—so, it's a bit of a stereotype, I'll admit. But there's something beautiful about watching two fighters dance around a cage. It's more than just an exchange of blows—it's a performance, using not only your primal senses and strength, but wits. As for the Karen skits, what can I say... It's a weakness. Especially the ones where they get put in their place.

Before I can reply, there's an almighty bang overhead, before the lights flicker twice, and the whole house falls into darkness.

"Shit," I murmur, heart racing. The crash was so loud that lightning must have struck a power station. I hope the hospital has backup generators.

I glance down at my cell to check how much charge I have when it starts ringing in my hand.

There's a small moment of hesitation as I read the name of the screen, but my finger quickly swipes the button.

"Hey," Rylan's voice comes through. "Did you just lose power?"

"Yeah," I answer. "It was pretty loud over here."

He sighs, the sound of him moving around catching my attention. "I tried to keep myself entertained since the fights got canceled, but now that's gone out the window with the power out."

"What were you going to do?" I ask, curious.

"PS5. Hunter, Tai and I were going to play COD."

Snorting, I adjust the pillow under my head. "Typical."

"Says the one scrolling social media."

"Don't diss my hobbies, Rylan. It's *educational*. I was learning a recipe for Boston Cream Pie."

He laughs softly, my ears laser focused on the sound despite the pouring rain and thunder outside. "I hope you plan to share."

"With you?" I question with amusement. "Aren't you worried I'll poison your food?"

"Nah," he answers casually. "Because I'd share my homemade chocolate chip cookies. Sharing is caring."

"Now you're just being mean and pulling my leg," I laugh. "The Rylan Astor does not bake homemade cookies. Or share."

I can just imagine the smug smirk on his face, his tone cocky. "There's a lot you don't know about me, Bex. I might surprise you yet."

You already are.

There's an unshakable urge to slap myself. I hate how easy we can talk in the safety of our own company, away from prying eyes.

Even last night on the rooftop, the tension was palpable, but I didn't feel uneasy at all. Just two leaders, seemingly letting our walls down for a brief minute while we bonded over a common battle.

"I'm surprised you haven't disputed the transaction with your credit card company."

Rylan hums thoughtfully. "I considered it. But given how disadvantaged the wildcats are, I wanted to be nice."

My lips twitch. "How generous of you, Rylan. Did you ever find your pants?"

A pause.

"What do you mean? You stole them when you took my shorts."

I quickly turn my laugh into a cough. "No, no—you're mistaken. I *accidentally* put them into the trash in the locker room. You just had to look."

More silence.

And more.

"What?" he near shouts, just as another block of thunder booms through both sides of the call. "They were there the whole time?"

"Yep," I grin. "I didn't force you into my shorts. You did that all on your own. But side note—why didn't you have underwear in your bag? Probably would have been a better look to stroll out in your jersey and tightie-whities."

Rylan growls low. "Tai bet me that I couldn't run gym while commando. So, I didn't wear any that day."

"Oh, so you *do* own underwear. Good to know," I mock.

There's a split second pause as Rylan's breathing hitches. "I'm wearing boxer trunks right now. In fact, that's the only thing I'm wearing."

"I—"

My sentence disappears mid-thought, the mental image of Rylan in only his boxer trunks appearing in my mind. I've seen all his muscles through his gym shirt, so I know that the guy is packing. And once again, my hormonal brain goes into survival mode as I try to permanently delete that image.

"You're thinking about it right now, aren't you?" he asks incredulously.

"No."

"Bexley," he drawls out. "Are you thinking about me... naked?"

I slap my hand on my forehead, squeezing my eyes closed. "Absolutely not, Rylan Astor. I have zero desires to ever see you naked—or discuss it. Tell me more about your baking skills."

Rylan laughs knowingly. "It's okay. We've all seen your ass hanging out in those shorts. It certainly fucks with the imagination."

"You're a pervert," I snap playfully. "And for your information, I've been trying to search Facebook Marketplace for a new pair since you haven't given mine back."

"If you want them, come and get them."

Shaking my head, I don't bother replying, letting the conversation fall into silence. As if sensing my stubbornness, Rylan clears his throat, tone suddenly weird.

"So..." he starts. "I can also bake brownies."

By morning, there was a small reprieve from the rain as it lingered off the coast for a bit. Using the opportunity like other motorists, I quickly jumped into my truck and went to the hospital to visit Mom.

Rylan and I had talked on the phone for over an hour last night. Once the awkwardness had passed, we found ourselves discussing music. He explained that music was a huge part of running for him, helping him drown out the thoughts and setting pace. Turns out, we had a mutual favorite band and fell down the rabbit hole of talking about the lead singer's recent Instagram post. The cryptic message had left fans scrambling to decode, but Rylan and I both decided that it was an Easter Egg for new music. *Lawless Dragons* often did things like that, to hype up their fandom before a big announcement.

I check my cell for Mom's admission details that she had sent through, following the directions until I reach the second floor of the hospital. I scan the room numbers until I find hers, the door wide open, facing the nurses' station.

"Good morning, sleepyhead," I grin, placing both hands on the doorjamb.

Mom pauses, a spoonful of jelly in front of her face. "Bexie! I didn't think you'd be able to come. The weather is meant to be terrible."

I skip in, leaning down to kiss her forehead. "It's just sprinkling at the moment. The heavy rain is just off the coast. So, I thought I'd come while I had the chance."

She smiles warmly, pushing the Jello tub away on one of those wonky, portable eating tables. "You're in a good mood today," she points out.

"Why wouldn't I be?" I gush. "You're getting better, and things are improving at school."

Her eyebrows shoot up in surprise, and when her eyes widen, it's the first time I spot the jaundice for myself. The sickly yellow color hides under her eyelids, making me feel relieved that she's in here getting help.

"I haven't seen you for one day and already Willowbrook has improved?" she murmurs in disbelief.

I nod, trying to figure out how to explain it. "We've come to an agreement," I say. "A treaty or something."

Mom's face pulls into a look of concentration. "That's good, sweetheart. Just stay on guard. And make sure you are looking after yourself. You spend too much time taking care of other people."

Her statement doesn't miss the mark. I cup her hand softly, settling in the seat next to the bed. "I like looking after you, Mom. You did it for me. That's what family does—through the good and bad times."

"And now I have Sandy to help, so you can focus on you," she muses, tilting her head toward the door.

My eyes fall on the petite nurse, her smiling face full of warmth and fondness at the introduction. I give her a quick wave before nodding toward a stack of papers at the end of the bed. "What's that?"

"It's a surprise," Mom answers with a chuckle. "No looking. Sandra knows she has to guard it too."

"That I do," the nurse laughs, stepping to the other side of the bed to press some buttons on the IV machine. "Top secret stuff."

Our hands squeeze together as I watch the machine pump drugs through the canula. Every time I ask for more information, Mom just smiles and says they are reversing some damage.

Not knowing everything makes me feel uneasy, but I trust her. I know this must be hard, having to face the reality of her spirals. But she has nothing to be embarrassed about. She's a survivor, like me. We'll get through it together.

Hopefully she opens up to me soon. When she comes home, I'm going to do all I can to support whatever option she chooses. Rehab, AA meetings, detoxes, psychiatrists... I'll be there every step of the way. We have so much lost time to make up, and she's not alone.

We have each other, and that's all that matters.

I'll prove to her that love is not the enemy. And that she's stronger than her demons.

Spencers don't go down without a fight.

Chapter Sixteen

Rylan

"I still don't understand why we have to back off," Hunter grumbles at me.

The cafeteria is extra busy today, with most students seemingly hiding inside from the rain. I don't blame them—it's torrential out there. But it makes it a little difficult to have a private conversation. Especially when eyes and ears are always on us here.

The three of us are sitting at our usual table, picking at the trays full of food. My eyes cross the room where Bexley is currently eating with her usual crowd surrounding her.

"I told you. Dad doesn't want to upset his political campaign," I murmur, unable to take my eyes off the purple-haired woman. She laughs at something someone has said, her hand covering her mouth to hide the fact that she's mid chew. She must have painted her nails again on the weekend—this week's color is a vibrant green, and I can't help but wonder if it's partly because of me.

After our chat on Friday night, I woke up yesterday to my socials blowing up with news about Lawless Dragons. Bexley and I were right—they are dropping a new album next month. When they posted the promo for it, I was instantly excited for the neon green and black steampunk vibes.

We spent all Sunday texting about it, sharing snippets of clips that we found online. And now her nails reflect the theme perfectly.

Like Friday, as soon as I met up with Tai and Hunter today, they bombarded me with more questions. When I told them Friday that we would be backing off from Bexley and the other Cedar Heights students, they asked me if I was serious. Well, I believe the words more accurately were, "Are you drunk?". But they settled for the bare minimum explanation when I held them off by saying I'd fill them in later.

And now unfortunately, later has come.

Tai fell on board pretty much straight away, indifferent to it all, even if he was skeptical as to the reasons. But Hunter is still in strong disagreement. Even worse, he's pissed at me for making a call without the input of the other two.

Our little wolf pack has been together for years, and as a courtesy, we agreed that we'd always make decisions as a team—or at least, best two out of three.

So, in Hunter's eyes, I essentially steamrolled them.

"We all know that the campaigns have no influence on votes," Hunter points out in annoyance. "He just doesn't want to piss off the Willowbrook alumni by being caught up in a scandal. This is all about saving face. But it does nothing to help our situation which should be the main focus."

"Look, I know," I sigh. "But our dads are upset. Even George got pulled into it."

Tai shoots me an apologetic look. "Sorry, Ry. On the plus side, he's still in Italy for another week. You can always come to mine if you need a break from Max. You know Mary adores you."

"Mary's the only good thing about your house," I joke. "Oh, and your sister."

"Leave my sister out of this," Tai warns, only half-jokingly. "Or I'll rip your balls off."

Hunter laughs, apparently delighted by the idea of my physical harm. After all, I'm the Brotherhood Betrayer right now. Shit—that would be an awesome name for a Lawless Dragons' song.

"Fuck their reputations," Hunter murmurs, getting us back on track. "Spencer needs to pay for what she did."

My brows pull together while I carefully navigate this. Neither of them knows I've been chatting to Bexley outside of school, or that we met last Thursday night. If they knew, I'd probably be chained to a tree and pelted with rotten fruit or silicone dildos.

"We deserved it," I say without thinking. I didn't mean to say it out loud... Obviously that was the wrong thing to say.

Hunter slams down his hand on the table, startling the people around us. "Fuck that," he growls quietly. "Cedar's little princess needs to stay in her lane. I found a picture of a chair inside my locker this morning with a note asking if the desk was lonely."

Tai snorts, quickly turning it into a cough. "Sorry, man. That sucks."

"Oh, save me the pity, T," Hunter groans. "At least you managed to block those numbers and find the source of your pain."

Grindr.

Yep—Bexley had plastered Tai's burner number onto a fake Grindr profile with the words, '*About to have a hard week. Make it better by sending hard, dripping cock pics. Desperate and needy little slut.*' Once we were able to get the profile taken down, the messages stopped. Though, Tai has made it his personal mission to stalk the Cedar Heights' Facebook group for info and dirty secrets. I'm surprised he hasn't leaked her number in an act of revenge.

But true to her word, no one from Cedar has said anything. The videos they shared inside the group were taken down and Bexley made an announcement post about trying for an amicable environment—though I couldn't help but notice she hasn't disclosed our secret little chats either.

I never thought I'd see the day where I actually enjoyed talking to her, but for some reason, we just click. Hell, in another life, we could probably be friends.

Yes... friends.

Except friends don't get hard thinking about their friends. Let alone their enemies.

What the hell is wrong with me?

Friday night I got carried away. The more playful our banter got, the more my dick started twitching and taking over my rationality. Every time she shot back some witty reply, challenging me, I found myself wondering if that carries over into the bedroom.

Then we got to the part about our attire. When I asked her if she was thinking about me naked, I quickly realized I was in the danger zone—*because I was suddenly thinking about her naked*.

Her soft, pink lips have been my focus all lunch break and I find myself itching to text her; to talk about music or how stupid the pop quiz was this morning.

But Hunter would kill me.

I would probably kill me too. That was essentially social suicide.

We agreed to be amicable at school, but apparently, that means *silence*.

She doesn't look at me. She doesn't speak to me. And she sure as hell isn't picturing me naked.

Yet, as I watch her converse at the cafeteria table, a hand from her boy-toy on her leg, I want nothing more than to go over there and rip it off her. Actually, that's a lie—I want to rip his hand off *his* body so he never touches her again.

"Earth to Rylan." Hunter snaps his fingers in my face, bringing me back to reality. "Why are you staring at their table?"

"Just reminding myself why we have to pretend to like them," I answer monotonously. "Besides, it's just until they leave. We'll still beat their asses on Friday night."

I have no doubt that the warehouse is going to be lit at the end of the week. The rain is making us all a little crazy, and I'm actually considering throwing myself into the ring to blow off some pent up steam.

Tai leans forward, lowering his voice. "We could still mess with her. If we land her back in detention, I could disable the cameras this time."

"No," I quickly reply. Clearing my throat, I elaborate when they both give me puzzled looks. "Okay, look..."

They wait as I take a deep breath and search for my balls.

"I spoke to her Thursday night," I admit, watching as Hunter's mouth falls open in angry disbelief. "People were getting restless, making accusations about us. I was pressured to smooth things over by Dad, but the only way that would work is if Cedar got off our backs too."

"Are you fucking kidding me?" Hunter gapes, clearly outraged and offended by this update. "You struck a deal with Spencer? *That's* why we have to back off?"

I resist the urge to scowl at his accusation—insinuating weakness. "I didn't tell you because I knew we'd end up in an argument. And it was better doing it one on one, instead of all three of us ambushing her."

Tai frowns, looking between us. "I don't know, Ry. I have to admit, I don't like this. I thought it was just because of your dad."

"Neither do I," Hunter agrees angrily. "We were doing damage control. Now people are going to think we're weak for making peace with her."

"That's exactly our problem," I say frustrated. "We need to stop showing that we care. When everyone saw us infuriated by the videos, they doubled down. This is our shot at control again—we show a united front, rising above. The others will fall into line and understand it was a leadership decision.

If we show we're the bigger threat by remaining unfazed, things will go smoothly and give us time to regroup."

"That decision should have come from all of us," Hunter rebuts. "I'm not playing house with Spencer. This is still our territory."

I nod, understanding. "She knows that, Hunter. But things will go a lot more smoothly for us if we play nice. Then, when it's all over and they are out of here, we can attack."

That seems to satisfy him—for now, at least. Though it does nothing to curb the sickening feeling in my throat.

He leans back in his seat, glancing over at Tai. "Any more information on those contacts of hers?"

Tai shakes his head. "I still can't find anything out about Lark Kory. It would be easier to jailbreak into her cell."

"We don't need the info," I exclaim. "Not at the moment, anyway. But I'll work on finding out information."

Hunter narrows his eyes suspiciously at me. "Just how *friendly* are you with Spencer at the moment?"

Too much, Hunter.

Way too fucking much.

This is a mistake.

Anyone could see and then I'll never hear the end of it.

Bexley Spencer has turned me into a damn stalker now.

Instead of going home during last period since I didn't have class, I decided to stake out the grounds, waiting to catch her. I knew from her arrival this morning that she had come alone in her truck, so I stood by the dinged-up, battered old blue thing, hiding out of sight of the main entrance as students flooded out.

My heart jerks when I spot her purple hair emerge, laughing freely with the chief fireman's son, before she waves goodbye and crosses the parking lot.

She gets closer, and just as she pushes her key into the lock barrel, I jump up from the other side.

"Jesus, Rylan!" she squeaks, stumbling back. "What the hell?"

"Sorry," I say sheepishly, offering a small smile. Her bright green eyes glare at me from across the hood, but slowly, they soften.

"I'm in desperate need of caffeine. You can't just scare me like that," she muses.

I raise an eyebrow, lips fighting back a smirk. "I scare you?"

"Very funny," she snaps playfully. "You know I'm not afraid of you."

Leaning against the hood, I strum my fingers along the paint. "I figured you might like your gym shorts back before class tomorrow."

That's a pathetic lie. But it's the best excuse I can come up with on the spot.

Bexley snorts in amusement. "You can keep them," she laughs. "Yours are way more comfortable."

"You like wearing my shorts?" I tease.

She stills before folding her arms. "Are you trying to start shit again?"

"Maybe."

Shaking her head, she unlocks the truck, slipping inside. I watch through the window, happily surprised when she leans over and unlocks the passenger door for me.

I quickly slink inside, leaning back against the old, torn seat. "How about you take these instead?" I say, hating how loud my voice sounds inside the cab now. But if I don't do it now, I'll probably chicken out. Reaching into my bag, I pull out a pair of brand-new Willowbrook gym shorts.

Bexley frowns, flipping over the clear plastic package that's still in my hands. "How did you guess my size?" she asks suspiciously, checking the tag.

"I just went up two sizes from the current shorts," I admit. "I figured you'd want a little room to move around."

"I—," she pauses, brows tugging together. "I'll pay you back."

There's an uncomfortable edge to her voice, one that makes me feel odd. But I swallow it, ignoring the strange feelings. "No need. I didn't pay for them," I lie.

Her eyes switch with uncertainty between the shorts and my face. "Why?"

It's easy to tell that she's not asking about my payment of them, rather, the gesture. Shrugging, I force a look of indifference over my face. "Even though we agreed to a truce, I can't have you wearing my shorts in gym tomorrow. What kind of message would that send?"

I wait for some snarky or witty response, but she just relaxes in her seat, laying the shorts in her lap. "Thank you, Rylan," she says sincerely. "That was really nice of you."

My hand rubs the back of my neck nervously. "It's fine. Just gotta save face."

Bexley starts up the truck, the whole damn thing shaking. I go to exit, taking it as a sign of her dismissal, but she laughs softly, the sound giving me goosebumps.

"Buckle up, Astor."

Chapter Seventeen

Bexley

I must be losing my mind. That would be the only reasonable explanation for what I'm doing. No, seriously... I might need a shrink.

Rylan glances over the front of my house, brows together, intrigued, as I ascend the front steps onto the porch.

"I'll grab your shorts," I tell him, watching as his eyes light up in astonishment. "You can come in if you like."

To be fair, I didn't realize I was going to do this either. My body decided to take charge and bring him here, which is ridiculous if you ask me. That's how all horror movies start.

Without waiting for a response, because I expect him to say no, I walk inside, leaving the door open. Before I can make it down the hallway to my room, the front door closes behind me, and I find Rylan standing inside. His eyes dart around with curiosity, checking out the living room to his left. At least I kept myself busy over the weekend with stress cleaning so it's pretty spotless.

"It's... cozy," he remarks, earning a snort from me.

"Probably tiny in comparison to the mansion you live in," I shoot back. But I'm not bothered by it—I like our house. It holds all my favorite memories, even the ones I try not to think about anymore.

Heading into my bedroom, I grab his gym shorts from atop my dresser, quietly gasping when I nearly bowl him over as I spin around. I didn't realize he had snuck in behind me.

"Nice bedroom," he grins, taking in the light blue walls.

My eyes scan it with his, giving a little shrug in reply. "It's not much but it's my safe space."

I have no idea why I'm telling him anything, or why I brought him here in the first place. This is Rylan Astor we're talking about, for fuck's sake. But still, there's an odd peace in our meetups, and I find myself finally able to drown out my own demons whenever he's around.

"It's nice," he says, eyes lingering on the double bed. "It's definitely *you*."

I'm not sure if he's referring to the purple bedding that matches my hair currently, or the random Lawless Dragons posters on the wall above my desk, but either way, I have to agree with him.

"Here," I tell him, holding out the freshly washed shorts. "Though, I'm sure you own multiple pairs."

Rylan grins, brushing my hands with his as he takes the neatly folded material. "I do. But these are my special pair now."

Oh, shit. The way his eyes are watching me, his words... it's enough to send flutters down my chest into my stomach. I need to control these strange sensations, because even though we agreed to peace, that's all it can be.

That's all we can allow.

Sure, the playful banter is fun. But being friends is not on the cards. Neither of us could survive that. Too many people rely on us, and we'd break a system that has been in place long before we were around.

Clearing my throat, I jiggle my car keys. "I'll drive you back to the school. I assume your car is there."

"It's not," he says quickly through a tight jawline. When he catches me looking at him in sheer confusion, he smiles brightly. "I got a lift with Tai this morning, but he had some errands to run so I said I'd find my own way home."

"Oh," I mutter, caught off guard. "Uh, would you like a lift back to yours?"

Rylan nods. "I'll give you money for gas if you like."

"No, it's fine," I say.

Famous last words.

Because why does it feel like there's alarm bells going off in my head?

I can't help but notice that when I pull into the Astor residence, Rylan's truck is nowhere to be seen. But I don't dwindle on that fact, pulling up at the wide-circular entrance.

There's a little turning bay on the gravel, surrounding a bronze statue of... something. It's very abstract, like the artist just took to the metal with a baseball bat until it warped into an acceptable shape. When I park in alignment to the front door, Rylan looks over from the passenger seat, eyeing me with a hint of uncertainty.

"Would you like to come in? I can give you back the shorts. You might want to use them for other things." There's nothing sinister or mocking about his tone, and for once, I actually find myself amused by his taunts. But seriously, fuck those damn shorts.

Laughing, I reply, "Sure," still questioning if I've left my sanity somewhere.

Turning off the engine, I slip out of the truck, staring at his house.

It reminds me of a large house from a fairytale, vibrant green vines lining the dark, charcoal cottage bricks. The wooden door is polished, reflecting our physiques as we approach.

There's a keypad by the front door, hidden from view by the shrubbery, and Rylan punches in a code without bothering to hide it.

Interesting...

I see the six digits easily, burning them into my mind for some reason. There's a beep of approval, and Rylan pushes open the door, holding it for me.

Stepping inside the entrance, the air whooshes out of my lungs, eyes rising as I take in the structure. It's absolutely beautiful, not like I expected—especially not from someone like Max Astor.

Similar to the outside, the inside is full of classic features, the interior renovated to bring life back to the wooden floorboards and bannisters. Family photos hang on the walls, giving it a homely feel. There are even pictures of Tai and Hunter when the three of them were younger, still looking as suspicious as ever. They were clearly up to no good in the photo, a secret hidden behind their grins.

"My room is upstairs," he says, gesturing for me to follow.

Kicking off my shoes by the door, even though he doesn't ask me to, my feet groan under the soft, plush carpet of the stairs as we ascend. My fingers run along the polished railing as I take note of the large sky-window on the roof. The crystal patterned glass welcomes the afternoon light, and when I reach the landing, I spot large windows at either end of the hall as well.

Rylan takes a right, and just before the glass panel, he stops at a door. Pausing for a moment, he gives me a warm grin, before opening the door.

Instantly, I'm breathless again. His bedroom is light and airy, full of blues and grays. There's a large balcony on the other side of the room, overlooking the front entrance of the grounds.

To my left, there's a large window above his desk, mounted bookshelves full of different kinds of literature. And on the right, his king-sized bed is donned with matte black matching bedding.

It's nothing like I expected, but it's still Rylan-coded.

In an open space between the bed and the balcony door, a 75-inch television is affixed to the wall with floating shelves holding his beloved PS5 in front of two beanbags.

"Your room is amazing," I murmur, glancing around. "I'm just surprised you don't have your own bathroom and staff in here." It's a joke, but Rylan walks back to the door, opening it.

"See that door across from us? That's my bathroom. It also has a walk-in closet attached."

Of course, it does...

Shaking my head, I head over to the beanbags, eyeing the console. "Still playing COD?"

"Yeah," he answers, making me jump when he appears right behind me.

I resist the urge to spin around, grossly aware of how close we are.

"I'll play you sometime," I offer, silently deflecting from the nerves that burn from our close proximity.

Rylan laughs, his breath tickling the back of my shoulders. "Think you can beat me?" he teases.

Finally, I turn around, facing him. There's no way I'm shrinking away from a challenge—even if I've never played COD before in my life. How hard could it be, really?

We're even closer than I imagined, barely three inches between us. My head tilts back so I can find his eyes easily. "Absolutely."

A wicked smile appears on his face. "Care to make a bet?"

"What's in it for me if I win?" I ask.

Rylan leans closer, and for a second, his eyes dart down to my lips. As quickly as it happens, the baby blues shoot back to my eyes. "Whatever you want."

"That's playing a dangerous game, Rylan."

"Maybe I like danger, Bexley."

What the hell are we doing?

So close, I can feel his breath on my lips. I find myself unable to tear myself away, despite knowing that I'm in trouble territory. My body is tense, urging me to reach out and touch him.

Every single reason why I shouldn't be here has vanished, and I'm mesmerized by his eyes and lips, wanting to just brush my fingers along the soft, pink edges to see if they feel exactly like they look.

For the second time today, my body just does what it wants, giving in as my thumb gently strokes his bottom lip for all of about two seconds before Rylan grabs my hand.

"Bex," he murmurs, running his finger along the inside of my wrist. "Don't tempt me. You'll regret the end result."

"And what's the end result?" I ask quietly.

Rylan's eyes darken, a storm brewing behind them. The baby blues become clouded, murky, swirling around as he holds my gaze.

"We'll—"

The words are cut off as his cell rings, the sound of Lawless Dragons' *Imaginary Insanity* blaring. He sighs, but doesn't let go of my hand, digging into his pocket.

"What's up?" he answers, still locking eyes with me.

Slowly, his brow furrows as he listens to whoever is on the other end, before he finally breaks the tension and looks away.

"Alright, I'll see what I can do," he says, hanging up.

Cold reality hits me like ice water, but before I can pull back, he brings my wrist to his mouth, placing a gentle kiss along it. "Duty calls, princess. I'll walk you out."

I don't sleep that night. Not even a wink.

After I left Rylan's house, the two of us continued to text like nothing had happened. But it had.

Something had shifted between us, and being in the unknown was not a place I liked to be.

It takes all my willpower to remember that this could just be a game to him, an excuse to gain leverage. Even when my body urges me to touch him.

Fuck. We almost kissed, I think. It felt like it.

We're not friends. We're still enemies. And even though we agreed on peace, it would be stupid of me to give in to temporary urges.

But also, why? Why do I feel like this?

There's no doubt in my mind that I'm attracted to him. Hell, I'd be crazy to deny the fact that Rylan Astor is gorgeous. They all are. But that's not an excuse to forget about my wits and risk everything.

I paid a quick visit to Mom afterwards, barely escaping the rain as it suddenly returned and pelted down on Ridgeview Valley. We were starting to hit the peak of this terrible weather forecast, and I was thankful for the excuse to stay inside. I tell myself that the rain is the reason I took pity on Rylan and let him get inside my car. As for the gym shorts? I can't explain that. And even more confusing was the new pair that now sit on the top of my dresser staring at me.

It's obvious he paid for them—I saw the receipt in his bag when he pulled them out. But the idea that he's being nice is so foreign to me that I begin to obsess over the reasons as to why he's doing this.

Blackmail. False sense of security. A game.

It can't just be out of the goodness of his own heart. Wolves don't change—all they do is fool people with sheep's clothing.

Pulling the covers over my body, I scroll social media for a bit, noticing that the posts of the fallen kings are becoming less frequent. I had asked everyone from Cedar not to share them anymore, and they hadn't. But in the Willowbrook public pages, a few people were still causing drama, but they quickly vanished, likely on the receiving end of scathing threats.

As darkness takes over my room, my mind is plagued with more thoughts, replaying things over.

I'm going insane searching for reasons, fighting back the feelings of guilty pleasure that want to take charge.

Especially since I keep circling back to one sure thing...

When I left Rylan's and drove to the hospital, I had to pass Willowbrook Academy.

And his truck was absolutely parked in the parking lot.

Chapter Eighteen

The warehouse is packed to the brim. It seems like every student from Cedar Heights and Willowbrook is here.

I'm not sure if it's because we made a display of allyship this past week and people think it's a load of shit and we're going to punch it out, or if they think there's news to be heard. But either way, people can barely move around. It's also Thursday night and I'm certain everyone is keen to blow off some steam before the weekend.

We moved the fights up a night when tension started to bubble over at school. People were getting antsy at the new dynamic, unsure how to react. The atmosphere was intense, and despite rarely holding the fights on a school night, we all agreed it was a good idea.

A fight finishes in the cage, and I clap enthusiastically, poking out my tongue in a mock gesture to Tai as he looks over from the other side of the room with a disgruntled look on his face. We're up three to one so far in the fights tonight, and I just know it's annoying the ever-loving shit out of them.

They can't say I didn't warn them.

The three guys are perched in their usual seats, while I hover and balance on top of a thick plastic barricade to get a better view of the cage from the other side of the room. From here, I have the perfect vantage point over the crowd, the fights, and best of all, I'm directly in the line of sight for Tai, Hunter, and Rylan.

I want them to see me. I've proven time and time again that I'm a force to be reckoned with, and despite their efforts, I'm not going to bow down. There's nothing more pleasing than being a constant reminder of someone's failure when they've tried to break you or make you fall into line.

But still, I find it weird that we're somewhat in *this* place. When Rylan suggested a truce, I could have fallen off the rooftop in shock. I was never going to back down, but if I'm being honest, I never expected him to crack either. I assumed we'd be in a frequent place of tension until we finally got the all-clear to return back to our own school. But his words surprised me. I still have no idea what his motives are, but if it means a better environment for my people, I need to consider their position in all this.

Two more people climb into the cage and the crowd in front of me starts to murmur. Of course, I knew what was scheduled, but for the majority of the folks here, no one knew he was going to fight tonight—or ever.

It's Parker's first time in the ring. He came to me yesterday, begrudgingly asking to fight. When I pressed for the reason, it turns out Millie is closer to breaking him than I thought.

Finally, he agreed she could fight but *only* after he tried it himself first.

To be fair, I know Parker's a protective big bro, but he and Millie are two peas in a pod. They both have wild personalities, and I can tell he's been keen to jump in for some time now. But he swallowed those urges, knowing full well that she'd lose her crap if he got to do it and she didn't.

Right on cue, Millie pushes her way through the crowd toward me, and before she can even open her mouth, I move to the side and motion for her to join me on the barricade. While I want a premium view, even in the crowd I'd be able to watch it relevantly easily. But my fun-sized shadow will never be able to see past all the heads.

"Thanks, boss," she grins, keeping her balance as she turns to face the cage.

I cringe. "Bex is fine," I say with amusement. "How are you feeling?"

Millie shrugs, the two of us watching as Parker stretches his arms. "Scared."

"Really?" I ask, surprised. "Scared for Parker?"

She shakes her head, a smirk appearing on her face. "Scared for the other guy."

A laugh bubbles out of me just as the bell rings. Parker instantly tenses for a quick second, but it's not with trepidation—it's the urge to control himself. The other guy from Willowbrook juggles his fists clumsily in front of his face, egging Parker on. Stupid move. I can already tell how this is going to go down. I don't need to have seen Parker's moves to know how good he is. The tall, bulky guy in white has already made it clear that he's too hot-heated to be in the ring. It's easy to pinpoint how good a fighter is based on their pre-fighting behavior. Of course, the logic doesn't always fit, but most of the time, especially in young males, their egos do all the talking.

Neither make the first move straight away. Parker raises his fists, but they are steady, covering his face if Ego-man decides to suddenly take a surprise swing. They play a game of chicken for a few seconds before the latter rushes forward, aiming straight for Parker's face. Rookie move. He's got that area protected, so Parker easily blocks him.

Ego-man appears stunned for a moment that his hit didn't land, angrily moving forward again. Even though his strategy didn't work the first time, the imbecile tries the exact same maneuver. To no one's astonishment, he misses again when Parker blocks, but this time, a return fist comes in his direction. Ego-man is too distracted and gobsmacked by his failure that he doesn't bother to block.

Next to me, Millie laughs manically, clearly pleased at herself for being right. I give her a playful shove with my elbow, grinning at her to behave.

I turn back to the cage just as Parker's fist connects with his opponent's cheek, and without giving him a second to recover, more blows swing out. Two, three, four—and on the fifth punch, Ego-man's eyes roll into the back of his head, his entire body stumbling backward into the cage wall.

From this angle, Millie and I have a perfect view, and my face scrunches up as I anticipate what's about to happen.

Ego-man falls into the fencing, his weight sending the rusty material barreling into the crowd along with himself.

People quickly scatter out of the way as he crashes through, no one bothering to try to catch the heavy, fallen fighter. He lands like a sack of bricks in the middle of the two cohorts and I watch as a few people from Willowbrook circle around to check on him. The three guys are on their feet too, watching with concern and frustration, and someone raises a hand, giving them a thumbs-up to signal their buddy is okay.

I feel his eyes on me before I see them myself. When I glance back over, Hunter is glaring at me. If I've learned anything about him recently, it's that he's a competitive little shit just like me. No doubt our four to one scorecard is bruising their egos after their confident word vomit earlier today.

And now, we have to call it a night. It's been a long-standing rule that the fights will only happen if the cage is enclosed. From previous experiences, accidents, like what just occurred, mean that innocent spectators get caught in the crossfire. They didn't consent to a fight therefore they shouldn't get injured from one. So, we're now on hiatus until we can rectify the damage.

Archie pushes his way through the crowd with Abby by his side, grinning from ear to ear. "Another victory, I guess," he shouts over the noise of the crowd.

I nod, offering a hand to Millie as Archie does the same. She grabs both of them for leverage, jumping to the ground.

"Told ya," she cackles, heading straight toward Parker who's climbing out of the cage.

She disappears in the crowd, and I jump to the ground myself, giving Abby a quick nod in greeting before turning to Archie. "They are pissed."

"Yep," he agrees. "Astor apparently wagered a huge bet that they were going to win tonight."

"It's cute that they were so confident," I smile, watching as people start moving toward the exits. "You realize we're going to have to let Millie fight next time."

Archie pulls Abby closer to his side as a group of people swarm past us. He keeps his eyes on me, almost like it was a natural instinct to protect her, one he did subconsciously. But with his attention focused on me, I get the privilege of seeing Abby's face light up with the same realization, her head turning to glance up at him, dare I say it... *lovingly*.

You know what else is cute? Seeing Archie so protective of his girl—the very one he's been pining over for years. And knowing that it's reciprocated means everything to me. If anyone deserves happiness, it's Archer Roberts.

"Ha, yeah," he says with a chuckle. "Parker had to have known that this would be the outcome. He's not the lose willingly type."

"I think he just wants to make her happy," I answer, shooting him a knowing look as my eyes drift to his arm around Abby's waist.

The both of them pick up on my vibe and suggestive words, cheeks turning red. I'm sure they want to lie and blame the almost unbearable heat in the warehouse—I'll pretend that's the reason too.

Giving them a wave of my hand, I glance over the crowd. "You guys head on out. I need to go speak to the Three Mus-keteers. You know what the rules say—we need to decide who's responsible for payment to fix the cage."

Archie hesitates for a moment. "I can come with you if you like," he offers.

"It's fine," I say, unfazed. "Go head to the beach with everyone else. I'll be there soon."

He nods, grinning down at Abby. "What do you say, baby girl? Ready to go?"

Abby smiles at him, my heart doing that weird melting thing again at the gesture. "Ready if you are, Sagg."

"Sagg?" I blurt out, trying to fight back a smile.

Archie blushes again but Abby beams at me. "Like *Sagittarius*," she says proudly. "Since that's his star sign and his name is—"

"Archer," I finish for her, holding back a laugh at his sudden shyness. "I like it."

"What's your star sign?" she asks excitedly. "I like comparing notes, just for the fun of it."

This time, I can't hide the grin from my face. She's so bubbly and happy—it's a contagious vibe. "Aquarius."

Her mouth forms an *O* shape as she nods with wide eyes. "Independent, loyal, logical, rebellious... and detached. Checks out."

"What?" I laugh. "Those are my traits?"

Archie clears his throat. "Well, I mean..." he trails off, smirking smugly.

"I'm not..." I start, ready to defend myself as I run through her list in my mind. "Wait..."

Abby waves her hand at me, trying to dismiss my train of thoughts. "Aquarians are good people. Natural born leaders and very smart."

"Okay, now you're just trying to suck up," I scold playfully. "Off you go, you pair of lovebirds."

They both laugh, giving me a wave goodbye as they disappear into the departing crowd. I lean against the plastic barricade as I wait for everyone to leave, making a mental note to ask Abby what her star sign is next time. My gaze flickers over to the other side of the room and for a brief second, I can't help but wonder what *their* star signs are.

Wait, what? I must be losing my mind. I don't care about them that much, or at all. Plus, I already *know* their personality traits. They are grade-A assholes with a complexity problem. Not to mention competitive, deviant, and lacking the smallest measurement of compassion between the three of them.

That's the story I'm going with—yep. And I certainly haven't rubbed my wrist a hundred times this week where Rylan placed a kiss in his bedroom.

This week has been oddly peaceful despite the growing tension, and I've been finding myself in constant daydreams, thinking about our encounter on Monday.

The past few days I've made sure to keep clear, not fully trusting myself to be near him. He has a habit of bringing my guard down. But we've still texted, talking about our usual things and exchanging quirky little details about ourselves in conversation. Like for example, Rylan hates the texture of Styrofoam. If he can avoid touching it, he will at all costs. And I stupidly admitted to him that the first—and only—time I walked the canyon trail, I was so exhausted that I accidentally flashed an entire group of tourists when I stumbled over my own feet.

It takes around ten minutes for everyone to disperse out of the warehouse, and when it falls deathly quiet, I realize how unusual this feels. We're the only four people left in this big room. Ego-man is the last to go, slumped over the shoulder of a football player, mumbling to himself with a clear concussion.

The three of them are watching me from across the room, and I know we're playing chicken again. They want me to come to *their side*.

Echoing my thoughts, Rylan lifts a hand, beckoning me with his index and middle fingers, a wicked smirk on his face.

I scoff, dramatically loud for effect, and cross my arms as I fight back a smile. "Why don't you come here?" I yell, internally cringing at how loud my voice sounds now that the room is empty.

"Easier if you come here," Tai shouts back. "There's only one of you."

Shaking my head with a little huff, I concede—but only because realistically it makes sense, much to my disgust. But also, I'm not afraid to step into their territory. Yes—that's the reason. Not because my body begs to get closer to Rylan.

Their eyes stay trained on me as I cross the room, and when they sit back down in their makeshift thrones, I roll my eyes. "Really?" I ask, pausing in front of them.

"What?" Rylan asks, feigning innocence. "Just resting our legs. We did a lot of standing."

"You did a lot of losing," I shoot back with a smug look. "In many ways. Lost some money, did you?"

Rylan's jaw tenses up, but it's Hunter who speaks next.

"Enough. I already have a headache forming and don't need you to add to it."

"Am I a headache?" I ask sweetly. "Shame."

Hunter stands suddenly, jumping down from the platform. "Let's just get this over with. You need to cover the costs."

"Me?" I repeat, somewhat offended by his demand. "It was your guy that destroyed it."

He shrugs. "Take the win and take the fall, Duchess."

My teeth grind together. They know very well that we don't have access to money as easily as they do.

"No."

Hunter's eyes flash dangerously. He takes a step toward me, and I tip my chin up, holding his gaze. "No?"

"Did I stutter, Hunter?"

"Fix it or else," he threatens.

I can't resist the urge. "Or what?"

"You're on our tuff, Duchess," he says, riling me up again with the nickname. "We'll move the fights to Willowbrook grounds. I'm sure I can swing my father's approval—it's convenient, after all. Since we're all there together anyway. I hold no guilt about having a home ground advantage."

"Do you really think your father is going to let you move the fights to his precious school?" I taunt. "Please—I see right through your bluff. We're *riff-raff* to him. It would draw attention from the authorities."

Hunter steps closer again. Our chests touch as he gets right in my face, unwavering. "He might be the dean but he's a Willowbrook Wolf through and through. He'd be willing to turn a blind eye if it meant putting you in your place."

I ignore the personal threat to his statement, raising an eyebrow. "Given Mayor Astor's current position in this town, I'm not the least bit surprised to hear that your father is corrupt. I bet they are in bed together too."

"Watch it, Spencer," Rylan growls from behind him.

Hunter shakes his head slowly, lips pulling up. "At least I have a father, Duchess. Mine actually stuck around for me."

Okay, fuck the personal attack on me before. *That* was uncalled for.

Since I can't slap or punch him from this angle, I have little choice but to just shove him back, trying to disperse some of this built-up frustration. My hands connect with his chest as I throw my weight through my palms.

Hunter stumbles back from the force since he has no time to prepare and find balance. Immediately, any sense of control and equilibrium he had vanishes from his face, rage taking its place.

"You fucking bitch," he snaps, lunging forward.

His hand wraps around my throat, squeezing all the air out of my body. I throw my hands up, one to his wrist and the other to his neck, digging all my nails in as I choke him back. We must look quite the sight, the two of us trying to dominate the other with mutual choke holds.

"Okayyyy," Tai says in a sing-song tone, jumping off the platform. "Let's chill, yeah? We're getting off topic. How about Hunter and I head home, and Rylan, you can sort this out?" He pushes in between our bodies, forcing us both to let go of the other.

Hunter and I glare at each other heatedly, neither backing down. There's a jingle of metal and a flash of silver as Rylan throws a set of car keys to Tai.

"I've got this," Rylan murmurs to Tai, the sound of his landing reaching my ears. He steps in front of me, blocking Hunter from view. "Come on, firecracker. Let's go negotiate."

Chapter Nineteen

Bexley

"I don't understand why negotiations need to happen outside," I grumble, following Rylan as we exit the warehouse.

After Tai and Hunter left, he took one quick glance at the broken cage before declaring we should step outside. How on earth he intends to figure out costs without properly assessing the damage, I'll never know.

"Inside is where we fight," he answers simply. "We're not going to do that—though maybe we should considering what you just said about my father in there."

I roll my eyes in a useless attempt at masking my guilt, wrapping my arms around my body as the night chill hits me. It's not a cold evening by any means, but after being in a stuffy warehouse with lots of warm bodies, it takes a moment to adjust.

I hate that I feel guilty—and I hate it more that it's only due to the fact that Rylan has managed to get under my skin recently. Despite my better instincts, I *care* about hurting him with my words.

"Maybe Hunter shouldn't have said what he did," I shoot back softly.

As I glance over to Rylan for his reaction, I'm surprised to see him nod in agreement.

"We should save the personal taunts for the school grounds."

And yep—there it is. For a second, I thought he might actually have a heart or conscience. That would have been a bizarre plot twist.

My eyes scan the empty parking lot, my response forgotten. "Ah, shit," I whisper to myself.

"What is it?" Rylan asks, pausing to look at me.

There's only one car left—and it's not mine. I clearly didn't think this through.

"I rode with Archie," I murmur, reaching into my pocket for my cell. "I'm just going to give him a quick call to come back for me and then we'll settle the cage issue."

"No need," Rylan says without missing a beat. "I'll give you a ride. I owe you one anyway."

Opening Archie's contact information, I shake my head with a laugh. "No, it's okay. If we get into an accident, it's better if our bodies aren't discovered together."

"Suit yourself," he shrugs, digging his hands into his pocket as he gives me a wonky grin. "But the offer is there. God—are you always this uptight when someone tries to do something nice for you? Just say thank you like the other day and accept the help."

Pausing over the dial button, I glance over at him with a witty smile. "Only when there's likely an ulterior motive. Don't pretend the *offer* is out of the goodness of your heart—you don't have one when it comes to negotiations."

"I keep the goodness limited to other body parts to make up for my lack of cardiovascular organs," he replies swiftly.

My cheeks heat up, mind drifting as I try *not* to figure out what body parts he's referring to. "I'm not budging on negotiations just because you are giving me a ride."

His eyes light up in amusement. "So, I *am* giving you a ride now?"

Fuck me. Remain focused, Bex. Just because this asshole insists on making sexual jokes constantly, it doesn't mean I need to fall down that rabbit hole too—I'm not Alice in Wonderland.

"Consider it your consolation prize. You lost the fights tonight, so you get my amazing company for a few minutes. How is your car even still here?" I ask, changing the subject. "Didn't you give your keys to Tai?"

"I gave Tai's keys to Tai. We came in two separate cars—the smart method for situations like this."

I lock my cell screen and slip it into my pocket. "A perk to having to share your kingdom," I snort. "Options."

"There's nothing wrong with not wanting to be alone," he says softly, surprising me. My body stills as I tilt my head up, frowning slightly.

"What is that supposed to mean?" I ask, immediately going on the offensive. "Another daddy joke coming in the punchline?"

Rylan's face falls flat. "I just mean there's nothing wrong with sharing strength and having trust in others. You might think that we are weak for being a team, but you'd be wrong."

I'm hit with a wave of exhaustion as the long day finally starts to get to me. I stopped at the hospital after school and promised Mom I'd go back to visit her after the fights were done and I'd stopped at the beach to check on everyone. I'm wasting time and bed is calling my name. Visiting hours will be over soon and now that the electric energy from the fights has departed, I'm crashing fast.

"Let's just get this over with," I murmur, walking toward his truck.

The sound of keys jingling reaches my ears before the lights flash orange as the vehicle unlocks. Rylan walks next to me as I step up to the passenger door, and for a moment, I almost think he's going to open the door for me, but he quickly pivots and heads to the driver's side.

Slipping into the car, I silently curse him for his cab being nicer than mine. I'm thankful to even have a vehicle that gets me around but damn it—these seats are comfy as fuck after a long day.

Rylan leans back, dropping the keys onto the dash. "We doing this here or on the drive?"

"Here, I guess," I answer. It's already embarrassing that he has to give me a lift. At least if we talk now, I can jump out of the truck as soon as we arrive at the beach. If I linger to chat, everyone will ask questions. Best to save that for text messages, away from prying eyes and ears. And where I can hide behind a screen.

"Alright," he says, twisting his body more towards me. "How much damage do we think there is?"

An exhausted laugh escapes from my throat. "You didn't give me time to check. But to be fair, it depends on how we want to rebuild it. I could probably source some second-hand material."

Rylan nods, contemplating my offer. "Personally, I think it would be better if we rebuilt the entire cage with new material. Otherwise, we'll just be back here again in a month of two."

"I know," I sigh, running a hand through my hair. "But it would cost a small fortune. We're not the UFC. I can ask around if anyone is willing to donate, but truthfully, we're hard pressed with our current situation. Students are already out of pocket at Willowbrook with having to buy new textbooks and supplies for stuff we didn't already have because of the fire."

"How about this?" he straightens up, like he's in a professional corporate meeting. "Willowbrook will cover the cost of a new cage, but you have to offer us something in return."

I raise an eyebrow. "And what would that be?" I ask, warily. "What could we possibly have that you want?"

"The beach," he suggests. "You let us use the beach every weekend for the next month or so until the cage is fixed. And," he pauses. "You have to tell everyone how *nice* I am."

Laughing at the stupid grin on his face, I shake my head. "Hard pass, Rylan. Beach I'll consider, but nice? I don't like lying."

"You wound me, Spencer."

"You'll survive," I smile. "You don't have a heart so I can only assume you're unkillable. Not that I haven't thought about it."

Rylan slaps his hand on the steering wheel with a chuckle, his silver rings reflecting the moonlight. "Fine," he concedes. "But you have to give us a proportion of your votes at the next town election."

The smile wipes off my face faster than a speeding bullet. "You're kidding."

"Just a percentage," he says. "I'll even let you pick it. If you're confident in your numbers, then it should be a sure thing."

"Zero is a percentage," I argue back.

"Has to have value otherwise the deal is worthless. Whole numbers too—don't be trying to pull a fast one on me with some bullshit decimal crap."

I run through my numbers again, like I have done a hundred times, counting all the new voters and weighing them up against the margin from last time. If I factor in a percentage of new voters for them too, I'm *fairly* confident we have the numbers. For some reason, we had a Cedar baby boom eighteen years ago—probably from all the giddiness of kicking Willowbrook's ass that year.

Dad used to love boasting about it, often telling me stories of his earlier days. You know, before he became a coward and took off without even saying goodbye.

"One percent of the new voters," I finally answer. "And you can't take your sweet time with the cage. It has to be done reasonably quick—we have a reputation to uphold. Plus, everyone will be antsy at having to wait to fight again."

Rylan runs his tongue over the back of his teeth, seemingly biting back a remark about his loss tonight. "Fine. No more than a month, beach is ours every Saturday until then, one percent of votes, and you don't have to tell people I'm nice. But I would appreciate it if you didn't tell them that I started at some ridiculous number like fifty percent of votes. I can't have them thinking I'm a pushover."

I laugh, holding out my hand. "Alright, deal. But you can't tell people I'm a pushover either. I might be alone, but I got here for a reason."

It's not a lie. I did get here because of a very good reason. But they can't ever know my pain, not to that level. Everyone might know I have daddy issues, but at the end of the day, I earned my place. I worked hard, fought with my life, and survived. My father doesn't get to steal that from me. He doesn't get to take my moment and diminish my credit.

"Deal," Rylan replies, shaking my hand.

Our joined palms stay connected, neither of us moving. That niggling feeling returns, the one that I've been trying to fight the past week.

I hate seeing this side of Rylan—because I can't *hate* it, no matter how much I try. I've spent my entire life being trained to hate them all, swearing to uphold our rivalry and believing they were nothing but assholes in flashier uniforms. We're not supposed to humanize them—not like this.

He pulls his hand back slightly but doesn't let go. My skin tingles when his finger caresses over my palm, our eyes locked. Neither of us move and before I realize I'm doing it, my palm curls inwards, our hands holding one another.

I need to let go; to remind him I've got places to be and to start the truck. But it's as if I'm having an out of body experience, frozen in place.

Rylan squeezes my hand, warmth spreading through me as he runs his thumb over the tops of my knuckles. "You know I still hate you, right?" he asks softly.

The words *should* jolt me back to reality, but his tone overwhelms my senses, and all I can do is nod once in response.

"I hate you too," I murmur, matching his timbre.

"Good," he breathes out in relief.

Before I can question the sudden change of topic, he slides forward across the seats, cupping the back of my neck and yanking me forward. I barely have time to register the movement before he presses his lips to mine. And instantly, my mind shatters into a thousand tiny pieces.

Sparks fly through my body as our lips touch, and I can no longer find a sensible reason to run. I'm sure it's there, lurking with my rationality and sanity, but the way our lips feel together, it's indescribable. I've kissed my fair share of men, but it's never felt like *this*.

It's saccharine and deadly. I can taste a hint of beer on his tongue while traces of wood and citrus linger around, overpowering me. And worst of all, probably the most dangerous part, is I feel *wanted*.

There's something about your enemy crumbling, abandoning his feelings and beliefs, that shatters my world and everything I know.

Rylan's tongue moves against mine, my body pressing snugly against his. His arm snakes around my body and he pulls me off the seat, hoisting me into his lap. My knees crush the soft seat underneath us as I straddle him. A moan frees itself from my body when his lips move to my jawline, finding a new home on my neck. He sucks and kisses my skin as his hand disappears under my shirt, stroking the small of my back.

I cup his head, holding it firmly enough in my grasp but not enough that he can't change direction. And he does just that, hot kisses moving to my clavicle as he pulls my jersey to the side to expose my skin.

"Rylan," I moan his name, eyes fluttering closed as his tongue traces my collarbone.

"Fuck," he whispers against my shoulder. "Say it again. *Say my fucking name.*"

My pussy clenches at his demand, his name slipping from my lips again without protest. He growls under his breath, hastily removing his hand from my back to slide it over our thighs.

Pushing his fingers against the front of my ruffled beach shorts, I gasp as an electric charge shoots up my body. Rylan massages my clit through the black flowy material while my head falls back.

Purple locks of hair cascade down my back and he scrunches them in his fist, yanking my head back once in warning before jerking me back upright. "Look at me, Bex. I need to see your eyes."

As soon as our gazes meet, he slips his hand under and up the loose leg of the shorts and shoves my hipsters to the side. I get all of a second to prepare before his thumb directly connects with my clit. His eyes flare at the same time as I let out a soft moan.

"Don't you dare look away from me," he breathes, sliding his fingers lower until they are pressing against my entrance. "I want to remember the expression on your face when I feel you for the first time."

First time...

The way it sounds, it's as if he intends to do this again. He could have just left it at *feel you*, but he didn't.

The thoughts are cut short when he slips his finger into my warmth. There's barely any light in the parking lot, but I swear his baby blue eyes suddenly look darker again. The cool metal of his rings do nothing to alleviate the hypersensitivity I'm feeling as he pumps his finger in and out slowly.

"Was it exactly as you had hoped?" I ask breathlessly, keeping my eyes on him.

Rylan smiles coquettishly. "Everything and more. But there's still a few more I need to see before I'll be satisfied."

"Oh, yeah?"

"I need to eternally memorize your face when *I'm* inside you and when you clench my cock as you come."

He lets out a groan when I give him a part-preview, my body tensing around his finger at his words.

"If we're doing it in that order," I murmur, sliding my hand next to his as I firmly massage his erection through his shorts. "Then you better hurry up and fuck me."

Rylan rips his finger out of me as his other hand moves up my pantleg to grasp the material between my thighs. The sound of fabric tearing renders me momentarily speechless as he turns my shorts into a skirt. The two of us suddenly turn simultaneously feral, a flurry of hands between our bodies working together to free the other from the confines of fabric prison. In the back of my mind, I vaguely recognize the sound of my cell slipping out of my pocket and onto the floor, but I don't care.

I tug down his zipper and pull his cock out of his shorts, only briefly acknowledging that he's bare under his shorts—just like *him*. I run my fingers over the smooth skin at the base before gripping his length firmly in my hand.

Rylan lets out a groan and when his head falls back, I grab his jaw, angling his face toward me. "Look at me, Rylan," I command, repeating his words. Blue eyes sizzle back at me with astonishment, and he crashes his lips into mine, blatantly ignoring my request. But I let it slide because his hand perches itself on the small of my back again, holding me upright as his other palm covers mine. He guides my hand up his length twice before positioning himself against my wet core as he pushes my hipsters aside.

"We can go back to hating each other tomorrow," he says with a gravelly voice, pressing the tip inside and making me bite back a moan. "But for right now, you're mine, Bex."

"You wish, Astor," I manage to mumble, tongue-in-cheek as I roll my hips.

He gives me an impish grin, and I start to slide down his length slowly with the mission to torture him. But Rylan has other ideas, thrusting up into me and burying himself until I'm sat back in his lap.

"Fuck," he drawls out, hands digging into my waist.

It's an instant wave of euphoric pressure as my body quickly adjusts to accommodate him. He's thick—like his ego—and just as generous in length. But he feels perfect, even if I need a moment to breathe through the way he stretches me.

I grab his face, bringing his soft, pink lips to mine as I start to lift myself up. His hands stay put on my waist, but he lets me have this moment of control as I set the tempo.

I'm falling apart inch by inch and when his fingers press harder into my skin, strong enough to leave bruises, I know he's fighting the same losing battle too.

"Fuck me, Rylan," I breathe into his mouth. "I'm yours."

I've never said anything like that before to anyone, my sense of self control vanishing in the cab. But he doesn't allow time for regret to sink in, his resolve snapping at my words. His hips spear up hard with precision.

I cry out against him, his tongue pushing into my mouth and silencing me. It takes all my strength to battle his tongue with my own as his cock plunges into me, over and over.

We're in a fog—in every sense—as my mind becomes a daze and the windows and windshield mist over.

My body starts to pulse around him and suddenly, he pulls back from the kiss, grabbing my face with his hands.

"Come for me, Bex," he demands. "Keep those pretty green eyes on me."

Our hips are molded together, his smooth skin rubbing mercilessly against my clit. I fall over the edge a few seconds later, screaming his name as my eyes roll into the back of my head, cunt clenching him so tight we might be stuck as one from this moment on.

"Fuck," he breathes out quietly before his tone does a sudden one-eighty. "FUCK!"

His hips slap against mine violently, jolting my body off his by a good few inches as he lets out a loud, guttural groan as he finds his release. I fall against his chest as his body shudders.

Exhaling unsteadily, Rylan runs his hand through his hair, trying to catch his breath. I'm entranced by the look of contentment on his face. His eyes are closed as he takes a moment to recover, before finally, I'm staring back into clear blue eyes.

Rylan scans my face for a few seconds, searching for something before he cracks a small smile. "Dammit," he says under his breath, leaning forward to kiss me again.

I kiss him back, mumbling against his lips. "I really hate to be this girl..." I trail off.

"Yeah, I know," he responds defeatedly, pulling back. "I better get you to the beach before Cedar sends out a search party."

"Actually," I say hesitantly, hoping I don't regret my words. "Think you can give me a lift to the hospital?"

Chapter Twenty

"Hey, Sandra!" I greet, horribly overcompensating my tone with warm pleasantries to mask my physical dishevelment. "Sorry I'm a bit later than usual. I hope you don't mind me visiting now. I know visitor hours have finished for the night."

Sandra peers up from the nurses' station, eyes wide at my flustered appearance. "Bexley—you're here."

"Of course I'm here," I say awkwardly with a dry laugh. "I said I'd be back to see her. I just got caught up with some stuff. How's Mom doing?"

Thankfully, Rylan didn't question why I wanted to go to the hospital, but he did crack some joke about me needing medical attention after what we did in his truck. I slammed the door shut in his face after he muttered the words '*ice pack*'.

Shit—that reminds me. I need to message Archer and let him know I'm not coming to the beach. Reaching into the pockets of my shorts—wait, skirt now—I tense up when I realize my cell isn't there. Double shit... I must have left it in

Rylan's truck after it fell out of my pocket. I'm sure Archie will be fine. I'll use Mom's cell to message him. *Mom...* I quickly turn my attention back to Sandra when I realize my thoughts drifted because she never responded to my question.

My eyes glance over at the door across from the desk, frowning. It's partially open, the bed shielded from view, but from this angle I can see the shelves that line the wall of the room. All Mom's belongings are gone, including the flowers I dropped off this morning.

"What the—" I mutter, stepping toward the room, feet near stumbling over themselves.

"Wait, sweetheart," Sandra shoots out in a desperate plea. "We tried to call you."

I push the door open without stopping for her, eyes falling onto the empty bed. It's made perfectly with fresh sheets—and no sign of Mom or her belongings anywhere.

"Where is she?" I ask, fighting back the urgency and nerves. Spinning around, I find the nurse that has brought me so much comfort recently. "Sandy, what's going on? Did they move her?"

Sandra braces herself against the doorframe, the look on her face sending every single nerve in my body into a full-blown panic. "We tried to call you," she repeats softly.

Nothing happens immediately because my brain refuses to connect the dots. "My cell—I left it in his... someone's car," I fumble over my words, pausing as I shake the thoughts and get back on track. "Where is she? Where is my mom?"

"I'm so sorry, sweetheart. She passed away about an hour and a half ago."

My heart clenches painfully in my chest. She's lying. She has to be. I just saw her a few hours ago. Mom wasn't doing great today, but she was sitting up and talking to me, joking about this stupid weather. The past week I finally saw the old version of her—happy and content, smiling like she wasn't destroyed four years ago. Like she hadn't wasted the last few years of her life, shattering all she worked hard for because one man decided to do irreparable harm. Besides, she was only in the hospital for monitoring... for a few tests. Wasn't she?

Oh, my fucking God.

It isn't until Sandra lets out a squeak and pain radiates up my legs that I've realized I've fallen to my knees. My hands reach out in front of me, pressing flat against the hospital floor, lungs struggling to take in oxygen as I start to get light-headed. "She's dead?" I whisper, failing to choke back a small sob.

This can't be right... The hospital was only temporary. We had a plan. She was going to come home and get help. She was going to get better. I have pamphlets of AA meetings and detox programs on the kitchen table waiting for her. *We had a plan.*

We had a fucking plan. It was going to change everything.

"Let's get you into the chair," she says, grabbing my arm.

"No!" I yell, making her jump. "I need... I need to get out of this room."

Pushing myself to my feet, I bolt past her. She calls out to me, begging me to stop but I ignore her, not bothering to wait for the elevator.

I sprint down the stairwell of the emergency exit as spots start to appear in the corners of my eyes.

I can't breathe. Why can't I breathe?

People stare at me with alarm and disapproval as I rush through the main reception of the hospital, not stopping until my feet hit the asphalt outside. Rain patters the ground, coming seemingly out of nowhere again. Large droplets start to soak me as I hunch over, bracing my hands on my knees.

She can't be gone. I just saw her. We had finally reconnected—exactly what I had wished for so long. She was battling her demons, ready to face life again.

We. Had. A. Plan.

Suddenly, it's like a brief second of clarity, my mind replaying the last few minutes. Sandra's words circle back through my mind, and I clutch onto the only tidbit of information that I deem important.

"She passed away about an hour and a half ago."

I'm nearly two hours late, held up by.... I can't bring myself to admit the words. I was in such a foreign, peaceful daze in Rylan's truck, the two of us chatting easily like we aren't mortal enemies. It was *something...* an intense feeling I've never experienced before. But if the cage hadn't broken and I hadn't gotten into a heated argument with Hunter, I wouldn't have ever been in his truck. I would have gone to the beach like I planned and been here on time.

I would have been with her in her final moments.

Sobs break out against my will, my frame heaving as I fight the wave of heaviness that threatens to send me to the ground again.

Forcing myself upright, I choke back the tears as I do what I've always done best. I push all the emotion away, compartmentalizing it until I'm nothing but a numbed, soaked mess on the curb.

My feet start walking on their own accord, my body no longer feeling the cold rain as I start the trek home in the dark. Cars pass without a care in the world, and it dawns on me the sickening realization that the world keeps turning. Just like when Dad left. Even at fourteen, I understood that life can be cruel, but I forced myself to turn off the grief, pushing on like it didn't tear me apart.

But...

I did that for *her*. It was never for me. I just knew I needed to step up, to care for her like she had done for me all of my life. That's what love is—it's about sacrificing your needs when someone you care about has greater ones. And now, I have nothing—no one.

They still need you, Bexley... You have to push it aside. Don't give up. Don't let this drown you. You're stronger than your demons and worst nightmares.

Getting home is an eerie daze. By the time I open the front door, completely drenched from head to toe, I have no recollection of my journey home, and it hits me again that I'm alone.

Did she lie? Did she know she was dying? Is that why things changed?

Was I not enough in life but I was in death?

The house is unnaturally quiet, and my feet automatically carry me to her bedroom door. Every time it was quiet in the past, I would find her here, sleeping peacefully. But now, her empty bed stares back at me, sending me spiraling into the icy cold grips of reality. The room still smells of her floral perfume, a pile of her clean clothes yet to be put away on the end of the mattress.

I slam the door shut when I can't bear to look at her room anymore, the hinges rattling with the force. Turning, I go to my bedroom, letting my body take the lead in autopilot mode while my brain shuts down and blacks out. And after that, it all becomes a blacked-out blur, and I remember nothing.

"Bex," Archie says, frowning from his seat beside me in American Lit. "Are you okay? You're... I don't know. You seem different today. And you never made it to the beach last night. I tried to call."

"I'm fine," I mutter quietly, cracking a forced smile. "Negotiations just took longer than expected and then it started raining again so I figured it was best to head home. I didn't sleep much so I'm just tired today."

Archie nods, his worrisome expression not faltering. "Alright..." he concedes. "You'd tell me if something was wrong, right? I can cancel my date with Abby tonight if you need anything."

My body jerks with a silent, sarcastic laugh that I quickly shove back down. I know he's asking about the negotiations—assuming something must have gone wrong since I never showed or answered any calls. Everyone probably just assumes we had a classic Bexley-Rylan fight and left it at that. They have no idea that the complete opposite happened in his car before he dropped me off at the hospital where everything went to shit.

"Everything is fine," I repeat, attempting to placate him. "Go on your date, Arch. It's been a long time coming. And you don't have to worry about the Willowbrook bastards."

A few people hear us, whipping their heads to glare at me, their white jerseys reminding me that I'm, in fact, still in Willowbrook territory. And just my luck, my comments will no doubt filter down the line of gossip until it reaches the people we're speaking about.

He nods again, finally falling silent. Even though he turns his head to face Mrs. Camerons, I still spot his eyes darting sideways to me every so often.

It takes everything in me to keep my body seemingly relaxed and fake a picture perfect expression of composure. I know I should tell someone or, at the very least, ask for help... but I don't know how. It's rare I ask for help, and even then, it's never for something personal. I don't know how to ask. The option has never been available to ask for help, and I'm left saddled with the fear that I'll be turned away if I do. What if I'm too much? What if my problems are too complex? What if someone takes my pain and tries to hurt me with it? I'm already in pain—I can't handle any more.

How the hell do I say to someone '*I need your support to plan my mother's funeral. Yeah, she was in the hospital for a bit. Died while I was at some shitty warehouse instead of being there with her in her final moments*'? I don't even know how I'm going to be able to pay for it. We had nothing, but we had each other, and that was enough. Now, I'm left with a gaping hole in my chest and I'm staring down the barrel of financial ruin at eighteen. Funerals are expensive, aren't they? That's why people often need to do Go-Fund-Me's and turn to family for help. But I don't have that option.

I don't have anything or anyone at all.

I can't do it. It's already hard keeping this information to myself. But to have people look at me with pity? To try to use her death to paint me as weak? No—just no. I can't. It puts everything at risk. I won't be able to cope with having people look at me like I'm a charity case. I'm already the girl whose father walked out on her. I don't need them slapping the alcoholic dead mother label on me too. I'll crumble, and truth be told, I'm not sure I'll ever be able to pick myself up again if that happens.

But if there's one thing I'm absolutely certain about, it's that I'll never forgive myself for having a moment of weakness with Rylan Astor when I should have been with her in her dying final moments on this earth.

After third period, I had officially reached the point of breaking. It was getting harder and harder to stay focused and
have conversations as if I wasn't falling apart. I faked being
ill with stomach cramps and went home. I lied to the school
nurse and said that Mom was in the hospital and that she
would be fine with me leaving. I hated having to admit that
she is—or was—in the hospital, but it was the only way to
keep my secret. Nurse Millar didn't want to call and disturb
Mom—jokes on her, I suppose—so she went against policy
and let me go home without making parental contact.

School has barely finished for the day when a knock pulls
me out of my catatonic state, forcing me off the couch where I
have been for several hours just gazing blankly at the ceiling.

When I open the door without thought, I immediately try
to shut it, but Rylan shoves his foot in the gap, blocking it
from slamming closed.

"What the fuck, Bex?" he grunts, wiggling his foot in pain.
"You slammed the door on my goddamn foot!"

"What do you want, Rylan?" I snap, not bothering with
pleasantries. "I'm really busy."

It's a lie—kind of. But if I want to lay and dissociate from
reality for a few hours, that's my prerogative.

He straightens up, huffing slightly as he glances down at
me, taken aback by my sudden change in attitude. "I tried

to catch you at school but apparently you left early. You left your cell in my truck. The damn thing hasn't stopped ring-ing." I finally notice it in his hand, seconds before he holds it out toward me.

It feels like there's a boulder-sized lump in my throat. He's being *nice* again, and on any other given day, I might have felt guilty for my cold demeanor.

"You didn't answer it, did you?"

That seems to catch him off-guard, face upturning. "Of course not. It's *your* cell."

"Funny," I say without laughing. "Never stopped you butting into our personal shit before."

On more than one occasion the Kings of Willowbrook have proven to be snakes. Why would I ever believe a word that comes out of Rylan Astor's mouth? At least... that's what I'm trying to tell myself. I'm trying to convince my mind again that he's our enemy, not the sweet guy he's pretending to be right now—or the past week. *Or last night.*

He has a way of bringing down my walls, and I can't let him do that. I can't let him see the broken person I'm fighting hard to hide.

"What the hell is up with you today?" he snaps back in frustration, folding his arms. "If this is because of last night—"

"Don't!" I yell, cutting him off as I shake my head. "Just... *don't.*" The last part comes out in a whisper because I no longer trust my voice not to crack and reveal my secrets. I can't have anyone knowing what happened, especially not him.

Rylan uncrosses his arms, bringing one up to the door-jamb as he leans forward. "Bex, talk to me," he says softly, the tone nearly unravelling me right then and there. "What happened at the hospital?"

"No," I respond quickly, clearing my throat. "I have nothing to say to you. And as far as I'm concerned, last night never happened."

His brows furrow, lips pursing as confusion and anger washes over his face. "I thought we were moving past all this animosity. Or was it all just a game to you? Some kind of ploy to fuck me over?"

I close my eyes, blocking him out of sight. Because truthfully, I don't want to admit that a part of me—a small part—*was* starting to *like* him. I had no regrets about last night until Sandra had to break my heart. I'm not sure where my mind was before that, but for the first time, peace looked a hell of a lot better if we had to co-exist in one school—a part of me even wondered if we *could* be friends after I left his truck. But now, I can't *do peace* while violence is raging inside of me.

But that's okay. Anger is easy. I can hold onto that, wielding it like a shield. But devastation? Sadness? I run from those types of feelings. They only lead to trouble.

Finally, I open my eyes again, still finding him staring at me with sharp blue eyes. "Don't kid yourself, Rylan. And don't insult me. We both know that it was just a game for you *too*," I linger and emphasize the last word, trying to make a point. "You even said it yourself: '*We can go back to hating each other tomorrow*'. It was just a moment of weakness, a means to an end. I had a need, and you were there to fulfill it."

His eyes flash, hurt reflecting back at me. But as quickly as it comes, it's replaced by burning hatred—and I know I'm on the right path. I cut him off again before he can respond.

"We're never going to be *friends*," I remark, spitting out the word like its poison. "A truce was never going to be a viable option. Let's just keep to ourselves until we're back at Cedar Heights and things return to normal."

"You're playing a dangerous fucking game, Bexley," he murmurs, voice dark and low. I know my words have hit a sore spot—just as I needed them too. "You're basically declaring war again."

I shrug lazily, still struggling to look him in the eye. "Then it's war time, Astor. Now, please leave. You're not wanted here."

Chapter Twenty-One

Rylan

What the actual fuck is her problem?!

Everything was fine last night when I left her. But now, Bexley has done a complete one-eighty so fast that I don't even recognize the woman who just slammed the door closed in my face.

I shouldn't have gotten comfortable or complacent, regardless of the reasons. It was a grave mistake to think we could be anything more than enemies. I had it right the first time when I said that Bexley was a snake.

We should have broken her when we had the chance. My one regret is not pushing back harder. Instead of punishing her for the acts against us, I took my foot off the throttle and changed strategies. It's a grave mistake, one that now plagues me.

Still, I can't shake the feeling that there's something missing here.

The way her voice shook, the dimness in her eyes... something happened. But what?

In spite of the urge to bang down her door and demand answers, I turn on my heel and stalk back to my truck. There's the unshaking feeling that she's watching through the window, but I don't dare glance back at the cream house. If I see her watching, I'll likely smash open the door until she tells me the problem, or I fuck her through a glass window or wall support beam.

My pride has taken a beating. A small voice in my mind taunts me, telling me this is my own fault—exactly like my father had said. How the hell am I meant to know which decision is right when I have everyone telling me different things? *Smooth it over, gain control, destroy them.* You can't please everyone, and now that my plan has backfired in my face, I'll never hear the end of it from any of them.

Things should never have gotten this far. The whole purpose of our truce was to keep her at arm's length, but close enough to keep a watch on things. I was meant to smooth things over so that we'd resume control. I just never expected to enjoy her company.

But I did.

And even though it hasn't been long, I feel like I started to get to know the real Bexley Spencer—not the one who hides behind feelings of tenacity and unwavering strength.

Blasting my Spotify through the speakers, I slam my foot on the gas, peeling away from the curb with a squeal. People in their front yards tending to gardens glare at my truck with annoyance, but I pay them no attention. I only have one thing on my mind.

Thankfully, Dad isn't home. He's on the road, visiting the State Governor as part of his beloved, all important electoral duties.

When I reach my bedroom, I waste no time hitting call on my cell, waiting for Tai to pick up. He's the only one I can speak to about this that might be able to help, even if it means potentially getting chewed out.

I know he doesn't agree with my actions, but he's less likely to give me shit. Plus, I need his skills. Regardless of what has happened or my motives for this, it's in our best interests to work out what has Bexley in a twist. If something has happened, maybe I can push her to open up to me. But if she's just playing the long con, then I can use whatever we find as ammo to crush her.

"Hey, Ry," Tai's voice comes through loud and clear. "Missing me already?" He makes kissy noises, and I cringe with a laugh.

"Absolutely," I agree. "But I have a weird question."

Tai chuckles. "Weird is my favorite. Hit me with it."

Taking a breath, I quickly get the words out before I can change my mind. "Total hypothetical, but do you know how one would go about hacking into some cameras if they wanted to, *hypothetically*, obtain footage from the hospital?"

Yeah—real smooth. Just dropping the old hypothetical mention twice... Not suspicious at all.

"A hypothetical, ay?"

"Yep."

There's a small pause before he says, "Nothing to do with your little trip to the hospital last night?"

My jaw tightens. I never relayed that information to him. But I know that he has trackers on our cells and vehicles. We agreed to it ages ago, so that we'd be able to locate each other in the event of an emergency. But I didn't share that little trip with them, which means he and Hunter were watching last night after they left us to negotiate.

And likely saw my truck parked at the warehouse for a questionable amount of time...

"Nope," I lie, not bothering to deny my spontaneous visit to the hospital entrance.

Tai chuckles down the other end of the line. "Right," he drawls out knowingly. "Also, nothing to do with the fact that her car wasn't at the warehouse last night. Or why you went to her house today?"

Motherfucker.

"Just how much do you stalk me, asshole?"

"It's a hobby—like bird watching."

I roll my eyes in annoyance. "And have you shared these updates with Hunter?"

I'm surprised when he answers, "Nope. It's our little secret, Brother."

"I appreciate you keeping it on the DL for now. I'm in Hunter's bad books," I murmur, rubbing my forehead. "So, about this hypothetical hospital..."

Tai hums thoughtfully. "Hypothetically, hospitals are easy. They don't bother with large and complex scale security—perks of being underfunded. And if someone has a father who works for the government and runs the town..."

My teeth grind at the idea. I really don't want to use that connection and bring this to his radar. Before I can think of a response as to why I don't want my father getting wind of this, Tai continues.

"But I could probably give it a shot. What am I looking for?"

Relief and appreciation fill me. "Find out where she went. A floor, a room... anything."

"Hypothetically," Tai starts, and I'm already sick of the word since we both know it's bullshit. "I think someone needs to watch himself. Anything you want to share with the class, Ry?"

"Just see what you can find," I growl, ending the call.

On the plus side, Tai will enjoy the task, and I know I can trust him. But I'll be hearing about this for days to come. After all, what are friends for if not to taunt the shit out of you?

About an hour after we ended our call, I received a text from Tai. When the notification first popped up, my heart raced momentarily, thinking there was a chance it could be Bexley—even if it was to chew me out about turning up.

It wasn't, of course, but at least I had some answers.

Tai was kind enough to obtain some grainy footage, sending it through with some basic notes—*floor two.*

The timestamp on the footage matched, and before I realized what I was doing, I was in the truck and driving to the hospital.

A few people linger around and give me passing glances as I stroll through the entrance. I take the elevator straight to floor two, heading to the nurses' station I see when I step onto the floor. I have no idea what to say or what to expect, but I'm on a mission to figure out why Bexley was suddenly cold as ice. Especially if there's a chance it could come back to bite us in the ass.

As I approach the desk, I spot a middle-aged nurse in scrubs, typing on a computer behind the desk. She looks up when I stop in front of her, offering a small smile.

"Can I help you, sweetheart?"

"Yeah, hi," I start, turning on the charm. "I'm here on behalf of a... friend," I force out, trying not to focus on the fact that we're not really friends. Or that friends shouldn't know what it feels like to feel other friends come—much less sworn enemies.

"Name?" she asks warmly.

Clearing my throat, I keep my voice firm. "Bexley Spencer."

The nurse pauses, and immediately, I know I'm on the right track. It's obvious she knows who I'm referring to. Now, it's just a matter of whether or not she's willing to provide any information. HIPAA aside, I just need a fraction of guidance, anything to explain the sudden shutdown that I can use to start looking for answers.

"Lovely girl," the nurse muses sadly. "Who are you in relation to her?"

"A friend," I repeat, still struggling with the word. "She asked me to stop in and... do... something."

The lie falls out like word vomit, but I'm toeing a fragile line here. If I give away that I'm not meant to be here, I'll be back to square one.

But to my surprise, the nurse stands, giving me a look of relief. "Oh, good. We were wondering if someone would be along to collect them. I've tried to call Bexley a few times, but she hasn't answered."

I nod, pretending I know what she's referring to. "She's a bit distracted."

"I can't say I blame her," the nurse responds, gesturing for me to follow over to a cupboard. "Poor girl. She was so distressed last night. Let her know we're thinking of her."

Frowning, I watch as she pulls out a plastic bag, a hospital sticker affixed to it. She hands it to me, and I take it, fighting my curiosity as I resist the urge to look at it. "I'll pass on the message."

"Thank you. I left her a voicemail, passing on the details for our hospital coroner. She'll be able to liaise with them to make arrangements for the funeral and transfer from the morgue."

"Right," I say, swallowing the growing lump forming in my throat. "I'll let Bexley know so she can contact them."

The nurse smiles sadly. "Look after her. She's heartbroken—I don't think she knew all the details, so it was a shock to her. But I'm happy to see she has a friend to support her."

I glance at her name tag, giving a firm nod. "I will. Thanks, Sandra."

I stare at the contents on my bed, eyes scanning the clothes, cell, sheets of paper, wilting flowers and purse.

Inside, I'm disgusted with myself. The normal, decent thing would have been to drive right over to Bexley's house and hand her the bag without snooping. But given her less than welcoming demeanor earlier, I knew that would end badly. And I wanted to know for certain myself.

So now, I'm stuck with a bunch of items on my bed, fingers rifling through the belongings to confirm my suspicions.

I'm a sick fuck.

I go straight for the purse, digging out a wallet. Opening the black leather, there's a picture inside; a younger Bexley with a warm, smiling face, hugging an older woman. Lifting the driver's license from the card slot, I check the name—*Savanna Spencer*. The ID photo matches the person hugging Bexley, and I let out a sigh.

Savanna Spencer... as in *Bexley Savanna Spencer.*

Shit. This is bad.

No wonder Bexley is out of sorts. Her mother is dead. Not just dead, but newly so.

Questions pop into my mind, leading to more unease and tension.

When? How?

We were just together last night, and she was happy. But the footage of her running out of the hospital haunts me.

Did she die when we were together?

It would explain a lot. Especially since the nurse made a comment that sounds like Bexley wasn't expecting it.

I quickly pack everything up again, feeling like an intruder. Shoving the bag under my bed, I take myself for a shower, hoping I can wash away the guilt that clings to me.

This is a clear violation of trust. Bexley's going to lose her shit when she finds out I stole her dead mother's belongings and impersonated myself as a friend there on her behalf.

After I get clean—which doesn't help ease the feeling at all—I sit on my bed, staring at my cell. Would she respond if I messaged her?

My fingers type out a message, delete it, write out another, and delete that too.

Eventually, I settle for the old trick of sending lyrics, hoping to gauge some type of reaction. I share the link to Spotify, attaching the Lawless Dragons lyrics in a text message to Bexley.

It sends, and I stare at the screen, hoping to see those three little bubbles appear.

My heart races when it gives the indication that she's read the message. And I wait.

But nothing appears. No bubbles, no response.

Sighing, I realize the only way I'm going to get a reply from her is in person. And it also means I might end up with something being thrown at my head. But that's fine.

I have fast reflexes.

Chapter Twenty-Two

By Monday, I realized that I couldn't avoid the world any longer. I spent the entire weekend curled up in bed, crying, until my body was incapable of producing anymore tears. A few times, someone knocked on my door, but I couldn't bring myself to answer. It was easier to hide, to blast tunes and temporarily take myself elsewhere mentally until I was able to shut it all off.

I'd finally fallen down that spiral where no matter how hard I tried my face gave everything away. So, I hid. The world kept turning and no one was the wiser that I was broken.

Monday morning, I feigned being ill again—this time with a swollen ankle—so that I could face the inevitable without being disturbed or distracted.

It just wasn't an option to put it off any longer. The thought of Mom laying in the hospital morgue, cold and alone, destroyed me all weekend. I went to the hospital and finally spoke to the team who handled *end of life trans-fers*—aka removal of deceased patients from the premises.

Did you know that hospitals can only hold bodies in the morgue for so long? Well, I just learned all the details. Never thought that I'd suddenly be equipped with the knowledge of those types of procedures, but here I am.

Part of my emotional breakdown was also attributed to the fact that I was about to face financial ruin at the ripe old age of eighteen. Neither of us had planned for Mom to die so early, and with little financial support, I had no idea how I was going to cover the costs to bury her. Or how I would be able to afford utilities and groceries now that she was gone. Her payments would be cut off, and without a job, I have no way to support myself. Having a roof over my head is one thing, but what good is it if I can't afford to eat or pay for electricity?

But not even that could beat the heartache and bitter reality of facing a life without my mom. I'd rather be hungry and cold with her than alone without.

Today, it was a matter of picking my poison—one destructive task at a time. And that was to deal with the hospital and contact the funeral parlor.

The Ridgeview Valley Funeral Home was situated in the central business district, not far from the crater. I'd never had the displeasure of meeting Mr. Morrison before, and truthfully, I hope I never do again.

Sure, he's a lovely old man, but even though it's not his fault, I can't help but associate his presence with my grief.

It was times like this that I really wish I knew how to ask for help. Having a friend with me, to help soak in the vast information would be beneficial. But I can't do it yet.

Archie keeps messaging, asking if I'm okay. Hiding behind my screen will only work for so long. Tomorrow, I need to return to school, to check on everyone. I just hope that I've broken my tear ducts so they stop working for the few hours that I have to socialize.

The last thing I need is those Willowbrook assholes seeing me cry. I'm not going to give them the satisfaction of seeing me broken. Or give them any ammunition to use against me.

I'm stronger than my demons. I'm stronger than the lies that haunt me.

I just need to take it day by day.

I had half a mind to throw out the new shorts that Rylan gifted me. The Willowbrook crowd enjoy that class, always ready to taunt my inability to purchase new clothes. And seeing the new shorts, they definitely had something to say about it last week.

But after weighing up my options, I decided it was better to have them mock my new attire and make snide remarks, rather than have them stare at my ass all morning.

Dumping my bag by the seats near the track, I take a final look at it, wondering if those vapid, bleach-haired cheerleaders will attempt to steal it again. Part of me hoped they would, so I had an excuse to punch someone and release some pent-up energy.

"Morning, sunshine!" Sophia beams, bouncing over.

"Hey," I reply, finding it easier than expected to feign friendliness with her.

Soph stops next to me, stretching her arms above her head. "I'm so happy the rain has finally disappeared. I just dyed my hair on the weekend."

My eyes fall to the tied-up strands, smiling at the freshly touched up pink tips. "Does pink fade as quickly as red?"

"Argh, yes," she groans. "I've stained too many pillowcases. My brother gives me shit all the time about it."

"You have a brother?" I ask, intrigued. "I didn't know that."

She nods. "We're twins actually. Though he loves to remind me that he's older—by a whole seven minutes." Her eyes roll, making me laugh.

"If you are twins, does that mean he's a senior too?"

"Yeah," she confirms. "You probably know him."

Given that I barely know everyone from Willowbrook, her statement makes me suspicious. Sensing my skepticism, Soph pauses, offering a sheepish, apologetic smile.

"It's Tai."

"Tai?" I gape at her. "As in *Tai Beckett*?"

Pain crosses her face as she scrunches it in response. "Are you mad at me? I promise I'm not as big as an asshole as he is."

I just stand there and stare at her wordlessly. To be fair, I have no idea how to feel. Betrayal is the first thought that comes to mind, but I quickly remind myself that neither of us owe the other any loyalty.

Anger is next, or at least it would be if I felt anything at the moment. The underlying numbness that I'm harboring seems to work in all scenarios. But I take the opportunity to voice the question that has been bugging me.

"Is that why you borrowed those library books?" I ask dryly.

Sophia blinks at me, pure confusion on her face. Either she's a really good actor, or she has no idea what I am talking about.

"The biology book?" she mutters. "What do you mean?"

I've always learned that you can't judge a book by its cover. And to her credit, she hasn't given me any reason to doubt her genuine friendliness these past few weeks. Hell, she even helped bring down Rylan. But while that still doesn't mean she's innocent, I'm willing to give her the benefit of the doubt depending on how she answers the next question.

"Your brother was the one who had my bag that first week," I tell her. "The cheerleaders gave it to him after they stole it. And your dear twin destroyed my textbooks. When I went to the library to borrow a copy, someone had suspiciously already checked them out that day."

My eyes stay on her face, unwavering as I watch for her reaction. Perplexity stares back at me, before her face twists in anger, mouth falling open with realization. "That asshole."

"Yes, but you're gonna have to elaborate."

Sophia groans, rubbing her template. "He told me he left his copy at home and asked to borrow mine. His classes for those subjects are earlier in the week before mine, so he asked to take mine and suggested I borrow the books from the library in case he forgot to bring them back to school. He's a forgetful ass sometimes. Shit, Bexley—I swear I had no idea. I'm going to smother him with my pink-stained pillow tonight."

Now that I'm looking at her closely, really closely, I can see the similarities. I'm not sure why I missed them before. While they both appear to have dyed hair, they have the same hazel eyes—even the random little spots of caramel in the irises.

Shit. This wasn't on my bingo card for this week, but it's a nice distraction from my own thoughts for a little while.

"Hey, Spencer! Who did you fuck to get the shorts?" someone calls out.

My body tenses as I slowly turn, spotting the hoard of males heading toward the locker room. To my surprise, Rylan isn't with them.

"Your father," I yell back without missing a beat. "He's disappointed in you, by the way. Wishes you'd been swallowed."

The guy gawks at my response while the group mock him and laugh, fucking me with their eyes and wolf-whistling. A few make quiet remarks about my shorts—which fit me perfectly to my displeasure. Rylan was spot on with his guess, and after hearing Sophia's confession, I'm now back to questioning his motives again.

I hate that I let him get close to me. Even removing the sex from the equation, I let him see parts of me that I normally keep hidden.

Blindsided by our supposed trauma bonding, I had let my guard down. And today is a reminder as to why I can't trust anyone.

As people start filing out from the locker rooms, I spot Rylan casually heading toward the field from the main building. As if sensing my eyes on him, he finds me easily in the crowd, eyebrows furrowing for a brief moment before his face becomes expressionless. He walks into the locker room without a word, my gaze glued to the doorway, even long after he's vanished from sight.

"Earth to Bexley."

"Hm?" I turn back to Sophia.

She grimaces. "You're mad. It's cool. I understand why you would be."

Sighing, I shake my head. "I'm not mad at you," I confess—which is the truth. Am I hurt? Yes, definitely. I thought I had found a friend in the snake pit, and I'm disappointed that she has ties to the Willowbrook kings. But it also explains a lot. It's why she and Rylan have a weird dynamic. Sophia is his best friend's sister.

At least they aren't dating.

Unlike last time, the thought brings a new type of relief. And I hate myself for it.

I shouldn't be relieved that Sophia isn't dating Rylan. He's not mine.

Sure, words were said in the heat of the moment, but the only truth that was spoken that night was that we hated each other.

We do *hate* each other. Right?

The coach calls for our attention before Rylan has emerged, and I welcome the distraction, making sure my back is facing the locker rooms. But even though I can't see him, I can feel his presence when he joins the group. My skin feels like it's being burned under watchful eyes, and for once, I want to run. Not away—but actual disgusting cardio.

When we're split into groups, Soph and I hang back, letting all the psychotic sprinters go first before starting our jog. But despite trying to keep pace, my body pushes ahead, making my running buddy curse under her breath.

"Jesus, Bex. Slow down," Sophia begs, panting as she tries to keep up.

But her words barely register in my mind. They sound faded, almost like they are being spoken under water.

Because all I can focus on is the wide back ahead, the dark brown hair ruffling in the breeze as light reflects off silver rings, beckoning me like death's version of the Bat Signal.

"I'm worried about you again," Arch says during fourth period.

"Why?" I ask, not glancing up from my textbook.

Despite meeting up at various times throughout the day, Arch apparently waited until we were in class together before questioning me.

We're at the back of the room, and even though I'm burning holes in the pages, I can't focus or absorb a single written word.

The Three Musketeers are in this class too, and every so often, they turn to look at me. But it's the difference in glances that puts me on high alert.

Hunter looks like he wants to bury me alive.

Tai throws bizarre stares that emanate *pity*.

And Rylan... He appears almost sad. With hints of... guilt?

If I didn't know any better, it's almost as if they have an idea of what has happened—well, Rylan and Tai anyway. But that's impossible. If my own people don't even know what happened on Thursday night, then they can't. I've made sure to cover my tracks.

"You've been sick a lot lately," Arch points out, ripping my attention away from Rylan as he glances over for the seventh time. Not that I'm counting.

"Probably just a little rundown," I offer pathetically.

He pauses, sparing a quick look at the teacher before leaning in. "Bex, I'm only going to say this once. You know I don't like to call you out on things, but something is going on. If there's something I can do to help—"

"It's fine," I snap, a little too harshly. His eyes widen, before narrowing in suspicion.

"Bex," he growls sternly. "That's bullshit and we both know it. Did *they* do something? Has someone hurt you?"

I laugh sarcastically under my breath. "No one has hurt me," I reply, monotonously.

Not really, anyway.

Arch reaches over, placing his hand on top of mine. "You don't have to deal with things alone. I promised you in fifth grade that I'd always be there for you."

"Don't you dare," I threaten, only half playfully, knowing what's coming.

He raises an eyebrow. "Nope. I'm initiating the pact. We promised to always be honest with each other—sealed with a pinky promise. So, tell me what's going on. You're legally obligated under the *Barchley* oath."

My lips twitch at our bestie name. It was one of those ridiculous things we did in elementary school, when I decided to adopt him as my friend forever. There was no escaping my grip once the scrawny little kid had stolen my favorite crayon by accident. Oh, Arch. Where would I even start?

I check to make sure the teacher is still facing the board before I pivot in my seat toward him. "Not here."

"Yes," he says sternly. "Because as soon as class is over, you're going to bolt, Bex. I know you too well. And I'm getting far too old to chase with my dodgy knees."

I'm fairly certain I'm on the verge of a mental breakdown, because all I do is laugh quietly in response. That and because his knees are far from dodgy. One season of basketball and a torn ACL that was repaired, and he thinks his knees are screwed for all eternity.

But I guess I just laugh, because my life is a joke right now. Laugh, because in about ten seconds, Arch is going to regret everything and he's going to feel as bad as I do. And then I'll feel ten times worse for bringing him into my mess.

And worse of all, laugh, because he might never look at me the same way and I don't know how I'll cope with that. I need him. I can't lose the one person in my life who is constant.

Taking a deep breath, I dissociate from my feelings, allowing that numb relief to wash over me like Lidocaine.

"Mom is dead," I finally say quietly. "She died last week. And I wasn't there with her because I was in bed with the Devil."

Chapter Twenty-Three

TAI

"Hey, asshole!"

My fingers hover over the keyboard, pausing as footsteps storm into my bedroom.

"Hello to you, too," I grin without glancing over.

Soph slams her hand down on the end of my desk before using her foot to kick my chair and spin me around.

Sighing, I lean back lazily. "If Calvin ate your shoes, I already warned you not to leave them out. You have no one to blame but yourself."

She glowers at me. "Did you end up taking your *biology book* back to school?"

"Yes, why?" I ask slowly, narrowing my eyes in suspicion at the question. Well, there's nothing suspicious about it to be fair. Twin telepathy and all. For example, right now, I know Sophia is pissed at me because she realizes I may have used her in a ploy.

"Did you accidentally leave it behind or were you just being an asshole?"

"You're gonna have to be more specific," I joke. "Tell me more about this asshole behavior."

Soph scans my face for a second before kicking the seat—right in between my legs. Yelping, I cover my balls, pushing the chair back into the desk to put some distance between us. Because that was likely just a warning. All's fair in love and sibling rivalry. She has no qualms with putting me on my ass.

"You lied to me for one of your stupid games," she scowls. "I told you to keep me out of your business with Rylan and Hunter."

Crossing my legs—for protection, of course—I fold my arms while holding eye contact. "Did dear Bexley tell you that?"

"Why do you all have to be such assholes? Seriously. Destroying her books? That's low, even for you."

"It's just business, Soph. Chill."

When she steps closer, I automatically cover my junk.

"Mom raised you better than that," Soph says. And now I'm annoyed.

Standing up, I tower over my twin, glancing down at the freshly dyed hair. She did mine on the weekend too, putting a new silver toner through it. Though I think that was just to draw my attention away from the fact that she stained my favorite towel. Yes—favorite towel. Everyone has one. And don't think I didn't notice, Sophia Louise Beckett.

"Soph," I warn with a hardened expression. "Don't drop the M word at me. Besides, what are you doing hanging around with Cedar trash?"

"Trash?" she laughs dryly. "You three are miserable ball sacks. Seriously, do you know how embarrassing it is watching how the Willowbrook students act at school? Since when do you care about shit like that at school? The Cedar students haven't even done anything."

I raise an eyebrow. "You don't know the full story, sis. Bexley isn't as innocent as she seems. Don't be fooled by her attitude and charm."

There's nowhere to go when she steps into me, hair tickling my nose as she flicks me in the forehead with her fingers.

"Ow!"

"Idiot."

Soph spins around and heads toward the door, shoving her middle finger into the air. "I like Bexley, Tai. And now she probably thinks I'm just like you."

"You have plenty of friends at Willowbrook. You don't need her approval," I call out, making me pause in the doorway.

She turns, glaring at me. "Do you know how nice it is hanging with someone who doesn't give a shit about their nails or reality TV? Someone who doesn't judge me for running like a D-list actor in a horror movie. If you involve me again, I'll tell Mary."

"Oh, come on," I groan. "Leave Mary out of it."

Soph knows she has hit a sore spot. I couldn't care less what our father thinks about me, but Mary? She thinks I radiate sunlight and lollipops. But she's also not afraid to scold me if she finds out I've been up to no good.

"Leave me out of your scheming or next time I'm turning your hair bright orange like the clown you are, asshole."

"Since when do you want a running buddy?" I groan, barely able to keep up with Ry as we run along the pathway.

When Ry asked me to meet up for an afternoon jog, I assumed that was code for beers or something—*not actual running*. What the fuck?

I can't give Soph shit for running like a drunk baby deer, because my workouts are strictly contained to weights. But right now, it's near embarrassing how little stamina I have compared to Ry, especially when he chose the scenic route.

Thankfully, we're just running the public track near the edge of the mountains, not up the path that weaves through the caves to the canyon. They would be carrying my carcass back down in a body bag if that was the case.

"Needed to talk," he replies, not out of breath at all. Psycho.

"We won't get much talking done if we're running," I wheeze back, relieved when he stops.

Rylan turns, shoving his hands into his gym shorts. "Fine. Happy?"

"Much better," I grumble, hunching over. "What is this about? Besides torturing me for your gratification."

"I fast-tracked the warehouse renovations," he says, smirking at my hunched frame.

Rolling my eyes, I straighten up. "This could have been an email or text message. Besides, why tell me and not Hunter too? He should be here for the torture-fest."

"Hunter won't like what I have to say."

I cock an eyebrow, amused. "To be fair, we kind of anticipated that she'd get the better of you with negotiations."

Rylan scowls at me. "That's not what I meant. And she didn't. We came to a mutual understanding."

"Meaning, your dick got the better of you," I laugh, freezing when his eyes widen slightly. "Wait—please tell me you didn't."

Silence falls between us, and I narrow my eyes, expecting the, "Ha! Got you." But it doesn't come.

... But Rylan did.

"Please tell me you didn't sleep with Spencer," I grimace. "I knew you were getting friendly, but come on, man—that's crossing the line."

"I don't know where the line is anymore," he admits firmly.

I stare at one of my oldest friends, trying to decipher what's going on in that head of his. Ry is right though—Hunter wouldn't like this at all.

To him, Spencer is still the enemy. And he hasn't forgiven Ry yet for forcing us into a truce.

As for me, I'm completely bewildered. First Sophia, and now Rylan. Spencer has managed to dig her claws into everyone around me.

"I should have known," I say lightly, trying to break the tension. "After all, you've taken up the habit of stalking her."

A pained expression crosses Ry's face. "Takes a stalker to know a stalker. But about that—I don't think we're going to be on friendly terms anymore."

I nod. "Because of her mother?"

He looks at me, surprised. "You know?"

Shrugging, we move out of the way as some joggers pass by. "After I checked the hospital footage, I did a quick search of her name in the system. Nothing on Bexley, but there was a patient there with the same surname."

"Her mom," Ry answers, confirming what I already know.

Despite the desire to know everything, I didn't delve too much into the personal information. It wasn't relevant and even I have boundaries I won't cross.

"Hunter's going to flip his shit."

"We're not going to tell him," Ry says.

My eyebrows shoot up into my ashy headline. "You can't keep secrets, Ry. It's bound to come out."

"I'll tell him—eventually. But right now, we need to figure out how to handle this. I'm going to speak to Dad to find out how the repairs are going at Cedar Heights. We need to get things back to normal as soon as possible."

"I can agree with that. Sophia already chewed me out for destroying Spencer's books."

Rylan gestures for me to walk with him as we start to head back toward the parking lot of the mountains. "Think Sophia would do me a favor?"

Fighting back a smirk, I shake my head. "If it's to do with Spencer, fat chance."

He sighs. "Fuck."

"So, circling back for a moment. When will the warehouse be finished?" I ask, ignoring the overwhelming curiosity at this so-called favor.

"We can fight this weekend," Ry answers. "And I'm getting in the cage."

That almost makes me pause, but instead, I keep walking, giving him a frown. "Things that bad?"

It's been ages since Rylan has jumped into the cage. It always coincides with his need to let out steam—usually when his dad is riding his ass.

"Yeah," he confesses. "And things are going to get worse. I need your help keeping Hunter under control."

"He won't go rogue," I say confidently. "But if he finds out what you did, you'll likely find yourself in the cage with him."

A smirk appears on his face. "No complaints here. An actual challenge is what I need right now. Someone to make me work for it."

Shaking my head, I snort. "Dividing us right now is going to cause nothing but trouble. You need to push her away. Whatever drama is going on, let it unravel on its own. Let Cedar Heights implode among themselves. We can still remain amicable but separate from the mess. It will help to keep control and pick up the ruins. We might even be able to make some of them fall into line."

When he doesn't respond, I glance over at him. Whatever is eating at him is starting to bleed through the cracks, and he knows as well as I do, that we need to keep doing damage control.

If shit is happening in the ranks of Cedar Heights, it will give us the perfect opportunity to capitalize on their weaknesses. But for whatever reason, Rylan seems hesitant.

Doesn't he realize that *she's* the one causing a rift between us? This is probably some ploy to separate us, to make us appear vulnerable.

Don't get me wrong, the whole situation sucks for her. I'm not sure what Rylan sees in her, but whatever she is going through, he needs to keep out of it. But given the look of concentration on his face, nothing I've said has gotten through to him.

Great. We're screwed.

Spencer has him by the balls and unless we do something, we're all in trouble.

Maybe I do need to go to Hunter. Of course, I'm not going to say anything about Rylan—his secrets are safe with me. But right now, we need a clear-headed approach. And if we have the opportunity to seize back power, we need to take it.

Rylan will thank me later.

He just has to rid himself free from Spencer's grasp before she poisons him.

"I'm getting sick of all these change of plans without the three of us consulting together."

Hunter glares at me, and if I were anyone else, they'd be cowering. But instead, I throw him a wink.

"Or are you just annoyed that I had a good idea, and you didn't think of it first?" I tease.

He snorts. "Be careful with that audacity, T. It's not as bulletproof as you think it is."

"Can you make it happen or not?"

"Of course I can," he replies. "But I'm still not completely sure why this is the best course of action."

Shrugging, I squat down and scoop up a crispy leaf, crushing it in my palm. The Ridgeview Park is fairly deserted. Only a few people are still around, getting their nighttime walks in before the sun fully sets.

After my little chat with Ry, I decided we needed to speed up things. The longer this drags out, the more damage Spencer is going to cause.

"Keep your enemies close," I tell Hunter. "Besides, I think it would be a good idea for Ry to take a step back."

As usual, Hunter doesn't miss anything. His brow twitches in annoyance. "Agreed. He's acting weird lately and I don't like it. Those renovations are going to set us back."

"There's something else as well," I pause, leaning against a bench. "The repairs at Cedar are still a while off. Rylan is going to find out if they have a more definitive timeline for completion. But I think we need to look into the fire."

He frowns at the suggestion. "It's not our problem, T."

"Except they made it our problem when Cedar had to merge with us. Whoever started that fire had motive. I want to make sure that it's not for our detriment."

Hunter considers the proposal, and a series of emotions flash across his face. I've got him on board before he even says the words.

"Fine," he begrudgingly agrees. "But you're the one who's going to have to deal with the new arrangement."

Grinning, I kick off from the bench, heading toward the parking lot. "That's okay with me. I think it's about time I find out what makes Spencer tick and why she has everyone in a choke hold."

Chapter Twenty-Four

"Thanks for coming with me," I murmur softly, keeping my gaze firmly locked on the outside world that passes by.

Arch glances over from the driver's seat, his sad look visible out of the corner of my eye. "Of course," he replies. "I'm so sorry, Bex. You shouldn't have had to do this alone."

All I can do is nod once. The secret is out—well, only to Arch. But it feels like the whole world knows. Even though it's impossible, now that I've voiced my new reality, it feels like everything has changed.

I know he's trying hard not to be overly pitiful or sappy. I'm thankful for that. But it still feels like someone has reached into my chest cavity with a burning fire poker and stabbed me in the heart repeatedly. Anxiety has become overwhelming. I'm waiting for the avalanche to come—the inevitable rolling effect of people knowing and tiptoeing around me in case I break at any given second.

Truthfully, I don't know how to act. Or how to feel. There's a huge battle of turmoil and rage lashing out. Part of me begs to break down crying again, while a bigger part is stoic and emotionless. But there's no running from this. Time is just not on my side. If I could dodge this forever, I would.

We pull up to the curb in the main town square, bile threatening to rise up my throat. There it is—the damn funeral parlor again.

The crisp white double doors are wooden and freshly painted. I wouldn't be surprised if they have to clean them often. The hand marks and fingerprints would be a pain in the ass to keep off. Alongside it, two colorful, frosted glass windows hide the inside. It gives an illusion—that life is technicolor. But all I see is black and white. Death.

"Are you ready?"

Slowly, I look over at my best friend, appreciative that he's now also mirroring a stoic expression. It's the silent strength I need, and I nod again, unclipping my seatbelt.

After my confession in class yesterday, Arch followed me back home. I'm not sure if it was just to solely get answers out of me, or if he needed to see it for himself. But the empty house took both of us by surprise.

It's been nearly a week. You'd think I would be used to the silence at home now. But every day when I walk in and nothing has been touched, nothing has been moved, and she's nowhere to be seen... it's a new wave of *'Fuck. This is real.'*

I had curled up on the sofa, filling Arch in about everything. Except it kills me because I don't know *everything*.

This was never the expected outcome. No one had voiced any concerns that Mom was terminally sick. If I had known... things would be different. Sure, the end result would have been the same—but I would be different. I could have prepared. I could have made better choices.

I have to hand it to him though. Arch handled it well—even when I admitted to what I had done with Rylan. Not that I expected him to say anything snarky. Arch isn't like that. But given our rocky situation at present, I thought for sure I'd see some type of resentment or judgement staring back at me. There was none—just sorrow and regret. Mom was family to Arch too. Before Dad left, we'd have sleepovers as kids. Mom would bake her amazing peanut butter cookies for us. She held that recipe close to her heart, guarded—and we were the only two people alive that she let in on that secret. It was special. Even Dad used to watch sports on the TV with Arch. But only one guy was man enough to stick around for me... and he's by my side as we walk through the doors.

Mr. Morrison comes hobbling out of his office when the door creaks shut behind us. His neatly trimmed white hair oddly matches the decor, and he gives me a soft smile.

"Bexley. It's lovely to see you again."

"You too," I lie.

Arch holds out his hand, introducing himself before we're guided into the office. I've already been in here, but I spot Arch glance around with curiosity.

We take a seat on the two single-sized plush leather chairs in front of Mr. Morrison's desk.

"I gave you some pamphlets the other day about different types of services. Have you had a chance to look through them or would you like to discuss them individually?" he says politely.

Shifting in my seat, I do my best not to hurl into the trash can that's in the corner of the room. "I haven't look yet," I admit. "I'm still unsure about what to do."

He nods, opening a folder. "It can be overwhelming," he starts, sounding apologetic. "But with our packages, all you have to do is pick one and we'll handle the rest. All we ask is you provide us with some personalized touches—such as any particular music or photographs you would like to use. Perhaps your dear mother had a favorite song or flower that we can incorporate into the service."

There's a giant rock sitting on my chest. Well, it feels like it. I have no idea how I'm meant to tell him that I can't afford to pay for Mom's service. All the packages are ridiculously expensive. If there's one thing I've learned, it's that weddings and funerals are horribly priced. At least with a wedding, you get to enjoy the day you pay for. Mom isn't here to see her funeral... if she was then I wouldn't be in this room. It still astounds me—the concept of funerals. I know it's a celebration of life, a goodbye to a lovely existence, remembering all the good that person put into the world. But how can you see it like that when someone is ripped from you so prematurely?

"Before we start on any of that." I take a deep breath. "Can we discuss payment plan options?"

I can't be the first person in this position. If anything, I'd bet that it's really common. It's not really a comforting thought, but there would have to be options in place for people like me. I mean, they wouldn't just dump a body and deny a service. Right?

Suddenly, my mind goes haywire with images of mobster-dressed funeral directors, dumping bodies into the Ridgeview Valley canyon. Shit. I bet there are actually bodies down there. Probably not from funeral parlors... but dead bodies, nonetheless.

"Payment options?" Mr. Morrison repeats, an air of confusion laced in his voice.

Arch reaches over and squeezes my hand, silently encouraging me to speak up. Bless him. He has a few thousand saved up for college and he offered it to me. I said no, of course. We're so close to graduating that I know there's no way I'd get the money back to him in time. I'm not about to shit all over his future just because mine is sinking to the bottom of the ocean in concrete buckets.

"I don't have any savings," I say. "And Mom didn't have assets. All we have is the house and I'm not in a position to sell that. I want her to have a decent funeral, but I'm financially stuck at the moment."

When his brows furrow, I quickly take a breath, continuing. "But I'm willing to get a job. I'll enter into a payment plan and work to pay it off. We can keep costs to a bare minimum—whatever you think is best."

My hand is squeezed again, and I shoot Arch a small smile, realizing just how much he's keeping me cool headed right now. If he wasn't here, I'd probably be on my knees, wailing like a newborn baby and begging for help. Or at home on the sofa, buried under a thick layer of blankets with music blaring so loudly that the cops turn up and arrest me for being a nuisance.

"Bexley, you'll have to forgive my reaction. But I'm a little confused."

Great. I have to explain all over again. I thought I was pretty clear. There's only so many ways you can say you are poor. I spent ages rehearsing my speech, searching for jobs on the internet. I even started putting together a résumé—not that I have any prior experience to list.

"What she means is we are keen to lay Savanna to rest as soon as possible. But we just need to be mindful of costs and work out a repayment schedule," Arch says for me.

Mr. Morrison gives him a bright smile. Seriously? He understood Arch's words and not mine?

Maybe I'm just rambling and in my head it makes sense, but out loud I'm slurring with nerves.

"Forgive me... but Savanna's services have already been prepaid."

It takes a few seconds before I even start to register what Mr. Morrison has said. Although I hear the words, I still fail to understand what he's trying to tell me. I haven't paid anything.

"Sorry, what do you mean?" I ask.

He reaches into the folder, flicking through the papers. "I'm certain that I have the details here. Ahh, yes—here you go. A lump sum has been paid. It will cover whatever package you choose."

I stare at the piece of paper he's holding out, frozen in place. Arch lets go of my hand, taking it instead.

"It's a receipt," he murmurs. "Definitely allocated to Savanna's account."

"That can't be right," I say, finally snapping out of my daze. Plucking the receipt from his hand, I glance over the words. There are very minimal details, the handwritten notes just listing an amount and Mom's name. "I didn't pay this."

Mr. Morrison nods, apparently agreeing. "A nice, young man stopped in yesterday. He paid with cash. It was a little odd. We don't see cash payments very often anymore."

My eyes snap up. "What young man?"

"I didn't get his name, unfortunately." Mr. Morrison looks crestfallen, as if he's personally wronged me. "But he was adamant about covering the services."

Arch frowns. "I thought no one knew except me."

"They don't," I answer. "You're the only one I've told."

"Are you sure?"

"Of course, I'm sure."

Who else would know? Sandy knows, but I very much doubt a nurse would randomly pay for a patient's funeral. Not to mention I'm fairly certain she's lacking a penis.

The other hospital staff wouldn't have any interest in this. Wait.

The hospital.

My eyes widen slightly as my mouth parts in disbelief. He wouldn't... would he?

No way. There's no chance in hell that Rylan knows what happened. He dropped me off at the hospital, but I never told him why I was there.

He swore he didn't answer my cell, but even if he had, the hospital wouldn't have disclosed personal information to a random person over the phone.

"What are you thinking?" Arch asks, his eyes locked on my painfully obvious shocked reaction.

Without replying, I look over at Mr. Morrison. "Did this young man have brown hair? Light blue eyes?"

Before he even says anything, my suspicions are confirmed right away as his eyes light up in recognition. "Yes, that's him! A friend of yours?"

I snap my attention over to Archie, whose color is quickly draining from his face.

"That fucking asshole," I whisper.

"No way... are you sure?" Arch murmurs back with a frown.

Shoving my chair back—which embarrassingly gets caught on the plush carpet—I stand up. Mr. Morrison looks momentarily horrified, stuttering out an apology as I storm out of his office. I feel bad for him, but I can't dwell on that at the moment.

Behind me, I hear Archie say something to him, before he joins me back at the car.

"Bex?"

"Take me home, Arch." My jaw grinds with anger. "I need my truck. There's someone I have to pay a visit to."

Chapter Twenty-Five

"What the fuck is this?" I hiss, storming into Rylan's bedroom without knocking, waving the receipt in the air.

If he's surprised to see me breaking into his house, he doesn't show it.

Looking up from his desk, he raises a perfectly shaped eyebrow. "How the hell would I know?"

"Don't treat me like I'm stupid," I snap, slamming the paper down in front of him.

Rylan casually leans forward to inspect the receipt, staring at it with disinterest. "That would be a receipt, Bexley. Businesses give them out after making a sale."

"Get up," I demand, kicking the side of his chair.

He pushes back with a little too much force, which tells me he's not as unbothered as he's pretending to be.

"Cool it, Spencer. It's not that fucking deep."

"Not that deep?" I repeat, astonished. "It's everything, Astor. I don't want your goddamn charity."

When I went back for my follow up meeting with Mr. Morrison, still completely lost at having to organize everything, the last thing I expected was for him to say that Mom's funeral services had been paid for in full.

I had spent days trying to figure out what to do. I had a plan walking into that meeting—it wasn't much, but it was something at least. Even though it meant no public service, cremation, and the basic, cheapest options possible, it was a step in the direction of handling this. After days of self-pity and drowning in my demons, I was ready to face everything and deal with the cards that had been given to me.

I would have been still up for a large sum of money, but after brainstorming with Arch and working on the résumé, I had come to the conclusion I would need to borrow the funds from the bank and start working to pay it back or enter into some type of payment plan with Mr. Morrison. Even if it meant eating nothing but raw pasta and canned vegetables for the next two years of my life. I was ready. To anyone else, it probably seemed insignificant. But I was damn proud of myself for not staying in the pity party and hiding from the new responsibilities that had been thrown upon me.

So, imagine my surprise when I found out an *anonymous donor* had gone to Mr. Morrison and offered to cover the costs. I could confidently rule out Archie as the culprit, especially when he looked just as shocked as I was. After getting the description from Mr. Morrison and putting two and two together, it was easy to figure out. Though I'm still stuck on the *why*. And it haunts me.

"It's not charity, Spencer."

"It sure looks like it from where I'm standing," I breathe out angrily. "You had no right to interfere with my mom's death."

Rylan crosses his arms, giving me a hard, expressionless glance over. "Then just consider it as payment for your services."

I move so fast that he has no time to react, my open palm slapping his cheek with a loud smack. I didn't even realize I was going to hit him until I felt the sting vibrate through my palm.

Something snaps in Rylan, his face twisting in red, blinded anger, and for a brief second, I wonder if he's going to hit me back. To be fair, I'd deserve it. I had no right using his code to enter his house and storm into his room, yelling at him—even if it feels totally justified.

Crash.

Shit flies everywhere as Rylan flips his desk over, laptop bouncing on the carpet along with a mug full of coffee. It stains the floor, but I barely have time to assess the damage as he steps into me, our chests connecting.

Rylan's chest heaves angrily as he presses his forehead to mine. For a brief moment, I catch his eyes darting to my lips, my breath stalling at the sight.

"Get out," he growls, pointing toward the door. "Just get the fuck out, Bexley. What gives you the right to come into my house and fucking hit me? So what? I did something nice for you. No wonder you are alone. You can't even stand your own company. Why would anyone else want to deal with you?"

All my pent-up rage vanishes in a mere instant at his words. It feels like I've had a bucket of ice water poured over my body, his words hitting places I had fought hard to protect and hide from.

He's right.

I am alone.

Shame and guilt overwhelm me. I'm better than this. I'm not this person.

Still, every fiber of my existence has fought against situations like this. It's engrained in me. I don't let people in, don't allow them to do something nice for me out of fear that it will be a favor, expecting repayment.

I purposely hide my personal life from everyone around me so I wouldn't have to deal with conversations like this. But I was so mad when Mr. Morrison said it had been taken care of. It felt like there was a price attached—like he'd own me. And it exacerbated the guilt that lingered from the night Mom died. It was already bad enough that I hadn't been there, and now, someone I didn't even like had stepped in to pay so I could say goodbye to her properly.

I hated it. I've never felt so weak and pathetic—so out of control.

Never in my life had I been unable to find a solution to a problem. Then she died. And it was beyond even me. It was a cold reminder that I had nothing in comparison to others, and for the first time, I was scared.

But I was also mad at Rylan. He was a huge part of my guilt, even if he didn't know it. I should never have been with him that night, never let myself give in to impulses and desires that made zero sense. And then he went snooping where he didn't belong.

How did he even know? He hasn't denied it.

"How?" I ask, voice cracking. "How did you find out?"

"Does it matter?" he challenges, taking a step back. His eyes are dark, locked on mine.

Shaking my head, I swallow the lump in my throat. "I'm going to make them refund it. I can't take your money, Rylan."

"Whatever," he responds monotonously. "Maybe you can do a funeral at your shitty little beach. Fire is free. Use the leftover material from the cage. It's been replaced now anyway."

He walks over to the bed, leaning down to pull something out from underneath. I watch, puzzled, when he stalks back over, thrusting the plastic bag into my arms.

Glancing down, it takes me a few seconds to realize I'm holding Mom's stuff. My mouth falls open as tears well in my eyes, and it takes every bit of fight in me not to let them fall. But I quickly fail, feeling the hot streaks glide down my cheeks.

"How did you get this?"

"I went looking," he snaps. "Because I was worried. But I was wrong to think you'd actually have the decency to be my friend."

A million words threaten to come out, but at the same time, I'm physically incapable of speaking. My eyes scan the floor, taking in the ruins of our argument, and I carefully put Mom's stuff on the floor, walking over to the tipped-up desk.

I pick it up, standing it back upright before reaching for his laptop. Dusting it off, I'm relieved to find it working as I place it back on the desk.

As I continue to collect the belongings off the floor, Rylan stands there wordlessly, just watching as his body remains tense and rigid with silent anger.

When there's nothing left but the coffee spill, I glance around for a rag or something, but Rylan's cracked voice stops me.

"I need you to go, Spencer. Now. Just go."

"Alright," I concede softly, pausing as I once again spot my handprint on his face. Something tries to compel me to apologize, but I choke on the words—they mean nothing right now. We've said all that we can, and it's not enough.

It will never be enough.

Not in this lifetime.

I'm the villain today. I let my sadness become my downfall. I've become everything I always hated.

Rylan refuses to look at me now, and the tension in the room is so thick, I feel like I could suffocate. And if I'm being honest, part of me wishes I could just die right now. It's a small part, still somewhat insignificant to the rest of the overwhelming feelings choking me... but it's there. Another moment of self-pity as his words cut deep like a knife.

I'm alone... because I made it that way.

Finally, I relent, turning on my heel and making my way toward the door. When I reach the doorway, I dare a glance over my shoulder at him, heart breaking as he leans over the desk, palms flat with his head hung low.

He looks just as broken as I feel, and I despise myself for being the one who did that. But it's his fault as much as my own for letting things get this far. It feels like a fitting goodbye—an ending to our short story.

Violent. Broken. Catastrophic.

Two ruined kingdoms realizing that the world is bigger than they can face. And the guilt is what drags me out the door and holds me back from running to him.

My footsteps echo softly through his house, more tears falling as I make my way outside. Thankfully, Mayor Astor is nowhere to be seen. And Rylan certainly doesn't try to stop me as I leave.

Whatever was growing between us is dead.

I made sure of it.

By the time I arrive for Algebra, I'm frustrated to find that the only available seat is next to Tai. Just my luck that we're desk neighbors in two classes. I swear he wasn't in this class initially. But at this point, I'm questioning my own sanity. The days are shifting into blurs, unrecognizable as I go through the motions with a fake smile.

Normally I'd have no qualms with sitting near him, but after my fight with Rylan last night, the idea makes me nervous.

I have no idea if he's told his best friends about what transpired between us. Part of me believes he has. No doubt it would give them a good laugh or fresh ammo to use against me. I keep waiting for the bullet to graze, my secrets to be unraveled in enemy territory.

But when I sit down, there's no snide remarks about it—just Tai's usual taunting demeanor.

"Someone got up on the wrong side of the bed this morning," he murmurs, cocking an eyebrow.

"I'm not in the mood today, Beckett."

Tai grins, scooting his chair and desk closer. "Don't be like that, Spencer. Besides, we're going to be spending a lot of time together. We should become friendly."

My head snaps toward him, grimacing as I try to surmise what he's referring to. But before I can question him—even against my will and sound state of mind—Mr. Valkov's loud voice booms over the class.

"Pay attention! As we are now nearing finals week, it is my duty to ensure you all pass—mainly because I don't want to see you here again next year."

Well, no one can disagree with that. Repeating senior year sounds like endless torture. I'd rather scoop my eyeballs out with a rusty spoon.

Mr. Valkov's eyes linger over the class, scanning each and every one of us as if he's trying to make a point. "Therefore, given the current climate, I have decided it is best to prepare you with additional assigned tasks. I understand the past few weeks have been difficult," he pauses, looking at a few Cedar students perched in the front row. "But there's no reason why that would stop you from passing. To ensure you achieve the highest grade possible, you will be partnered up with a study buddy for the remainder of the semester."

What?

Since when do you need a study partner for *algebra*?

Murmurs float through the room. Everyone, including the Willowbrook students, appear surprised by this late addition to the module.

"I will be placing a list by the door, assigning you to a partner. You will notice that I have attempted to pair up students together from each academy. This is beneficial," his voice raises as the murmurs turn angry. "It will allow you to explore each other's knowledge, perhaps giving you an advantage. It is also my hope that it will teach you unity, removing any distractions upon finals week."

Ahh—essentially, they are forcing us to be friends.

Once again... what the fuck?

Mr. Valkov walks over to his desk, plucking up a piece of paper. "This is mandatory. Should you not comply it will be an automatic failure as the task is now worth a percentage of your final grade. Now, we're going to continue where we left off—trigonometric functions. I'm about to hand out a pop quiz so I can ascertain your current level of knowledge. This topic will be in the finals, so pay attention to the questions and take them seriously."

There's a chorus of groans as he starts walking the rows, handing out the quiz papers. Once distributed, he makes tracks to the door, slapping the partner list on it with a heavy thud.

I have no idea how I'm supposed to concentrate on this pop quiz when all I want to do is check the list. But I manage to push through, mainly because I'm gifted with some mild entertainment. Tai cusses quietly next to me, muttering something about cotangents being shoved into anal orifices.

By the end of class, people shove past one another to get to the door, a line forming as people survey the list. I hang back, not keen on being stampeded. I want to know as soon as possible so I can prepare for inevitable torture, but at the same time, I'm in no rush to meet my fate now that I have the opportunity to check.

Finally, the line dissipates. Approaching the list hesitantly, I grip my bag strap in my fist as my eyes run down the list. Behind me, Tai peaks over my shoulder.

"Well, this is going to be fun," he grins, making my back muscles tense up.

I wish I could feign ignorance, but there's no denying what I'm seeing on the paper. It's exactly what I had silently prayed against. But it's there for us, in black and white.

Tai Beckett (W) and Bexley Spencer (Ce.)

Chapter Twenty-Six

Grumbling, I can't hide the disdain from my face as I ring the doorbell. There's only one small consolation to me voluntarily coming to this hellhole, and somehow, I manage to crack a smile when the door swings over and I'm tackled by Soph.

"I'm sorry!"

"Can't... breathe," I choke out.

She pulls back with a sheepish grin. "Sorry—*again*."

After begrudgingly agreeing to unblock Tai's number, I had no choice but to admit I was at the mercy of the curriculum. I'm still not entirely sure why algebra requires us to partner up. Even more confusing is the so-called project that's now been assigned to us. Each pair has been issued with an equation to solve. I miss the days where mathematics didn't include the alphabet, and for a split second, I was certain that we'd probably be able to just solve the equation on our own—but I was wrong.

If I had to bet money on it, this bullshit series of numbers is more complex than at first glance. Not only are there at least two dozen steps to complete it, I'm almost certain that the equation in itself is unsolved. But we still have to work through the series of steps to find some definitive answer that we both agree on. Trying to come to a consensus with Tai... *that* will be the real test.

"So, this is your house," I mutter awkwardly, gazing up at the two—no, wait—three storey home. Well, it's not so much of a house as it is a mansion. It's even bigger than Rylan's place, and once again, I find myself a little annoyed that these men continue to dazzle in luxury and rub it in our faces like a weapon.

In other circumstances, I would have firmly stated that we stay at the academy to work on the project. There's no way in hell I'd let Tai into my house. But apparently, the academy decided to limit access to facilities outside of school hours. But I'm not stupid—I'd easily guess that it's to stop Cedar students from snooping around or being on grounds unsupervised.

As I said, the only consolation to agreeing to come here is that I have Sophia present as a witness in case I *accidentally* murder her twin brother. I'm still in dumb disbelief that I managed to befriend the one person that's tied to the three men that serve to make my life a living hell. Talk about luck.

Speaking of the Devil, he trots down the staircase with practiced ease, locking eyes with me from over the top of Soph.

"Spencer. A pleasant sight as always."

"It's as pleasant as a pap smear," I grumble, Soph snorting as I waltz past her. I'm keen to just get this over with. The less amount of time I need to be around him, the better.

Swinging my bag dangerously high, I nearly manage to connect with his precious face. He doesn't flinch though, just grinning at me like he's caught a mouse in a trap.

"Follow me. We can study in my room."

I don't immediately follow, instead turning to Soph. "You'll be nearby, right?"

She nods, words cut off as Tai gapes at us, offended.

"I'm not going to cause bodily harm," he protests.

"I might," I quickly answer, squeezing his sister's shoulder for good measure—a silent plea at making sure I don't leave here in handcuffs. Normally, I'd like being cuffed... just not under these circumstances.

He grumbles under his breath, leading the way as we climb the stairs. I gaze around, taking in the pastels—well, it's mainly just a lot of white. I guess Willowbrook Wolves never change colors. It's no secret that his father is an esteemed alumnus, making Tai and Sophia legacies. They care about their dumb rollcall as much as they do their funding.

But his house is so eerily different to Rylan's. Even though Max Astor is a Wolf too, their house still felt *homey*. There were pictures lining the walls, the smell of floral accents, and welcoming furniture. This house reminds me of a museum—cleaner than any building I've ever seen, smelling horribly of disinfectant, and not a single trace of livelihood. There's no pictures, not even any artwork on the pale white walls. It's as if they forgot to decorate it, and someone just cleans vigorously all day.

My stomach clenches at the smell and color. Flashbacks of the hospital spring to mind, and when Tai disappears through a doorway, I have to take a small breath to steady myself. But when I walk in, preparing to face more blank canvases, I'm surprised to find the opposite.

If you showed me a picture of Tai's bedroom next to a photograph of any other communal room in this house, I'd never know they were in close proximity. Where the walls are bare downstairs, Tai has photos, artwork and trophies lining around the room. My eyes fall to a large black and white canvas on the far wall, the charcoal streaks of wax pastel weave into shapes—the face of a beautiful woman.

Throwing himself into his computer chair, he swings around to face me, frowning at my hovering figure by the door. "You can come in. I don't bite. Well, not unless you ask nicely of course."

Ripping my eyes away from the canvas, I cross the room, sitting in the second chair on the other side of the computer desk. It's clear that it's not its usual place, and I'm silently thankful for the hospitality. Maybe this won't be so bad after all.

"Have you looked over the equation yet?" I ask, dumping my workbooks and notes onto the desk.

"I figured you could just do it all for us."

Scratch that. It's going to be bad.

"I'm not doing the project solo," I snap. "You might have a free ride to graduation, but I don't."

"Chill, Spencer. I was just kidding. It's a joke, not a dick. Don't take it so hard."

My eyes snap up, face awash with frustration. He just grins in response, leaning back in his chair like he doesn't have a care in the world.

"And what does that mean?" I ask sternly, reading between the lines.

Tai cocks an eyebrow. "Whatever do you mean, sweet Bexley?"

I might not know how to do this algebra equation yet, but I can add things together. The smug smile, the dancing eyes—a lot can be said about someone's facial expressions. And clearly, Tai knows. It doesn't take a psychiatrist to figure out he's taunting me with unspoken secrets.

"Get over it," I answer sharply. "What's done is done."

He leans forward, folding his arms on the desk. "I'm intrigued though. Tell me this—how did you manage to *woo* Ry?"

Sitting down, I ignore him, adjusting the workbooks so they are all symmetrical on the desk. Picking up my pen, I finally glance up, expressionless.

"Have you looked at the project?" I ask again.

Tai grins, folding his arms. "No, I haven't."

"Well, we may as well start there," I reply, annoyed.

Putting the project paper front and center, I pretend to examine the jumbled mess of numbers and letters. Fuck—there's brackets too. I feel like this is the one time that PEDMAS is going to fail me. Why teach us one thing just to have it completely contradicted later on in a different subject? Academic torture at its finest.

"I'm going to assume this relates to trigonometric functions somehow," I start. "It doesn't say outright that we're finding an angle, but Valkov has probably snuck it in there somewhere. Do you have a scientific calculator?"

When he doesn't answer, I glance up, ready to give him a good tongue lashing at his lack of interest. But instead, I find him staring at the paper, looking almost green.

Frowning, I put my pen down. "What's wrong? Are you that repulsed by my presence that you're on the verge of vomiting?"

"I hate math," he whispers painfully.

The tone is almost pathetic, full of indication that *the* Tai Beckett is on the edge of a nervous breakdown, that I nearly laugh.

"I don't like it either," I admit. "So, maybe Valkov was onto something when pairing people up. Suffer together, you know?"

Tai looks up. "We're going to fail, Bexley. This was a mistake."

What the hell is going on? There's something off-putting about his sudden change of behavior. But regardless of whatever crisis he is going through, I don't have it in me to fail. Not after everything else that has happened. The very least I can do is graduate after I lay Mom to rest. I still haven't sorted out the whole funeral mess, but I'll be damned if I don't pass senior year and fully implode my life into irreparable despair.

"We're not going to fail," I say firmly. "We have two weeks to finish this. It's not the end of the world. Truthfully, I don't think there's even a correct answer. We just need to show our working out process."

He doesn't answer, just remains frozen. Seconds continue to pass and part of me wonders if this is some type of ploy to catch me off guard. But the longer the silence takes hold, I start to genuinely panic that he's having some medical emergency and may need to get Soph to assist.

"Snap out of it." I wave my hand in front of his face.

A little head shake is all I get in reply. Sighing, I'm about ready to give up when there's a knock on the door.

Turning my head, an older woman walks in, carrying a tray of cookies.

"I thought you might like a study snack," she beams, pausing once she catches sight of Tai. "What's wrong, Bear?"

Her words seem to snap him out of his trance, cheeks reddening slightly as he gazes at her in alarm. "Nothing!"

She looks at me, offering a warm smile. "Is he doing mathematics? Poor child can code all day but the moment he has to multiply—" she trails off, laughing softly.

The tray gets set down on the edge of the desk, my stomach grumbling at the smell of freshly baked cookies. Holy fuck—they look amazing.

"You're not allergic to peanut butter, are you?" She asks suddenly. "Oh, goodness. I should have asked beforehand. I'm so sorry."

"No, no it's fine," I quickly say, reaching for one. "I love peanut butter."

I nearly choke on the words. Nostalgia threatens to send me into a spiral alongside Tai—what a pair we would be. Beckett breaking down over math while I wallow over peanut butter cookies. The smell reminds me of Mom and better times, but surprisingly, I find myself overcome with emotion-fueled fond memories instead of living night-mares.

A wave of relief crosses her face. "I'm glad. They are Tai's favorite. I'm just not used to having new faces in the house. When he said he had a study partner, I was expecting Rylan or Hunter. Though I'm not sure how much studying those boys get done. Boys and their videogames."

"I don't have the correct anatomy for that, I'm afraid," I joke, taking a bite of the... *best fucking cookies I've ever tasted. Holy shit.*

My eyes widen in surprise, causing her to laugh. I swallow, turning to her. "These are incredible," I boast. "Did you make them?"

She nods. "My secret recipe." Her smile is infectious, and I can't help but return the gesture. She reminds me of Mom in her better days—putting me at ease as I take in her delicate features and contagious happiness.

"I love to bake but this puts me to shame," I grin.

My gaze drifts back to Tai, momentarily forgetting his presence in my euphoric cookie moment. "Your mom is amazing."

He blinks before breaking out into a smile—one without sinister motive. The sugar starts to rush to my head because for a moment, my stomach clenches at the new expression.

It's so different from his usual smirks and grins, that I almost forget about the cookie in my hand.

"This is Mary," Tai murmurs warmly. "She's our designated house queen and carer."

"Oh." Embarrassment floods my face. "I'm so sorry. I shouldn't have assumed."

Mary laughs again, the tone so warm and friendly that it makes me think of hugs and cozy Sundays. She reaches out and pats my shoulder gently. "It's lovely to meet you—?"

"Bexley," I answer, rising to my feet to shake her hand. She beams back at the gesture, letting me greet her properly.

"Bexley," she repeats with a smile, and I'm surprised to hear the lack of acknowledgement that usually comes from anyone associated with Willowbrook when they hear my name. "Pleasure to meet you, sweetheart. If you need anything, I'll be downstairs."

Mary makes her way back to the door, pausing to shoot Tai a final look. "Shall I take Calvin for a walk?"

"I'll do it," he answers softly, his face full of adoration. "He's too strong for his own good."

"If I can handle you, I can handle Calvin," she muses. "But he'll like that. He misses you during the day."

She vanishes down the hall and I hold back a laugh at Tai's flushed face.

"She seems nice," I say, amused. "Who's Calvin?"

In an instant, Tai's face changes again, a big grin reflecting back at me.

"Come on." He abandons the study papers. "I'll take you to meet him."

Chapter Twenty-Seven

Tai

Calvin comes barreling out of the kennel not a second after I open the back sliding door.

I hold back a laugh as Bexley freezes in disbelief, not even bothering to move out of the way as the giant furball lunges at us—well me, anyway.

"Oof." The air is forced out of my body as Calvin tackles me, his big pink tongue leaving a trail of saliva up my cheek. I have to take a step back to steady myself, wrapping my arms around the big fluff monster. "Bexley, meet Calvin."

At the mention of their introduction, Calvin jumps down, tail wagging as he sniffs Bexley's ankles. Most girls who have seen Calvin tend to squeal and stumble away due to his sheer size, but I'm surprised when Bexley leans down, putting her face right in the firing line as she gasps excitedly.

"Oh, aren't you just the cutest thing ever?" Bexley mumbles between slobbery licks.

"Incoming."

There's no time for my warning as the second large pup-sicle crash tackles us. Between the two of them, both Bexley and I end up on the lush grass outside the door, pinned down while the two behemoths attack us with hugs and canine kisses. In theory, perhaps I should have fore-warned her before opening the door, but is it wrong that I wanted it to be a surprise?

The sound of free laughter reaches my ears and every nerve ending in my body stills, captivated by the noise of pure joy. Pushing to my feet, I glance down at Bexley sprawled on the grass, her purple hair surrounding her like a halo. Her eyes are squeezed shut to protect her emerald irises from the extra moisture, but even closed, her whole face is lit up like a Christmas tree. She looks carefree and happy, and I realize in this moment that I've never witnessed this side of her.

Sure, I've been on the receiving end of many smirks and shit-eating grins from her—usually at the warehouse or school—but this is different. And coupled with the recent information that Ry filled me in on, I'm not prepared for how much it affects me. To see her genuinely happy, walls down... I'm starting to see why Ry became so captivated by her.

I let out a sharp whistle. "Alright, down boys!"

On my cue, the two pups scoot back, sitting down above her head. I step over, glancing down at the grass-angel spread out beneath me. She pries her eyes open, face not changing as she smiles up at me.

Shit. I really don't like the way it's making me feel. I need to remember this is Bexley Spencer I'm dealing with. She's our sworn enemy, the nightmare in my daydreams. Except for a split second, the nightmares don't seem like a bad place.

Maybe this is how she charmed her way into Ry's mind. Fucking succubus.

I offer her a hand because it's the polite thing to do. She grasps it, using my weight to help pull herself to her feet.

"You have dogs," she remarks breathlessly. "They are gorgeous. And very friendly."

"Too friendly," I reply with a laugh, looking at the two who are awaiting my next command. "Meet Calvin and Klein."

Bexley raises an eyebrow in amusement. "Calvin and Klein?"

I nod, fighting back a smile. "Calvin is mine. Klein is Soph's. They are brothers."

She glances over at the two, eyes dancing as they turn their attention to her. Their asses stay grounded, but their tails wag aggressively when they spot her watching. Traitors. Clearly, they are also taken aback by her attention.

Suddenly, a look of perplexment appears. Her gaze shifts between them a few times, before turning to me. "They look like wolves," she states, her tone somewhere between impressed and annoyed.

This time, I can't help it. My laugh bursts out, my lips pulling into a Cheshire grin. "I know," I reply simply. "Quite fitting, don't you think?"

Bexley rolls her eyes but steps forward, patting the tops of their heads. "Ego much?" she mumbles.

We adopted Calvin and Klein three years ago as puppies. Well, adopted in the guise of parental bribery.

Dad was leaving the country for work, and around the anniversary of Mom's passing, I was quite vulnerable. We were no strangers to having him away, but between the date gutting me and Soph being depressed from some of the stereotypical schoolyard bitches, I unleashed a decade of locked away thoughts. Still, my pleas and demands weren't enough to convince Dad to stay. After all, business comes first. He's never been hands-on, and the idea of dealing with teenage emotions was enough to scare him onto a plane without the bullshit excuse of work. So, we woke the next morning to his car gone from the driveway, but a quick handwritten note to check the backyard. That's when we found Calvin and Klein tied up, waiting to meet us.

For a man who is nothing but meticulous, he gave no thought as to the requirements of owning such brute pets. This was nothing more than a payment of his *generosity*, an excuse to call himself a good father. But thankfully, Mary was already onto it. She helped arrange the proper fencing and kennels, making sure our new family members had everything they needed.

As much as I still detest the coward move, I have to admit, Calvin and Klein were a great addition for both of us—man's best friend indeed. You can't buy a child's love, but he did give me someone else to love since you can't love an absent father. He may as well be a ghost too, but at least my remaining memories of Mom still existed deep down. The memories with Dad are few and far between.

Soph fell in love with Klein straight away, obsessed with his fluffy white ears. Something about the canine helped her grow a backbone. Well, that's what she believes. It was a team effort.

That same week, I pulled Ry and Hunter together, demanding we take control of Willowbrook. Our predecessors were too busy with their dicks buried in the senior cheerleaders to care, and with Hunter's Dad already a strong presence as the Dean, we easily dethroned them. It was unheard of, freshman students taking over as leaders. But with our plan in place, we had successfully taken over before sophomore year. And with that, I scared the shit out of anyone that dared look at my sister the wrong way. The bitches who tormented her suddenly became intoxicated with our power, instead throwing themselves at us. And in turn, they tried to befriend Soph, hoping to use her as leverage to weasel their way into importance. But Soph's too smart for that. I wish I could say the same for other students. Some never take notice of the warning signs—a fatal mistake.

My favorite memory was taking Calvin and Klein to a pep rally for the first time. Jay Bereman was trying to hit on Soph, refusing to take no for an answer. The egotistical bastard was in senior year and one of the few that refused to acknowledge us as leaders. He looked down on two things—girls, and anyone who wasn't a senior. Calvin tackled the piece of shit in front of the whole school, pissing on his chest which made Bereman vomit like a little bitch. After that, we never had any trouble again. We cemented our place as the head of Willowbrook and no brainless dickheads tried to target Sophia ever again. Occasionally, I watch the video recording of that momentous event whenever I need a pick-me-up.

"What are they?" Bexley asks, pulling me from the fond memory.

I stand next to Calvin, scratching behind his ear. "Tamaskans."

"I can't get over how much they look like timber wolves," she replies.

Calvin throws his head back, desperate to run his sandpaper tongue on my palm. "Like I said—fitting."

It's easy to tell the two pups are from the same litter. Both have the same gray hues throughout their coats, mixed with shades of white, black and brown. Where Klein has pure white ears, Calvin's are black. The patterned coats blend the colors seamlessly, resembling wolves. Their honey irises stand out against the monochrome colors, and without seeing them as the big slobber goblins they are, you'd probably shit yourself coming face to face with them.

Bexley shakes her head at my response, but her hardened expression barely lasts as the two twins give her literal puppy-dog eyes. She melts instantly, squatting in front of them to offer dual pats.

I unhook their leashes from the nail hanging by the door, offering one to her. "Come on. Let's procrastinate from that disaster of an equation a little longer. You can walk Klein for Soph. She's deep in a book at the moment. I tried to talk to her earlier and she threatened to throw her Kindle at my head if I disturbed her again."

"That's why I like her," Bexley murmurs playfully, taking the lead from me. She clips it easily to Klein's collar, while I do the same to Calvin.

"Yeah, well if it's any consolation, I think my own sister likes you more than me. She was more than willing to greet *you* at the door. But heaven forbid I try to talk to her while she's reading about dragons."

Bexley laughs, like she's remembering something funny. "She's a good woman."

"Because she's likely to maim me?"

"That's a bonus."

I beckon for her to follow me to the side gate, the two dogs leading the way. They know our afternoon path better than anyone, and once we hit the pavement on the street, they guide us with ease.

Emerald eyes skirt around, taking in the various houses in the gated community. It's a quiet neighborhood, and at this time of day, the only people around are house staff finishing up their outdoor jobs and people driving by as they return home from corporate roles in expensive suits in even more extravagant cars.

As we approach a familiar looking home near the entrance, I nod toward it. "That's Hunter's house."

Bexley frowns, observing the large house that's similar size to mine. "Dean Lannister's?"

Shit. On reflection, it probably wasn't the greatest idea to tell someone from Cedar where the dean lives. But for some reason, the words had slipped out before I could stop them.

As if sensing my anguish, Bexley laughs. "I'm not going to set it on fire."

"I wouldn't put it past you," I reply dryly. "After all, your own school got burnt down."

She suddenly stopped, much to the displeasure of Klein who gives us both the side eye. I pause as well, watching her curiously.

"You think we burnt down our own building?" she asks sternly. "I'm fairly certain it was someone from Willowbrook."

"Us?" I scoff. "Why would we be interested in destroying it? In case you haven't realized, we're not exactly loving your presence at school."

Bexley cocks an eyebrow. "Well, someone burned it down. And we're going to find out who."

"Be my guest."

Shaking her head, she continues walking, jolting a little when Klein takes off enthusiastically. "Why do you hate math?"

I groan at the change of subject. "It's a bullshit subject that makes no sense."

"It does if you apply formulas correctly."

"The only formulas I care about are in computers."

"Then why did you pick it?"

"I didn't," I shoot back quickly, realizing my mistake.

Bexley stops abruptly again, this time pivoting her body to face me. She's tall, but I still glance down at her, keeping my face free of admissions.

"I knew it," she snaps. "You weren't in the class when I arrived. Did you switch classes?"

"That's none of your business, Spencer."

She tilts her head, eyes narrowing. It's a little unnerving. I know she's trying to read me, ready to pull my mind apart until she finds the answers that she's looking for. "You changed classes. Why?"

Her tone is all business, demanding. I grin, unbothered and immune to her death stare. Reaching out, I grasp her chin with my fingers, giving her head a little wobble. "Because I was so keen to keep an eye on you. We can't have you causing problems now, can we?"

Her hand slaps mine away, eyes flashing dangerously. "You asshole. You three will really go to extraordinary lengths to be a pain in the ass."

"Yet, you're the one who fucked Rylan. We must have something going for us if even you wanted to jump on that joyride."

Bexley shoves Klein's lead into my chest. "Walk your own damn dogs. And solve your own fucking equation," she snipes, turning around and heading back toward the house.

I readjust the leads to make sure I have both dogs securely. "Oh, come on, Spencer. Don't be a sad little dick rider."

All I get in reply is her middle finger, flipped over her shoulder as she storms back toward the house. Sighing, I look at Calvin and Klein, their beady eyes pleading for more pavement time.

"Well, I guess it's just us three now," I murmur, tugging the lead to signal them to start walking. "Protect me from Soph's wrath when we get home and I'll give you extra treats."

Chapter Twenty-Eight

Who knew that applying for a bank loan or a job would be so difficult?

I spend most of the new week pleading my case to loan officers and emailing off job applications, but to my disappointment, no one is interested in hiring or loaning to an inexperienced full-time schooler. I guess I shouldn't be surprised, but with each day that passes, I realize I'm out of options. Which only means one thing.

Wind whips my hair around, the cool gentle breeze making my skin tingle as I lean against my truck. This has to be the single lowest point of my existence. And if he doesn't turn up soon, I might just consider a run along the canyon since it would be less torturous.

But to my utter surprise and relief, headlights turn into the warehouse parking lot, the familiar sound of wheels flicking up gravel and roar of an engine sizzling my nerves.

Rylan pulls up next to my truck, wasting no time to disembark. The driver's door slams shut a bit too harshly behind him, and I know he hasn't forgotten our last conversation.

"Well, I'm here," he proclaims with a huff, leaning against his pickup, facing me.

That stoic, expressionless look is back, his mental walls up as he scans my frame. But despite being in the one place we come to spar, I'm not here to fight. It's ironic, really, but I didn't choose this place because of its significance to our feud, or because it's neutral territory—I choose it because it's where we found a truce in a savage world.

I'm hoping to dig deep; to find the courage and strength I normally have in the cage, to step outside my comfort zone. And if that fails, Arch is on standby if I need rescuing.

It was a bitter pill to swallow, asking Arch for help and letting him see my broken-down mind. This next conversation will be even harder. But I've quickly realized if I don't do this—don't ask for help—the only place I'll end up in is Failure-Ville.

"Thanks for coming," I murmur, wrapping my arms around my frame.

Rylan nods sharply, the lights from the eternal warehouse bulbs reflecting off his silver rings. "What's this about?" he asks coldly.

Sighing, it takes every ounce of strength not to automatically snap back at his tone, but I remind myself that he has every right to be mad at me. I did break into his house and cause him to trash his room after all.

"I'm sorry," I start, voice shaking. I swallow, clearing my throat as I attempt to strengthen my words. "For the other day. You were right—I shouldn't have done that. Any of it."

He doesn't answer, but his eyes soften slightly, silently gesturing to continue.

"My mom died," I admit, even though he already knows that. "It wasn't expected. She passed while we were here that night..."

The words cut off, grief gripping my insides like steel vines. I hate talking about this—to him—but he needs to know. He needs to know the extent of my pain, why this is so hard for me. Especially if I need to do what is required.

A deal with the Devil.

I'm still not entirely sure I can even trust him. But so far, I'm the only one who's given any reason for distrust. Except of course for the whole Tai being a know-it-all asshole. But that's an issue for another day. And when I'm finished having this *minor* crisis, I fully intend on interrogating Rylan to ask how he ended up with Mom's belongings.

"I'm sorry," he finally says. "That must be hard."

I nod. "It is." My eyes meet the ground, no longer able to face looking at him. "But you already knew that."

There's an intense need to know more. It's been painstaking, driving me insane trying to figure out how he found out when my own found family didn't even see the signs.

A gruff sigh breaks the silence. "I'm sorry for sticking my nose into your business."

I laugh quietly, shaking my head. "I tried so hard to figure shit out on my own. But I can't."

His eyes focus on me. "What do you mean?"

"I can't get the money for the funeral. Turns out I might be the queen of Cedar Heights, but in the real world... I'm a nobody."

The admission out loud sends a sharp stab through my chest. His feet come into view, hand tipping my chin up. The movement forces me to face him straight-on.

"You're not a nobody. You're Bexley fucking Spencer."

Our eyes lock together. For some bizarre reason, the words ricochet through my body, and for the first time in a while, I feel that old fire again. It's small, insurmountable, but there's a flicker of something.

"Come on," he says, dropping his hand. "I want to show you something."

Nodding, I follow him. Rylan heads straight to the warehouse doors, pulling out a key identical to the one on my keyring. He opens the side door to the building, slipping inside into the darkness. We both know the path well despite being shrouded in complete darkness. Little scraps of moonlight trail over the concrete floor of the main arena, the windows lining the tall tops of the walls letting in the faintest of light.

I reach the power switches first, yanking down the lever. The room explodes in a furious array of fluorescent light. It takes a second for my eyes to adjust, blinking rapidly until the room fully comes into focus.

A gasp escapes my lips. There, in the center of the room, is a large, fully enclosed cage. It could easily rival a proper

UFC ring, the thick black fencing almost glistering under the industrial bulbs.

"Holy shit," I mutter, stepping toward it.

The white floor is pure and unmarked—though I have no doubt it won't stay that clean for long. The side door is open, inviting, and I step inside, still mesmerized by the perfect structure.

"Do you like it?" Rylan asks, stepping in behind me.

"Like it?" I repeat. "I love it. This is amazing." Spinning around, my body buzzes with excitement. I'm fairly certain in all of the warehouse history, there's never been a cage of this magnitude. It would have set Willowbrook back a pretty penny.

"I had them fast track it. But I still want the beach for the month as promised."

Turning to face him, I relax at the visible smirk tugging on the corners of his mouth.

"I suppose you still want the votes too," I joke.

"A deal's a deal."

My fingers run along the fence, the black vinyl-coated chain-link metal surprisingly warm. "Shit. Well, you've really outdone yourself, Astor."

"Impressed?"

I shoot him a smile. "Don't let it go to your head. We both know I'd be able to kick your ass in here."

Rylan steps toward me. "Want to put your money where your mouth is, Spencer?"

"Like a bet?" I laugh. "I didn't take you to be a losing man."

He snorts. "I'll go easy on you."

"I don't like things easy."

"Evidently."

His knuckles grace my cheek intimately. Our eyes are locked, both burning with need. But I can't make the first move. Guilt still eats at me, the silent fear that if I give in to my temptations, something bad might happen again.

"Stop overthinking," Rylan murmurs. "I can see the cogs turning in your mind. Fight me, Spencer."

Stepping back, he pulls off his shirt, tossing it to the side of the cage. Muscles ripple under the orange glow, and I'm not sure if I want to fight him or fuck him. Both seem equally enticing in my mission to escape reality.

I repeat the move, trying not to pay attention to the way his eyes flare at my bare torso. We're even now, both in shorts, though it's obvious my sports bra is a distraction for him.

Idiot.

He's still staring at my chest when I rush forward, punching him square in the pec. Rylan's solid frame stumbles back slightly, eyes shooting up. Only two seconds pass before he moves forward, throwing a hook toward my face. I block it with ease, annoyed that he's going easy on me like promised. I don't want easy. Or pity. I want to feel something other than the gut tearing pain that pulls apart each thread of my heart.

"You can do better than that," I taunt, the two of us circling off.

"I don't make a habit of hitting girls," he remarks.

"Spare me your nobility. Gender has nothing to do with this right now."

To prove my point, I swing my leg around, the top of my foot slamming into the side of his ribcage. Rylan growls in pain, the last piece of chivalry fading as he charges forward.

The two of us exchange blows carelessly. Even when my knuckles hit his flesh and his hand finds my face, I know we're both holding back still. But it's enough. The air rushes in and out of my lungs, chest heaving as we spar. Pink patches blossom on his torso with each hit, and I have no doubt my own skin is flushed. But the slight ache feels like home.

In a sickening way, it feels like justice. Allowing myself to feel pain. I can't help but continue to regret that night, but I know I can't hold onto that forever. Nothing I do will bring her back, and the longer I let myself fall into these feelings, the more I lose myself.

I can't do that.

I'm still needed.

I still want to live.

Somewhere in my hazed, adrenaline-fueled rush, I lose track of my control, my fist connecting with Rylan's jaw harder than anticipated. He stops instantly, rubbing his jaw with an amused look.

"Jesus, Spencer. You have a mean right hook."

"Shit." I step forward, pulling his hand down to survey the damage. Thankfully, it's just a pink mark, but it's probably going to bruise a bit. "I didn't mean to hit you so hard."

I let out a squeak when Rylan snakes his arm around my body, pulling me flush against him. My eyes widen when I realize just how little he cares about his face, erection pressing into my thigh.

There's a small calm before the storm, the two of us staring at each other. It's electrifying, and I'm not sure who moves first, but when our lips smash into each other, I find I don't care.

Our teeth clash together in our intensity, tongues battling for dominance as my hands waste no time in slipping down the waistband of Rylan's shorts. I grasp his hardened cock, stroking him from tip to shaft as his lips trail down my jaw, feasting on my neck.

The rest of our clothes get thrown around the ring, creating a makeshift circle around us. Rylan's foot attempts to sweep me off my feet, but I quickly turn the tables, swinging him around until he lands with a heavy thud on the floor.

Straddling him, I hold him down, my hands pressing against his rock-hard chest. Rylan doesn't fight me though, his own hand slipping past mine to grip his cock. I feel it pressing against my entrance and I slam myself down, impaling my body with his.

Rylan hisses softly, hands gripping my hips. I roll my body, little gasps of pleasure mixing with his rugged breathing. It feels like we're back in his truck again, two dominant forces, and once again, he's giving me control—like he knows it's what I need.

Raising myself on my knees, I slowly draw him out before sliding back down. It's agonizing for both of us, but the speed keeps me level-headed. I don't get lost in a frenzy. And when his head tips back, eyes closing tight, I realize he needs it too. We're almost cut from the same cloth, except his is designer while mine is thrift store. There's nothing wrong with our differences, and I think we're both starting to see that. Here, we're taking what we need—polar opposites.

I need control as much as I need pain. The unwavering desire to feel a hold of something is all I have left to cling to right now, while Rylan clearly needs someone else to take the reins for a minute.

We're perfect, in complete unison as our hips smash together. We chase our releases as one, my nails digging into his chest as I start to feel the coil tighten in my stomach.

"Bexley," he says, deep and low, and already I know what he's asking. Not realizing my eyes had fluttered shut, they open, locking with his. And when I come, I don't hold back, letting him see everything wash over my face—the pleasure, the destruction, the agony. It's all one, and I allow myself a reprieve to enjoy a moment of weakness in the safety of his tight grip.

As soon as my orgasm finishes, Rylan is right there with me, groaning deep in his throat as his hips finally jolt up, taking control as he falls over the blissful edge.

Flattening myself against his chest, I feel the thudding of his rapid heartbeat through his chest. It's soothing, hearing it beat, and a tear slips out and splashes onto his skin.

He doesn't point it out or make a big deal of it though. His arms wrap around my back, holding me against him while I silently cry.

And there, in our new ring where we will return as enemies, I find some short lived peace.

Chapter Twenty-Nine

Bexley

"What's that?" I ask, amused.

I shove back a laugh as Soph frantically waves a flyer in my face. Arch and I are at our usual lunch table on Friday in the cafeteria, joined by Parker, Millie, and Abby. They don't seem surprised either at Soph's insane arrival, Arch moving down to make room on the bench next to me.

"It's our annual dance," Soph replies, throwing herself into the space. "You have to come. Please."

"A dance?" Abby gasps excitedly, and Soph squeals at her enthusiasm. New friendship incoming.

Arch starts choking on his Caesar salad, reaching for his bottle of water as he attempts to clear his airway. That boy will do just about anything Abby asks, but dancing? That's going to take some convincing. For as long as I've known Archie, he's had a strict no dancing policy. Go figure that he ends up in a relationship with a cheerleader.

"It's themed too," Soph says, elbowing me. "You have to come, Bex. I've never been and it's our last year here."

"Why haven't you been?" I ask, deflecting. Me and dancing? I'm kind of on Arch's team here. Pretty certain I was born with two left feet and the last thing I need is to fall over in front of everyone at Willowbrook.

Soph falls quiet for a second, seemingly embarrassed. "I didn't have anyone to go with. But now I do! You'll come, right?" she turns to Abby. "New person..."

Abby laughs warmly. "I'm Abby. And you are?"

"Tai Beckett's twin sister," I interject playfully.

Arch has already met Soph, but I see the rest of our group stare on in disbelief. Soph, on the other hand, elbows me again, making me wince. Unbeknownst to everyone at the table, I'm currently sporting some interesting bruises from my *fight* with Rylan.

"Don't associate me with that asshat," she grumbles. "And don't think I know that you two had some type of argument. He got home with the pups and I realized your car was gone."

I shrug nonchalantly. "To be fair, I have arguments with everyone."

"It's true," Arch interrupts. "It's a right of passage. You have to have at least one argument with Bexley before graduation."

Millie pipes up, intrigued. "I haven't had an argument yet."

"That's because I'm a little scared of you," I joke. "And Parker too."

"Oh, please." Millie rolls her eyes. "I've seen you fight. You could handle me. Speaking of fighting—when do I get my turn?"

Parker's face hardens. I can see the battle behind his eyes but he's out of luck. A deal's a deal.

"Next fight night," I answer, glancing over at Sophia. I wonder if she knows that her brother's best friend arranged the best damn cage I've ever seen in my life.

My cheeks heat up at the memory, deliberately knocking my fork off the table so I have an excuse to duck underneath. As I reach for the fork slowly, I catch sight of Arch and Abby's hands linked in her lap, and I snicker, tickling his hand with the prongs. A foot swings at me in retaliation, and I reappear from under the table, grinning at his annoyed look.

"Way to change the subject," Soph mumbles, turning to Abby. "I'm Sophia. Bexley's new BFF."

"Only because we share a common enemy and I can use you for intel."

"What common enemy is that?"

The whole table turns at the sound of the deep voice, eyes landing on the three men who haunt my nightmares in different ways. For a second, Rylan and I lock eyes, his blue irises dancing slightly. Quickly, I look at Tai, replying, "You. Obviously."

His mouth snaps shut, glaring at his twin with some weird loving-hateful sibling glance. "Traitor."

Surprisingly, there's zero malice in his tone, but he's still annoyed at her presence at our table. Sharp eyes grab my attention and I cock an eyebrow at Hunter, who lingers on Tai's left.

"Lannister," I greet coolly. "Got something on your mind?"

His eyes narrow, a stark contrast to his blue-eyed friend. I'd almost say that the hatred comes from fucking his best friend, but I'm fairly certain it's just pure hate.

"This isn't over yet, Duchess," he quips. "Not by a long shot."

My lady boner at Rylan's presence is instantly eradicated, anger taking its place as I stand up from the bench. Hooking my leg over, I stand toe-to-toe with Hunter, silently telling myself not to throw hands.

"You started this mess. Don't blame me because you don't like the consequences of your own actions."

His bicep flexes as he pushes back his hair, the red tips melting into the obsidian mess. "You'll have to do better than a little glue. I'd sleep with one eye open if I were you."

Smiling, I gently press the tip of my nail into his chest—today's color is a bright shade of pink. It reminds me of the pink hues on our skin after our tumble in the new cage, but I'll never admit that to anyone.

"I sleep soundly, Lannister. In fact, my dreams often feature tubes of superglue and your ass on Mrs. Smythson's desk."

I can feel Rylan's gaze on the side of my face, but I ignore it. I don't trust myself to break character if we lock eyes.

"Are you going to the dance, Sophia?" he asks, and I can still see him watching me through my peripheral vision.

She jumps up, picking up the flyer and waving it excitedly again. "Hell yes. We're all going. Aren't we, Bex?"

Is it possible to get away with murder? I mean, I know I have a room full of witnesses, but a little homicide can be disguised... right?

"Soph," I warn.

"Oh, come on," she whines. "Senior. Year." The words annunciate with such force that I break my gaze with Hunter to look at her over my shoulder.

"You haven't told us the theme yet."

She grins. "Villains and sinners."

I roll my eyes, noticing that Arch does the same. Could the Willowbrook administration be any more obvious? I'm surprised they are even still holding a dance with our attendance here. It seems like the last thing they would want is to have all of us in one big room together—probably with spiked beverages.

Rylan plucks the flyer from her hands. "Villains and sinners, you say."

My eyes turn to him on their own accord, finding brief release as he scans the paper. When he looks up, his eyes dart to me. I turn back to Hunter. We're in some weird fucked-up version of I-Spy.

Thankfully, he doesn't seem to notice. Hunter sneers in disgust, finally turning away to read the flyer too. "The cheerleaders certainly have a weird sense of humor."

"Cheerleaders?" Abby asks, piping up with interest. "They picked the theme?"

Soph nods. "The staff give them a list of options and they pick one they like. It's a fundraiser for them."

"You omitted that information," I grouch. "Count me out. I'm not donating to those psychos' funds."

"Oh, come on," Soph groans. "We can hang by the food table. They don't come near it."

At the table, I catch sight of Abby giving doe-eyes to Arch, and when he sighs in resignation, I know we're both screwed. He turns his face, pursing his lips together in a silent conversation that says, "Well, if I have to go, you're fucking coming too."

"Fine," I relent, folding my arms. "But can we get to the purpose of this visit so I can return to my cheeseburger?"

Tai hands the flyer back to his sister, who snatches it for no reason other than she can. He holds up his hands in defeat before turning to me.

"Fight night tonight," he says. "The new cage is ready. No point waiting," he finishes with a grin.

Millie gasps excitedly behind me, and I swear I hear Parker curse under his breath. "Fine," I nod. "I'll let my people know."

"And don't think I've forgotten about the project," Tai grumbles. "We only have a week left. I'm not letting you be the reason I fail."

I raise an eyebrow. "Seriously? You're the idiot that near cried when seeing the equation."

"I had something in my eye!"

Soph leans closer to me, lowering her voice but ensuring Tai can still hear her. "Not true. He's been raging all week about it."

"Shut up, Sophia."

"Make me, Tai."

"Alright," I sigh, intervening before the siblings can draw any more attention to our small crowd. There's already a bunch of eyes watching the exchange. We can save that for tonight. "We can meet Monday after school."

Tai shakes his head. "We need more time than that. We're running out of time."

"Just take what you can get," I snap suddenly.

The table falls silent. I'm surprised that even the Three Musketeers are also biting their tongues at my random outburst. A flash of concern crosses Rylan's face, but it's quickly hidden with expert precision. We've been texting again this week but even he doesn't know why I've had a moment of weakness.

A hand touches my shoulder and immediately, I know it's Arch without looking. Mom's funeral is tomorrow. Rylan doesn't know. A part of me feels guilty, like I've been playing a persona all week in our conversations, purposely hiding a secret and making sure only to put forward the best parts of me—if they exist anymore. Only Arch knows the intimate details—just how I need it.

Mr. Morrison was nice enough to accommodate my schedule. After missing my fair share of classes lately, I was grilled by Dean Lannister at the start of the week and warned that any more absences would affect my graduation. I know

I had ammo, a genuine reason, but I kept it to myself. If I was still at Cedar Heights, I probably would have owned up to my secret. But not here. So, we organized for a small service to take place at the Ridgeview Community Gardens over the weekend. Originally, I was going to go with Sunday since it's meant to rain tomorrow, but Arch made a good point—I'll want Sunday to myself, to grieve and come to terms with shit.

All in all, their suggestion of a fight night couldn't have come at a better time. I've been in a daze this week, doing everything I can to distract myself. But I can only run until tomorrow. At least tonight, I can find peace again... even if it's only temporary. I probably deserve to be locked up in an asylum. What sane person finds peace in violence? Humans are meant to have emotions, but I run from them like a person with commitment issues. It's the only cardio I'm good at—well, besides fighting. And I'm keen to get my knuckles bruised tonight.

Our card is already getting full. Between Mills and me, it won't take much to fill the other spots. Hell, Parker looks ready for round two as well.

"Alright, Monday," Tai concedes, staring at me as if I've suddenly spouted two heads and turned green. "But no more funny business."

"Fuck yourself with a cactus, Beckett," I whisper angrily, clearly still not in control of my temper as I grab my bag, abandoning my now-cold cheeseburger. "Arch, start spreading the word. I'll take care of the rest."

Chapter Thirty

Hunter

"Are we all set for tonight?" I ask Perkins.

The man is utterly useless at the best of times, except when it comes to causing a distraction. Or stealing things. I'm not sure how he manages the art of theft so well when he was called 'Butter Fingers' all last season. Seriously, they resemble Twinkies. You'd think having such large fingers would make for steady hands to catch a football, but until this year, it was an ever-loving miracle that he was even first string on the Willowbrook Wolves football team.

After our little encounter with Duchess today, I knew I would have to take charge of things. I'm not sure what's gotten into Rylan and Tai, but clearly, they still want to take a step back with things.

That can't happen.

They will thank me later. Once I can prove that Spencer is nothing more than a snake, it will become apparent that the only reasonable tactic is total destruction. The longer we let those Cedar freaks have any type of power, the harder it will be to regain control.

We're on the verge of a crumbling empire and I'll be damned if I lose everything I worked hard for. Dad agrees as well, and with his blessing, I'm going to make sure tonight is one to remember. It's time to make them fall into line once and for all. I'm tired of this bullshit charade, pretending we're co-existing in peace. It's all an act. The other two might not be able to recognize what's happening in the background, but I can.

People are questioning things—us. Word is filtering down the grapevine, making its way back to parents and alumnus members. The board is demanding answers, and someone even had the nerve to ask Dad if his son was even capable of being in charge. And of course, he's quick to remind me that my status reflects directly back on him.

Rylan and Tai have easily forgotten that even though we earned our place, there's still people who would be happy to see us get burned alive and take our spot. Every decision affects all of us. Which is why I need to do this. I'm saving all of our asses.

"Yep," Perkins confirms, handing the warehouse key back to me. "The new cage looks fire. I wouldn't mind having a go tonight."

Sighing to myself, I pocket the key, hardening my expression. "Maybe next time. I need you on call tonight. And remember—don't breathe a word of this to anyone."

He nods in resignation, but the idiot has no idea what's in store for him if he steps into the ring. His ego wouldn't last two minutes. I've tried to explain to countless people that there's more to fighting than just throwing punches.

We need to win the fight card tonight, which means playing smart. I've just finished the list and have to meet up with that guy who follows Bexley around everywhere like a pathetic little puppy dog. We'll exchange lists, taking a copy of the matches and opponents.

Part of me wishes that I was handling this directly with Bexley, but for whatever reason, she's opted out of the meeting.

She can only run for so long though. And now that I've set a trap for her, she'll regret ever stepping into Willowbrook territory.

"Are you sure you want to do this?" I ask for the fifth time.

Rylan alternates between stretching and bouncing on the balls of his feet. "Of course. What's wrong, H? Don't trust me to secure a win?"

"You know I do," I retort. "I just figured you'd want to be on the sideline when Spencer fights."

We're in one of the many rooms at the side of the warehouse. I assume it used to be an office judging by the power points and worn-out desk. Fighters use the rooms to get ready before a match. There's three on each side of the warehouse main floor, and we're in the end one of our set, waiting for his fight to begin.

Rylan probably thinks I'm doubting his ability by asking repeatedly. But in foresight, my question extends to a bigger picture.

He just doesn't know it yet.

Tai enters the small room behind me, holding two bottles of beer. He passes me one, grinning at Rylan. "You inspired me, Ry. I placed a bet."

"Odds on me, I hope."

"Nah, I bet against you. Kidding," he adds when Rylan stops bouncing and throws him a death glare.

I'm surprised that Rylan hasn't wagered his own bet. The man has a serious gambling problem. Though, is it a problem if you always win? He's ruthless—always playing the odds and analyzing every possible scenario. It's at the point where he can usually tell you the outcome before something has even begun.

Flicking the top off the beer, I take a swig, leaning against the wall. "You're up against someone called Steele Turner."

"Bexley's fuck buddy," Rylan answers. "We saw him at the beach."

"I thought he looked familiar."

Tai jumps up, sitting on a dusty, abandoned desk. "He's a footballer. I stalked his Facebook profile."

"Even better," Rylan says. "They're my favorite to knock down a peg."

My eyes narrow at his tone. There's something about it that seems... *personal?*

Neither of them look at me, and I fail to believe that torn up, pale green carpet is that interesting. Tai usually talks all our ears off, but he's quiet too.

I pull out the card details from my back pocket, skimming it for dramatic flare. "Spencer is fighting too, I see."

Waiting for their reaction, I study them both carefully. Rylan's face is the perfect picture image of empty emotion, but his posture fails him. He tenses slightly, quickly recovering by rolling his shoulders as if it's a deliberate move.

"Oh, really?" Tai asks. "I had no idea."

Bullshit. They knew—both of them. I caught them looking at the list when we arrived.

"She's fighting Tamara," I say casually, pretending I'm not catching onto their act. "Not sure Spencer will win this one."

Even I have to admit that when it comes to fighting in the cage, Spencer is lethal. To my knowledge, she's never lost a fight—at least not in recent years. The few times I've witnessed her matches I've been mildly impressed. I can still hate her and respect the hustle. But part of my plan tonight is to bring her down a notch. If she wins, I'll accept it, but Tamara will give her a run for her money. I've personally been coaching her for this very reason.

Thankfully, there's no shortage of footage from previous matches. I studied Duchess' form, her tactics. She's smart—much like Rylan in the ring. The best way to catch her off-guard is to make sure she never knows your next move. That, coupled with Tamara's sheer size, will make it difficult for her.

Our last fighter had the size advantage, but they lacked agility. Tamara is good at both. Our women's volleyball team captain, she's equally strong as she is fast. All we had to do was tweak my strategy. And assuming we stick to the plan, Duchess will be in no position to rush out of here at the end of the night.

We don't want her too injured though. Just enough that she stays back to recover, but still mobile to decline any offers for assistance. She's stubborn, but beside that, I want her to fully be aware of what I'm doing to her—so that she understands the consequences of fucking around.

I'd have her leave in an ambulance if I thought it would end well for us. I just need to get her alone, away from prying eyes. Whether we win this particular fight or not is a bonus. At the end of the night, as long as I have Spencer here by herself, then it's a victory.

"Hamilton?" Rylan asks. "She's good but do you think she'll really beat Bexley?"

And there it is.

Not only has his body language given him away, but now his mind has too. The way he says her name—her first name—normal people wouldn't pick up on it. But it's clear she's gotten to him.

Tai's eyes dart up at Rylan before swinging to me, giving us both a wide grin. "It will be interesting either way."

I shrug. "I wouldn't be surprised if Spencer gets quite hurt. But maybe she'll learn her lesson then. Plus, you taking out that boy-toy of hers will just be salt in the wound."

Pausing, I decide to poke the bear once more for good measure. "I guess they won't be able to fuck for a while."

Rylan's jaw hardens. My suspicions are spot on. If I offered a bet with him right now, to wager that they haven't slept together, I know without a doubt that he'd turn it down.

Because they have.

It's written all over his face. And if that wasn't proof enough, Liv's been stomping around the academy complaining at his lack of attention to her. We're men—simple creatures. If Rylan isn't fucking Liv and has stopped paying attention to her, it means he's drawn to someone else. Who else would have the kind of power to make Rylan turn his back on his oldest friends? I'm sure he means well and believes it isn't causing harm. Normally, I'd probably agree. But in our present situation, we need a strong front, and Rylan has made decisions without us recently. He's protecting her—probably from me—but he's the only one in that little dynamic I give a shit about.

I'm not entirely sure what's up with Tai. Maybe Sophia has wielded her twin leverage on him. There are very few people that Tai will listen to in this world, but she's one of them. And I don't think she'd be appreciative of her brother tormenting her friend. I heard Soph gushing and blabbering on about the dance to Spencer. I also know that she helped instigate some of these heinous acts against us. I'm surprised that Tai hasn't thrown that back at her. But sibling love is a tough nut to crack—or so I've heard. I have no qualms about being an only child.

"I'll see you out there," I finish, kicking off the wall. "Good luck."

Rylan doesn't need luck—not when I've dropped that mental image of Turner and Spencer fucking in his mind. Spencer might be shown some mercy from Tamara, but I can't say the same for her *friend*. I've been close to Rylan and Tai for so long that I know them better than they know themselves. We've joked about sharing girls before—hell, junior year was a wild time. But sharing someone with a person he hates? He won't let that go. Steele Turner will be lucky if he doesn't leave here in a body bag.

As I join the edge of the growing crowd, I lock my sights on the target across the room. People around me murmur pleasantries, some tapping my shoulder, but I'm laser focused on Spencer. I expected her to be in a changing room, getting ready for her fight. But she's stood on that damn barricade again, towering over the Cedar Heights landfill.

Dressed in skin-tight black shorts and a royal blue sports bra, her torso shakes as she laughs at something. Her eyes are drawn to someone in the crowd, and when people part for a brief second, I realize it's Turner.

It's like the depths of Hell want me to succeed, everything aligning perfectly as I whip my cell out. I lift it high, zooming in and snapping a quick picture of their smiling exchange before the crowd compacts into one giant mess again, blocking him from view. Texting the photo through to Tai, I have no doubt he'll share it with Rylan.

The speakers in the corner suddenly come to life, signaling it's time for the first set of fighters to make their way over. As the crowd cheers with excitement, I head over to my usual seat, sipping my beer as the cage door is closed behind the inaugural match in the new ring.

I should probably feel guilty for deliberately making sure Ry was placed with Turner.

But I don't.

BEXLEY

"Ouch. That's going to leave a pretty, little mark."

The crowd simultaneously groans as one of our fighters smashes into the ground inside of the cage. It seems like Willowbrook brought their A-game tonight. We're down two-to-one, but Millie is up next so I'm confident we'll get a win.

As predicted, the pure white flooring didn't stay untarnished for long. Splatters of blood are already creating stains and decorative victories.

I'm using Steele's head to balance on the barricade. As more fights progress, the crowd becomes restless. Especially on a night like this when tensions are high.

After Mills' match, I'm up. And then the real party begins.

When Arch handed me the list of matchups, I had to do a double take when I saw Steele and Rylan's names together. I shouldn't care, but something tugs at my insides uncomfortably. Of course, I want Steele to win—but I can't move past that small fragment of... *unknown emotion* I feel about Rylan.

Steele seems awfully confident. I've already warned him to play it smart. This will not be an easy match for him. Despite my advice, he remains cocky, hand running up my bare leg and wrapping around my thigh.

I feel on edge myself. I'm doing my best to not think about tomorrow but my body is filled with nervous energy. Hearing the crowd grow more restless, it almost sends me over the edge. My empathy radar is at max capacity, and I want to blame the humid conditions in the warehouse for making sweat drip down my body. It's probably half true but it doesn't explain why my hands are shaking.

My eyes land on the side of the cage, spotting Mill crash through the door in record time. She's already bouncing like an energized bunny, eyes blown wide.

A tall, green-haired girl enters after her and immediately the two start checking each other out. I can see their mouths moving and judging by the way Millie's eyebrow cocks and a smirk appears, the Willowbrook fighter appears to be taunting her.

The bell rings through the room. I'm not sure why I expected more dancing and dodging, but Millie shoots across the cage, crash tackling the girl with force. Apparently, she wasn't expecting it either, and despite my fun-sized fiend lacking the weight advantage, the two of them smash into the ground.

Millie throws blow after blow into her opponent's face, swinging so fast that it feels like I'm watching a sped-up

Tiktok. The crowd of people around the cage are unsure how to react, several of them pressing against the fencing to get a better look and shout jeers.

But it's obvious neither of the girls hear them—mainly because the green-haired girl passes out. I spot Arch rush into the cage bravely, tapping Millie's shoulder to grab her attention. Finally, she realizes and stops, blinking for a moment before jumping to her feet.

My eyebrows spring up high in disbelief. Even after unleashing all that power, she's still *fucking energized*. Talk about good stamina. Cardio makes me fight for my life.

"I better head over," I say to Steele, jumping off the barricade.

He nods, grinning at me. "See you on the other side, babe." When he presses his lips to mine, it takes me a few seconds to respond.

Our kissing has never been the *sparks flying, feels like I'm floating* kind of thing, but it was always enjoyable. Now, it feels like I'm tasting ash or bland mashed potatoes. The usual tingling is missing, and I pull back, forcing a smile. "Good luck," I offer awkwardly, doing my best to hide my strange reaction.

Pushing through the crowd, I arrive at the cage as Millie finally steps out. She grins at me, slamming her hand into mine with the hardest high-five possible.

"You did great," I smile, shaking my palm to clear some of the sting.

"Oh, my God. That felt so good. I need to find Parker," she gushes, disappearing into the crowd without a backwards glance.

Arch turns to me, fighting to find words. "Well, that was... something."

"At least we're two-all now."

He nods. "Go make it three," he says warmly, hand patting my back as I climb the two steps and head into the cage.

My eyes inspect the floor, amused at the sweat and blood. And then I'm flooded with images of Rylan's naked body pinned under mine.

Well, that's a little alarming at a time like this...

Thankfully, my opponent steps into the ring and distracts me. I'm actually pleasantly surprised to see she's as tall as me—not a very common trait I come across in my matches.

"Spencer," she greets coolly with a sharp nod.

"And you are?" I question politely. *Good sportsmanship and all.*

"Tamara Hamilton."

I nod, acknowledging her. "Ready?"

The two of us circle, waiting for the buzzer to kick us off. I've got my hair tied back in Dutch braids, while her brown hair is poised in a tight bun. Thankfully, she doesn't seem like the type to pull hair. Some opponents fight dirty, but she doesn't give that impression. Her glance is sharp, cool, and calculated—trying to get a read on me as much as I'm doing to her.

Excellent. A worthy opponent for once.

Neither of us move or strike when the signal to begin rings out. Our footsteps match perfectly, circling and sizing the other up. I try to focus on her movements to gauge and anticipate what's to come, but she hides it well.

I sense the watching eyes grow restless, the need for blood spurring on loud taunts and gestures. Finally, we collide in the middle of the cage, a flurry of hands and limbs striking. I manage to get a hook into her jaw at the same time as her fist hits my rib cage.

We don't come up for air, intensity only increasing as we exchange blow after blow. Blood trickles down my face from a cut above my brow. Wiping it away quickly, I land a kick to her outer thigh, pain ricocheting up my foot and calf from her firm muscles. Jesus—what are her legs made out of? Bricks?

Despite the pain in my foot, Tamara didn't walk away from the move freely either. She stumbles slightly, rocking the pressure to her other leg for a second. Then, she's back on me again, foot flying forward and connecting with my left quad.

Her aim is perfection. She's definitely had training or some type of martial arts background because the force sends me to the ground.

I know I need to move quickly, and I manage to roll onto my side as she jumps on top of me. I throw my hands up to protect my head as her blows rain down onto my skull. Spots are quickly appearing in my eyes, my surroundings shaking as I try to focus.

I'm not going down like this. I can't.

My shoulder nearly dislocates as I swing it up, curling around the back of her neck in a lame attempt to get her into a reverse choke hold. The move forces her weight into my side more and I try to bring my knee up, but she has them pinned down. My arm screams in pain but I swallow it back, tightening my hold around her neck until she has to roll off me to alleviate some of the pressure. I only have a few seconds to roll away, springing to my feet just as her body crash tackles into me.

The crowd behind us groans as we slam into the cage wall, the metal branding my back as I grip her shoulders to try to get her off me. A knee comes up, catching me in the lower stomach and a sickening feeling washes over me as I hunch over involuntarily.

Using the opportunity, Tamara throws a sharp jab at my face. My cheek explodes in pain as her knuckles bruise the skin.

My vision starts to swim. I know I'm in danger, and I'm suddenly faced with the realization that I'm outmatched. Maybe on a better day I'd have a chance, but even I can tell I'm lacking tonight.

Her fists pummel down on my head and I attempt to block them, waiting for either my body or mind to give out. But she pulls back to my surprise, grabbing my wrist and using it to fling me to the ground again.

Before I can contemplate her strategy, my stomach is flat against the ground, shoulder yanked back as she presses a knee into my lower back. Shit—she's trying to make me tap out. That's even worse. A knock-out is the ultimate prize normally, but against me? She's trying to make me give up.

It feels like the cage is shaking as people scream from both sides. Pain bursts through my body as I once again feel my shoulder threatening to dislocate.

Everything in my body and mind beg to make it stop, but I clench my teeth, fighting back the waves of agony. Squirming beneath her, I pathetically try to throw her weight off me but it's futile.

Her warm breath tickles my ear, surprising me. "Just tap out, Spencer. I don't want to hurt you."

Her tone startles me. There's nothing mocking or sinister about it—she's genuinely begging me to end this. We both know that I don't have a chance in hell at recovering, but my pride fights back, refusing.

Shaking my head, it's all I can give her. My jaw is locked, teeth nearly snapping as I clench hard in pain. She lets out a hiss, pulling my arm further behind my back. "Please—just tap out." Fresh pain rips through my body, my vision finally giving out as white light blocks everything out.

I'm on the verge of passing out, every fiber screaming, begging, pleading to end this. Somewhere in the back of my mind, I weigh up my options. I either tap out and admit defeat, walking out with my head held high. Or I black out, escaping the pain for a short while and lose my dignity.

And suddenly, realizing what both will do to my reputation, my shaking hand slides forward, gently tapping the ground three times.

Immediately, Tamara lets go, rolling off my body. Even without my arm being pulled back or her weight into my spine, I'm still in a world of pain. Except now, I also have to face the reality that I just lost.

It's a new feeling, and I fucking hate it.

A shadow rolls over my face, and I brave a glance toward it, seeing her concerned frown. Slowly, I push myself up, ignoring how my legs threaten to buckle.

She offers me a hand which I take, letting her help me.

"Good match," I murmur quietly.

Tamara nods sharply, dropping my hand once she's confident I'm able to stand on my own.

My eyes check the door, meeting Archie's. His are blown wide with horror and I make my way over, avoiding looking directly at anyone else.

He shoves the door open for me, offering his forearm as I carefully climb down the steps.

"Shit, are you okay?" he asks, wrapping an arm around my waist when I sway in response.

Suddenly, Parker appears on my other side, grabbing my arm.

"I'm fine," I tell them both, shrugging in an attempt to get them to let go.

"Help me get her to the rooms," Arch says to him, ignoring me.

The crowd parts as the three of us stumble through, the feeling of disappointment drowning me. Taking a deep breath, I force myself to look up, holding my head high as we weave our way through the Cedar bodies.

I try not to let it get to me. Many look devastated by the result, but to my surprise, everyone appears concerned. People try to offer well wishes of advice, saying I'll get her next time and asking if I'm okay. All I can do is nod, forcing a small, pained smile before reaching the rooms.

Away from prying eyes, I collapse onto the ground, Arch dropping to his knees beside me.

"What the hell happened?" Parker asks, shocked, from the doorway.

Neither of us answer him. Because truthfully, I don't have anything to offer.

And it's too hard to admit the truth.

Chapter Thirty-Two

It takes a lot of convincing to get Arch to leave when the night is done.

I stayed in the room for the rest of the fights, recovering and waiting for the pain to diminish as much as possible. He popped his head in occasionally, giving updates after I asked—well, insisted—that he wait outside.

There's something about being at your most vulnerable that makes you want to hide. I know he's already seen my vulnerable side many times recently, but having a babysitter right now is like rubbing salt in the wound.

Steele lost his match too.

Badly.

According to post-match feedback, my injuries look like a walk in the park compared to Steele's. At least I walked out of the cage—Steele had to be carried, barely conscious.

The fights have now finished and the voices from the main room are slowly getting quieter. I asked Arch to look after Steele, making sure he gets medical attention.

Since I drove here, I intend on waiting until everyone has left before I make my way out. It's not a pretty sight. Dried blood is stuck to my face while bruises are already flourishing on my skin. There's a particularly sore spot on my upper cheek that's going to be a pretty black and blue tomorrow.

Arch and Abby pop their heads in for one final check before taking off. Everyone is making their way to the beach, to drink away their sorrows. Willowbrook are using it tomorrow, so it's our best opportunity to let loose and lick our wounds—no pun intended.

We lost fair and square tonight, but it's still a bittersweet pill to swallow.

When the sounds outside fade away to nothing, I slowly force myself to stand, using the wall as stability. Everything hurts, and I wouldn't be surprised if I'm a bit concussed myself. Truthfully, I probably shouldn't be driving, but I'll take it easy.

Grabbing my keys to lock up, I head out of the room, happy to see the warehouse empty.

I need to cross the main floor to get to the side door, and despite only being a small distance, it feels like a fucking mile.

Reaching the other side finally, I'm just about to switch the lights off when footsteps draw my attention. My head pops up toward the Willowbrook rooms, heart racing as I expect to see Rylan—but it's not him.

"Duchess."

Hunter stands casually in the walkway, hands deep in his pockets with a shit-eating smirk on his face.

"What are you doing here?" I grumble, pausing.

He steps forward, scanning my body. "Rough night, I see. That must hurt."

I want nothing more than to wipe that smug look off his face, but even I know I don't have the strength to fight him. I could get a second wind and all he would have to do is poke my arm or face and I'd topple over like a house of cards in a breeze.

"I'm not in the mood, Lannister," I say instead. "If you're hanging back, lock up."

Hunter cuts into my path as I step toward the side door, eyes dancing in amusement. "Before you go, Rylan would like a word."

Frowning, my eyes instinctively dart toward the rooms. "Why doesn't he just come out here then?"

"He's recovering from his fight."

My gaze flickers between Hunter and the rooms, desperate to see Rylan, but also not wanting to be ambushed by the three of them. But surely, Rylan wouldn't let that happen?

"Fine," I agree warily.

He steps aside, gesturing with his hand for me to walk past. It takes everything in my power to stay upright, acting as if every step isn't pure agony.

The first room is empty, and the second, so imagine my surprise when I reach the third one and find it equally vacant.

Before I can ask where Rylan is, someone shoves me hard in the back.

I fall into the room, feet catching on the old carpet before landing stomach first on the ground. The cry of pain wheezes out as I brace my hands, ready to push myself up when Hunter's shoes appear in my peripheral vision.

There's a flash of something shiny and metallic, but before I can register what it is, I'm cuffed with them.

"What the fuck, Hunter?" I sneer, staring horrified at the metal handcuffs binding me to the leg of the abandoned desk.

Tugging them, I wince as they tighten around my wrist. Hunter squats down next to me, proudly exclaiming, "Not bad for a cheap pair. I guess you have that in common."

That second wind I was waiting on finally emerges as I use my entire body weight to yank on the chain. They don't budge, and neither does the desk I realize with horrifying disbelief. The metal legs are deadbolted into the ground through the murky green carpet. Without a key, I'm stuck.

"Very funny," I snap. "Unlock them."

Hunter reaches out, softly brushing a piece of fallen hair off my forehead. "I don't think so. It's about time you learned your place, Duchess."

"Don't touch me!"

He laughs as I jerk my head away, standing up. "Hopefully it doesn't get too cold for you."

I squirm frantically as he quickly grabs my cell and keys from my pocket, holding them out of reach when I try to snatch them back.

"You're pathetic," I shout, pulling the chain again. "This is low, even for an asshole like you."

Hunter shrugs. "Maybe you shouldn't have fucked with us—and certainly not with Rylan."

I freeze. He dumps my keys and cell in the corner of the room, out of reach.

"Give them back!"

"I don't think I will. I'm going to find out all your secrets soon, Duchess. When I do, you're going to regret the day you stepped foot in my academy."

This can't be happening. I know he hates me more than anything, but of all times, leaving me half naked, bound in an abandoned warehouse, the day before my mother's funeral... that's cruel, even for him.

"Don't do this," I murmur low, shaking my head. "Not today."

"No time like the present, Duchess. Maybe this will make you think long and hard about trying to tear us apart."

"I didn't do anything!" I argue. "Maybe you should be taking this up with Rylan."

Hunter smiles. It's cold and hostile. Maybe on the surface it can be mistaken for a gesture of warmth, but deep down, he's ruthless. There's nothing pleasant about his lips upturning like that. Behind his eyes, I see his hatred for me, pouring out in waves.

He wants to break me. To punish me for what I did to him in the detention classroom and to make an example of me for fucking his friend.

There's no going back after this. He's ensuring my compliance—not necessarily to bow down to them, but to stay away from Rylan. We both know that if Rylan has to choose, he's going to pick his friends, his legacy. This is a cold reminder that I'm just a notch on his bedpost.

"Don't worry," Hunter says, standing. "I'll be sure to lock the door behind me, so no one takes advantage of your *vulnerable position*."

"How noble of you," I snap back sarcastically.

Grinning, he says nothing further as he vanishes from the room. I listen to his footsteps fade away, the lights turning off before the sound of the side door slams closed.

"Hunter!" I shout unsuccessfully. "Get back here, Lannister!"

Outside, an engine roars, unmistakable dirt and gravel kicking up underneath tires, and then there's silence.

He's not coming back...

No one is.

I hate to admit it, but when the faint whispers of birds chirping and soft morning glow slithers into the room, my face is red and puffy from crying.

There was a small period of time where I passed out—a result of the pain in my body and exhaustion—before I woke up again to continue this nightmare.

Bereft and devastated, I struggle to understand how everything happened. Today is meant to be about saying goodbye to Mom. Last night was hard. Losing doesn't happen to me often, and I'm humble enough to admit defeat, but I know in my heart I don't deserve this.

Unless someone finds me, the chances of me missing her goodbye are growing higher with each passing hour.

My bladder is screaming at me, made worse by the violent shivers from the morning chill as I lay against the coarse carpet in my sports bra and shorts.

It could be days until I'm found. Monday, someone would have to take notice that I'm missing from classes. I try my best not to panic. All it will do is make things worse. But in the back of my mind, I'm terrified. Injured and dehydrated, there's no telling what condition I'll be in if I'm left here alone until Monday. To make matters worse, my stomach rumbles with hunger, also reminding me that I may be without food for several days—if I survive that long.

If you asked me yesterday, I'd say that Hunter isn't that cruel—that he wouldn't leave me stranded that long. But now? I don't know what to believe.

You'd think that missing my mom's funeral would be cause for alarm. But I'm known for hiding from emotions. My friends would just assume I need space. Hell, at the moment, it's only Archie who knows. The chances of the alarm being raised are smaller again. He'll just believe I couldn't face saying goodbye, probably off somewhere drowning my sorrows with music.

This is my own fault for isolating myself. And now, Hunter Lannister has exploited my weakness. What used to be my strength is now my downfall, and I have no one to blame except myself.

Well, and Hunter. This is all his doing. But if I discovered someone was sleeping with the enemy, I'd probably react strongly too.

It's comforting to know one thing though. I'd never do this to someone. That's the difference between me and Hunter.

Still, the semi-comforting thought does nothing to improve the situation. I could be dead in two days.

Exhaustion creeps into my bones again, body curling up as hunger pains exacerbate the feelings of affliction. It's been nearly twenty-four hours since I ate anything—too sick with nerves to have lunch or a snack before the fight.

I don't have to fight long. The darkness pulls me under again, providing temporary relief from reality as I pass out on the ground, numbing the aches and pains that throb through my entire body.

Chapter Thirty-Three

Rylan

There's very little I take for granted in this world now.

Beneath the wilting promises and torturous expectations, I've come to love finding beauty in the smallest things.

Pure, untainted beauty is the key and cornerstone of life. It balances out all the challenging pressure that continues to surmount on a daily basis.

The Ridgeview Canyon is the epitome of all things good in my world of bad. Soft, amber glows bathe the shrubs and orange dirt. Little floral structures pop out of the ground, rising from nothing into the most incredible spectacles of nature.

Sweat drips down my skin as I run along the track, relishing in the feelings of nerves exploding. Even though it hurts to run today, I easily get lost in the pain, coupled with the blaring of music coming through my headphones.

Last night was something else.

I stayed inside the room until it was my turn to fight. Tai had ducked out not long after Hunter, only to come bursting back in a short time later to tell me that Bexley lost her fight.

To say I was surprised would be an understatement. We knew that Tamara would give her a run for her money, but after everything Spencer has been through lately, I would have thought for sure that she would come out on top.

After all, that's what happened to me.

Turner didn't stand a chance once we got inside the cage. I almost felt sorry for him.

Weeks of pent-up rage and frustration came charging out through my fists, the feeling of aching, battered flesh only spurring me on.

It was over before it had even begun.

He tried to put up a fight—I acknowledge that much. But from what I remember, he was barely able to touch me.

As soon as the buzzer rang out, I blacked out. It wasn't until someone was pulling me off him that I realized the match was over. The crowd loved it, of course—well, at least our folk did. Not long after that, the Cedar pack slowly disappeared with their tails between their legs. To say they were annihilated would be an understatement. Not only did we win the fight count, but their leader lost.

Sure, we could argue that a better result would be a whitewash of wins, but Bexley's loss superseded everything else. It's embarrassing for them, even though everyone loses from time to time. I guess the problem is timing. It's a critical point for all of us, and we all wanted that victory.

I feel bad for her though. With everything going on, I'm sure she's feeling the hit. But that's just business. She'll bounce back.

Nodding to some fellow early morning runners that pass by, I jog back toward the parking lot.

As usual, she's on my mind. Normally when I run, my brain turns off, giving in to the endorphins and entering into primal mode. But lately, the thought of Bexley has been able to break through even my toughest of restraints.

It's like a virus. Images infiltrate my vision, flashing back to cool nights and naked bodies. The taste of her, the feeling of her body on top of mine.

When I stepped into the cage last night, that's all I could think of. In fact, I'm willing to bet that whenever I look at that ring now, it will always be pleasantly tainted with the ecstasy feeling and memory of us together.

I've fallen so far down the rabbit hole that I doubt I'll ever emerge again. I'm in too deep, and a part of me is concerned. But another part, that grows bigger every day, never wants to be saved.

Getting back to my truck, I pause my music, shooting off a text to Bexley. Maybe I should go to her house and check on her. It can't have been easy for her. I know if I was in her shoes, I'd be pissed.

I wanted to see her last night, but by the time I calmed down enough to be around the crowd of people, Hunter told us that Bexley had already left. I assume she went to the beach with the other Cedar Heights students.

That's where we'll be tonight.

I have half a mind to invite her—not to rub it in her face, but to enjoy the sound of lapping water, gentle breeze, and heat from the bonfire with her. There's no way she'd ever agree though. She hates being around anyone from Willowbrook at the best of times, let alone after last night.

The engine revs as I buckle my seatbelt, checking my cell for any replies. Nothing—which is disappointing. Maybe she's still asleep or busy.

Maybe she's busy with Turner.

Clenching my teeth, I'm angry at myself for the visual. The thought of the two of them licking each other's wounds has me on edge again.

Before I know it, I'm heading in the direction of Cedar's side in Ridgeview Valley, following the road I know too well now.

Bexley's house comes into view when I turn down her street, and to my relief, there's no other cars there.

Except... there's no cars or trucks at all.

That's weird.

I don't slow down as I pass, but I hit the call button on my car touch screen, listening to the ringing sound that echoes throughout the cab.

"Good timing," Tai laughs, answering.

"Why's that?"

By the speed of his voice, I'd deduce that he's had a few cups of coffee already. Reaching for my water bottle, I wait for him to fill me in.

"I was just about to call you."

"Oh. Maybe we're developing twin telepathy now. Hope Sophia doesn't mind sharing."

Tai snorts. "She'd sell me off for books any day of the week. But that's beside the point."

"Well, you go first. Lady and all."

"Ha, very funny, Ry," he pauses. "I just found some updates I thought you might be interested in."

Pulling up a red light, I relax in my seat. "Hit me."

"Spencer's lapdog just posted in their Facebook group. Apparently, the funeral is today. He's asking for people to turn up to support her."

"That's not surprising," I mumble, spotting the Starbucks up ahead and trying to decide if I want caffeine after my run. "But it explains why she was out of it last night."

Tai hums in thought. "You should have seen it, Ry. Spencer was a mess. You could tell her mind wasn't there."

"You feel bad for her," I point out, astonished. It's the first time I've really heard him have sympathy for Bexley, other than when we discovered what happened to her mother.

"Just being a caring algebra partner," he says back quickly. "That's not all though."

"Okay..."

He stops for a moment. "I may have driven past the warehouse this morning on my way to get coffee. Spencer's truck is still parked there."

I frown. "Are you sure?"

"Of course I'm sure," he grumbles, annoyed. "Despite being tired and a little delirious, I'm not hallucinating motor vehicles now."

Ditching the lane to Starbucks, I rejoin the traffic, heading toward the outskirts of town. "I'll go check. You said she was hurt last night."

"Not badly," he argues weakly. "But probably wouldn't be a bad thing to check."

A smile forces its way onto my face. "Are you starting to care for her, T?"

"No."

His quick response makes me laugh, but who am I to judge?

Tai stays on the call until I arrive at the warehouse a few minutes later, obviously tracking my GPS coordinates. He tells me I'm there before I even voice it out loud, and I promptly end the call much to his annoyance.

But he's correct. It's definitely Bexley's truck in the parking lot.

Pulling up beside it, I peek through the windows first to make sure she's not inside, before heading to the warehouse door.

I find it locked, which is suspicious, and when I enter the building, it's dark except for the late morning light that manages to creep in through the tiny windows on the high walls.

My nose upturns at the stench of sweat from last night. My eyes wander to the cage as I pass, spotting the bodily fluids on the white floor, before I reach the Cedar Heights rooms. All three are empty to my surprise, as are the bathrooms, but to be safe, I head toward our end.

I nearly skip the last room when I reach it since it was mine last night and to my knowledge, I was the only one who used it. But I do a double take through the doorway at the body curled up on the floor.

"Shit. Bexley?"

Still dressed in her shorts and sports bra, Bexley is hunched over on her side. At first, I think maybe she's passed out from the fight. But as I step closer, an invisible hand claws at my throat, choking me.

Silver handcuffs catch my attention, one end wrapped around the leg of the desk, pinning Bexley in place.

Her head lifts slowly, peering over at the doorway with swollen cheeks and blood-shot eyes. "What do you want? Come to gloat?"

My initial relief is short-lived at the cold, harsh tone. Dropping to my knees beside her, I cringe at the dark bruise on her cheek, along with the cut above her brow that's congealed with dry blood. It looks like a streak of blood had dripped down her face from the fight, but it stops on her cheek bone, seemingly washed away by fallen tears.

"What the fuck happened?" I demand.

Bexley tries to sit up but is immediately pulled back down by the shortage of chain. "Why don't you ask your friend?" she spits out, hurt evident in her voice.

Shaking my head, I force her to meet my eye. "I'm not playing these games again, Bexley. I'm not a mind reader. Tell me what's going on."

I wait for the cold reaction, the dismissal like what she had done previously when I confronted her the night after we first had sex. But instead, she sighs, animosity vanishing from her face to make room for exhaustion.

"Hunter."

I recoil as if I've been slapped. "Hunter did this?"

Bexley smiles sadly. "Of course, he did. He knows about us, doesn't he?"

"What?" I gawk. "I haven't told him anything."

"Well, he knows."

Her voice is barely above a whisper, confirming my worst fear. If Tai figured it out, then perhaps I was wrong to assume that Hunter wouldn't. This is my fault. In attempting to keep our... *whatever it is...* secret, I didn't stop and think of the consequences if he found out.

Hunter was already mad that I entered into a truce. Hell, he hates Bexley with a passion. Even before she glued his ass to a desk, he despised her. But we've been friends for so long, he'd never punish me for it. No—he'd want to make a statement, unleashing fury on her.

"I'm so sorry," I murmur sincerely.

Bexley shrugs dismissively. "Have I missed it?"

"Missed what?"

"Mom's funeral."

I swallow, wondering if I should play dumb or drown her in empathy. But Bexley is so similar to me, I know that's not what she needs.

"No, you haven't," I tell her. "It doesn't start for another hour."

Reaching into my back pocket, I pull out my Swiss Army Knife, jabbing a pointed end into the keyhole of the cuffs. With a bit of force and manipulation, I eventually manage to jam the lock, releasing the cuffs.

Flinging them aside for her, I offer Bexley a hand. To my surprise, she takes it, trembling as she slowly pushes to her feet.

Seeing her shaking body, I quickly take off my black hoodie I had slipped on when I finished my run. I drape it around her shoulders, and once her arms are in, I zip it up.

"Thanks," she says softly, unable to meet my eyes.

"Are you going to ask how I know?"

The question leaves my mouth before I can stop it. I don't know why, but I want her to interrogate me. It's not normal to know the things I do about her, and even though most people would say I'm a fucking stalker or psychopath, I want her to know that I follow the events of her life—but we won't get into the reasons why.

Bexley shakes her head. "I assume you just find out everything to hold power. After all, if I was going to ask why you know the details of her funeral, I should probably start with the obvious question of how you came to have her belongings."

True. She raises a valid point.

"I did initially obtain information to hold an advantage over you," I admit. "But then I got to know you. After that, it became a matter of caring."

"You don't care," she points out weakly. "You just need to know everything. We're exactly the same."

I cock my eyebrow at her. "We are similar. Which is why you know that's bullshit."

"It doesn't matter what I know." Bexley sighs. "We keep finding ourselves in this position. It's wrong, Rylan. People are going to get hurt."

"Then we make sure they don't," I argue back. "I'll talk to Hunter and straighten this out."

Finally, her eyes snap to mine. I'm relieved to see some anger staring back at me. At least I know she's not broken because of him.

"There's nothing to straighten out. He's your friend. You can't fix this with him. I'm the enemy. He even said it—that I'm trying to come between you."

I shove Bexley against the wall, boxing her in with my arms. She lets out a tiny whine as her sore body hits the cold wall, but I barely register it. "I make my own goddamn choices, Bexley. I don't need anyone dictating what I do or who I fuck. You're mine now. You have been all along. This ridiculous feud means nothing to me. If you want to slap a label on us, sure, call us enemies." I lean forward, brushing our noses together. "But this body is mine. And I'm not going to just give that up because my friends decide that you're off-limits."

Her eyes flash back at me—a mix of anger and defiance. "I'm not yours, Rylan. And it's not just your friends. It's your father too. Your legacy, your leadership. I'm a nuclear bomb that could destroy everything."

Shaking my head, I grip her chin with my fingers. "And I'm a fucking grenade that could detonate at any second. But you're the only person who gets me—really fucking gets *me*. Not the leader, not the legacy... just me."

I feel her body relax against mine, that anger dissipating with my words. She looks like she wants to say something back, but she fights it, biting her tongue.

Finally, she just sighs quietly, tilting her head back, unfazed that I'm still caging her in and holding her face. "I need to get ready. I'm heading to the bathroom, then heading home."

"Fine," I concede, stepping back. "But I'm coming with you."

Chapter Thirty-Four

To my surprise and astonishment, when we arrive at the Ridgeview Valley Gardens, I'm taken aback by the number of people waiting.

In my mind, I knew I should have fought Rylan on his demand to come with me, but I couldn't bring myself to do it. But now, seeing the Cedar Heights crowd, I can't help but wonder if I've made a mistake.

He followed me home after we left the warehouse, and when I was ready to leave, he insisted on driving me, stating I'd be in no position to drive myself. As much as I wanted to refuse, I gave into the uncomfortable feelings and let him take charge. Today of all days, I need to not be in control.

When we arrive, I can't stop the emotions from flowing at the group of people, standing next to the gravesite for support. Arch is front and center, and while others give Rylan a weird look, he just smiles.

Thankfully, no one says anything. Mills rushes forward to pull me into a hug, and out of the corner of my eye, I spot Steele sporting some matching bruises. He looks worse for wear like me, but he gives me a tight smile, gaze flickering to the tall man next to me. There's a flash of confusion, anger, and resignation, but he gives me a little nod.

"How are you feeling?" Arch asks quietly.

"I'm okay," I reply, tugging on my black dress nervously.

It's one of those old pieces of clothing that stay buried in the back of the wardrobe, only breaking out for unique occasions. I didn't bother with my makeup and the best I could manage with my hair was to chuck it into a bun to hide the knots.

My face is still blotchy and red from crying, but after the beating I took last night and the fact I'm at a funeral, no one knows the truth.

I don't know where to go from here. After briefly giving Rylan the rundown of Hunter's antics last night, I was ready for him to be indifferent. But he still insisted on accompanying me.

He's a master of disguising emotions, and he's doing a great job at hiding it, but I can't help but wonder what the fallout will be for this. Who will be the victim? The three guys go way back—I'm just the archnemesis who sometimes bangs him. But even though he's masking his true feelings, I catch little glimpses of anger when he thinks I'm not paying attention. It's obvious it's directed toward Hunter, and I just know there will be further consequences to pay.

Mr. Morrison is standing at the foot of the grave, holding a battered black book. It must be filled with so many memories from deceased folk, telling tales of livelihood and victories, detailing every milestone in a person's existence from birth to death.

I wonder if he remembers most funerals. Or if any have stuck with him.

This will probably be a fading blip on his radar. Sure, he might remember me for a few weeks—particularly as the girl who had a stranger step in to pay—but then life will move on, and I'll be in a dusty file somewhere.

Rylan gives Arch a sharp nod, offering his hand to both our surprise. Arch takes it, shaking it firmly. Before I can process the interaction, a car door slamming closed grabs our attention, and when I turn around to glance at the parking lot, my eyebrows shoot up in surprise.

Soph comes bouncing over, Tai in tow. For a seemingly confident dickface, he's barely looking up, acting shy.

"Bex! I'm so sorry," Soph rambles, hugging me. "I had no idea."

Words are caught in my throat, and seeing my confused expression, Rylan places a gentle hand on my back. "I hope you don't mind, but I told Sophia. I figured you could use a friend."

When his head scans the Cedar crowd, I can tell he's just as perplexed as I am at the mass gathering.

"Sophia dragged me," Tai mumbles. "My condolences."

My eyes switch between the two Willowbrook men, welcoming the distraction from what will be a rough morning in a few minutes. Rylan cocks an eyebrow but doesn't say anything, the two of them sharing a silent conversation.

I turn back to Arch, starting to feel overwhelmed. He smiles softly, reaching out to rub my arm.

"We just want to support you. We're your family too."

Choked up, all I can do is nod in reply, signaling to Mr. Morrison that he's free to start.

Everyone falls quiet, and despite originally wishing I could keep this quiet, there's a feeling of peace around me as I stay flanked by the group.

I can't bring myself to speak for once, tears slipping down my cheeks as I throw a red rose on top of the casket as it's lowered into the ground. A portable speaker plays a collection of Mom's favorite songs, and when Arch stands up to say a few words, recalling some of our fond memories with her, I'm relieved to feel an arm around my waist. Rylan tightens his grip, holding me up as my legs shake. I let myself lean into him, swiping tears away with the back of my hand.

And there, in death, the enemies wave the white flag, laying their weapons to rest as we farewell a life that deserved better.

When Monday rolls around, I've officially entered the Twilight Zone.

I don't remember anything from yesterday, and the funeral is all but a blur.

After the service finished, Rylan, Tai, and Sophia stuck around for a bit to make sure I was alright before heading to set up Willowbrook's night at the beach. Arch stayed with me at the house, and Abby cooked us dinner. I had no idea the girl could cook but I'm so appreciative of her. Most girls would be jealous of their partner having a female best friend, but not her. She shares Aquarius Instagram reels with me. But on the plus side, I'm allegedly coming into wealth, a new relationship, and prime opportunities for my career.

Despite everyone from Cedar Heights knowing that Mom was gone, no one mentions anything. In fact, it appears Rylan, Tai and Sophia also keep it under wraps. Besides the usual taunts and glares from Willowbrook peers, I manage to escape pretty unscathed.

Rylan continues to text me in the evenings while Soph has made it her mission to join us at lunch. She seems completely immune to the whispers, people deeming her a traitor. But as Tai's sister, it doesn't go beyond that. No one is brave enough to voice their concerns or opinions to the three leaders.

And speaking of which, they look as snuggly as ever. The three of them stalk around the school, apparently unfazed with the brewing trouble in their inner circle. Hunter glares at me whenever we cross paths and today, I've already flipped him off three times—making sure to flash my black nail polish at him. I can't tell what's annoying him more—my seemingly unbothered attitude to his little stunt, or that Rylan and Tai give me a little wave whenever we see each other. But he's not the only one pissed off. A few times I found Liv seething, steam almost billowing from her ears at Rylan's attention toward me. Soph told us that she was expecting him to go to the dance with her, but when she brought it up, he was dismissive of the idea.

At least three times a day, Ms. Power Suit makes an announcement over the speakers, requesting volunteers to help set up the dance for Friday. As expected, I don't have a choice in attending. When tickets went on sale, Soph purchased one for me. And Arch has been sucked into it too. Apparently, that friendship guess between Sophia and Abby was accurate. They purchased the tickets together, and now Arch is being dragged there as well.

I have no choice but to bite back a groan and give my blessing when Cedar students come and ask if they should go to it. It would be wrong of me to advise them not, just for photos and rumors to emerge that I was there.

So, anyway, after classes, the two girls practically kidnap me, forcing me into Soph's little yellow Mazda. I silently curse Archie for being able to get out of this impromptu shopping trip, but I make a mental note to send him teasing text messages about Abby. I'm not going to suffer alone.

We arrive at the Ridgeview Valley Mall, the two of them linking arms with me on either side as they drag my flailing dead-inside corpse to the nearest formal wear store.

The shop assistants can see them coming from a mile away, offering glasses of non-alcoholic bubbly the moment we step foot inside.

I have to admit, even though the idea is daunting, seeing all the dresses hung up in colored order makes me oddly happy. I try to ask the question of why we need formal dresses when the theme is Villains and Sinners, but they just shush me, throwing sequined prisons at my head.

"Whyyyyyy?" I groan, digging my heels into the plush carpet as Sophia attempts to shove me into a changing room.

"Because everyone deserves to feel like an evil temptress. Get in there!"

I'm ashamed of the squeal that rips out of me as a second pair of hands shove me in the back. The last thing I see before they close the curtain is Abby and Sophia's grinning faces.

"I could end you both in the blink of an eye!" I half-threaten.

"That's the evil energy we are looking for!" Abby calls out with a giggle.

Sighing, I have a look at the pile of dresses they have thrown into my hands and hung up on the hook inside the changing room. They range from black and navy-blue to bright red. Shit—how am I going to be able to decide? One... I can't even afford a dress. And two, I don't have character inspiration yet.

As I shift through the dresses, my ears strain to listen to their conversation, the two women also ducking into adjacent rooms.

"Did you see that one on the mannequin?" Soph calls out. "That's what I want for prom."

"It's so pretty. Except those mannequins are too tall. I'd drown in the floor length skirt."

My head swirls in circles, an image popping up. Darting my attention back to the dresses, I ignore my preferred colors, reaching for the bright red dress.

It's quite stunning, I have to admit. The thin spaghetti straps blend into a cowl neckline, before a sequin corset-style bodice cinches the waist. Blood-red silk flows to the floor, hiding everything except for the side slit.

Slipping into the dress, I'm pleased to find it fits perfectly, and oddly enough, I can breathe even with the corset. I call the assistant in to help tie up the laces and by the time I'm done, so are Abby and Soph.

"Alright, ready," I tell them, stepping outside the curtain.

Sophia rips back her fabric doorway, a scowl on her face. "We were meant to countdown—to be dramatic." She pauses, gasping. "Holy shit. Look at you. Evil temptress indeed."

"Wait—I want to see," Abby says, stumbling out of her room. Her eyes lit up upon seeing the dress, nodding vigorously. "That's the one, Bex."

"I haven't tried on the others yet," I argue, though if it gets me out of trying anymore dresses on, I'll consider it a win.

"No need," Soph murmurs, walking to stand in front of a mirror. "It's perfect. What do we think about this?"

The dark navy dress shows off her cleavage, the v-neckline plunging toward the fitted bodice. Below, a voluminous tiered skirt with asymmetrical ruffle layers spins out around her. She circles slowly, popping a hand on her waist. "I'm the Evil Queen from Snow White."

"It's good," I tell her with a nod of approval. "Your tits look amazing, by the way."

She grins. "I know."

We turn to Abby, and it takes everything in my power to hide the smirk that fights its way to my face. Unlike us, she's opted for a cotton-candy pink dress that hangs just above the knees. It's covered in patterned sequins with floral lace and tulle. I'm not quite sure villains wear bright pink, but then again, I'm not sure I can imagine her in dark or monochrome colors.

"And what are you meant to be?" I laugh, grinning.

Abby hops up onto a step next to Soph, flattening her hands over the tulle. "I'm going to be Cruella de Vil. I have the perfect faux fur white coat that my parents got me from Europe."

"Cruella doesn't wear pink," Soph points out, equally amused.

Forever the unfazed queen, Abby smiles fondly, giving a tiny twirl. "This version does. I'm Cruella 2.0. Besides—she was a fashion icon. Pink is the new black."

I fold my arms, smiling at them both. It's the first time in weeks I feel truly happy, and even though life goes on, the two of them have reminded me that living can be a beautiful thing with the right people in your life.

"What about you, Bex?" Abby asks, turning around to face me. "What villain or sinner are you?"

Staring at my own reflection in the mirror, I smirk. "Everyone from Willowbrook seems to think I'm insane. So, that's easy. I'm Harley Quinn."

Chapter Thirty-Five

"Are you sure he said four o'clock?" Hunter grumbles at me, checking his watch.

Nodding, I stretch against the warehouse wall, groaning happily when my back cracks. "He's not that late. Chill."

Rylan messaged our group chat earlier, telling us to meet him at the warehouse. H and I arrived a few minutes before four, but now, ten minutes have passed and there's still no sight of Ry.

H looks more annoyed than usual, pacing the warehouse floor while occasionally rolling his eyes. Finally, we hear the gravel kick up outside and the roar of an engine before a car door slamming shut announces Ry's arrival.

When he power walks through the door, his gaze immediately falls onto Hunter, a scowl appearing on his face. It's not unnoticed by H, who stops pacing and straightens up.

"About time."

"You'll survive," Ry shoots back, crossing his arms.

The two of them glare at each other, and I sigh, throwing my hands up. "Alright. What crawled up your asses?"

"Ask *him*." Rylan nods toward Hunter, who just scoffs.

"I knew this would be your reaction. I'm disappointed, Rylan."

Both of them ignore me. I need a spray bottle or something. If I squirted them in the face, surely that would bring them out of whatever testosterone fueled match-off this is. Perhaps H found out about the funeral on the weekend. I wasn't going to go but Soph insisted I tag along with her. Apparently, I *owed it* to Spencer. While I didn't necessarily agree, my mathematical panic kind of drove me to go. The last thing I need or want is to be stuck with that stupid equation. Which I'll never get done if these two don't hurry up.

Soph mentioned something about dragging Spencer to the Mall. Then after they are finished, we have to study. The deadline is fast approaching, and I can't afford to fail this class. Especially since Hunter thought it was a great idea to change classes last minute.

"You have no idea what the fuck you are doing," Rylan snaps at Hunter. "You took it too far."

"Took what too far?" I interject, annoyed. "Someone tell me what's going on."

H rolls his eyes, twirling his hand in Rylan's direction. "Go on then. I know you're chomping at the bit to throw me under the bus."

Ry's darkened glare finds my face. "Hunter kidnapped Bexley."

"What?!" I shout.

"Oh, spare me the theatrics, Rylan," Hunter groans. "It was not a kidnapping."

"Then what would you call it?"

"A lesson."

I rub a hand down the side of my face. "When?"

"Friday night," Rylan says sharply. "After the fights. Hunter handcuffed her to that shitty, bolted down desk in our changing room. Not even touching on the fact that she was half-naked and injured, but she nearly missed Saturday morning."

I suck in a breath, finally realizing the seriousness of this. No wonder Ry is pissed. He's gotten close to Spencer lately and despite what people think, he's a protective little shit.

"Her truck?" I direct at Ry, remembering our conversation on Saturday morning.

He nods in reply. "She would have missed it if you hadn't seen her truck in the parking lot."

Hunter huffs, listening to our exchange. "Nice to see you are both still against me."

"We're not against you," Ry shoots back angrily. "But Bexley isn't our enemy anymore."

"Of course she is," he argues. "You're just too blind to notice. Which is also why you didn't bother to tell me that you were fucking her."

My eyebrows dart into my hairline. We should have known that Hunter would figure it out. He's too clever and a master of reading between the lines. And that's exactly why he didn't say anything either—he wanted to prove a point.

"Is that what it's about?" Ry whispers heatedly. "Jealousy or something?"

Well, at least he's not denying it. They are close to butting heads and the last thing we need is a punching match.

"I'm not fucking jealous! You're just blind to what's happening in the real world!"

"Hunter..." I warn, shaking my head.

He turns to me, eyes flashing dangerously. "I'm not surprised you knew, T. But you are just as guilty here for not saying anything. You led me to believe that you were on my side."

"I'm on both of your sides," I groan. "But Ry is right. There are bigger things to worry about right now. Spencer isn't the threat."

"You idiots can't see what she's doing to us."

Rylan crosses the floor, making a beeline for Hunter. I hold my breath, nearly expecting him to tackle his childhood best friend but he stops short, shoving a finger into Hunter's chest. "Her fucking mother died, you moron. Your little stunt nearly made her miss the funeral on Saturday morning."

The three of us fall silent, Ry and I waiting for the information to process in Hunter's mind. I can practically see the cogs turning as he assesses what to do with it, placing it into some mental alignment with the rest of the recent events.

"That doesn't change things," he answers, softening his tone slightly. "Our priority is our position. She's weakening us." His eyes fall to me, narrowing slightly. "And she's getting to you as well."

"You need to stop listening to Marcus," Ry scoffs. "Fuck his reputation."

Hunter scowl. "Our reputation is all we have. Your father would agree."

Ouch. Playing the daddy card. This is turning messy. But surprisingly, Rylan doesn't react like I expect. He just laughs, amused at the idea that his father would be on Team Lannister.

"I don't give a shit anymore." Rylan pauses, deep in thought. "What has that ever really done for us?"

"Everything—" Hunter starts but Ry cuts him off.

"It's not, H. We're forced to follow in their footsteps. To our fathers, we're just extensions of them. Everything we do, everything we say, it's all for their benefit. We deserve better."

For once, Hunter doesn't know how to respond. He looks confused at the idea, like being a pawn in his father's career success is unfathomable.

I feel for them both. To be under scrutiny every day, it must be exhausting. Having an absent father is secretly a blessing in disguise. I don't care how much money he makes or how important he is in the legal world. None of that matters when we should be his priority. When I was younger, I looked up to him. Being rich and successful opened a lot of doors for our family. But it wasn't until I realized that Sophia was struggling without an active parent that the price wasn't worth paying.

All Dad cares about is his image and reputation. And Rylan is correct—Marcus Lannister and Max Astor are exactly the same. The only time they offer any praise or guidance is when it benefits them. If we do something that's deemed a failure, we are punished and belittled.

"I don't even know who you are anymore, Rylan," Hunter mutters. "Listen to yourself."

"H," I start, tone gentle. "He's right. We've spent too much energy looking at this the wrong way. We turned our attention to Cedar Heights when we should have been focusing on the events that got us here."

Hunter shakes his head. "It was needed. We had no choice but to mark our territory when they arrived."

"Maybe so," Rylan agrees. "But what does that get us? All I see is expectations and a life that's not my own."

I frown. I never realized just how much he was struggling. Hunter seems surprised too, letting out an exhausted sigh and rubbing his temple.

"I thought we suspected that someone from Cedar started the fire."

"I don't think so," I shrug. "There wasn't any benefit from them attending Willowbrook. All it did was cause chaos and mess with everyone."

Rylan nods. "Besides, Cedar are under the impression that someone from Willowbrook started it."

Hunter snorts. "Not our circus, not our monkeys."

"See. That's why we need to be careful. Someone out there is out to get all of us," I finish.

Pacing again, Hunter's face pulls up in concentration. "This still doesn't excuse either of you for befriending the enemy. After what she did to us..."

"Fuck's sake. Let the damn ass table go," Ry groans. "At least she didn't steal your credit card and make you wear booty shorts."

"Or post your number on Grindr," I say.

A smirk breaks through Hunter's concentration. "She really got to all of us in one go. I have to give some credit."

"We did worse to her," Ry sighs. "But honestly, she's not so bad when you get to know her."

I choke back a laugh as Hunter's head snaps to the side, glowering at Rylan. "I'm not being friends with her."

"You don't have to," he grumbles back. "But if we're going to find out who started this mess, maybe we need to work together."

"Absolutely not," Hunter replies. "We've got more than enough power to find out answers on our own. Plus, if Dad catches on..."

Rylan folds his arms, eyes glued to the pacing ball of energy. "He won't find out. But we need all the help we can get. Bexley knows Cedar Heights better than anyone. That insider information will come in handy."

I can see the moment that Hunter begrudgingly gives in, his eyes tightening and fists balling up. "Fine!" he snaps. "But I'm still not being friends with her. I don't care if her mother just died or that she has a mountain of daddy issues. If she gets in my way, I'll destroy her, regardless of your dick's needs."

Rylan smirks, shooting me a quick glance. "Trust me—if you were ever lucky enough to have her, you'd understand."

Shaking my head, I dig into my pocket for my car keys. "Well, this has been enlightening and all, but I have a study date with a certain Cedar Heights pain in the ass. We'll work out a plan. But for now, I better go before Spencer cuts off my head. Or Sophia. Those two together are a bit scary."

"About time," a voice snaps as I walk into the house.

My head turns to the side, finding Bexley sitting in my living room. Her crossed arms are tense as she glares at me, clearly annoyed that I'm late.

Damn. I honestly thought I'd beat them back. Don't girls take forever when shopping?

"Where's Soph?" I ask, ignoring the annoyed stare coming my way.

"Walking Calvin and Klein with Mary," she answers, standing up. "It's nearly dark and they were getting restless."

I snort. "And you didn't go with her?"

Bexley rolls her eyes. "I assumed you'd be back before now so we can sort out the project. It's due this week."

Cringing, I fight back the bile that threatens to rise. How the hell can mathematics cause such a visceral response to my body?

"I'm here now," I sigh. "Let's get this over with."

Waggling my finger at her, I motion to follow as I head for the stairs. Her soft footsteps echo behind me and when

I enter my bedroom, I hold the door for her, closing it behind us.

Bexley grabs the spare chair, pulling it to the desk. She sits down and digs into her bag, pulling out a notebook and the project paperwork.

I sit down across from her, reaching for a pen before I can chicken out.

My eyes stay trained to her face, watching her expressions as she focuses on setting up. It's quite remarkable how different she is from Saturday. I expected her to be a sappy mess—especially after hearing that Hunter fucked around with her after the fights. But to her credit, no one would be able to tell. It's as if she's locked everything away, straight back into that leader mode she portrays constantly.

Now I get it. Rylan being exhausted and fed up with everything, I can only imagine what goes on in that brain of hers. We underestimated her, but perhaps Rylan is right—we need her.

"I'm sorry," I quickly say before I can change my mind. "For your loss."

Bexley pauses, lifting her head slightly to meet my gaze. "Thank you." She stills, eyebrows furrowing. "And thanks for being there on Saturday with Soph."

I nod, grabbing the project paper. "Alright. The sooner we can get this finished, the better. Let's begin."

Chapter Thirty-Six

Bexley

After fighting for my life running the track, I'm promptly reminded of my own mortality. It can't be normal to have such pathetic stamina when I'm meant to be at the prime of my life. I'm fairly sure that I'm one more lap away from going into cardiac arrest and pissing myself in front of the cheerleaders.

On the plus side, Soph equally struggles and if it wasn't for her helping hold me up afterwards, we'd both be on the ground mimicking grass angels. To be fair, I also held her up, which was a little embarrassing when Rylan jogged past, barely a hair out of place as he flaunted his cardio God-like abilities.

Shamefully, I did spend an unhealthy amount of time perving on his ass as he ran ahead. But what can I say? I appreciate good muscles.

Even the catcalls couldn't bring me down, which was surprising. Sunday had been a blur, but I didn't expect to suddenly feel so different this week.

I still ache for my mom, but knowing she's at rest now, free from her demons, makes it a little easier. I don't think it will ever stop hurting, and in my mind, I still one-hundred percent blame Dad. But she's free now and I cherish those last few days where for a split second in time, things were normal.

Maybe she knew something was wrong and that's why she won against the demons, her old self reemerging to make me feel seen. Still, too many questions linger that keep me up at night.

On my break, I call Dr. Lavings and book in for that annual check-up I'm due for. I'm also planning on bringing up Mom. I deserve answers—I need to know what went wrong that things ended so quickly. If Grey's Anatomy has taught me anything, it's that shit can hit the fan awfully fast. But in my mind, it doesn't make sense. But then again, I'm not a doctor. And at the end of the day, Mom would want me to live—to take the chances that she never got.

Thankfully, I'm able to squeeze in an appointment tomorrow afternoon. Normally we have to wait for ages, but the receptionist said there had been a cancellation.

Cancellation, my ass. It was one-hundred percent a pity appointment. I'm not stupid enough to believe that divine timing has fixed the atrocious healthcare system. But I'll take what I can get. The sooner I can get peace of mind, the better.

The rest of the day goes relatively quick. There's a weird change of atmosphere around Willowbrook as the dance approaches. The cheerleaders are walking around, acting all high and mighty, while staff still beg for volunteers. I'm surprised they haven't just told Cedar Heights students that it's mandatory to assist. After all, they do love their free labor.

When I walk into my last class of the day, Biology, I'm surprised to see a familiar face. Mr. Martin hasn't changed in the slightest over the past two months, still rocking a mismatched jacket and lavender hair. He smiles at me when I enter, giving a little wave before scanning the rest of the class.

I can see the Willowbrook students sneering, some baffled at the newcomer. But the shit-eating grins on the Cedar students are the icing on the cake. Suddenly, I'm filled with hope. We might survive this torture after all.

"Hello friends!" Mr. Martin grins when I take my seat. "I bet some of you are wondering who I am." He pauses, winking at me.

I can't help but smirk in response, shaking my head as I look down. There's nothing but silence in response, quiet enough that you'd hear a pin drop.

"I'll be taking over from your regular Biology teacher for the next few weeks. As you might have guessed, I'm from Cedar Heights."

My hand covers my mouth quickly, muffling a laugh as someone scoffs in disgust. Mr. Martin grins in their direction, tugging on his jacket lapels. The black jacket has patches of blue sewed onto it—all different shapes, the quirky attire appearing out of place in the building of snobs.

I meet the eyes of a few Cedar peers, happy to see them react in the same way as me. Scanning the other faces, I realize where the sound of disgust emerged from. Liv is in the front row, leaning on one elbow as she sneers at Mr. Martin while whispering to Sierra. It takes all my willpower to stay calm, knowing if I start cackling like a hyena it's going to send the room into chaos.

It becomes my favorite lesson to date, and by the end of it, I'm practically skipping out of the room with a dopey grin on my face.

When I get back to my truck, I catch sight of Sophia sprawled over the bonnet, eyes closed like some kind of reptile in the sun. She cracks an eye open at the sound of my approaching footsteps, still not moving.

"Carry me home," she begs.

"Still fucked from gym?"

All I get in reply is a long groan and the sound of flesh sliding down metal. Crawling into the cab, she drops her head back with a frown.

"I'll never recover from that. My legs were already sore from Klein chasing a fox yesterday. And then Coach Carter had to make it worse."

"Well, at least you get to go home and rest now," I laugh.

She sighs blissfully. "Thanks for the lift again."

Pulling out of the parking lot, I put some music on. "I'm heading to your house anyway. Saves you from having to carpool with your brother."

"We should carpool on Friday," she says, finally straightening up. "You, me, Abby and Archer."

I groan playfully. "If you insist."

Sophia elbows me. "You're going to have fun. Don't try to bullshit me otherwise."

"A night with Willowbrook's finest? How can I resist?"

"Why, thank you! I am pretty fine."

We pull up in front of Sophia's—and Tai's—house, the two of us disembarking mid-conversation about hair and makeup for Friday. For a girl that hates attention and is a living definition of introvert, she sure is bossy. I guess when she has her sights set on something, she'll take charge and wear you down until you give in. Huh—She's like Tai after all.

Speak of the Devil and he shall appear. The crunch of gravel has us both turning our heads as we watch his car pull up behind mine. He flashes both of us a grin as he heads through the front door, apparently in a better mood than yesterday for our study date.

"Let's do this!" he excitedly shouts, grabbing my arm and yanking me toward the stairs.

"Jesus, Beckett. Chill!" I beg, managing to catch my footing as I'm dragged toward his room.

I look over my shoulder, watching as Soph shakes her head with a snort before disappearing out of view.

"Why the madness?" I breathe out when we're in his bedroom. "I nearly died in gym today. You can't force me up stairs at that speed."

Tai flops down in his computer chair, placing his hands behind his head. "Because we're going to finish this stupid project today. I figured it out."

Laughing, I walk over and sit down at the desk. "Did you now?"

"Okay—maybe I overheard someone talking about it. But I think I know what to do."

"So, you cheated."

"I didn't cheat! He was just talking about the calculation steps. Sshh—trust me, Bexley."

I cock an eyebrow. "I trust you as much as a loaf of moldy bread."

"You wound me," he replies, and I'm hit with a sense of déjà vu.

"Alright, Einstein. Lead the way," I snort, pushing the paperwork toward him.

To my surprise, Tai *did* seem to know what he was doing. And I think he was equally as shocked.

Together, we managed to work through the series of steps, showing our working out strategies until we reached an agreement on our answer. I have no idea if we are right, but I'm fairly confident we've done it to the best of our ability. Tai looks like a little kid, grinning wildly as he writes his name on the top of the sheet.

"Done!"

"See... it wasn't so bad," I laugh. "Plus, you got to hang with me and learn from my wisdom."

"You're so full of yourself, Spencer," he snorts, relaxing back in his chair. "But yes. Solid teamwork."

I reach for another mini quiche. I've eaten five now, but who's counting? Mary brought them up shortly after I arrived and after I tasted one, I couldn't stop. I don't want to insult her cooking by leaving any crumbs behind. Yep—that's my story and I'm sticking with it.

As I shove an entire one in my mouth, Tai blinks in disbelief. I must resemble a squirrel, cheeks blown out and puffy but instead of nuts in my mouth, it's bacon and cheese quiche.

"What?" I grumble, words slurring through my full mouth. Oops—probably need to work on being more lady-like.

"I didn't think it was humanly possible for a mouth to stretch so wide," he taunts.

Chewing, I hold eye contact, determined to make him as uncomfortable as possible. Except the idiot just stares back with a smirk, waiting patiently for me to swallow.

"I'm not disrespecting Mary by sending food back," I start. "It would be rude of me. I'm the perfect guest."

Tai breaks out in laughter, messing up his hair with his hand. "I gained ten pounds in freshman year. I kept eating everything even though I was full. Eventually Mary caught on, realizing she was overcooking. Man—she scolded me good for not telling her. She thought I was just a *growing boy*. But it was enough to feed an entire class."

"I wish I had someone to cook for me," I murmur thoughtfully. "But I do love baking. Except I have zero self control and will eat an entire tray of cookies if I'm not careful."

"Cookies don't have calories," he says dismissively with a wave. "That's the rules—I don't make them."

I feel oddly at ease. Relieved that the project is done, I'm able to just relax. Thoughts of heading home quickly exit my mind when the bedroom door opens, and a new face surprises me.

"Knock knock," Rylan mutters, walking in without waiting for a reply. "You better be finished. I've been waiting all afternoon so we can get this sorted."

My gaze shifts between the two of them. "Sort what?"

Tai gives me a sheepish smile. "We're extending that team effort. Dream team and all."

"You've lost me," I mumble, turning to Rylan. "Please explain to me... in English."

I let out a yelp when Rylan lifts me off the chair, plonking his own ass down. Before I can rip him a new one, his hands grab my hips, pulling me down to his lap.

"Rylan!" I hiss, looking at Tai in alarm.

"Oh, he doesn't care. Do you, T?"

Tai shakes his head, amused. "I'm cool. Just try not to get too distracted. We need your full attention for this."

My eyes widen when Rylan jerks his hips slightly, absolutely pulling my focus to him. He laughs in my ear, tapping my thigh in resignation.

"We think it would be a good idea to join forces to investigate the fire. The three of us and you."

"I don't need your help," I start but the two of them just laugh like they are sharing an inside joke.

Tai strums his fingers along the desk. "I have no idea why they don't get along. They are practically the same person."

I narrow my eyes at him. "You better not be talking about Lannister."

Rylan hums in my ear, squeezing my thigh. "You seem stressed."

"About working with you three? Absolutely," I shoot back, ignoring the flames that travel through my body and light up my face.

"You need us," Tai points out. "We have access to things that you don't."

Rolling my eyes, I slap Rylan's hand—not that it does any good. He just squeezes tighter. "I'm more than capable of finding resources."

"We need you," Rylan answers sharply.

I can't help but focus on the husky tone, suddenly feeling like he's talking about more than a joint arson investigation project. I suppress a shiver, darting my gaze to Tai to assess his reaction. There's no way he didn't pick up on the same vibes. Men are idiots but not complex creatures.

Tai grins. "I know I need your expertise. No one knows Cedar Heights better than you."

Fingers dance up my skin, ducking under my Willowbrook skirt. I go to grab Rylan's hand in warning, but his other arm swings out, pinning me.

"Come on, Bex," he whispers, his warm breath sending goosebumps all over my skin. "Are you scared that you won't be able to handle all of us?"

Chapter Thirty-Seven

My body tenses up under his touch but it's not out of fear. He knows what he's doing to me, and I refuse to just cave in.

"I can handle the three of you just fine," I shoot back. "It's just a matter of whether I want to or not."

Rylan chuckles in my ear, brushing the loose tendrils off my neck. His fingertips graze my skin gently before they are replaced with his soft lips. My eyes flutter closed for a brief second before I promptly force them back open, darting a glance in Tai's direction.

Hazel eyes watch me closely with a smug smile accompanying them. When Tai notices I'm staring at him, he leans forward in the chair, resting his elbows on his knees.

"Come on, Spencer. Are you afraid of showing me how you handle Ry?"

This asshole *did not* just say that. There's a lot of things I let slide, but insinuating that I'm afraid of them? He knows just what buttons to press to get a reaction—and I hate him for that. It's practically a dare, a challenge. They know I won't back down from something like that.

As if to emphasize the point, Rylan's hand disappears up my skirt again, not stopping until his fingers are pressed against my hipster briefs. He draws little circles around my clit, my body heating up even with the layer of fabric between us.

"I'm not scared of you," I answer. "But you should be afraid of me."

Rylan flattens his hand against my sensitive skin, his palm pushing into my clit. I can't stop the jolt of my body or the arch of my back as I lean against him. Our bodies mold together, perfectly as always, and his teeth nip my throat. "Is that a fact?" He murmurs, slowly pushing the material aside.

Skin upon skin and my mind starts to feel a little hazy. I'm not letting him get the upper hand here. I'm already outnumbered, but I'm not outpowered. Reaching behind, I slide my hand between us, grasping his growing erection through his black shorts.

My mouth tugs into a smirk when I feel him stiffen. He rests his forehead against my shoulder; a small growl caught in his throat as I palm him.

Cocking an eyebrow at Tai, I shoot him a sickly-sweet smile. "See how fast I can take back control? You can't do that."

The words have barely left my mouth when I feel Rylan move beneath me. I'm thrown forward fast, chest landing on the computer desk as a strong hand grabs my wrist and pins it to my back.

"You might want to rethink that," Rylan says, voice deep and low.

I turn my head to the side so I can glance at him out of the corner of my eye. "I meant every word."

Still holding me down with one hand, he flicks my skirt up with the other, sliding his warm palm over my ass. "We'll see about that."

Tai scoots his chair forward, moving directly into my line of vision. I raise an eyebrow at him, keeping my face expressionless as Rylan slowly slides the lace to the side.

In... out... in... out.

I focus on my breathing, taking controlled, timed inhaled breaths. But then his finger pushes inside me, mimicking my oxygen exercises. In and out. Slow. Perfectly timed.

Somehow, I manage not to react. But then, Rylan grabs the back of my hair, fisting it as he yanks my head back.

"Watch him," he orders, making sure I'm facing Tai. "I want him to see the moment I break you."

I shake my head. It's directed at Rylan but I'm looking straight at his best friend. "You can't break me."

Tai grabs my chin, forcing my head to stay still. "Come on, Bexley. *Break for us.*"

At his words, Rylan adds another finger into my warmth, slamming them into me. He fucks me fast with his fingers, making stars appear in my vision. But I still resist giving in, even as my body starts to lose the fight.

I clench down around Rylan, swinging my face hard out of Tai's grip. Meeting Rylan's baby blues, I croak out, "Is that all you've got, Astor?"

He pauses, knuckles still buried deep inside me. Blue irises narrow at the challenge, and with his hand still fisted around my hair, he pushes me forward, so my top half drapes off the desk, depositing me face first into Tai's lap.

"Hold her still for me," he growls.

With my lower half now sprawled on top of the desk, I've lost control of my legs. Hands softly run up my hamstrings before they shove my thighs apart. I quickly place my hands on Tai's upper legs to steady myself, and in retaliation, he grabs the sides of my face, tilting my head up.

"Still sticking with the same story?"

I quickly bite back a snarky remark as I feel Rylan press against my entrance. He gives me no time to prepare, cutting off any words as he spears forward, stretching me from the inside out.

"Fuck," I hiss as my body betrays me.

My head drops into Tai's lap as Rylan rolls his hips, moving his cock in and out of my body.

They have me helpless and they know it. I can practically feel the smugness rolling off Tai in waves as he watches over my body as his best friend fucks me.

"How does she feel?" Tai asks.

"Fucking incredible as always," Rylan replies, jolting into me harder.

A moan breaks free from my lips and I dig my nails into Tai's thighs. To my surprise, he groans, his fingers bruising my jawline as he presses tighter. He barely flinches at all as I claw at his legs.

"I bet she does," Tai mumbles, still holding onto me tight. "Did you hear that little moan? She's falling apart for us already."

My jaw clenches at his words. I'm currently powerless against Rylan's brutal thrusts, but to hell with the both of them if they think I don't have power still.

Under my chin, I can *feel* my power as it practically stares me in the face. The bulge in Tai's pants confidently sides with me and when Rylan chuckles darkly in agreement to his comment, I decide that three can play this game.

"Go on, Bex," Rylan says. "Beg for us. Give in and I'll let you come." He slows down, finding a torturous pace, promising to make good on his threat.

"Over my dead body," I breathe out, my hand speedily disappearing under the waistband of Tai's shorts before either of them can register what I'm doing.

Tai sucks in a breath when my fingers curl around his shaft. Giving them the same courtesy as they gave me, I rip the shorts down just enough to pull his cock out fully, before I wrap my lips around the tip.

"Fuck, fuck, fuck," Tai groans, jerking underneath me.

Rylan's movements stammer for a moment as he catches sight of Tai's length disappearing into my throat. Keeping my hand firmly around the base, I pull back, looking at Rylan over my shoulder.

I offer him a quick smirk before I shove my foot into his muscular torso—not hard enough to *really* hurt him, but the force does make him step back.

Sliding my body off the desk, I drop to my knees on the floor, kneeling in front of Tai. His eyes are blown wide, still in disbelief, and blatantly ignoring the stunned man behind me, I pull Tai into my mouth again.

I'm not surprised to hear he's quite vocal, his groans bouncing around the room. The man never shuts up.

As I hollow out my cheeks and pull him into the back of my throat, I cup his balls, intensifying the sounds that I'm ripping out of him.

Powerless, my ass.

I hum in the back of my throat, holding back a laugh as he flinches under my touch, the vibrations shooting along his sensitive shaft.

Quickly, I pull back, my hands and mouth vanishing from his skin. He curses and groans in protest, looking down at me.

"Go on, Tai," I smile. *"Beg for it."*

Conflict flashes through his eyes, and when he hesitates, I spin around, fisting Rylan's glistening cock instead.

His hand presses against the back of my head as I slide my tongue over him, tasting both of us. Tai tries to reach for me, apparently feeling left out, but I swat his hand away.

Taking Rylan into the back of my throat, I shift over, making sure Tai can see everything I'm doing. I wink at him, amused when he pouts back at me.

I lift a hand away, motioning with a single finger for Tai to lay on the floor. This time, there's no hesitation, as he scrambles to the plush carpet, leaning back expectedly.

Deep throating Rylan for a split second, I pull away while he's still mid-groan, crawling over to Tai.

His hazel eyes light up excitedly but I shove his chest, sending his back to the floor. Before he can react, I climb over the top of him, my thighs straddling his face.

No words need to be exchanged when I lift my skirt up, pulling the lace aside. Tai's tongue darts out, lapping at my slit before landing on my clit. I grab my tits through my blue jersey, grinding my hips into his face as the tip of his tongue draws patterns over and over.

Tai grabs my hips, pulling me harder into his face, and for a moment, I do question his ability to breathe. But he doesn't seem to care, so neither do I.

The familiar rumble of pleasure curls in my lower abdomen, bringing me closer to bliss, until finally, it explodes. I ride out my orgasm against his tongue, hips swiveling until it fades away.

Climbing off him, Tai lets out a breathy moan before grinning at me proudly. I smile back, leaning forward to ruffle his hair with my hand.

"Good job," I taunt before pushing to my feet.

The grin drops instantly, alarm crossing his face. I turn to look at Rylan, eyes slowly darting down to his throbbing length.

I was right in my assessment the night we were at the warehouse. The blue in his irises has turned stormy, a dangerous look of heat and lust staring back at me.

But before either of them can see it coming, I scoop up the study notes, shoving them into my bag. Stepping over Tai, I make tracks to the door, smirking at them over my shoulder.

"Have fun taking care of those," I say, amused. "Thanks for a good study session."

"Bexley," Rylan warns.

Opening the door slightly, I lean against the doorjamb, feigning innocence. "What?"

Tai looks speechless, still sprawled out on the floor, looking at me upside down.

"Get back here and finish what you started," Rylan answers.

"I didn't start that," I say, playing with the hem of my skirt. "But I sure finished it. How's that for power?"

Their eyes widen, but before they can reply or come after me, I'm out the door, laughing.

I pass Soph at the bottom of the stairs, her arms full of snacks while she balances her Kindle on top of them.

"See you at school tomorrow," I grin, letting out a meek sound of surprise as Tai's bedroom door bounces off the wall behind us, signaling their incoming presence. "Gotta go!"

"Uh—" She freezes, unsure of what she's witnessing.

"Bexley! Get back here!" Rylan's voice floats down the stairs, getting louder. But I'm already out the door, jumping into my truck.

The whole cab rattles as I start the engine and I hit the gas, the two men appearing in my rearview mirror as I venture down the gravel driveway.

I can't help but laugh at their wide-eyed, stunned faces and I give a little *beep beep* on the horn as I pull out onto the street, still cackling when I finally exit the community gates.

Chapter Thirty-Eight

Usually, I'd love to say that I was right. But not this time.

I guess cheerleaders have some weird pull over the staff because those requests for volunteers to set up the dance soon turned to mandatory requirements. It was not in my mid-week plans to be balancing on a ladder, hanging black and red streamers from the large glass windowpanes in the auditorium. Not to mention their sexist attire means I'm trying not to flash anyone that walks past.

At least it's not just me suffering. There's a mixture of Willowbrook and Cedar Heights students in here, all dragging decorations and muttering curses.

Dean Lannister lingers by the door, a pleased sneer on his face as he watches us work. Ah yes, the thrill of free labor. The only thing that gets rich people off besides more money... is saving money.

"This sucks," Arch grumbles from the next window. "Did you notice that there's no cheerleaders in here?"

My eyes scan the room. "I'm not surprised. They probably blew the dean under his desk for this."

As I focus my attention on him, I spot Soph skipping through the doorway. She pauses, doing some weird curtsy to him while holding a stack of floating red balloons.

The ladder shakes as I double over, holding in a laugh. Dean Lannister smiles fondly at her, obviously not recognizing that she's mocking him. The vision that one of his own is taunting him is a safety hazard.

"Jesus, Bex! Chill," Arch hastily whispers.

I grab the window, taking a deep breath. "It's fine. I'm all good. But hey—if I fall, maybe I'll get a payout?"

"No broken bones. Your bruises are only just starting to fade from last Friday. As if we need any more injuries."

Climbing down the ladder, I intercept Soph, plucking a strand of black ribbon.

"I'll give you five dollars to pop it and suck the helium," I dare.

She snorts. "And risk a video of me floating around social media? I plan to stun everyone on Friday, not torment them."

"I do both," I shrug with a grin. "It works well when you mix them together."

We walk together to the other side of the room, passing the balloons to one of the footballers. I can't help but notice that he body scans Soph, clearly interested in more than just her latex presents.

I throw her an amused expression, and when her nose crinkles at him, I swing my arm around her shoulder. "Come on, baby girl. I need you in my bed soon."

His mouth pops open as Soph leans into me, the two of us walking away from the horny, drooling jock who looks like he wants nothing more than to follow.

Back at the ladder, Soph makes a gagging sound. "Argh. Did you see him staring at my chest? Why do they think we like that?"

"They don't. They couldn't care less what we think. We're just bodies to idiots like that."

She nods. "He's not my type anyway."

Her head turns, gazing at someone across the room. I follow her line of vision, doing a double take when I realize who she's looking at.

"Parker?" I whisper heatedly. "You like Parker?"

"Shut up!" she hisses, cheeks flushing bright red. "I didn't say that."

"You're staring right at him."

Soph buries her face into her hands. "Argh. Stop."

"Oh, my God. You like him," I grin.

"I will end you, Bex. Stop talking."

"Aww," I tease, pinching her cheek. "You're so cute when you're angry."

She narrows her eyes on me, before the expression changes and she's back to being all embarrassed. "Don't tell him. I know he runs in your circle."

"I won't," I promise. "But maybe you should ask him to the dance."

Soph blinks at me, perplexed. "We're going together—you, me, and Abby. And Archer too, but he's non-negotiable baggage."

"I can hear you!" Arch grumbles from his ladder.

"I meant for you to hear that!" Soph shoots back, poking her tongue out.

I lean against the ladder, taking the opportunity to glance around the room. It's slowly coming together. They really went for the dark theme—every decoration is red, black, or dark blue. Streamers are making their way across the roof, while dozens of balloons turn up spontaneously.

A group of jocks start dragging tables and chairs in, and when the bell finally rings, we all breathe a sigh of relief. Now it's the next group's turn for torture.

The three of us head past Dean Lannister, his eyes turning cold when they land on me. Pausing, I glance at Soph, and she reads my mind, the two of us curtsying at the same time.

The older man gapes at us, looking like he's been clam-slammed in the face. Archie groans, grabbing both of our arms and dragging us away before we end up in detention.

We're still clinging to each other, laughing loudly, that I don't see the body approaching before I smash into it.

"Watch where you're going!" the shrill voice yells.

Straightening up, I cock an eyebrow at Liv. Dressed in her usual cheerleader uniform, I spot her minions behind her. Sierra sneers at me, dramatically flicking her hair over her shoulders. Peyton seems reserved as always, eyes glued to the floor.

"Oh, are you going to hang decorations?" I ask.

Liv scoffs at the idea. "I don't think so. We don't do manual labor."

"I guess that explains why Rylan got sick of you," Soph mumbles loudly.

Sticky pink lips part in anger, and I see a blur of white and black. My body reacts on its own, pushing Sophia out of the way of the charging cheerleader.

Apparently, Liv seems happy with the alternative, her hands darting straight for my hair. She rips on my ponytail, yanking my head down.

She did NOT just fucking do that...

I hate stereotypical bitchy girl fights. There's no honor in them. Nail scratching and hair pulling is a cheap tactic.

Launching an uppercut into her stomach, Liv groans, doubling over. Sierra jumps in, likely remembering the last time Liv and I got physical with each other.

The two of them throw punches and grab my arms, attempting to pin me down. To my surprise, Soph lunges at Sierra, jumping onto her back. The two of them squeal, falling to the floor in a heap of flailing limbs.

Liv doesn't care about the welfare of her friend, going straight for my face with her sharp acrylics. Just as I go to block it, a hand snaps out and grabs her wrist.

"That's enough, Olivia."

Everyone freezes. I quickly find Arch, annoyed to see him blocked from us by two giant footballers who must have followed us out of the auditorium. They don't appear to have touched him though, so they can live... for now.

"But Rylan!" Liv whines. "They started it."

At the mention of his name, I snap my head in his direction. Rylan towers over Liv, still clutching her wrist tightly. He locks eyes with me, lips twitching slightly.

"Bullshit," Soph interjects. "You tried to attack me."

Rylan cocks an eyebrow at Liv, who immediately starts stuttering pathetically. "It's not like that."

"You tried to lay a hand on Tai's sister?" he asks darkly.

I guess that explains why Soph and Rylan were always immune to each other. Friendships go a long way—never mess with someone's twin.

"No..."

"Yep!" I cut her off, folding my arms. "She sure did."

Liv glares at me. If looks could kill, I'd be dead three times over. She scowls at the smirk on my face, and to be fair, I should have seen it coming.

"No wonder your father left you and your mother died. I wouldn't want you either."

"Olivia!" Rylan snaps loudly, but I barely hear him.

"What the fuck did you just say to me?" I ask quietly, stepping toward her.

She rips her wrist out of Rylan's grip, wiggling her fingers like she's about to claw my eyes out. "You heard me. We all heard what happened to your mother."

Sophia quickly steps in front of me, staring daggers at the head cheerleader. "Back the fuck off. Now."

"Why are you even wasting your time with this loser, Sophia?" Liv scoffs. "You're supposed to be better than that. Tai—"

"Keep my brother's name out of your dick sucking mouth!"

I find Rylan's gaze again, his baby blues watching me closely, silently trying to calm me down.

This is the mother of all self-controls. I want nothing more than to pound her face into the floor. No one speaks ill of my family. It's been less than a week since I buried Mom, and I'm not about to let someone who's destined to peak in school talk about her like that.

But despite my body shaking with rage, I know the moment I lay a hand on her again, she's going to go running to Dean Lannister. I'm surprised he hasn't appeared from the auditorium with all the commotion. It will be an immediate expulsion. Her bruises will fade but my future and graduation will be ruined forever. She'll have won.

Soph's words come back to me, an idea flashing to mind.

If Liv is going to hurt me where it hurts... then I'm going to do it right back to her.

Pushing Soph gently out of the way, I watch as Liv stiffens, prepared for me to come at her. But at the last second, I step to the side, brushing my chest against Rylan's. Snaking my hand to the nape of his neck, I tug him forward, pressing my lips to his.

The fallout is instant.

All the gasps are still no match for the banshee scream that comes from Liv, the sound ricocheting around the hall.

Behind me, I hear Soph's stunned gasp before saying, "Well, fuck. I didn't see that coming."

To my relief, Rylan kisses me back while casually placing a hand on my waist. It's short-lived though, as Liv shoves us apart, rounding on Rylan.

"What the *hell* are you doing?!" she demands, voice cracking. Tears well up in her eyes, like she can emotionally blackmail him into providing the perfect answer.

He glances down at her, unfazed. "Kissing?"

For once, Liv is rendered speechless. Her eyes shoot over to me, shock, anger and embarrassment registering all over her face. A single tear manages to spill before she hastily turns around and takes off down the hall before everyone can see her crying. Sierra quickly follows, calling out her name.

My eyes fall to the lingering girl, her hands nervously fidgeting with her cheer skirt.

"I'm sorry to hear about your mom," Peyton murmurs so quietly that I barely hear it. Without waiting for a response, she turns and follows her friends.

When they are out of sight, I face Rylan, annoyance on my face.

He looks at me, amused. "What?"

"Don't you *what* me," I say. "How the hell did they find out?"

Rylan's face drops, turning serious. "I didn't say anything."

"You better not have," I reply, still shaking with fury. Looking over my shoulder, I glare at the footballers. "Move."

They hesitate, peering over at Rylan. He must give them a look or nod because they quickly move, freeing Archie from the body cage they have formed around him.

As I go to step past him, Rylan grabs my arm, halting me. "I didn't do it, Bex."

"Let me go," I mutter sternly.

He releases me straight away, watching as I walk away with Archie.

Soph looks unsure if she should follow, gaze flickering between us and Rylan. Finally, it appears she decides to stay put, probably realizing that I need space to cool down from the clusterfuck that just happened.

I'll talk to her later about it. But right now, I need to get out of this hellhole.

I need to go somewhere quiet and peaceful.

Arch follows me to the doors, waiting for me to tell him what I need. Pausing on the front steps, I turn to him, allowing myself a moment to let my walls down.

"Go hang with Abby," I say softly. "I'm going to go to the beach for a bit."

"Are you okay?" he asks.

I nod. "I will be. But I need to leave before I commit a cheer-homicide."

Chapter Thirty-Nine

The gentle, lapping water is exactly what I need to calm the storm exploding in my body.

There's not a single soul here except for me. Warmth still emanates from the sun even though it's high over the mountains on the other side of town.

My toes dig into the sand as I hug my knees, pleased that I found a tiny rock-free part to bury myself in.

I can't believe that Liv said those things. I have no idea how she managed to find out, but I shouldn't be surprised. Secrets never last—I learned that the hard way.

But what's even more shocking is the fact I kissed Rylan in the middle of the hall, in front of multiple witnesses.

I mean, sure—it had the desired effect. Liv was crushed and humiliated, and I'm not on the chopping block for expulsion. I haven't escaped the consequences of my actions though. People talk. That's never going to change. Everyone in both Cedar Heights and Willowbrook will know we made out. The fallout could be disastrous for all of us. And shit... if it gets back to Mayor Astor then things will really turn nasty.

Oh, well. It was worth it to see the look on her face. She walks around thinking she's better than everyone, that she can have anything she wants—people included. Clearly, Liv has never been told no in her life, and now, someone she deems trash has taken something that she wants. That has to sting.

I guess I was never destined to keep a low profile at Willowbrook.

The sound of a car door slamming shut pulls me from my thoughts. Glancing over my shoulder, I half expect to see Arch or even Rylan, but it's not.

My brows furrow as I watch him cross the parking lot before tiptoeing over the rocks.

"Fancy finding you here," he grins.

I shake my head. "Sophia and her big mouth."

Tai sits down beside me, nearly landing in my lap as he wiggles into the sand patch to avoid taking a rock in his asshole. "I heard you caused quite the stir. Shame I missed it. Someone needed to put that crazy girl in her place."

"Well, she started it," I mumble. "Did you hear—?"

"That she tried to attack Soph? Yeah. Ry filled me in."

I snort. "So, you're everyone's go-to-guy."

Tai shrugs playfully. "Soph is stuck with me. We did share a womb together for eight whole months. As for Ry, my witty charm keeps him around."

"I think you mean ego."

"Well, if I did have one, you made sure to bruise it."

Smirking, I turn to face him. "Are your balls on the verge of falling off? I did warn you on day one that I'd go after them."

Tai laughs. "And I'm not surprised that you know how to use your mouth. You do talk a lot of shit."

"Is this our version of foreplay? Complimenting each other."

"I hardly think this counts as foreplay. I'm not a masochist, Bexley. I'd prefer my balls stay attached to my body."

"Are you sure my mean streak doesn't turn you on? Not even a little bit?"

He puts his hand on my knee, squeezing it. "Just makes me want to shut you up to be honest."

My body shakes with quiet laughter. "Lucky for you I'm not really in the mood to talk." I turn my head back to the water, mesmerized by the lapping, gentle waves that crest and fall into nothing before retreating back.

Out of the corner of my eye, I see Tai nod in response. He mirrors a peaceful expression, at ease with our silence.

I find that I don't mind just sitting here with him. A few weeks ago, it would have been difficult to be relaxed around them. But now, their company doesn't bring the feelings of needing to be vigilant. It's stupid really. Even I can admit to myself that it's not the smart thing to do. I barely know them, and while our dynamic is shifting into unknown territory, I can't help but let my guard down sometimes.

It helps that they do the same—whether or not they realize. Rylan definitely knows. At the academy, he's different. Exactly like he's always been—cool, calculated, watching everyone as if they are prey. But when it's just us, everything is different. We'll never get over our blessed personality traits of needing to fight for control, but we at least have a silent agreement that sometimes it sucks. No one else knows what it feels like to play a role, sacrificing your own needs for the sake of others. I think that's why we are able to pull back our walls and be ourselves for five minutes—allowing ourselves a moment of peace to enjoy what we love, like music.

With Tai, I'm starting to see a similar vibe. His smart-ass attitude and playful demeanor are his true nature—that's not an act. But what I saw as darkness and sinister intentions is nothing more than protectiveness. All the threats, promises of destruction, it was nothing more than someone trying to protect the people he loves. We have that in common.

We may come across as cold sometimes, brutal, even to our own people. But that's the only way Tai and I know how to protect and love. I see it in the way he guards Sophia, without needing to lay a hand. And that same possessiveness crosses the threshold to Rylan and dickhead Lannister. In turn, he plays that part for his people.

I sense him staring and give in, facing him. In the light, his hazel eyes shine a vibrant green, little swirls of caramel captivating me like molten honey.

"I don't know if Soph ever told you, but our mom died too," he says.

I'm not sure what surprises me more—the news or the way he relays it so easily.

"I had no idea," I murmur softly. "I'm sorry."

Tai smiles, gazing back to the water. "It was a long time ago. But I understand what you're going through. It makes you want to implode and rage, but you can't. So, you just ignore it because there's no other option."

My eyes stay locked on him, even as he continues to look at the shoreline. "Does it get better?" I ask quietly.

"Yeah," he breathes out. "Every day it gets a little easier. Some days it all comes rushing back, but then it hurts a little less again. Then one day, you just suddenly accept it, and the sadness becomes different. It's always there but you learn how to live through it."

I rest my head on my knees, pulling my legs further into my chest. "It's exhausting."

"The only way to get through is to remind yourself that nothing you could have done would have changed the outcome."

"I don't know if I believe that," I mutter sadly. "But thanks."

Tai reaches out, resting his hand on my knee as he links our fingers. "Don't let Olivia get to you. People will try to throw it in your face, but it's just words. Thanks for protecting Soph though."

I squeeze his hand. "I would protect her with my life—just like I would for any of my Cedar Heights people. She's a good kid."

"Don't let her hear you calling her that," he laughs.

Snorting, I can just imagine the verbal beatdown I'd get. But I mean every word. I had a feeling that Soph would grow on me, ever since our first encounter in the locker room. If

I'm being honest, she practically forced me to be her friend, but I have no regrets. Soph was the first person to treat me as a human and not a rival, and never once gave me shit for my background. In a world full of judgmental stereotypes, she refused to stay in a box given to her by birthright.

"I won't tell if you don't."

"Deal."

Pulling out my cell, I check the time. "I have to go. There's an appointment I can't miss."

Tai slowly releases my hand, stretching out his legs. "Give me your cell."

"Why?" I ask, though I'm already handing it over.

He grins. "I'm going to give you my number."

"I already have your number."

"My real number. That was my burner phone."

I slap the top of his arm playfully.

"Ow. What was that for?" he groans, punching his details into my contact list.

"For making me listen to a documentary on whales," I shoot back, snatching my cell back when he's finished. "I could have done without the lesson on semen. Or the ass picture."

My suspicion of a pity appointment is confirmed when I'm immediately ushered into Dr. Lavings' room. He offers me a tight smile, swinging his chair to face me.

"How are you going, Bexley?" he asks sincerely.

I feel bad but all I can focus on is anger toward him. I know he's trying to be polite and caring, but this man probably knew about Mom's condition. Of course he did. He had the test results. And realistically, I understand he wouldn't be able to call me and disclose them, but it still stings. Maybe I'm just looking for someone to blame, someone to be angry at.

"I'm wonderful," I mutter sarcastically. Ouch—not cool, Bexley.

Dr. Lavings nods. "I imagine you have questions."

"How?" I ask, and we both know I'm not referring to his previous statement.

He grimaces, letting out a sigh before turning to his computer. Clicking a button, the printer beside it whirls to life, spitting out paperwork. He hands it to me, letting me scan over it for a few seconds before diving in to what I'm sure is a well-practiced speech.

"When Savanna presented with jaundice, I organized for the blood tests to check her liver function. Her markers came back indicating liver failure, so I had her admitted to assess her liver health with imaging and a biopsy. Unfortunately, subsequent testing found she had cirrhosis, likely caused by heavy alcohol consumption. Based on her results, I would say that she had this for some time, which continued to worsen and shut down her liver function."

I stare at him with hollow eyes, understanding the words but struggling to process anything.

"By the time we conducted the biopsy, she was already in end-stage liver failure. The only treatment would have been a liver transplant, but unfortunately, it is incredibly hard to find a match in such a short window."

"Why didn't someone ask me?" I question sharply. "I could have been tested."

Dr. Lavings offers me a tight smile. "Savanna declined that option."

My heart drops. It literally feels like someone is cracking open my chest with bare hands. "She declined having me tested?"

"I'm sorry, Bexley. I know this must be difficult to hear, but I truly believe she was trying to protect you."

"Protect me?" I gape at him. "She left me. There was the potential option that I could have been a match and saved her. But she purposely chose not to pursue it."

He sighs, regretfully. "This is not my place to say, and to be fair, we didn't discuss her reasons for declining. But I honestly believe she didn't want you to—using your words—'save' her. She didn't want to place that burden on you."

"No. Instead, she placed a whole other burden on me." I swallow hard. "She took away that choice from me. That was a decision that should have involved me."

Dr. Lavings nods, leaning forward to pat my hand. "I know, sweetheart. People make decisions at the end of their life that don't always make sense to us."

Shaking my head, I focus on a spot on the wall, silent tears sliding down my cheeks. I don't know how to feel. I'm so angry, but at the same time, I feel broken again. She knew she was dying and didn't say anything. The little white lies she fed me from her hospital bed changed the course of my life. It altered my decisions and shattered the vision of a future I had in mind. I was preparing for things that were never going to happen. She had me believe in hope, knowing that it was never coming.

I close my eyes, squashing the crushing feeling that's suffocating me. When I open them again, my voice is robotic and empty.

"I'll arrange another appointment for my annual. But thank you for the information. At least I have some answers now."

CHAPTER FORTY

BEXLEY

I'm completely in autopilot mode driving away from the clinic. That familiar rage is back, along with several other emotions, all drowning me at once. The moment I compartmentalize one, another slips back out, and it feels like I'm close to losing control.

There's a small fragment of relief that I have answers now, understanding how everything went to shit so quickly. But there's also guilt and hatred at myself for feeling so angry at my dead mother.

What does that say about me as a person? You're supposed to mourn the dead, not be angry at them.

I can't help it though. And without even stopping to ask myself if this is a good idea, I screech to a stop in front of the large house.

Ringing the doorbell, I compose myself, hanging onto that thread of control before the door swings open and I'm greeted by a bright smiling face.

"Bexley! How lovely to see you," Mary gushes, brushing her hand over her apron. It's covered in flour and I can smell the lingering scent of vanilla wafting from inside. "Sophia isn't home yet but Tai is upstairs."

"Thank you," I forcefully smile. "Can I head up to his room?"

She steps aside, opening the door fully for me. "Of course you can. Let me know if you need anything."

I knew she was a beautiful soul before but now knowing that Tai and I share the same feelings of heartbreak, I have a new appreciation for the woman. Soph and Tai are very lucky to have her in their lives. The three of them care about each other a lot and I have to admit, I'm a little envious. But on the same token, I'm so relieved and happy for them.

"Thanks, Mary," I mutter and without realizing I'm doing it, I launch forward and pull her into a hug.

"Ohh." She laughs softly, hugging me back. "I'm probably getting self-rising flour all over you."

"I don't care," I whisper, taking a moment to live vicariously through the Becketts. "It's worth it."

As I pull back, I notice her tinged cheeks, her eyes matching her lips as she beams at me. Giving her a tight smile back, I head up the stairs, straight for Tai's bedroom.

There's music coming from inside, and I hesitate for a second, wondering if I should knock. But I keep with my habit of storming into bedrooms, twisting the handle and inviting myself in.

Tai glances over casually, before doing a double take, eyes widening in surprise. "Bexley."

I close the door, leaning my back against it. "Can we hang for a bit?"

He nods, slipping off his headphones. "You have flour all over your skirt and jersey," he muses.

When I don't move or respond, he frowns, standing from his chair and walking over.

"What happened?"

I shrug. "Remember how you said there was nothing I could have done to change the outcome?"

Tai tilts his head curiously. "Yeah?"

"Well, I turned out to be the exception."

His jaw tightens, as if he's silently reliving his own memories. "Come over here," he says, holding out his hand.

I slip my palm into his, allowing him to pull me toward the bed. Reaching for my waist, he guides me around, sitting me down on the mattress edge.

"The appointment?"

"Hmm."

Dropping to his knees, he cups his hands together, resting them on my leg before putting his chin on his knuckles. "Wanna talk about it?"

"Not really," I murmur.

He nods, standing back up. I watch, expecting him to go to the computer but he walks to the side of the bed, climbing onto the mattress. Wiggling forward, his legs slide past either side of mine. Hands move into my hair, carefully extracting the hair tie and letting my ponytail loose. His fingers comb through my hair, untangling it before separating it into three sections.

"Are you braiding my hair?" I ask with sheer amusement—which is a nice one-eighty change from all the other emotions.

"Yep."

I smile, letting my eyes close as he starts weaving the locks together. There's something so relaxing about having your hair and scalp played with. It's my goddamn weakness and I melt into putty in his hands.

"You do this for Soph, don't you?"

Tai laughs. "Is it that obvious?"

"It's brother-coded for sure."

He wraps the hair tie around the end, securing it. "I taught myself with Youtube tutorials. But I draw the line at makeup application."

"Yeah, I wouldn't trust you with a mascara brush near my eyeballs."

We seem to move at the same time, Tai shifting forward as I lean back. He wraps his arms around me, encasing me in a bear hug.

The two of us stay quiet for a moment, simply enjoying the moment of physical touch, until I ask the question, "Just how close are you to Rylan?"

"He's like a brother to me. But you already know that. So, tell me what's happening in that head of yours?"

As I sink further into him, Tai plops his chin on my shoulder, waiting for my reply.

"Because I think I might kiss you," I answer without hesitation. "And as much as I used to love the idea of bringing you all down, I'm not in the habit of breaking friendships."

He brings his hand up to my face, fingers gently tilting my head in his direction. "We don't have a problem with sharing, Bex," he whispers against my cheek, sending shivers down my body. "Which is why Ry was more than happy to watch you ride my face."

In a perfect world, I'd do my due diligence and hear it from the horse's mouth as well. But right now, I take his word for it, twisting my body and angling my face to find his lips. He kisses me back, and unlike the intensity I have with Rylan, this is slow and all-consuming.

Our lips caress gently, building in pace until I'm flipped onto my back with Tai straddling me. With our new position, we're closer, bodies pressed together as his tongue darts into my mouth seeking mine out.

Like the night in the cage, there's a weird sense of nirvana. Rylan knew what I needed that night and today, Tai senses it too. As usual, that uncomfortable feeling tingles, largely masked by perplexity that someone like him could be the answer and the calm to my storm. But I lean into it, taking what I want and need since he's offering with no questions asked.

His warm hand slides up my waist, bunching my jersey under my chest. Fingers dance along my rib cage, seemingly asking for permission to go higher. And fuck me, there's nothing sexier than consent.

I mimic his movements, grasping his white jersey and tugging it up. Sliding my hand over his toned stomach, I let out a little groan of appreciation. Of course he's ripped too—why wouldn't he be? Devils are meant to be creatures of seduction. If they weren't, how else would we sin?

Muscles tremble under my touch as my fingers trail downwards, stroking the skin above his waistband. It's all the confirmation he needs, hand disappearing under my jersey to cover my tits. He gropes them firmly, massaging me through the lace bra, before tugging on my nipple. My back arches on its own accord and he loops his arm around, lifting me off the bed.

There's a flurry of hands as we both reach for our jerseys, pulling them off and slinging them to the ground somewhere. He kisses my neck while gently grabbing one of my bra straps, taking his sweet time to drag it down my shoulder before doing the same to the other side.

Everywhere he touches burns with need despite his feather-like pressure. Soft lips cover every inch of my neck, occasionally sucking the tender skin.

I wasn't expecting this. In my mind, we were going to fuck hard and fast. But this slow, intimate dance has my thighs clenching together to try to relieve the ache begging to be fixed.

I need him—now.

My hand slides into his shorts, a tiny gasp leaving my mouth when he quickly snaps my wrist up, pinning it above my head instead. He lifts my other arm up, locking both wrists together with one hand, while his other glides over my torso and skirt to my thigh. It disappears under the tartan material, rubbing me through the lace.

"You tasted so good yesterday," Tai murmurs against my lips. "I can't wait to see what you feel like too."

"Then do it," I mumble through the kiss.

He kisses me harder at the same time as his fingers slip underneath, pushing into my body. My hips jolt into his hand as he swallows my moan.

The pace still doesn't change, torturously slow movements that drag pleasure out of me but refuse to push me over the edge. It's driving me insane in the best way possible. We both know that the relief is a disguise for what I really need. There's so much more that I crave, that only someone like Tai can give because we've been through the same thing.

Affection. Touch. Love.

Pulling out of my body, I lift my hips so he can help remove the rest of my clothing before doing the same with his. He covers me with his naked body, pushing my legs apart with his knee.

"Protection?" he asks, trailing kisses over my chest.

"Birth control."

"Good," Tai answers and I feel the head of his cock inch into my entrance slightly. "Because I want to feel you completely." He finishes his sentence with a jolt of his hips, burying himself inside me until our hips clash.

I wrap my arms around his neck, pulling his face closer as our lips move with our bodies. He grinds against me, reentering my warmth with slow precision, making sure to rub his pelvis against my clit.

One leg locks around his back, keeping him in place as we chase physical and emotional freedom. I start to get close, feeling my climax building and my pussy tenses around him. Tai moves out of me, ignoring my moans of protest. Before I can scold him, he rolls off me, laying on his side. Scooping me up in his arms, he drags me back until his chest is flat against my spine.

He lifts my leg, looping it over his muscular thigh, spreading me open. He grabs my tit, using it to hold me against him as he thrusts back into my cunt.

His movements are faster finally, but without the direct contact to my clit, I'm still caught in limbo, hanging on the edge of the cliff. I start to move my hand down my body to relieve myself, but he quickly grabs it, replacing his touch with my own over my chest. He pins my palm to my tit, taking control of my hand to tug on the hardened, pink tip.

"Tai," I breathe out, desperation in my words.

"Soon," he promises, letting go of my hand to tilt my head back.

Hot kisses distract me as he rolls his hips harder, slowly gaining momentum. I'm so lost in the feeling of everything that I can't focus on anything except for him. Our mouths move wildly, urgently seeking each other out while the sound of skin slapping together echoes around the room.

And just when I start to forget about my aching need to come, my mind letting go and being in the moment, his fingers land on my clit, touching me hard and fast. It's the equivalent to a bomb detonating, my climax ripping through me with no notice. A scream tears from my throat, body shuddering as I clench down tight around his cock.

"That's it," he whispers proudly next to my ear. "Scream for me, pretty girl."

Fuck. It doesn't stop coming—quite literally. Tidal waves roll and crash through my body, white spots appearing in my eyes and blinding me as I ride out the high that doesn't seem to end. His fingers keep moving against my clit, dragging it out as he thrusts mercilessly into me.

It feels like I can't breathe. I must be spiraling out of control because all I can focus on is how good it feels to drown and suffocate. It's freeing, the white dissipating into black as I fall into a calm darkness and I realize that my eyes have closed. Behind me, I hear Tai groan loudly, holding the sound in his throat as his movements turn jerky and I feel his hot release spill into me.

We're both breathing heavily, panting as we come back to reality. His arm moves back to my chest, tightening his grip as he holds me against him.

The two of us lay in comfortable silence, a wave of exhaustion washing over me. I know I should move before I fall asleep, but for the life of me, I can't see a reason as to why I should. Tai's steel grip doesn't loosen either, so I just let go, drifting off into a peaceful sleep in his arms.

Chapter Forty-One

Friday rolls around and there's a strange atmosphere looming over Willowbrook today. These guys really take their dances seriously.

Teachers barely make any effort to teach, even the Cedar Heights ones that joined the staff this week to assist. With the auditorium apparently set up and ready for tonight, I'm thrilled to find that we're all given an early mark to go home and get ready. Hey, no complaints here.

Finding myself back at Soph and Tai's house is a bit unnerving if I'm being honest. Even though the plan was always to get ready here, my mind can't help but think back to Wednesday.

Sleep has been hard to come by lately, but in Tai's bed, I took the best nap of my life. The only reason we ended up moving was to shower and join Mary for dinner—because fuck missing out on her awesome cooking. Soph seemed a bit bewildered to see me there—probably since I had just admitted to the whole school, well both schools, that I was banging Rylan. And now here I was, hanging out with her brother. Well... that's the story I went with. It's the tame version at least.

Not much gets past that girl. I was a bit worried how that conversation would go down, but whenever Mary left the room, Soph would make sexual innuendo jokes at the pair of us. So, safe to say she's not *that* upset about it. If anything, I've given her enough ammo to tease me for the rest of the school year. I'm sure she'll bring it up tonight in one way or another, but that's a problem for near-future Bexley. At the moment, she's in my good books, so I'll let her taunt me, since she paid for my dress against my will.

I'm just hoping that she doesn't bring it up in front of Abby. I doubt she'd care or have a problem with it, but she's too innocent to be corrupted by my antics. And now I'm stuck picturing her and Arch in kink outfits. Fucking hell.

"Stay still. I don't want to get anything in your eye," Soph directs, tugging on my hair.

"This is going to be fixable, right?" I eye her through the mirror, tensing as she applies more bleach to the ends of my hair.

She raises an eyebrow, attention locked on her hairdressing skills. "Well, if your hair wasn't purple this would be a little easier. But don't be surprised when you love it," she says in a sing-song voice.

"I have the boxes!" Abby announces, strolling into Soph's private bathroom. "This is going to be amazeballs."

"Well, at least one of you has faith in me," Soph grumbles, making me laugh.

Abby stands beside her, playing with the other side of my head. "If she can make her ends pink, she can do yours too."

"I'm all about the pink bits," Soph replies with a grin. "Like someone else."

She meets my gaze in the mirror, biting her bottom lip to stop herself from cackling.

"Shut up, *Sophie*," I tease.

"Oof. Playing with fire. You're game to make a death wish while I'm applying chemicals to your head."

"I'm all about the thrills in life."

Dumping the box on the basin, Abby fluffs her hair with a smile. "Save some of that aggression for the dance, you pair. If I have any chance of getting Sagg on the dance floor, I have to make it there first and not be witness to a double homicide."

In the evening light, there's a slight charm about Willow-brook. Maybe because it's partially hidden by the dark and for a moment, I can pretend I'm not in hell.

The four of us walk into the auditorium, eyebrows raised at the in full swing dance.

Hundreds of red lights have been strung around, making the room glow eerily. Bodies are pressed together on the dance floor in the middle of the room while large circular tables line the walls. We manage to find a free one, sliding into the seats while music booms from the stereo loudly.

Black silk cloths lay over the tables, with red LED candles lingering in the middle. The entire roof is covered with floating balloons, their latex skin reflecting strobe lights that slowly project Bat signals around the room.

As soon as we sit down, I hear Abby turning on the charm, begging Arch to go dance. Cruella in her pink dress manages to persuade him in record time, and I muffle a laugh as his eyes shoot me a cry for help. The themed attire of the dance doesn't help his cause as I watch Cruella drag a terrified Magneto into the crowd of people.

Soph suddenly fans out her dress around her, nervously adjusting the bust. Instinctively, I glance around, amused when I find Parker standing in a dark corner, scowling at the crowd of dancers with a drink in his hand. Turning to her, I raise an eyebrow. "Are you getting turned on by Lex Luthor's presence?"

She freezes, eyes blowing wide. "I didn't do anything."

"Just go talk to him," I laugh. "Do you want me to take you over there?"

"Would you?" she whimpers. "I promise to fix your hair if you do."

Shaking my head, I stand, holding out my hand for her. She did a fucking good job, and she knows it. After lightening up the tips, she applied bright pink dye, before adding a few streaks of the same color throughout my head. It's not exactly Harley Quinn hair, but it's close enough. The multi-colored strands are tied into two pigtails and together, the colors are just chef's kiss. But this is her version of bribery, so I'm rolling with it.

Even though she takes my hand, I practically have to drag her over to Parker. He notices us coming, offering a tight smile.

"Bexley," he greets warmly before turning to my cowering companion. "Soph."

"Dance with the Evil Queen. Please and thanks," I say, yanking her arm forward to jerk her hand into his.

Before either of them can speak, I turn on my heel with a shit-eating grin and head back to the table. Only when I'm sat back down do I dare a glance, pleased when I see them heading to the dance floor nervously, like the two introverts they are. You'd think they were on their way to be sacrificed by the looks of horror on their faces. But despite being un-comfortable at the concept of whipping out some moves in front of their peers, their obvious attraction to each other seems to override it.

I scan the room curiously, checking out everyone's cos-tumes when I pass a faceless body staring at me. I double back, snorting as I push off my chair and make a beeline for him.

He watches me approach, hands in his pockets and a smirk appearing out of the corner of the mask.

"Phantom of the Opera," I murmur, gazing at Rylan's sparkling blue eyes through the mask. "How fitting for you."

"Should have known *you'd* turn up as your alter ego."

"Hilarious," I mock, catching sight of his eyes drifting down my body. They land on my waist, cinched by the corset before falling on my chest—typical male.

"Hey," I say, using my index finger to tilt his chin up. "My eyes are up here, buddy."

Rylan grins. "I know."

Rolling my eyes, I shake my head, looking around. "Where are the other two?"

"You'll see them soon enough," he replies coolly. "No doubt Tai will come hunt you down."

This dynamic is weird. I don't have the spoons to put a label on it or to even consider what it could be. But I ask the next question regardless, getting it out of the way. "Did he tell you we had sex?"

"He did," Rylan agrees, and I'm happy to hear there's no resentment or animosity in his voice. Well, at least I think I'm happy. Relieved, mostly.

"Good," I answer, spinning around to face the dance floor. "Saves me having to do it."

He steps up behind me, leaning down to my ear. "But yes, Bexley. We're fine with sharing. So don't worry about getting your panties in a twist."

Looking at him over my shoulder, I casually smile. "I'd have to be wearing panties for that to happen."

I stalk off, leaving him open-mouthed as I weave my way through bodies to the drinks table. Staring at the punch bowl, I can't help but wonder if it's already been spiked. Deciding I'm fine with it either way since I need something to get me through this evening, I pour myself a cup.

When I spin around to head back to my table, I stumble, nearly colliding with someone. Green eyes narrow at me, a sneer crossing his face.

"Duchess."

Without responding, I stare him down, drinking the entire thing in one go, eyebrows shooting up when I taste the unmistakable taint of vodka—thank fuck.

"Hold that thought," I murmur, filling my cup again and drinking that as well.

Hunter scowls, obviously catching on to my tactic, that I need to be buzzed to be in his presence. "Seriously?"

"Yep," I shoot back calmly. "Feel free to do the same. I won't be offended."

He cocks an eyebrow. "And drink that cheap shit? No, thanks. I brought my own."

My eyes fall to the cup in his hand. I wonder what his poison is. Probably something expensive and fancy like scotch.

"What is it?" I ask, making a poor attempt at conversation. I guess we should try to be amicable since we're going to be working together. The thought of being civil with this man makes my skin crawl, but to be fair, I thought the same about Rylan and Tai before they grew on me like the plague. And the three of them are a package deal, so I'm a bit screwed either way—pun intended.

Conflict appears in Hunter's eyes as if he's equally trying to mentally peptalk himself into being nice to me. It's quite entertaining to watch, waiting to see if he caves in as well.

"Scotch."

Ha! Called it.

"Cool."

The two of us stand awkwardly. I continue to look around for a familiar face—anyone really, I'm not picky—but Hunter keeps his eyes locked on me. It's probably some lame effort to make me uncomfortable, but he's going to have to work on his stalker tendencies if he wants that to happen.

I can't even see Soph or Abby anymore, and my eyes start to hurt the longer I stare into strobe lights and reflections of red.

Finally, I relent, giving him my attention. "The Devil, huh?"

Red horns poke out of his head, matching perfectly to the dyed tips of his hair. But that seems to be the extent of his outfit, like he couldn't be fucked trying any harder. Though, I'll never admit it out loud, but he looks *fine*. He's dressed in black fitted jeans and a black buttoned-up shirt. The sleeves are rolled up to his elbows, his bulging forearms sticking out looking like God himself carved them. In an alternative universe, I'd say he looks hot. But in this lifetime, no chance of that.

"Harley Quinn doesn't have purple and pink hair."

Sighing, I'm just about running out of patience for this walking butt plug when another voice chimes in.

"Well, *my* version of Harley does."

We both turn at the same time to find Tai, grinning widely at me. His eyes run slowly down my dress appreciatively, but I'm too stunned to react to that.

"You're fucking kidding me," I mumble, taking in his costume.

Gone is his silvery ash hair. Bright green strands are slicked back; white makeup smeared messily over his face with red lipstick climbing up his cheeks. Dressed fully in a royal-purple suit and green tie, I'm both horrified and impressed to see the Joker standing before me.

"I'm going to kill Sophia," is all I manage to say.

Tai laughs, ignoring Hunter as he snakes his arm around my waist and yanks me into him. "Don't be mad," he muses. "Just get even."

Hunter makes some type of gagging noise, muttering, "Gross," before turning and walking off. Well, I guess that answers that question about how much the three of them share news of their bed conquests. I'm actually surprised Hunter didn't murder them, but I guess he's outnumbered anyway.

"Come dance with me, Pumpkin Pie," Tai grins, dragging me toward the dance floor.

"I thought I was Peach Queen," I laugh.

"That too," he answers, blissfully unaware of the confused and alarmed eyes on us. "But tonight, you're my partner in crime."

Chapter Forty-Two

I manage to finally slip away from Tai after a few songs, needing to get off my feet. Whoever invented heels knew what kind of torture they were inflicting and if my calves didn't look so good, I'd curse them with lukewarm coffee every day.

There's still no one at the table when I sit down, and that alone makes me happy. Things must be going well for the new couples, even if Arch and Parker are probably fighting for their lives on the dance floor. Poor souls.

Steele walks past at one point, and I have to do not one, not two, but three takes at the person on his arm. He gives me a shy grin as he passes, seemingly impressed with his companion.

Peyton has her arm threaded through his, blushing nervously as they head into the sea of people. For a moment, I question just how strong the vodka is in the punch and whether I should have had a third cup. But no, it's not a hallucination. One of Liv's besties is dancing with Steele to *Look What You Made Me Do* by Taylor Swift, and I can't think of a more fitting song. The head cheerleader would have a meltdown if she saw.

I'm surprised I haven't seen her yet. She seems like the type to be the center of attention at a function like this. But I'm not complaining. Any time spent away from her is a victory I welcome.

Hopping up from the table, I head outside the auditorium in search of the restrooms. My eyes light up when I spot Millie outside the restroom door, leaning against a locker while chewing her nails.

"Mills."

She glances over, relief flooding her face as she kicks off from the locker, running over to me. "Bex, thank God you're here."

"What's up?" I ask firmly, immediately on guard.

Millie's eyes dart to the door with a frown. "Jenna from freshman year just told me that she overheard a conversation in the restroom. I'm trying to see if they come back."

"Who?"

"She didn't know. She was in the stall when she heard them come in and start talking about our school."

My face scrunches up in confusion. "What were they saying? I'm sure it's not uncommon that someone from Willowbrook would be ranting about us tonight. We're crashing their dance."

Millie shakes her head, and it's the most worried I've ever seen her. That alone puts me on edge. "They were talking about the fire."

"What did they say?" I ask with a hint of urgency. Shit—the people who lit the fire could be here right now.

"They said that the first fire didn't do enough damage—that the repairs will be done in a few weeks. So, they started discussing ways to destroy Cedar Heights. They got real quiet after that but Jenna thinks they were talking about another fire... tonight."

My eyes widen. "Is she sure?"

Millie's face hardens, and my little shadow is back, anger on her face. "No. But we can't let them do that."

I nod. "We won't," I tell her, giving her shoulder a gentle squeeze. "Leave it with me."

Heading into the restroom, I check to find it empty. They won't come back—not if someone is already on their way to Cedar Heights.

Knowing that everyone is here, it would be the perfect time to attack the school. We need to move now.

I storm back into the auditorium, foot pain forgotten, as I carefully scan the swarm of bodies. The whole place is crowded, but I just need to find one—then we can take care of this.

Walking along the edge of the room, I weave through laughing, painfully obvious drunk people, searching. Finally, I spot one, and I groan, irritated at my options.

"Hey, asshole," I say loudly, watching as Hunter slowly spins around, boredom across his face.

"What now, Duchess?" he snaps back. "Sick of Rylan and Tai already?"

I don't have time for these games, so I grab his wrist, pulling him roughly toward the door. To my surprise, he follows, but definitely rips his arm out of my grip at the first possible second.

I find an empty classroom, motioning for him to enter. He sneers at me, annoyed, but does anyway, closing the door behind him.

"What?" he growls lowly.

"We think someone is on their way to Cedar Heights to finish off the arson job," I quickly tell him, not bullshitting around. "I need to head over there. Where are your other two minions?"

Hunter stares at me in astonishment. "I don't fucking know. Probably on the dance floor or walking around the grounds."

"Look," I sigh. "I don't have time to find them. I'm going to head over now but if you could locate them, the three of you could meet me there."

His face hardens. "You're shitting me, right? I'm not letting you get behind the wheel of a car after drinking."

"You've been drinking too," I point out. "Besides, I feel fine."

"I had one shot," he argues back, voice raising. "You drank at least three cups of that vodka punch. I'll drive."

Trust me to find the asshole of the group during an emergency. Every fiber in my body wants to decline the offer, but time is of the essence. Begrudgingly, I agree, mentally promising to come back from the dead and kill the mother-fucker myself if he kills me in a car crash.

"Fine," I snap. "Hurry up and move."

As I stalk out of the classroom, Hunter follows, huffing to himself. "Are you always such a raging bitch?"

"Are you always such a hormonal hemorrhoid?"

He doesn't answer me, which is probably a good thing. We're on the cusp of murdering each other, forced to band together for the sake of all our sanities. The sooner we can get back to Cedar Heights, the better.

Hunter leads the way once we hit the parking lot, orange lights flashing on a black Escalade as he hits the key fob in his hand. Neither of us speak as we climb into the car and once we're on the main road, I pull my cell out of my bra.

"What the fuck?" Hunter grumbles, doing a double take.

"Keep your damn eyes on the road, Lannister!"

He seems almost offended that I had my cell stuffed inside my dress—as if his entire existence has been tainted with the secrets of girlhood. Christ, what else did he think tits were for?

I start typing out a message to both Rylan and Tai, hitting send and hoping that they can hear or feel their cells through the loud music and thudding of the stereos. "I've texted the other two."

"Hm," is all I get, making me shake my head. Asshole.

As much as it pains me to disturb Arch's cardio adventure, I also send him a text, alerting him of the situation. Hope-fully, they can be our ears and eyes at Willowbrook while we are across town.

The ideal scenario would be that this is all for nothing. Perhaps Jenna heard wrong or misunderstood, but we can't leave anything to chance. If I have to spend any more time with Dean Satan and his son, I'll probably shrivel up.

There's not even any music as we sit in silence, my foot tapping impatiently as Hunter drives annoyingly slow. I mean, sure, he's going the speed limit. But fuck him anyway. Any excuse to be mad at him works for me.

Finally, I spot the familiar cream and brown building coming into view, shrouded in darkness except for the streetlights. Hunter scoffs under his breath as we pull into the Cedar Heights parking lot, but for me, it's like a breath of fresh air seeing home.

I jump out of the car before he's turned off the ignition, taking a few steps toward the main entrance. Pausing, I gaze over the building, inspecting the previous damage and searching for any signs of embers.

Hunter strolls up next to me, straightening up a jacket he's just shoved on, hands deep in his pockets as he scowls at the building like it's personally wronged him. I cock an eyebrow at the addition to his attire, baffled that even in the presence of a damaged building, he's still trying to make a statement with his ego.

"I don't want to hear one single comment from you," I mutter, eyes landing on some boarded-up windows outside the administration building.

Before he can reply, I take off, lifting the hem of my dress as I walk up the steps. I half expect him to turn and leave, but as I'm fidgeting with the giant padlock on the front door, he comes up beside me.

"Move," he grunts, thrusting a key forward.

I raise a brow, which only seems to go higher when the key turns effortlessly, and the padlock unlocks. I stare at him in question, receiving a bored look in return.

"Your principal gave us a spare key," he says simply, as if I'm stupid for being confused.

"You mean he gave your father a key."

"That's what I said."

Elbowing him out of the way, I remove the padlock and open the door. "I don't know if I should be impressed that you have our key or pissed that you stole it from the dean's office."

"You have a funny way of saying thank you," he shoots back. "What was your plan? Break a window and scale the building like fucking Spiderman?"

Ignoring him, I step into the darkness, immediately gagging at the strong stench of smoke and burned materials. Even two months later, it's still overwhelming, and part of me wonders if it will ever be truly gone.

I head down the corridor, using my cell torch as a light. I bypass the main admin office which has large sheets of plastic draped all over the walls and construction materials dumped on the floor. My eyes fall on the lockers as we pass, and my chest tightens as I see the damage for the first time.

They really did it. It's... destroyed. We were told that the lockers were largely intact—I guess not all of them. The ones near the admin office are all but gone.

Warped melted metal disguises the fact that these used to be lockers, charred books fallen on the floor, completely unrecognizable.

As we head further toward the classrooms, I stop suddenly, staring.

"What is it?" Hunter asks with a pressing tone, swinging his head around to figure out what's stolen my attention.

I reach out and touch the mangled mess, surprised when the locker door swings open with ease. The lock is broken, and everything inside has turned to ash. Lifting a blackened Polaroid, my shoulders droop. I can still see the picture in my mind, but in front of me, it's non-existent. The fragile film crumbles under my touch, a small gasp escaping my lips before I can stop it.

"Your locker," Hunter says knowingly.

I suppose that explains why they weren't able to recover more of my stuff. It dawns on me that the textbooks given to me to take to Willowbrook weren't mine to begin with. Someone provided me with copies so that I'd be able to start classes.

Nodding, I tip my hand, letting the ash fall to the floor. "That was a picture of my parents and I," I answer quietly, stepping backwards.

Without elaborating, I keep walking, blinking back the tears that have formed in my eyes. Whoever did this will pay.

I hope they are here—trying again. Because when I get my hands on them, they are going to wish they were swallowed and shit out.

Hunter follows silently and I can't help but notice, much to my annoyance, that he seems to know where we are going. I glare at him out of the corner of my eye, shooting daggers. He pretends not to see me, still wearing that bored expression that I long to wipe off.

As we enter the library, I stumble for a moment, really overpowered by the smoke smell. It's stronger in here than the admin office, to my surprise. The whole area is completely decimated, and it appears they haven't even started repairing this section.

There's a pile of supplies in the far corner, neatly packed together. My feet carry me over, curious as to why they are there when nothing has been secured and prepped in here. For a second, I suddenly wonder how structurally sound the building is and whether it's going to collapse on top of us.

My fingers skim the packaging, still perplexed. It's brand new, unopened. I have no idea how repairs are supposed to be completed in a few weeks because judging by the state of what I've seen, it's nowhere near done.

Because maybe they don't intend to finish it...

I scan the library, pausing for a brief second to look at Hunter. He's glancing down an aisle, fixated on something.

"What is it?" I ask, moving next to him.

Through the dark, I flash my light, spotting something out of place. There's a giant hole in the floor and as we approach, I realize it's a trap door.

"Where does that go?" Hunter questions, peering into the hole.

I shake my head. "I have no idea. I've never seen it before."

Old memories run through my mind. All the visits to the library, wondering how I missed a trap door. If it was hidden, it was done well.

Bending down, I start unbuckling my heels. Hunter's eyes widen in disbelief. "You can't be serious?" he huffs, looking between the hole and my hunched over body.

"What if that's how they broke in?" I offer, annoyed. "Someone could be down there right now."

"You don't even know where it goes. It might not be safe," he snaps back. "You really want to go underground in a burned-out building?"

Kicking off my shoes, I straighten up. "This probably means nothing to you, but this place is everything to me."

"Don't be stupid, Duchess—"

His words are cut off, both our heads spinning toward the library doors. The sound of metal clanging echoes outside, like a pipe was dropped heavily on the floor. We both freeze, listening intensely, and when more banging comes, I abandon my shoes, taking off toward it.

"Bexley!" Hunter snaps behind me. But even his use of my real name doesn't deter me.

Someone is here.

Chapter Forty-Three

Damn this fucking woman.

I want to strangle her. Even as I call out to her to stop, she refuses to listen, running barefoot through ash and broken bits of building.

At least she's easy to spot in the darkness, the red sequins on her dress reflecting the little amount of light in here.

Taking off after her, I catch up quickly, nearly colliding into her back as she pauses in the hallway, head turning rapidly.

"This way," she breathes, and I'm not entirely sure it was said to me as she charges off toward classrooms.

I hate that I know the layout of this place. Dad had blueprints in his office of the existing structure as well as the reconstruction plans. I studied them meticulously, learning everything I could about this academy in case I ever needed the information. Perks of being dragged into this mess, I suppose.

I just didn't think I would need it for *this.*

Spencer stumbles a few times, trying to lift the long hem of her dress which gets caught on numerous things. Her feet must be in Hell, but if she's stupid enough to run through here barefoot then that's on her. I'm not saying she should have kept her heels on, but I guess we didn't really have time to change into appropriate attire.

Sounds of banging keep echoing further away, and as much as I hate to admit it, she's right. There's obviously someone here and we need to find out who.

Judging by the way the noises keep moving ahead, they know that we're here too. I just hope that they are fleeing and not leading us on a wild goose chase. Maybe our presence has scared them, and they will abandon their efforts to commit arson. But the stubborn woman running next to me won't accept that—she wants to hunt them down.

My cell buzzes in my pocket but there's no time to answer. It's likely Rylan and Tai, responding to Spencer's text messages and trying to find out what the fuck is going on.

I have no idea what they see in her. She's insufferable and a pain in the ass. But for whatever reason, they seem to like her now—or her cunt at least. I still don't agree with it, but I have no choice but to honor our Wolf Pack.

Hopefully they know what they are doing. We're risking a lot by teaming up with her, and it's even more painstaking when I seem to have drawn the short end of the stick tonight.

Spencer bursts through the doors to the Cedar Heights auditorium. They bounce off the wall with a loud bang and I cringe. There's nothing fucking subtle about her. We should be approaching these people like predators—slowly, in silence. But no. She's charging around like a bull in a room full of red. Ironic really given what she's wearing.

Finally, she pauses, breathing heavily as she scans the room. The windows around the auditorium are all boarded up even though there's minimal damage in here. As we stop moving, I can't help but notice it's gone eerily quiet.

There are no sounds at all except our breathing, and it starts to alarm me. It very much feels like we've just walked into a trap. Whoever is here couldn't have vanished that easily, and it feels like eyes are upon us.

Spencer appears to sense the same, her body twisting to turn toward me. "Hunter," she whispers with a frown.

I'm not sure what she's asking of me, but I step over to her, our arms brushing. "They're here somewhere," I answer under my breath. "Where could they be?" It's a direct question to her, urging that brain to use her knowledge of the building. I may know the blueprints but that's the extent of my participation. Spencer will know things that I don't—places where people could hide.

Her eyes focus on mine through the dark, face hardening as she gives a nod. I stay close to her as she crosses the auditorium toward a side door. For a second, I think she's going to go through it, but she walks past to the stage, climbing a set of stairs. The blue curtains are open, nothing seemingly out of place, but she heads to some draped curtains lining the back wall.

Peeling them back, I'm intrigued to find there's a door behind the stage, hidden from sight.

There we go. Smart girl.

I give myself a little internal praise for directing her before I follow Spencer into another dark room. I realize it's not a room per se, but a corridor, leading to a multitude of dressing rooms. They don't look like they have been used in some time, even before the fire. Everything is covered with white sheets to protect from dust, and a stale smell lingers in the air.

Our footsteps echo as we walk slowly, scanning empty rooms and listening to sounds. When we reach the wall at the end of the corridor, Spencer turns around with a frown.

"Not here," she mutters in disbelief.

"Think," I tell her, stepping in closer. "Are we certain they came in this way?"

I see uncertainty cross her face, but she nods. "Yeah."

"What about that side room in the auditorium?" I ask.

She shakes her head. "It's just a prop cupboard. Practically the size of a shoebox."

"Maybe we should check it out anyway," I offer, reaching into my pocket.

Extracting my cell, I see the missed call notifications from Rylan and Tai. That seems to jog Spencer's memory too, lifting her own cell and temporarily blinding me with the torch.

"They are on their way," I say to her, reading a text from Tai. "We should head back to the entrance and wait for them."

"But there's still someone here," she replies, disappointed. Her face wrinkles and I see guilt plastered all over it, as if she's taking this personally.

Sighing, I reach out awkwardly, patting her shoulder like I'm consoling a wounded animal. "We've probably scared them off. Best we head back and wait for the others."

Spencer gazes at me, my breath hitching as her eyes shine at me in appreciation. It catches me off-guard, not used to seeing this side of her. I don't know how to feel about it—other than confused as fuck.

"Okay," she agrees, motioning with her head for me to follow as she treks back toward the stage.

We walk in silence, neither of us knowing what to say to the other. As we start to near the secret door, my body stiffens, and I take a whiff of the air. This whole building reeks of smoke and charred materials, but the auditorium was largely undamaged. The smell of smoke seems stronger now, puzzling me.

As we push through the curtains onto the stage, we quickly discover why.

Spencer stops abruptly and I crash into her, my hands instinctively gripping her shoulders to steady us both. Our eyes are glued ahead to the other side of the auditorium, horror filling me.

Smoke billows under the cracks of the door, flooding into the room at an alarming speed. But that's not the most concerning part. It's a draw—somewhere between the fact that we left the now-closed doors open, and the goddamn orange glow that illuminates through the gaps.

We rush forward in unison, standing on the edge of the stage. Before either of us can speak or process what we are witnessing, flames lick through the wooden doors, disintegrating them before our eyes.

"Shit," I hiss, grabbing Spencer's wrist.

She's tensed up, eyes blown wide. After a few seconds, she finally reacts, turning to look at me with speechless, unbridled panic.

"Bexley!" I say sharply, yanking her wrist. "Emergency exit."

Slowly, she raises her other hand, pointing a finger toward the fire that's now completely engulfed the main doors. "We're looking at it."

"What?" The yelp that sounds from my mouth would leave me embarrassed on any other given day. "There has to be another exit! It's literally part of any good fire plan."

My tone seems to temporarily snap Spencer out of her panic. "Well, I don't know what to tell you," she barks at me. "There isn't another door!"

"Okay, okay," I mutter to myself, closing my eyes for a second as I try to ignore the rising heat and smoke that's quickly filling the room. Punching a few keys on my cell, I crash it into my ear, cursing until I hear the voice pick up on the other end. "Rylan! The fucking building is on fire. We're trapped inside the auditorium."

His voice pauses for a moment, before he lets out a string of curses as well. "Fuck. We're nearly there. Tai, call for help. Hunter, where's Bexley?"

"Here with me," I answer, realizing that I'm crushing her wrist in my grip. She doesn't seem fazed though, eyes scanning the room for a contingency plan. When she stops, narrowing her eyes on something, I spin around to follow her line of vision.

The door to the prop room is wide open. Anger rips through me as realization dawns that I was correct—it was a trap. Whoever is here led us to this room, deliberately locking us in.

And wants to burn us alive.

"Call me when you get here!" I yell before hanging up the cell before he can respond and shoving it into my pocket.

Spencer suddenly breaks our contact, flying across the stage. She disappears out of sight for a moment, reemerging out of an exit onto the floor. My eyes widen as she darts toward the flames, my body springing into action as I take a shortcut, jumping off the stage to chase after the insane woman running toward fire.

She runs over to a boarded-up window, hands clawing at the wood as she tries to pry it off. As thick smoke starts to surround her, hiding her from sight, I sprint forward, eyes watering and stinging. I follow the sound of violent cough-ing, hands blindly finding her waist through the smog.

I hastily shrug off my jacket, thrusting it at her face. "Breathe into this," I yell, and through the haze, I see her gawk at me in disbelief.

"No, you use it," she argues back, flinging it at me in some noble attempt to sacrifice herself. I growl when she starts violently coughing again, gasping for air as my own lungs scream as heat starts to sizzle our skin.

The fire is getting closer, and I grab the jacket, holding it against *her* mouth and nose myself since the stubborn woman won't do it. I can feel her body tremble against mine as she fights for air, the two of us pressed together. My free hand feels the board, searching for a weakness in the wood, but nothing comes up.

I snake my arm around her waist, ripping her back toward the stage. We're not getting out through the window, and the longer we try, the closer we get to suffocating and passing out—or being burned alive.

Dragging Spencer at lightning speed, I pull us both through the secret door to the dressing rooms, slamming it closed behind us. We lean our backs against it for a second, wheezing as we desperately suck in oxygen.

She makes an odd choking noise, and I gaze through the shadows at her. I grimace and panic when I see her eyes start to roll back, fighting to stay conscious.

"Don't you dare!" I shout at her, doing the only thing I can think of. I shove my mouth over hers, administering a few rescue breaths, ignoring the taste of smoke on her lips which are a horrible shade of blue. She's limp between the door and my body, but after a few seconds, I feel her tense up, becoming alert again.

I pull back as she sucks in a ragged breath, relieved when her eyes focus, blinking rapidly a few times before her brain finally kicks into gear. She looks at my jacket, draped over my arm, ripping it toward her. I watch as she bends down, shoving it under the door to block the smoke.

"Come on," she mutters, voice hoarse and cracking from the smoke inhalation. Grabbing my hand, she pulls me down the corridor to the last dressing room, pushing me inside before grabbing a fire extinguisher from the corridor wall. Closing the door behind us, we both reach for one of the white sheets, plunging it into the gaps around the doorjamb.

When we've done all that we can, the two of us walk backwards, staring at the door with wide eyes. Our backs hit the wall at the same time, and I feel her slouch next to me in resignation.

"For what it's worth," she murmurs quietly after a few minutes. "I still think you're an asshole."

"I still think you're a fucking bitch," I grumble.

Spencer laughs sadly, the weird contradictory sound making me feel uneasy. "Well, shit. I'm going to die here with you."

"We're not going to die," I snap firmly, but even I don't truly believe my own words.

She turns her head to look at me, offering a tight smile. There's a sickening rumble in the distance, the sound of roaring, hot flames getting louder. I feel her small hand link with mine, our fingers entwining together. And for the life of me, I don't have the will to let it go. I close my eyes, squeezing her hand back with a sigh.

"Fuck."

"Hunter?" she asks quietly.

"What?" I grumble again, but the usual coldness toward her in my tone is gone.

Spencer doesn't say anything straight away, and I open my eyes, checking to make sure she's okay. Our eyes lock and I find watery green irises staring back at me.

"Promise you won't let go?" Her voice cracks. And suddenly, I don't see my enemy in front of me. I just see a peer, an equal, in all her raw emotion, begging me for a fraction of humanity.

"I won't let go," I tell her, squeezing her hand as a loud bang shudders the building, something exploding nearby in the flames. "You're not alone, Bexley. I got you."

Chapter Forty-Four

My heart is pounding painfully in my chest. This is not the way I thought I'd go out.

I'm not sure what's worse—the idea of being burned alive or waiting for it, trapped with no way out.

The roaring outside grows more intense, windows smashing under fierce heat and loud banging as parts of the auditorium collapse. Terrifying creaking sounds echo around us, my eyes flitting to the ceiling as my breathing gets heavier. It still hurts to breathe—my lungs screaming in pain while the taste of ash lingers in my mouth.

Maybe the roof will fall down on top of us, crushing us to death. That would be the humane, peaceful way to go. I almost start internally begging for it, just to get this nightmare over with.

Hunter squeezes my hand again when something explodes nearby, a frightened whimper escaping my lips.

I can't help but glance around the dressing room, cataloguing all the wood inside. The cupboard in the corner, the dressing table with white lights surrounding the mirror. So much flammable material.

A buzzing sound distracts me from my thoughts for a moment, and Hunter flinches. He digs into his pocket, letting out a dry laugh as he glances at his cell. From here, I see Rylan's name easily, flashing across the screen. And it hits me—just how fucked up this is.

"Hey," Hunter answers, in an eerily calm voice. It's as if he's just casually picking up the call on a normal day.

To my surprise, he puts them on speaker, Rylan's deep voice mid-conversation as Tai rants in the background. The sound of sirens weaving through their voices should calm me, but I think my mind already knows that it's too late.

"—Out the front. Emergency services are here. Tell me where you are exactly so I can tell the Chief," Rylan demands, in a bossy tone that even in my life-or-death panic makes me still want to fight him.

Hunter holds out the cell under my chin, nodding at me. He's handing control over, knowing I have a better understanding of this building.

"We're behind the stage in the auditorium," I recite clearly, a little stunned that my tone is so strong. "At the back of the room, toward the West side of campus, there's a set of dressing rooms, accessible through a door behind the stage backdrop. Last room on the right."

There's a sharp inhale on the other end of the line before the two voices clash together, both Rylan and Tai shouting my name at the same time.

Next to me, Hunter laughs quietly to himself, shaking his head. More voices grow louder, seemingly as they get closer to firefighters, and we hear Rylan repeat our location to someone. Shit—Archie's dad.

I barely have a handle on this disaster, doing my utmost best to purposely block my emotions so I don't spiral and end up in a blubbering mess on the floor. But realizing that people who know us—people who care—are outside, about to witness our deaths, that is a hard pill to swallow.

And suddenly, it all makes sense.

I've nearly torn myself apart trying to understand why Mom locked me out, why she hid the truth of her illness from me.

Now, I know why.

It wasn't to exclude me or deny me any input.

She was protecting me from the pain of what was about to happen. Minimizing my grief so our last moments together weren't tainted with fear and sad goodbyes.

A tear rolls down my cheek, which doesn't go unnoticed by Hunter. He glances over with a concerned look, pulling the cell back toward his own face as he answers whatever Tai just said. Their conversation is muffled, the world around me distorted as I have one of those ridiculous end of life epiphanies. People always say that things become clearer at the end. I thought that was just something people said to make the grieving process easier. But right now, I don't have some profound sense of peace and acceptance like I'm allegedly meant to have.

I'm not ready to die. And I sure as hell don't want anyone hearing it through a cell.

As I take a deep breath in, my chest constricts and tightens, sending me into another coughing fit. Hunter pauses his sentence with alarm on his face as Rylan's voice booms through the speaker.

"Hunter, is she okay?!"

"She's fine," he snaps back, but his lingering gaze contradicts his tone.

I'm not imagining it. As I stare at the door, waiting for it to blast open in one way or another, I notice smoke trickling through the cracks. Almost immediately, the smell intoxicates the room, Hunter pivoting to look at it as well.

It must be getting close if the smoke has managed to get through the stage door and travel down the hallway. Coming in thick and hard, the white sheet seems to do little to stop it.

I see resignation appear on Hunter's face as he notices too, a grim expression forming.

"Give me the cell," I say to him, holding out my hand.

He passes it over without question, and I bring it to my face, taking a deep breath. "Rylan... Tai?"

"Bexley," Rylan answers instantly, a chill to his tone. "Tai's here too."

"I'm here, Peach Queen."

Hunter makes a final scoff of what I assume is meant to signify disgust, but there's no heart in it. Holding his gaze, I offer a tight smile, hating what I'm about to do but having no regrets.

"Look after yourselves. Tell everyone we love them."

"Don't you fucking dare hang up, Bexley—" Rylan snaps back but I'm already hitting the red button, ending the call.

Slowly passing the cell back to Hunter, he wordlessly pockets it. Within seconds, we hear the buzzing and vibration as they attempt to call back, but Hunter doesn't reach for it.

Smoke continues to flow into the dark room, that eerie orange glow returning through the gaps in the door. It's only a matter of minutes now. Hopefully it will be quick. I think I read somewhere once that burning is one of the most painful ways to go—but eventually, the nerves reach a point where they stop hurting. Unless we suffocate first. I guess that would be the merciful way to die in this situation.

A brief thought crosses my mind, making me laugh.

Hunter raises an eyebrow. "What's so funny?" he asks, perplexed that I could be laughing at a time like this.

"I could kill you," I smirk through the shadows. "Two birds, one stone. Save you from the fire killing you but also... you know, getting to end your existence."

"Good to see that death hasn't affected your warped sense of humor."

"Who said I was joking?"

Hunter drops his head back against the wall, humming when he suddenly pauses, stiffening.

"Bexley."

I eye him through my peripheral vision. "What?"

"Look," he nods his head toward the ceiling.

Lazily I follow his direction, frowning as small flashes of red and blue hit the corner of the room. It's faint, a reflection from nearby emergency vehicles parked further up near the entrance.

Hunter spins around, slamming his hand on the wall. He knocks a few times, placing his ear to the panel. "What's on the other side of this wall?"

"The grounds," I answer, trying to decipher what's going on in that thick head of his.

He sprints over to the dressing table, shoving his weight into it. "Help me push this to the wall."

My face wrinkles in confusion, eyes darting up.

The window...

Well, it's not so much a window as a porthole. It's barely wide enough to shove a child through. Back in freshman year, the academy removed all the unused A/Cs to relocate them to other parts of the building. You know, saving costs and all since the State doesn't like to part with funding. I had forgotten about them since no one has come down here in years. Instead of replacing the A/Cs at the later date, they installed glass panels to seal up the holes.

The dressing table crashes into the wall and Hunter wastes no time climbing onto it, reaching up high to bang his fist on the tiny glass pane.

"We're not going to be able to fit through there!" I yell, smoke irritating my eyes. I can barely see him in front of me, even though he's only a foot away. "Nor are we going to be able to reach it."

"We have to try! Where's the extinguisher?"

I fumble around in the dark until I feel cool metal, lifting it up and passing the extinguisher to Hunter.

"Cover your eyes," is all I hear before there's a loud thud as metal hits tempered glass.

The pounding continues, and on the fourth attempt, I hear a different sound—a crack, followed by a shatter.

Before I can even move, rough hands grab my shoulders, hoisting me up onto the dressing table. I barely feel the sharp, stabbing pain as I stand barefoot on broken glass. Hunter wraps his arms around my waist, lifting me up toward the hole at the top of the wall.

Sweet, cold air hits me in the face, and I make an ungodly wheezing sound, chest rattling as I feel blood vessels explode with oxygen.

I start panting uncontrollably, breathing hard and fast as my body works overtime to suck in much needed air. I reach for Hunter's shoulder, squeezing it.

"Your turn," I say, wincing when I land on glass again. My senses have returned with the literal breath of fresh air, and before he can comprehend what I'm doing, I barge my shoulder into his ass, pushing with all my strength to lift him up. He's not as close to the window as I was, but I hear him taking deep breaths, my pride relishing in the beautiful sound.

Another thing I read was stories of people exuding super-human strength in the face of danger. I'd like to believe that's what's happening as I lock my knees and arms, holding onto the wall so we both don't crash to the floor. My body shakes, and just before I finally drop him, my strength giving out, Hunter yells, "Hey!".

He lands heavily next to me, the dressing table wobbling as we both throw our hands against the wall to catch our balance.

"Why did you yell at me?" I grunt, hissing as I flick more glass off my feet. "I did the best I could."

"I wasn't yelling at you," he answers abruptly, and I hear a flurry of thudding coming our way.

Rylan's face appears on the other side of the hole, eyes blown wide and that odd stormy color again. He growls as another figure crashes into him, their heads colliding painfully as Tai comes into view—apparently proving that Rylan is indeed the better and faster runner out of all of us.

"Hunter," he chokes out, suddenly coughing as smoke billows through the shattered glass into his face.

"We need to smash the rest of the glass out of the way," the man pressed against me says with urgency. "Quickly."

The tone of his words starts to unnerve me. Or is it because we're so close to safety that suddenly my body is in full survival mode?

Blue eyes meet mine through the smog and I'm horrified to find a tangerine glow in them. Spinning my head around, I gasp as I see the door in flames—well, what used to be a door.

"Move!" Tai shouts, an unusual darkness taking over his playful voice. There's just enough reflection through the black fumes to see a purple ball hurling toward the edge of the glass, his fist wrapped in his Joker jacket as he punches shards toward us.

Tiny fragments of glass slice my face but that's the least of my concerns. The two men outside barge their fists into the shattered window, clearing the rest of the hole as unbearable heat starts burning up my skin. It's so hot in here, sweat pouring off my body as Rylan attempts to squeeze his shoulders through the gap. Shit—we might just fit after all.

There's a tiny break in the smoke as a breeze rushes through and I see his eyes darting between the two of us, panic on his face. Suddenly his face is gone again, replaced by the sound of violent coughs as black smoke engulfs us all.

I get it.

He's trying to choose. Trying to decide who to save first.

I don't envy him, having to pick between the girl who's broken through his walls and sees the real him or his life-long best friend. But lucky for him, I already know the right choice.

Holding my breath, I crouch low, repeating my self-proclaimed impressive move from before as a surge of power rushes through my body. Hunter flinches against me, immediately tensing up and sandbagging his weight to try to stop me.

"Bexley!" he shouts. "Stop."

A hand rips me up, and for a brief second, I let him, reaching blindly through the dark to cup his face. It's amazing I can get any words out at all, white spots appearing in my eyes as my lungs scream and cry for air.

"It needs to be you," I manage to croak out, knowing the pain of losing their best friend would kill Rylan and Tai. I'm replaceable in their dynamic, not him, and before he can respond, I'm back low, shoving him again.

One of the guys must manage to grab him at the same time as I push his feet off the ground, probably unaware of our dispute below. Between their grip and my push, Hunter gets dragged up, legs brushing my face as I thrust him with all my strength until his weight is gone.

And there it is.

That weird feeling of peace and acceptance.

Even as flames light up the room, my body sags, exhausted against the wall with one arm still raised and resting above my head. I'm too tired to move it, a moment of relief as I realize I'm about to pass out before the fire can touch me. The heat from the flames is burning me, but slowly, the pain starts to fade, my consciousness floating away in static waves.

It sounds like someone is screaming my name, but I have no energy to respond, my sweaty body starting to slip down as my legs give out.

Then, it stops.

And my world goes black.

The Monster I Am - Book Two

Follow Bexley, Rylan, Tai, and Hunter's journey in book two
https://mybook.to/IwFhMLd
THE MONSTER I AM

Acknowledgements

Thank you for reading The Devils They Are! I hope you enjoyed book one in the Boys of Willowbrook series. And I'm sorry about the cliffhanger.

I'm so appreciative to all of you for supporting me. My sole purpose is to bring stories to life, to create a world that you can immerse yourself in. Reading is my escape and a part of my soul—and I hope my books bring you as much joy as I have writing them. I truly fell in love with Bexley, Rylan, Tai and Hunter writing this. And of course, our side characters! Sophia is a force and Arch is the supportive best friend we all need!

I'd also like to give a shout out to my bookish family. The people who go above and beyond as part of Team Macca. My husband Pete, my supportive loves Kyani, Cameron and Chris, my amazing and seriously out of this world awesome PA Kat who hypes me up and supports me through everything, my author friends who are my circle, my incredible beta team who laugh at all my Australian slang and EM dashes – Teresa, Meagan, Kaja, Sherry, Jacci, Amber and Aliss, my agent Nikki who believed in me from the start and fought hard in my corner, my wifies who put up with my crazy antics but cheer for me no matter what. And lastly, my two adoptive besties who have become such light in my life, always screaming my name on their socials and sending me voice notes – Ness and Jana.

Also, a huge thank you to all the ARC readers who gave this new series a chance! I was blown away by everyone's excitement.

And finally, to all my readers. Whether you've been with me from day one or whether you've just found me—thank you. You mean the world to me. I could type forever and there still wouldn't be enough words to express my gratitude and love for you.

About The Author

Steph Macca is from the East Coast of Australia. She writes all shades of romance but has a special love of contemporary why-choose dark romance.

Morally gray men are her favorite – anything questionable that makes you pause, usually followed by cliffhangers that may be hazardous to Kindles.

She has a remarkable talent of entering into the vicious cycle of binging reading until she regrets her alarm, promising to go to bed sooner, and returning to step one.

You can find and stalk her here:

www.stephmacca.com

Steph Macca's Reader Group

(Steph Macca's Asylum for Pectoral Perves)

Facebook (Author Steph Macca)

TikTok (@authorstephmacca)

Instagram (@authorstephmacca)

<hr>

ALSO BY STEPH MACCA

<u>Contemporary Series</u>

DANCE WITH MY DEMONS
(Dark romance, why choose, asylum, secret society)
Book One: Unhinged
Book Two: Echoes
Book Three: Ravage
Book Four: Exile

THE LIES WE KEEP
(Dark romance, why choose, college, MC, stepbrother)
Book One: Vicious Games
Book Two: Pretty Savages
Book Three: Recklessly Damaged
Book Four: Sweet Anarchy

THE BLACK SPADES
(Dark romance, why choose, high school 18+, mafia/gang)
Book One: King of Spades
Book Two: Queen of Fire
Book Three: Aces and Ashes

Novella: The Hunter

THE CHRONICLES OF MAXWELL

(Dark romance, why choose, mental health, enemies to lovers)

Book One: A Day of Ruin

Book Two: A Day of Chaos

<u>Paranormal Series</u>

MIDNIGHT PSYCHOS

(Dark romance, why choose, omegaverse/shifter/wolves, competing alphas)

Book One: Ruthless Savages

Book Two: Ruthless Redemption

Book Three: Ruthless Reign

Book Four: Ruthless Fate

<u>Standalones</u>

Wickedly Sweet

(Dark romance, Halloween, masks, brother's best friends)

All Too Well

(Romance, fake relationship, healing after heartbreak)

Sleigh

(Romance, stepbrother, Christmas)

Beautiful Deceptions & Sweet Miseries

(Dark romance, why choose, college, DV, BDSM)

Rayne

(Dark romance, MFM, adopted siblings, key party)

www.ingramcontent.com/pod-product-compliance
Lightning Source LLC
Chambersburg PA
CBHW070342170726
48291CB00001B/146